STERLING TOUCH

L.B. DUNBAR

Model Cover Design: Lori Jackson Designs

Photographer: J. Ashley Converse Photography

Cover Models: Brady and Lori

Mountain Cover Design: Jillian Liota/Blue Moon Creative Studio

Couple Cover Design: Megan Dunbar

Character Image: Erika Plum

Editor: Nicole McCurdy/Emerald Edits

Editor: Gemma Brocato

OTHER BOOKS BY L.B. DUNBAR

<u>Sterling Falls</u>

Sterling Heat

Sterling Brick

Sterling Streak

Sterling Clay

Sterling Fight

Sterling Touch

Sterling Stone

<u>Chicago Anchors</u>

Elevator Pitch

Catch the Kiss

Parentmoon

<u>Holiday Hotties (Christmas novellas)</u>

Scrooge-ish

Naughty-ish

Grouch-ish

<u>Road Trips & Romance</u>

Hauling Ashe

Merging Wright

Rhode Trip

<u>Lakeside Cottage</u>

Living at 40

Loving at 40

Learning at 40

Letting Go at 40

<u>Silver Foxes of Blue Ridge</u>

Silver Brewer

Silver Player

Silver Mayor

Silver Biker

<u>Sexy Silver Fox Collection</u>

After Care

Midlife Crisis

Restored Dreams

Second Chance

Wine&Dine

<u>Collision novellas</u>

Collide

Caught

The Sex Education of M.E.

<u>The Heart Collection</u>

Speak from the Heart

Read with your Heart

Look with your Heart

Fight from the Heart

View with your Heart

The Heart Remembers - a sequel

BOOKS IN OTHER AUTHOR WORLDS

<u>Smartypants Romance (an imprint of Penny Reid)</u>

Love in Due Time

Love in Deed

Love in a Pickle

<u>The World of True North (an imprint of Sarina Bowen)</u>

Cowboy

Studfinder

THE EARLY YEARS

<u>Legendary Rock Stars Series</u>

<u>Paradise Stories</u>

<u>The Island Duet</u>

<u>Modern Descendants – writing as elda lore</u>

Thank you to Vale and Cortland, whose story stayed alive in my imagination during a difficult time when I needed to pause writing their romance.

FOREWORD

Warning:
Memories of, and reference to, child abuse. Off the page
suicide.

PROLOGUE

[Vale]

Ten years old

My mother's death had been my fault.

Even though I'd never met the woman.

Even though I understood the biology behind her death.

Her passing has haunted me and my six older brothers.

However, the ghost I'd been more afraid of during my life was a living one: my father.

While he appeared to hate my brothers, ranging on a spectrum of fire and brimstone toward the younger set to a flame-throwing dislike of the older ones, he was simply indifferent toward me until I was ten years old.

That was the year of big changes.

From birth, my eldest brother Stone was the only father-figure I had, which was a lot of pressure to put on a boy who was twelve years older than me. Hero worship hardly described my feelings for him.

But there was another boy who became equally important to me. He'd been the true hero in my story.

No one ever forgets the day they fell in love. I can still recall the heat of the black asphalt shingles on the sloped roof outside my bedroom window. My butt aching on the hard, scratchy surface and my worn gym shoe-clad feet planted at an angle to keep me steady, to prevent me from slipping off the covering over the extended porch. My knees were tucked up to my chest, skinny arms wrapped around my shins. My chin was lowered, but my gaze never wavered from the stables. A space devoid of horses since the passing of my mother a decade earlier.

With my eyes focused on that weathered barn, I couldn't help thinking my father's death had equally been my fault.

A whisper in my ear.

Sebastien hollering.

Knox swinging his fists.

I'd close my eyes, but I was afraid of what I'll see. Every memory of that slow, slurred voice waking me from sleep sent a shiver rippling down my spine.

"There you are." A deep masculine voice pulled me from my haunting thoughts. *He* knew my hiding place, which wasn't much of a hidden spot considering the roof of the overhang was fully visible to anyone who'd look. Plus, it was broad daylight, and the early May sun was beating down on me.

Even the wind seemed to be dead that day.

However, my heart was hammering, reminding me I was very much alive. The sensation was becoming more and more frequent whenever Cortland Haven was around, which seemed kind of silly considering he was Stone's age—twelve years older than me and a grown-up at twenty-two. Not to mention, he was

Stone's best friend, and a figure in my life as constant as my brothers.

In the last year, though, something in my brain flipped whenever I was around Cort. Like a lightbulb switched on, only it intermittently flickered. Like the electricity didn't quite catch, missing the connection between the bulb and the socket or something. Still, a blink of light glowed here and there.

That fluttering illumination was Cort.

"We've been looking all over for you, Little Bee."

My name is Vale, short for Valentine. Little Bee was the nickname he'd given me, claiming I was always buzzing around Stone and him, eavesdropping or under foot.

The name seemed silly to me as I was almost a teenager. Officially in the double-digits, soon enough I'd be grown, and leave Sterling Falls like Stone and Cort had. I'd go off to college and put this small mountain town behind me.

Cort lowered himself to sit beside me, practically mirroring my position, only his knees were spread wider when he bent them, and his arms casually looped around his legs, one hand circling his opposite thick wrist to lock his arms in place. Cort reminded me of the Vikings I'd seen in an old picture book. Dirty-rust hair that hung to his shoulders and a smattering of facial scruff. He was big and burly, and always a little sweaty, but I didn't mind.

"Why you hidin', Little Bee?" His voice was much lower than it'd been when he was younger and running around our property with Stone.

"I'm not hidin'. I'm in plain daylight," I sassed, not looking over at him until his bicep bumped into my thin shoulder, nearly knocking me over.

I whipped my head in his direction, prepared to scold him for touching me. Like when Sebastian points his finger in my direction, and I swat it away. My brother right above me in birth order could be so annoying.

Only, when I looked at Cort's big face, his expression turned from tease to torture in the flap of a heartbeat.

"Bee," he whispered, reaching out for my face and swiping his callused thumb underneath my eye.

I blinked, caught off guard by the sudden, yet tender, touch. The firmness of the pad of his thumb. The featherlike stroke. I realized then I'd been crying. Crying tears I hadn't even felt which seemed stupid.

I wasn't sad that my father was dead. Wasn't sorry he was gone. Maybe that's why I was crying, because I felt guilty that I wasn't more upset, which was downright backward.

I couldn't possibly mourn the loss of a dad, because I'd never really had one. I had Stone.

Surprising me again, Cort hoisted my tiny frame onto his lap, wrapping his arms around me like a giant bear and pressing my head to his chest. His heart thumped beneath his worn T-shirt. One that smelled a little stinky. Heat emanated through the threadbare cotton against my cheek.

He also felt like an emotion I wouldn't recognize for a while longer.

On that day, I hadn't known how badly I'd needed that hug until it happened. Something inside me clicked. The lightbulb tip hit the socket just right and the bulb finally illuminated to its full capacity.

A one-hundred-watt crush on Cortland Haven burst into brightness.

A crush I dreamed of acting upon, doodling our names together in my secret journal for months, before Cort and Stone had a major falling out.

Until Cortland Haven became the enemy.

Unfortunately, my heart never got the memo.

1

[Cort]

Forty-six years old

"Sylver." The sharp call of that last name turns my head in the direction of my younger brother Clint.

Together, Clint and I run Haven Exteriors, proud roofers and house painters which is a far cry from my previous life. One where I was more athletic and much younger, full of spunk and spirit like the thirty kids currently trying out for the travel baseball team we sponsor and coach.

Haven Hitters is the result of my love of baseball and Clint's desire to give back to our small-town community of Rogue River. Personally, I think it's his way to live vicariously, never having athletic success on the level of our brother, Tate, or myself. Clint is organized, encouraging, and less of a hard ass than I am which is ironic considering his hair is redder than my lion's mane once was. Currently, he's checking in the kids trying out for the twenty-five spots on our 12U—twelve and under—team.

The team is typically all-boys, but this year we have one girl trying out. Legally, she can play with the boys until she's twelve years old, and we don't believe in discriminating. If she has the skills, she's on the team.

In some ways, I might be living vicariously as well, as I missed out on these years with my own son, Josh. When he'd been roughly this age I'd been at the peak, and subsequent valley, of my career in professional football. An injury to my leg took me out of the game completely. That was almost a dozen years ago, and at the ripe age of forty-six, my knee still flares in rainstorms like I'm some old fucker with an ache in my limbs afflicted by the weather.

I'm no stranger to bodily harm.

My latest injury is all Valentine Sylver's fault.

If she hadn't parked her car across the street from the Hartford house while I'd stood on top of the roof of their two-story home, I wouldn't have fallen nearly twenty feet, like Icarus blinded by the sun.

But as I stood tall atop that pitched roof, a sunspot blinded me for a second, and I was caught off guard by the sudden sight of Vale—the sway of her supple hips, the firmness of her ass in athletic leggings, and that dried-cornstalk-blond hair I swear I'd recognize anywhere. Her beauty was at fault for the loss of my footing and me slipping from the roof I was supposed to be repairing. Thus, I fell two stories and landed in a set of overgrown junipers.

I have no idea if Vale saw my graceless tumble.

The doc said those damn bushes saved my life. He claimed the fall was from my old knee injury.

Tumbling that distance also tweaked my back, and I've been struggling with back pain in one form or another ever since, which is not great when you are the other half of a partnership with your youngest brother.

Clint continues assigning the potential players a number for the unbiased judges to rank the kids' skill level. Irony in a small town is that there isn't anyone without an opinion or a connection to someone in some manner, so it's difficult to find impartial adults to measure the competency of our potential team members. Typically, we use our brother Tate who is the athletic director at the local high school, and another buddy from our adult softball team, Master Batters.

However, I'm stuck on that last name. *Sylver*. The family is one you cannot help but recognize in the Milton County community, especially as Stone Sylver is the county's Sheriff. He's also my *former* best friend. The Sylvers primarily reside in Sterling Falls, the sister town to our current location in Rogue River. The two communities share many things, including the local high school, the mountain peak, and Haven Hitters travel team.

Without questioning my brother, I reach for the tablet in his hand and double check the name he just read off.

Stone Sylver doesn't have a child, and until recently most of his siblings didn't either. Out of his brothers, most of their kids are girls and under the age of ten which leaves only one option.

Hudson Sylver, age eleven. Valentine Sylver's son.

I've known for a long time Vale had a child. I've seen her around Sterling Falls the few times I've ventured into the town next to mine. Motherhood agrees with her. She always looks happy when she's around the kid. That's all I'd ever want for any of the Sylvers. *Happiness.*

Hudson is on the younger side of our twelve and under qualification, and possibly under-skilled for our team as most boys—correction, most potential players—will be twelve years of age within the year, if not already. Hudson just turned eleven.

I hand the tablet back to Clint without a glance in his direction. Instead, I focus on the collection of boys seated on the ground, scanning from face to face, as if I could pick Hudson out of the crowd.

The truth is, I can.

He looks exactly like his mother. Same wicked blue eyes. Same dusty blond hair. A dimple to boot as he laughs at something the kid beside him says.

He's wearing a Chicago Anchors T-shirt, probably a fan of the professional baseball team because his uncle used to play for them. Being the nephew to a world-famous, all-star athlete isn't going to win him brownie points. He'll still need to prove himself.

Flicking my gaze from the skinny kid sitting with his legs extended in front of him, leaning back on scrawny arms, I scan along the row of parents standing a few feet back.

Anxious dads wanting to relive their glory days through their progeny.

Frazzled moms with to-go coffee mugs and a cell phone in hand. Some have another kid on their hip.

However, one woman stands apart from the rest. Her arms are crossed in front of her chest, one hand lifted to her lips, where she appears to be biting her thumb nail. Her gaze is laser-focused on her son.

Looking at Vale is like the glare of that sunspot. Or getting hit by a defensive back at top speed.

I should look away from her, but that's the thing about Valentine Sylver. Despite our age difference. Despite the riff between our families and the loss of friendship with her brother, there came a point where I couldn't pull my gaze from her. When I'd noticed that Vale Sylver wasn't my best friend's annoying little sister, but a grown woman. A young lady on the verge of a new chapter in her life. A story I'd never be a part of, and yet something inside me stung at the thought.

And then I'd made a foolish and reckless decision and sealed our forbidden fate forever. Thus, putting me on the periphery of her life and never within her line of sight until today.

Until this moment.

When I catch her glance up at me, watching me watch her, like the moment that got me in trouble with her in the first place.

2

[Vale]

While I knew this was a bad idea, I didn't have a choice. Hudson really wanted to play for a travel baseball club, and Haven Hitters was the closest team, even if the coaching staff was less than ideal.

I don't have anything against Cort or Clint Haven as human beings. Both men are unfairly attractive with bodies that are probably a crime beneath their athletic wear. Cort had once been Stone's best friend; Clint had been my brother Sebastian's. When the older boys severed their friendship, Sebastian's strong ethic for loyalty pulled him away from Clint, cutting off their relationship as well.

Boys can be so stupid sometimes.

Just my luck that having six older brothers, I'd have a son. However, Hudson is the reason for my being, and I would not trade him for anything. I love him, plain and simple. He's a good kid, having grown up without an actively involved father, just as I had, but having the love of his Uncle Stone, serving as his mentor and protector, also like me.

Which makes it difficult to deny him anything, especially when he begged to try out for this team.

At eleven years old, he barely makes the twelve and under requirement for the club. He's young and skinny, and compared to a few of the other boys, a little scrawny. However, with an uncle like my brother Sebastian, Hudson has learned to be a scrapper. He has drive and determination to be the best he can be, and I never want to squash that fortitude.

There's a saying for mothers of boys: *son up to son down*. The phrase embodies my kid. High energy, enthusiasm for each day, and sometimes, utterly exhausting. He also has a huge heart and a wise soul. And I really want him to make this team despite my apprehension about the coaches.

Well, one coach, at least, because regardless of my brothers' circumstances with the Havens, declaring their family *our* family enemy, I have my own history with Cortland Haven. One I'll take to the grave with me.

Thoughts of that moment give me pause and draw my attention to the man clouding my memories to find him glaring back at me.

Dark eyes narrowed. Thick arms crossed over his broad chest. Making a statement with his wide-legged stance. *Don't mess with me.*

Ha! Too late for that message but one I've never repeated, not once in twelve years. In fact, I hardly look at Cort Haven, feeling blessed that he lives one town over and rarely ventures into Sterling Falls where I reside. If his stare down is meant to intimidate me, it won't. It has the opposite effect where bubbles go off in my belly. Actually, it's more like a soda being opened and the fizz releases. And I hate that I'm not more indifferent toward him. That after all this time, I can pretend on the outside that I don't care if he glares, but on the inside, I'm a bubbly mess.

I always knew there'd be a day when Cort's path might cross mine, but I also always thought it would be more like an intersection and then diverge again in opposite directions. However, if . . . *no, when* . . . Hudson makes this team, I'll be seeing Cort more often in the next six months than I've seen him in the past decade.

I'm a big girl now, compared to the child who grew up around Cort, and that means I wear big girl panties. I can face him. I can even be cordial toward him.

I do *not* need to recall how his hands were once on my waist, or his breath tickled my ear when I was in my early twenties.

Glancing at Cort again, I catch on his eyes for a second before dragging mine away. I hate feeling like a coward, accepting defeat by pulling back first. I'm the queen of stare downs, having mastered the skill with my brothers and I've picked up a steely glare as a mother. But there's something intimidating about Cort looking at me. Not in a frightening sense. Not in a threatening way. The sensation is more of a weird magnetism that had us meeting eyes across a crowded bar twelve years ago. A time when I just *knew* he was checking me out and I wasn't shy about staring back at him.

Then there was the day after and—

A loud clap snaps me out of my revelry, causing me to flinch a little at the suddenness of two firm hands slapping together.

"All right, everyone. Let's hit the field and give it all you've got." Clint's masculine tenor isn't as dominant as his eldest brother. His cheerful voice is full of positive encouragement and the kids respond by climbing up to their feet, gathering what they need for their assigned stations, and heading to the locations marked by cones for fielding, hitting, catching, and pitching.

Hudson wants to be a pitcher, which worries me. There's a lot of pressure on the mound, and my brother Ford, a former Chicago Anchors baseball star, has tried to convince my son that centerfield is an equally important position on the team.

"How's he gonna get the girls in the outfield?" my brother Knox had teased.

"What do I care about girls?" Hudson answered.

I smiled at the exchange. *That's right, baby. Don't grow up too fast.*

While I silently pray romantic love will find Hudson one day, for now, I want his eyes on the ball and his heart on the field, enjoying his time as a kid. Love complicates everything. Plus, I'd grown up too fast and I never want that for Hudson. I was pretty confident he was right where he should be. At eleven, his life was easy.

With that in mind, I watch the kids scatter while Cort approaches the parents. When he comes to a full stop, his legs spread again. He's wearing a straw cowboy hat instead of a baseball cap, which contrasts with the athletic pants he's sporting. Up close, I notice that he's cut his once chin-length hair, so it curls around his ears. Salt peppers the thick dirty rust coloring along his jaw line.

Somehow, he still looks like a Viking to me.

"Parents," he addresses the adults, offering a crooked smile that does little to dispel his unease. His expression suggests dealing with the parents is his least favorite part of hosting this team. "We only have a few rules for you during these tryouts. Let the kids do their job. And let them have fun."

Cort's eyes drift to one particular dad. Henry Stanton is a stern-looking man and a bit of a loudmouth, always thinking his kid is better than the others, always thinking *he* knows it all. How to play baseball. How to win a science fair. How to cheat the system.

He rubs me the wrong way, and unfortunately, we keep

bumping into each other because Hudson has developed a new friendship with his son, Atticus. The boy is one half of a fraternal set of twins. With Henry being a single dad while I'm a single mom, there's a camaraderie he thinks we have, which we don't. Single parenthood is the only line we share, and one I'm not interested in crossing with him.

Next, Cort's gaze roams to Veronica Archer. Her daughter Kennedy is trying out for the team, and I'm impressed by how progressive Cort and Clint are by allowing her here. Ronnie is a buxom brunette in her forties, who lost her husband two years ago and since then she's made quite a reputation for herself, constantly hitting on the few available single men in our community. There is no reason for her to stay home, dressed in black, weeping for the remainder of her days. But her penchant for also hitting on married men gives Ronnie a bad reputation.

Cheating is a hard limit for me and the thought draws my attention back to Cort a second.

My eyes narrow when I glance back at Ronnie, who is twirling a long strand of hair around her manicured finger. Slowly blinking her eyelids at Cort, she curls her lips like a hook that suggests she'd like to catch him and eat him for dinner.

I hate how my gaze pings back toward Cort like I'm watching some reality television show playout. An announcer voice goes off in my head: *Will he fall for her charm?*

Cort's eyes only remain on Ronnie for a second before he flicks a glance in my direction again, glaring at me like *I'm* the one looking for trouble, when I'm standing here all innocent and anxious over my boy.

"We'd prefer if you kept all cheers and jeers to yourself." His head whips back in the direction of Henry Stanton, pinning him with another hard stare. "Let the kids concentrate. And have fun."

Henry's mouth falls open, and God only knows what might

tumble from those loose lips, before Cort adds, "I'm not opposed to throwing any parent who violates these requirements out of this tryout."

For some reason, his gaze comes back to me, and I roll my lips inward, fighting a willful retort of my own.

What the hell did I ever do to him?

But then I remember exactly what happened between us, and how it made Cort weep afterward.

3

____

[Cort]

Fuck. Why does Vale Sylver have to be so beautiful? Women have this fear that growing older ages them in ways men might find unattractive, but there is something about Vale that just makes her more stunning with each passing decade of her life.

I don't know if it's the two-tone shades of blond in her hair, glistening in the sunlight, or the soft lines around her mouth as she smiles at her boy, but Vale just takes my fucking breath away.

"That was fun." A slap on my shoulder and Clint's low voice in my ear does nothing to distract me from watching Vale walk away. Her body is the perfect shape of infinity. Her legs look toned beneath her leggings. Her arm is around her son as she leans into him and says something I wish I could hear.

Scrubbing my thick paw down my face, I drag my thoughts away from Vale.

"Yeah. We have a good crop of kids this year." The tryouts are over.

Clint smiles while Tate adds, "And some hot moms as well."

Clint's head pops upright, jerking his gaze from the tablet in his hand to glare at our middle brother. Even in his forties, Tate can be a real punk, which might explain why he's single.

"What is wrong with you?" I snap, turning on him. He's my height but I'm broader than him. He's all lean muscle while I'm bulk, and his hair has a hint of gray in the sandy locks which I love to razz him about.

"What? I'm just saying that Ronnie Archer is fine."

Clint snorts. "And from what I've heard, she isn't too discerning about her partners."

Far be it for any of us to judge her choices, though.

Tate grins. "Good news for me then, huh?"

Clint scrunches up his nose in disgust at the manwhore ways of our middle brother.

"Parents are off limits," I remind Tate.

He pouts like I've told him he can't have dessert before dinner. I don't care what order he eats his meals as long as he doesn't hunger for any of our parents. Especially one particular single mom.

"Vale's looking good," Tate adds, driving in the steak knife, and my entire body shifts to face him, realizing too late he's addressing Clint.

Clint lowers his head, staring down at the tablet in his hand like it holds all the secrets on how to win a baseball game, or a woman. His cheeks flush. As a single father of a precious five-year-old, I suspect it's been a while since our brother has hooked up with anyone. He's closer in age to Vale, being only three years older than her, and once a playmate of hers as he hung out with Sebastian Sylver before everything fell to shit between our families.

And the last thing I want is Clint lusting after Vale.

Despite the separation of families almost twenty years ago —twenty-three to be exact—we never reconciled. I've seen Vale be cordial to my brothers and even develop a friendship with our only sister, Trinity, through their ladies-only book club. Stone has always been fair, as a sheriff should be, not that we Havens have caused any unlawful disturbances or trouble. Still, an invisible wall exists between the men in our two families.

Sadly, I'm the one who built it, and I've never forgiven myself.

"Beer?" Tate asks, which is the first smart thing he's said in the last five minutes. "Milton Roadhouse," he adds, confirming the location of the main drinking establishment in Sterling Falls. The former hotel and bar on the intersection of Main and Corner in the downtown area looks like a Western saloon inside.

I cringe a little at the suggestion, preferring the privacy of Randy's which is just outside town, wedged between Rogue River and Sterling Falls. It's more of a locals-only, get-lost-in-your-head kind of place, and less crowded than the Roadhouse.

Not to mention, I'd be less likely to run into one unavail-able-to-me single mom.

I've done my best over the years to avoid the place that got me into trouble with Vale.

Then again, the spot that pushed me over the edge was next to the famous falls themselves, and a location I avoid as well.

"THOSE SYLVERS ARE LUCKY BASTARDS," Tate mutters as I'm taking a seat on a bar stool inside Milton Roadhouse.

I almost topple off the tall, wooden seat, while craning my neck to scan the bar for what Tate is talking about. Or rather, whom, as four women sit at a table on the opposite side of the place.

Milton Roadhouse is rather dark, with wood-paneled walls and hard wood floors. A three-sided bar takes up a portion of the space with several high-top tables scattered here and there, and regular tables made from whiskey barrels located closer to the slim stage. The Western décor is complete with giant wagon wheel chandeliers and country music piped through overhead speakers despite baseball games on the large screen televisions behind the bar.

Adjusting my ass on the stool between my brothers, I stare across the space at the table where Vale sits, along with Halle Reynolds, a slim redhead who is Knox Sylver's girlfriend. Also at the table is Mavis Grant, a Native American woman with sleek black hair with thin strips of gray in it, who is engaged to Clay Sylver.

"Heard Knox finally married his girl," Tate states, sliding onto the seat beside me, while clarifying the relationship status of the former high school sweethearts.

"It was a family-only affair," Clint adds. Roughly two years ago, when Halle inherited her grandmother's house, Clint took on the job of painting the exterior of the historic home located on the boulevard outside the Sterling Falls' downtown business district.

Clint is the painting side of our business; I'm the roofing.

On that thought, my back pinches a little, and I sit up a bit straighter on the hard wooden seat attempting to stretch out my spine.

"That so?" I mutter, responding to Clint's expanded information about the Sylvers and their love lifes.

Continuing to stare at the table, I notice our sister, Trinity, a blonde-headed spitfire of a woman who can scare the crap out of me sometimes, among the ladies.

"Must be Thursday." Tate wiggles his brows.

"What's special about Thursday?" I ask.

"Every Thursday, Trinity has *book club*." Clint air-quotes the final words, and I turn my head wondering just what the fuck these two are talking about.

"Book club?" I mock back at him like I'm missing the obvious.

"You know, the code word for what Meredith Mulligan is doing above her store," Clint explains.

Now I'm really lost and not certain I want to know, but laughter from the other side of the bar draws my attention and I glance across the space to find Vale's head tipped back. Her throat exposed. Her hair dangling down her back. The rich timbre of her laugh shooting up into the air like a volcanic eruption.

I want to feel the heat of that sound on my skin.

Instead, I shift my gaze to the television above the bar, fighting the unwanted sensation in my chest, and the urge to ask my brothers for clarification.

Fuck it. "What's Meredith Mulligan doing above her store?"

Meredith is the owner of The She Shed, a knitting supply store across the street from the Roadhouse. As a widow in her early seventies, she's a good friend to our widowed mother, and the two of them get up to all kinds of trouble.

"Selling sex toys," Tate blurts.

"What?" My head turns so sharply, my neck cracks and I cup the back of it.

Clint chokes on a sip of beer that mysteriously appeared before us. "Would you keep your voice down?" he chides.

I continue staring at Tate, blinking like it will help me clarify what I've just learned.

"Everyone knows that book club is not just about books, if it's even about books at all. It's a way for Meredith to hustle her side gig." Tate rubs his hands together like he's in on the business. "And I am not complaining. Her profit is my gain."

"Isn't the saying 'her profit is your loss'?" Clint asks.

I've never heard such a statement and I'm not certain I want to have this conversation. Where have I been that I don't know anything about this so-called secret side to the local book club?

"Nope," Tate corrects. "The more she sells, the more *invested* I become." He wiggles his brows, insinuating the sexual benefit he receives from Meredith's sales.

A thought hits me hard. "Ew. You're talking about *our mother's friend*." And I do not want the image of Meredith Mulligan pleasuring herself with a dildo in my head, let alone our brother assisting her.

"Not Meredith," Tate clarifies, scrunching up his face as well.

I glance at Clint like he can help me, but his elbow is on the bar, his forehead in his hand, shielding his eyes like he can hide himself from this discussion.

"What am I missing?" I finally admit, sounding like a dumb ass.

Tate responds. "It means, the ladies of this town seek gratification by having sex toys." He chuckles at his own pun. "And Momma taught me to share my toys." Tate double taps his hands on the wooden bar.

"You mean *they* share their toys with you," Clint clarifies.

Tate only smiles wider, exposing his perfectly white teeth. "Exactly."

My head swivels again toward the table of women, and I'm grossed out for half a second considering our sister fits the bill of ladies in this county that partake in this book club slash sex toy store.

But then another thought strikes, nearly knocking me back off the stool again.

If Vale is a member of the book club . . .

And Vale attends the meetings which include the sale of sex toys . . .

Then Vale must own—

Aw, fuck.

I scratch underneath my chin with my knuckles like I can erase an image, because the very last thing I need in my head is the vision of Vale Sylver pleasuring herself with a little assistance.

Or a big one.

4

[Vale]

I live for Thursday nights. It's the one night of the week I get to forget I'm a mom for a little while and feel like a woman. At thirty-four, I'm still young, but not as wild as my teenage years. Back then, if there was a party in the woods, I was present. And if there happened to be a cute guy flirting me up, I didn't balk at heading behind the trees to make out with him. In my early twenties, I had my fair share of one-night stands and short-term romances, always hopeful for more in both physical satisfaction and emotional connection.

The best result of one of those experiences is Hudson.

My son is the lasting benefit of misplaced romanticism, but I don't regret him one bit. I've been a single mom since his birth, and grateful once again for the love and support of my eldest brother who took us in. Long gone are my days of one-night stands and dating apps. I'm just not that person anymore. Unfortunately, I've been living in my childhood home with

Stone ever since Hudson's birth, and sometimes I just need a break.

From a boy on the verge of adolescence.

From a grown man with a heavy weight on his shoulders.

From that old house full of conflicting memories.

Thursday nights are my night off from everything. As much as it pains me at times to be reminded I'm lonely without a life partner at my side or ring on my finger, I'm *not* alone. I have good friends, some of whom are also single, and I have book club.

AKA the town's secret: The Sterlets.

Named for the starlets of this community who recognize their worth as women. As in, women who deserve sexual gratification, even if some of us need to bring it upon ourselves. *Thank you, sex goddess*, for Meredith Mulligan and her side hustle of selling pleasure-inducing adult toys. The She Shed is a knitting store on the first floor of her business, but upstairs, in Meredith's private apartment, our book club revolves around romance novels, copious wine, and conversations about the best dildo.

Before the official club meeting, a new tradition of getting together with the women in my brothers' lives has evolved. Most weeks, Enya, Sebastian's wife, is here, along with her sister Cadence, who happens to be my brother Ford's fiancée. But Enya and Sebastian just had their second baby, sweet Annabelle, and Sebastian is being a beast of protection and love over the second-time mom and their new bundle of joy. Cadence recently announced she is pregnant and tonight she's somewhere with Ford and his three young daughters.

Halle, Knox's wife, and Mavis, Clay's fiancée, have met up with me instead. Since I saw Trinity Haven outside Milton Roadhouse before I entered, I invited her to join us.

As the only sister in each of our families, we both agree boys can be stupid, and the long-standing riff between our eldest brothers is an example. I understand all too well the pain Stone suffered at the hands of Bailey Cummins, but my brother has been better off without her. He dodged a bullet, as they say. Unfortunately, Cortland caught the shot, and he's been injured from that decision.

Maybe the former friends can never forget the situation, but forgiveness seems long overdue. Then again, I learned a long time ago that forgiveness *doesn't* always need to be granted to others. Forgiveness is more important to give to yourself.

For awkward situations.

For painful experiences.

For poor choices.

I've made them all and glancing across the bar, catching on the eyes of one such decision sends a tingle down my spine. Because Cortland Haven is staring back at me and it's exactly how we got in trouble the first time. The only time.

Quickly, I pull my gaze away from him but too soon I'm glancing back in his direction again. He's changed his clothes since the baseball tryouts into a flannel shirt and jeans. A baseball cap graces his head instead of the straw cowboy hat from earlier. My memory flashes back to a night more than a decade ago when he was dressed in a similar fashion, minus the hat and with a little longer hair. His eyes were on me just the same that night, sending shivers over my skin back then, like his gaze does now.

Then, the tickle was a thrill; now, the shudder is confusion.

What are the odds that for nearly a decade I haven't seen Cortland Haven in more than casual passings and rare sightings, but today, I've encountered him twice? And of all nights, on my book club night, when I am looking forward to what Meredith calls her Spring Fling collection.

My gaze flicks away from Cort but almost like my eyes have a will of their own, they draw back toward him.

"What are you looking at?" Trinity squawks, laughter in her voice as she glances over her shoulder. "Ugh."

The feisty blonde turns back in my direction and rolls her eyes. "Brothers."

I chuckle, but the sound is a mixture of choked strain leaving my throat. Brothers can be overbearing and annoying, and sometimes, it sucks to be loved so much by them. *Insert sarcasm.* Because most of their concern comes from a good place, even in the years they never picked up their smelly laundry and spent a little too much time in a locked bathroom using all the hot water.

Boys.

Only, our brothers are now all men, especially hers, and dammit, I cannot stop myself from looking over at Cort again. Instantly, I'm reminded of catching him watching me once upon a time in this bar on a night not so different from tonight. I'd been surrounded by friends, content with my life, full of plans for my future. His eyes were appraising, assessing, even appreciative of my then-thin, twenty-two-year-old body.

Now, I'm a mom, and while I keep myself in shape, knowing the importance of movement and strength training, my frame is not as sleek as it once was. I'm more curves and dips, thighs and ass.

And I no longer have the desire for a quick hookup.

"We should probably get going," Halle says, interrupting my thoughts, pulling my attention back to the table and the redhead my brother loves.

Halle and Knox have one of those romantic tales where high school sweethearts reunite, and I'd be jealous if I ever had a high school sweetheart. Instead, I have a pithy history of hookups and teenage mishaps, chasing something I have yet to experience.

Love. And decent orgasms with a man.

Nodding in agreement with Halle that we need to get a

move-on, I also need a moment to reset, and announce, "I need to use the bathroom quick." That first glass of wine is running right through my system.

I double tap my hands lightly on the table and slip from my chair, heading around the bar for the restrooms in the back corner. At the same time I'm passing one side of the bar, I look up to see Cortland leave his barstool.

For some ridiculous reason, my heart begins to beat faster as he walks toward the corner of the bar. The same corner I'm headed toward. My belly flutters and I press my hand to it to quell the flapping.

We intersect at the same time.

"Valentine," Cort says, his voice low and rugged, and rinsing over me like fine sand slipping between my toes. He dips his head, nodding once as he nears me.

"Cortland," I reply, my tone just as formal as his, using his full name in response to him so firmly using mine.

But something even stranger than my accelerating heart beats behind my ribs, and the thickness in my throat occurs as our bodies pass a little closer than necessary considering the space around us.

Cort's pinky finger brushes against mine as we cross paths. Electricity ripples up my arm, and a trigger of shock forces my smallest finger to twitch, crackle, and then dull.

And I desperately want to hold onto those initial sparks. That little reminder that Cortland Haven once had his full hands on me. His palms holding my hips. His lips against the side of my neck.

I shiver again, like I've felt a singular ray of the sun's warmth after a long, cold winter. I'd spin to face Cort, to see if he felt a similar response, felt the unnerving sensation, but I remember all too well how Cort ran away from me. How he never looked back.

He'd never feel a giddy, tingling connection with me.

He never felt about me how I once felt about him.

Which makes it all the stranger that he's been glaring at me today. *Twice.*

As I near the hallway leading to the restrooms, I fight the desire to glance in Cort's direction one more time, knowing I'm damned if I look and damned if I don't.

Because I don't want to see he isn't looking back at me.

I also don't know what to think if he is.

5

[Vale]

"Hudson Sylver. Hurry up." I holler up the staircase of our family home. The one I share with Stone and my son. For a few years, Knox lived with us when he returned from the Navy. Sebastian even spent a brief stint here before he moved into the apartment above his bakery and then into Enya's house.

Our old farmhouse has more space than three people need, with five bedrooms on the upper level, many of which were once shared by my brothers. I'm still in my childhood room, although it's been updated extensively from the yellow of my youth and walls covered in posters of teenage heartthrob hotties. The entire house has been renovated over time to include a green tin roof, replacing the worn black shingles, and a fresh coat of bright white paint on the clapboards. A new porch was installed replacing the rotten original one. I've been told the place looks like the house in *The Waltons*; however, the classic television program was before my time.

"Hudson," I groan, pinching the bridge of my nose, needing my boy to get a move on. I need to get him to school and get myself to work, all while nursing the twinge of a headache which is the aftereffects of a little too much wine last night, despite sleeping like a baby thanks to the self-induced stimulation I gave myself with my newest purchase from book club. The conflicting part of my night was the fantasies of Cortland Haven using my new B.O.B. on me, causing me to come hard, and provide a second release quickly following the first. Which never, *ever* happens.

"Headache?" The low tone and quiet concern in the masculine voice has me lifting my head.

Offering a soft smile, I greet Stone. "Good morning."

Stone looks a little like that guy in those Dr. Pepper commercials during college football season. It might be the sheriff's uniform or the striking combination of salt and pepper on his jaw line. Heavy on the salt. Could also be that he was once a college football player himself. He'd been a favorite among his team, and a strong contender for the professional league.

Between the apprehension on his face and his still-fit physique, I'm always reminded of the two sides of Stone—who he could have been and who he is.

"Good night?" He arches one bushy brow, the corner of his mouth turning up slowly. His smiles are rare, adding to the stern sheriff look he's mastered.

Sighing, I hang my head and pinch my finger and my thumb together. "Just a little bit. And I need Hudson to hustle."

On cue, feet thunder down the staircase before my son takes a final leap from the third step to the floor, giving me a near heart attack as he stumbles on his landing.

"Hudson. Careful," I warn, reminded of when my brothers did the same thing in this house.

Back then I'd hold my breath, waiting for my father to start yelling about the racket, followed up with insults like *bunch of shitheads* and *pains in my ass.*

In comparison, Stone offers Hudson a warm smile before scrubbing his hand over Hudson's hair.

"Not the hair, Uncle Stone."

Hudson flicks his fingers through the short tuffs, making the front stand upright and the sides smooth down.

Stone glances at me again, arching that brow once more. A silent conversation ensues between us.

This new?

Guess so.

At eleven years old, Hudson is on the cusp of being a teenager, which means his body odor can sometimes be rank, but his hair has become an important feature.

I'm curious if this has anything to do with Amelia Stanton, the fraternal twin counterpart to Atticus.

Amelia is a sweet thing, quiet and shy, unlike her brother who is the spitting image of his father's know-it-all attitude. I'm not thrilled about the new friendship Hudson has with Atticus, but I hold my peace about it. The twins have blond hair and bright blue eyes reminding everyone of their beautiful mother who was killed when they were six.

"See you later, kid," Stone says to Hudson, whose hair is now back in place.

"Breakfast," I holler after Hudson who rushes toward the kitchen where his school bag is waiting by the back door along with his jacket on a hook, which he'll ignore because he's *too cool* for a coat.

Hudson knows nutrition is important, though. Breakfast being the most valuable meal for a growing boy and an active brain. He picks up a protein bar—new breakfast of champions

—as he passes the basket of them sitting on the kitchen counter and continues toward the back entrance.

Within minutes, his stuff is gathered, he calls goodbye to Stone, and we are out the door.

Phew. Let Friday begin.

~

As a physical therapist, I work at Reflexology located in Rogue River. The clinic includes physical and massage therapy, where the massages are more about healing after injury. I'm rather passionate about my line of work and especially love helping older people.

Edwin Hamlin is typically my first patient on Fridays, but he graduated out of physical therapy, so my first session this morning is now open.

Gratitude. Because I'm two minutes late.

"Hey," Derrek greets me as I rush past the check-in desk. Our front desk attendant has better eyebrows than me and perfectly styled, jet-black hair with enough product in it to give him the appearance of a Ken doll. A few weeks ago, he decided he wants his name to now be pronounced *dare-reek* instead of the crisp *dare-ick*. I love the guy.

"I scheduled a walk-in for you. He had a referral." He tips his head toward the hallway leading toward the massage rooms. "I put him in room 4."

As I've always considered four an unlucky number, dread instantly fills my gut which still sloshes with last night's wine and the addition of my morning coffee. I flatten my hand against my belly as I hustle toward the room, opening the door with a bit more flourish than necessary, causing my toe to catch upon my entrance. But the thing that really causes me to stumble is my new patient.

"Cort?"

6

———

[Cort]

*F*uck.

I knew this was a bad idea. Even told my doctor there was no way I was going to massage therapy.

However, my back is acting up again. When I bent for a laundry basket on the floor, my lower left side seized. It sucks getting older. I didn't think I could stand upright and can't say I am at a perfect ninety-degrees. More like seventy-nine. Which is the position I'm seated in—hands wrapped around the edge of the sheet-covered massage table, shoulders hunched forward, head lowered—when the door to the room opens with a *whoosh* and Vale Sylver stumbles in.

Her wheat-under-sunshine hair is pulled into a loose bun at the base of her neck, exposing her throat, and she swallows hard as she says my name.

I attempt to sit upright, both in surprise at her rapid

entrance and the suddenness of her appearance, and then wince, gripping the table beneath my hands harder.

"I—" Vale looks up at the number on the door and then back at me.

"Sorry, this room's taken," I snark, gritting my teeth through the sharp pain on the left side of my lower back.

"I'm . . ." Vale glances back at me, then steps forward and closes the door behind her. A giant tote is hooked over her arm. She's wearing a plum colored, light-weight jacket while holding a travel mug in her hand. She stiffens her shoulders. "I'm your therapist."

I scoff. She looks like any mom in a school pick-up line. Not that I'm familiar with that situation lately, but I remember how Bailey used to look. The harried appearance of a rushed morning.

"You're kidding." My voice is low, almost a snarl of disbelief.

Dropping her bag to the floor and stepping closer to the table, she sets her mug on the nearby counter and addresses me. "I'm not."

Her blue eyes are wide and clear, like the waters of Sterling Falls in early morning sunlight. The liquid is pure but fierce as it cascades from the upper river to the lower one. The falls always remind me of Vale and not just because of what happened with her beside it.

Little Bee has grown into an incredible queen of strength.

"There must be some mistake." I'm here for a massage. The doc told me once upon a time to get them regularly to help keep my back loose, but I'm not a fan of strangers touching me.

I'm actually not in favor of *anyone* touching.

And I'm really not looking forward to the possibility that Vale will lay her hands on me.

I lean forward like I intend to hop off the massage table. With my hands still gripping the edge of the table for leverage,

I swing my upper body forward, and almost double over. Reaching for my lower left side, I let out an elongated, "Fu*uuck*."

Vale rushes toward me, hands outward, and I snap upright, struggling to pull my shoulders back and my chest away from her. I hiss again as pain shoots across my back.

Concern fills Vale's clear eyes. Her brows pinch, forming a divot between them. Thankfully, her hands don't make contact with me, and she stands to her full height.

"I can get another therapist for you." Resolve settles on her shoulders, and she drops her gaze.

"No." As much as I'm not certain I can do this with her, I need help, and I *know* I can't do this with someone else.

Her expression shifts to something stern with a side of no-nonsense. "Then I want you to get undressed and slip under the sheet." She points at the covering partially folded back, inviting me to slide beneath it. "Lay down on your stomach, head on the circular pillow at the end, and I'll be back in a few minutes."

With that, she spins, picks up her tote and exits the room, closing the door gently behind her.

I hang my head knowing this is a terrible idea, but a sharp pinch in my back reminds me why I'm here.

Within minutes, I undress and slide gingerly beneath the sheet, pulling it up to my chin. A light knock on the door and the soft call of my name forces me to respond, "Come in." My voice is rougher than necessary. My throat a bit thick, both from the ache in my side and the anxious anticipation of Vale's hands.

Vale opens the door and steps quietly inside before dimming the lights a little. She does a double take at my position before reaching for a tablet on the countertop near where she set her to-go mug.

"Why don't you tell me why you are here today?" Her voice is controlled. She's down to business, acting like I'm any other patient.

For some irrational reason, a rush of envy fills my chest. *How many men has Vale laid her hands on?*

Attempting to shut down my thoughts, I answer her although the scratch in my throat still makes my voice rough. "Tweaked my back. Doc says I should get a massage regularly to see if it helps."

She types into the tablet. "Did you suffer a previous injury?" Her voice is still distant, disembodied even.

"I fell off a roof." I stare up at the ceiling as I answer but sense Vale on my right spinning to face me. A soft gasp follows. "It happened about a year ago." *I was staring at you and lost my footing.*

"You're very fortunate." Her voice softens.

Fortunate. That's what the doctor said but I haven't felt fortunate in years. Over a decade, actually.

Vale steps closer to my right side, holding the tablet in her hand. "So what areas of your body would you like me to concentrate on or stay away from?"

My dick. And my dick. Can you answer with the same body part twice?

Of course, the last thing I need is Vale anywhere near that appendage that's slowly coming to life from her closeness. The second she lays her hands on me, I'll be tenting this sheet. Then again, the second she touches me, I'm going to tense up.

"Uhm . . . just anywhere is fine, but my back is the issue."

"Of course." Vale spins for the cabinet again and sets the tablet on the counter, before turning back toward me.

I still can't look her in the eye and instead focus on the dull glow of the recessed lighting overhead.

"I'm going to need you to roll over to your stomach."

Right. She'd initially mentioned that.

"So, I'm going to lift the sheet and then if you'll roll to your left . . ."

Suddenly, Vale is holding up the sheet like a privacy screen and I attempt to shift but let out a sharp hiss as my left side seizes again. With my hand on the edge of the table for leverage, I lug myself sideways to roll over, while Vale speaks from behind the raised sheet.

"Do you need my help?"

"No." Again, too terse. Too strained. But the longer I can delay her touching me, the better, which is counterintuitive to having a massage.

After an awkward pull and flip, aware that my dick is instantly soft again from the ache in my back, I belly flop on my stomach and place my face against the donut pillow at the top of the table.

Vale drapes the sheet over my back but when her hands come to my spine and smooth down the covering, I stiffen. Shoulder blades tight. Back concave. Even my legs are like hurricane resistant telephone poles.

Vale stills and instantly lifts her hands. Clearing her throat, she says, "Maybe we should start slowly. I'm going to lay my hands on your back. You tell me if I hurt you."

She places her hands against the middle of my spine and holds. Her touch is not too hard, not too soft, but I'm not certain if it's right. Something inside me feels . . . off.

Trying to concentrate on the warmth of her palms through the sheet and the delicate press of her small hands and ten firm fingers, I breathe in. I breathe out. And Vale waits. One heartbeat. Two.

She doesn't so much slide her hands, as move them apart a few inches, and I'm incredibly aware of one between my shoulder blades and one on my lower back.

My heart hammers harder, anticipating the residual effects of being touched in a place on my body I cannot see. The fear is ridiculous and unwarranted with Vale. She wouldn't hurt me. But old haunts never die.

"You doing okay?" Vale asks.

My response is a grunt.

She moves her hands one more time, resting one near the top of my shoulder blades by a scar and the other near my ass, just above the curve. She pauses again, waiting as I take another deep breath.

"Good."

I'm not certain if it's a question or praise before she removes her hands and returns them to the middle of my spine again, pausing another beat or two before repeating her deliberate, patient movements.

"It'd be better to have skin to skin contact, but I don't need to, if you are uncomfortable."

It's strange to me that she can sense my discomfort, and yet stranger still is how I'm not entirely uncomfortable with her.

"It's good." I hesitate. Am *I* asking a question or giving her permission?

"I'm going to move the sheet then," she warns me like I'm a caged animal.

And fuck, I do not want to admit the fear sawing at my chest.

I nod against the donut pillow as Vale slowly moves the sheet downward, folding it over once, and then once again, and finally bringing it to the top of my ass where she pauses.

"Um . . ." She chuckles but covers it with a quick throat clearing. "You could have kept your underwear on."

I want to argue that she told me to get undressed.

"I don't wear underwear." Not necessarily true, but the comeback pops out in place of my argument.

The silence that follows is thick before Vale clears her throat again.

"You might want to for any future appointments." Her voice isn't as steady as she might have hoped because she sounds a little distressed.

Victory or defeat at knocking her off balance is erased when she smooths the sheet along the base of my spine, just before the swell of my ass. I stiffen again as if her touch offends me when she's been nothing but cautious and kind, warning me with every movement.

Get a grip, man. This is Vale.

She isn't a stranger, even if I no longer know her, not as the adult woman she's become. Deep down, I know I can trust her. She isn't leading me on. Isn't acting inappropriate. Isn't hurting me.

Her bare hands return to the middle of my back. Again, the pressure is strangely comforting, and the skin-to-skin contact is even warmer than minutes ago. I relax just a little as Vale waits on my breathing to settle. Then she repeats the measured movements, setting her palms higher and lower along my spine at the same time.

Closing my eyes, I inhale and exhale again with each pause she gives me.

With her hand just at the base of my spine, she adds pressure to her fingers on my right lat. "Does that hurt?"

I shake my head despite the awkward cushion holding it.

"How about here?" She rolls her hand backward, forcing the heel to push gently against my lower left side.

I grit my teeth. "There."

"I'm going to apply some light pressure. Tell me if it's too hard. Or if you want it a little harder."

The mere thought of Vale using those words in another manner has me closing my eyes. If I wasn't in so much pain, I'd find humor in the moment. I might even flirt. I'd like to take

Vale hard, push a little harder into her. Bring us both back to that moment beside the Falls and have a do-over.

But as Vale applies more pressure, I grind my molars despite the pleasing relief, and I release any thoughts of a second chance with her.

Like the water cascading down Sterling Falls and drifting toward a larger sea, I had my moment with Vale and then lost it.

7

———

[Vale]

After Cort's session, in which he offered me a grunt of gratitude, I slip out of the room to allow him privacy to dress. Once inside the staff kitchen, I rest my hands on the counter, flexing my fingers, while bowing my head. I take a large inhale, hold, and then exhale slowly, as if I'm blowing out the nerves doing a jig inside me. Rolling my shoulders back, I try to release the tension and energy lingering after touching Cortland Haven.

The relief lasts only seconds before images of Cort, naked on my massage table, resurface in my mind.

That strong back. The firm curve of his ass. The strength in his arms.

Shaking out my fingers and tilting my head side to side, I fight the images dancing in my head.

Be professional, Valentine.

With that thought, I reach for my tablet and write up my report on the session before heading to the front desk.

"Well, that was interesting," I state, setting the tablet on the counter near Derrek's computer.

Cort was clearly uncomfortable having my hands on him, and as much as it might have been about me, I also think it was about him. He apparently doesn't like being touched.

"I don't think Cortland Haven should be assigned to me again, *if* he even comes back," I warn Derrek. I highly doubt Cort will return to Reflexology.

"Funny, because he scheduled for next week and requested you." Derrek raises one of his perfectly sculpted eyebrows. "He'll be back Wednesday at eight A.M."

"What?" Slow to form, the question expresses how dumbfounded I am. What is Cort thinking? Better yet, what is he doing requesting me again?

"And Mrs. Cougar is here," Derrek says distracting me. The patient's name isn't really Mrs. Cougar, he just likes to call the older-than-him woman such a thing because she's a shameless flirt with everyone.

Shaking my head, I pick up my tablet and brush away thoughts of Cortland Haven.

By four, I've been on my feet most of the day. My hands are tired from massaging others, and I need to pick Hudson up from Atticus Stanton's house. I wish the two boys weren't friends for two reasons: Atticus himself *and* his father. The boy wouldn't be so bad if he didn't have the negative influence of his dad. I try not to fault the twins. Being a single father, Henry is probably doing the best he can. Lord knows I have no room to judge as a single mother. Still, Henry's pigheaded attitude is starting to rub off on his son.

Once I have Hudson in tow, and gratefully bypassed an encounter with Mr. Stanton, Hudson asks if he can check Haven Hitters website for the tryout results. The decision wouldn't be posted until five and Hudson promised to wait until we were together to look. With only twenty-five spots on the team, there will be a few broken hearts this evening. I don't want Hudson's to be one of them.

"Number 312. That's me," Hudson shouts from the back seat. "*Yes.*"

"Way to go, bud. I knew you'd make it." In my heart of hearts, I believed in my boy, but I was also a bit nervous that Cort would bypass Hudson because of me. Not that he'd actually do that or even have a reason to do such a thing, but I was still anxious yesterday afternoon when I first saw Cort. Now, I've seen him three times in less than twenty-four hours.

And with Hudson making the baseball team, I'll be seeing a lot more of Cortland Haven.

"Number 475. That's Atticus. He made the team, too." While Hudson sounds happy, his voice takes on a softer tone, and I peek at him through the rearview mirror. He lifts his head and stares out the side window with a sly smile on his face.

"Huh. Guess that means Amelia will be at your games."

Hudson turns his head to glare at me through the mirror a second. His mouth pops open like he's about to argue that he doesn't care about Amelia. But then he clamps his lips and turns toward the side window again. His lips twist the slightest bit to fight another smile.

I don't want to tease my son about his budding crush . . . *but oh, who am I kidding*, I absolutely want to razz him about crushing on a girl. Still, I remember that gooey sensation. That moment when you first notice someone as something other than a friend. As someone other than simply kind. As someone truly beautiful on the inside and the out.

Shifting my eyes back to the road, I chew on my lower lip, already worried my boy will have his heart broken one day, probably from more than one girl.

Live and learn, they say. Love and learn as well.

At my age, I know I haven't experienced the kind of love I want. The kind I believe I deserve. That all-consuming, only-want-to-be-with-you desire, resulting in spending my life with my person.

My *person* right now is my son; however, that's not healthy or wise. Hudson will grow up, and too soon he'll be out of the house and living his own life separate from me. The thought can bring tears to my eyes, and I quickly blink before they build.

"We need to celebrate," I say. "Pizza?"

"Definitely." Hudson pauses, still staring out the window. "But do you think we could also stop at Uncle Sebastian's bakery for a cookie?"

Sebastian owns Curmudgeon Bakery, a fitting name for our once-grumpy brother who lived a rough decade before he pulled himself together and started his business in downtown Sterling Falls.

When we were kids, and Sebastian was still friends with Clinton Haven, we spent quite a bit of time at the Haven's house, attempting to stay out of the way of our father. There, Sebastian and I learned to bake under the guidance of their mother, Mary Haven. My brother has taken the art of baking to a new level.

His wife loves his lemon baby bundt cakes while Hudson loves what Sebastian calls a monster cookie, made with peanut butter *and* oatmeal plus butterscotch chips *and* chocolate candy bits.

My mouth waters just thinking about the treat although I try to curtail myself when I'm around those delicious baked goods. Still, Hudson deserves the celebration.

"Definitely," I finally respond, turning my SUV back toward town.

AFTER ENTERING the bakery for our celebratory cookie, Sebastian mentions how Enya would love some company. I don't want to detract from Hudson's big moment, but I could use some time with my beloved sister-in-law and a baby fix. Sweet little Annabelle is only a few weeks old.

Hudson making the 12U team is another reminder that he's growing up so fast.

"Why don't you let Hudson come out with the guys?" Sebastian adds. "We can take him out and get him drunk to celebrate."

Not that my brother would ever consider doing such a thing with an eleven-year-old. Sebastian doesn't drink anymore. Doesn't do drugs either after years of being both a user and a dealer. The end of his rebellious years came to an abrupt halt because of me.

One more fault of mine, where I'll gladly take the blame.

Not that I wanted my brother to serve time for committing a crime. He took his anger too far, just like our father used to do. My brother needed help, and I was the last person to offer assistance. Back then, I was following too closely behind him and his reckless ways, chasing my own demons and personal drug—sex—and coming up dissatisfied at every turn, every touch.

"Funny," I counter before my mind heads down a slippery slope.

"Drunk on pizza and root beer, of course." Sebastian winks at Hudson.

While I was looking forward to just the two of us celebrating, Hudson loves to spend time with his uncles. Some days I almost *don't* feel bad that he doesn't have his father around because he has six amazing uncles who love him and show him how to love others. Also, as Hudson has grown older, he's fallen into deep admiration of his uncles and any opportunity to hang out with them makes him feel special.

The second Sebastian suggests Hudson go out with him, Hudson's head is turning toward me, eyes wide, begging me to let him hang with the adult men in our family.

"If you want to . . ." I knock the ball into his court, knowing a time will come when he won't pick me to continue being our team of two.

He's already nodding and glancing back at Sebastian, who winks again.

"Well, as long as I'm getting dumped for the night, I'm gonna go corrupt your wife."

Which is how I end up at Sebastian's beautiful modern farmhouse outside of town.

"Give me that baby," I whine, holding out my arm and wiggling my fingers at Enya to hand over her baby girl.

Enya's acorn colored hair is swept up in a messy knot on the top of her head. She's wearing her glasses, and an oversized shirt that looks like it belongs to my brother, and she still looks beautiful.

"I brought reinforcements." I hold up a bottle of wine. "Trade ya," I prompt again, wanting that little bundle in my arms.

"Bless you," Enya teases, taking the bottle from my hand and passing over her precious newborn.

Enya isn't much of a drinker on a good day and she won't drink more than a glass because she's nursing. She looks tired but happy. Her friendship has been a bright spot for me the past couple of years. Our family needed more women. For my brother, Enya's been pure sunshine, lightening his dark days and bringing joy to his life.

With Annabelle in my arms, I sway side to side, inhaling her baby scent of special laundry detergent and lavender body wash. At only a few weeks old, she gazes aimlessly up at me and then fixates on the low lights overhead. Her dark hair is a reminder of Sebastian, although it's probably baby fuzz she'll lose. Her eyes are still dark blue, a signature trait of being a Sylver. Looking at her brings the burn of tears again. My brother has come so far from who he was and truly deserves the happily ever after he has earned.

"How are you feeling?" I ask as Enya opens the wine bottle in their open concept kitchen and living space. The living room is an explosion of baby contraptions and toys for their soon-to-be two-year-old, Adara, who is quietly playing with a baby doll.

"I'm . . . exhausted." But she smiles with a dreamy look in her eyes. At forty, she has two children and a husband, when she thought she'd be going it on her own with just Adara.

I'm not envious but I want what they have. That look in her eyes. That sigh of contentment. At thirty-four, I don't think another baby is in the plan for me. For now, I'll just snuggle up the one in my arms.

Lowering my head, I run my cheek across the top of Annabelle's downy crown.

"So how are you?" Enya pours me a glass of wine. "How are the Sterlets? What's the latest gossip?" She laughs, knowing all too well how our book club works.

"I don't know if it's gossip, but Hudson made the Haven Hitters baseball team."

Enya finishes pouring my glass of wine and sets the bottle on the counter. Glancing up at me, she confidently states, "As we knew he would."

Damn straight. "But the gossip part might be that the Haven brothers are the coaches."

Enya tilts her head, forcing the knot of hair on top to wobble to the side. "But we also knew this."

"I know. I just . . ." I lick my lips. "In my head, it didn't seem like an issue. I could separate church and state. I mean, Trinity is a good friend, and boys can be dumb, but . . ."

Enya continues to watch me and I almost chicken out on mentioning my fear.

"I just think it might be awkward being around Cortland."

Her brows lift. "Cortland? The oldest one?" She continues to watch me like she can't figure out why *he'd* be the issue. "I thought you were worried about Clint, Sebastian's old friend."

I snort. "Clint is cute but he's not my type."

"Oh." Enya's hairline rises. "And do we have a type?"

I laugh at how she continues to reference *we*, instead of me. Yes, I'm the problem. I'm picky, and for good reason. While Hudson has often been my excuse for not wanting to bring a man into our lives, concerned that he will disappear like Hudson's father did, the real reason is a deeper secret. A personal one.

Again, I'm the issue.

"Of course. Tall, buff, and bearded." I sigh.

Enya laughs. "Sounds a lot like Cortland and—" Her head flinches slightly, taken aback a second, like the truth hit her in the face. "Oh my gosh, you have a crush on Cortland Haven." Her mouth falls open before her smile grows wide. I can almost predict what she'll say next and hear the teasing tone of her voice.

You love Cortland. You love Cortland.

Only her expression sobers, and her voice softens, as she quietly repeats, "You have a crush on Cortland Haven." Like it's the worst news she's heard all year.

"How does that work with Stone?" she adds.

"Hopefully, Stone doesn't have a crush on him?" I shrug and wince, knowing that my brother would be so hurt to learn that I've crushed on Cortland Haven most of my life. Even when he married that bitch Bailey, I forgave Cort. How could I not. I was ten when it happened. But in my heart, Cort was always going to be mine.

Unfortunately, he has already proven he isn't.

With a heavy sigh, I shake my head. "It's silly, really."

"What's silly?" With concern in her eyes, trusting Enya

should come easily. She is a no-judgment zone. Entering into all our lives two years ago, Enya was the first stitch in expanding our family. Enya and Adara, that is. From one single mom to another, we became friends instantly, but there's an even deeper connection between us now. She really is like the sister I always longed to have. The sister I wanted to share secrets with and bounce ideas off.

Hell, when I got my period in my early teens, I had to go to Trudy Wallace, one of our mother's best friends, for advice on why I was bleeding *down there*.

Now my heart is erupting in a way I can't define. A way I don't understand.

Why Cort? Why now? Why, after all this time, are those old feelings buzzing about again?

I could chalk it up to unresolved business between Cort and me or I could conclude the results are lingering side effects. Ones that never truly disappeared and are resurfacing again.

Like a bleated warning, telling me to finally admit the truth, I blurt out:

"I had sex with Cortland Haven twelve years ago."

8

[Cort]

aven Hitters' practices are Saturday mornings and early in the evenings on Tuesdays and Thursdays. I didn't see Vale at either the first official practice or the Tuesday afternoon one.

Despite our interaction during that initial massage therapy appointment, I know I need additional sessions. While I'd like to believe the laundry-basket-mishap was just a tweak, my back has been spasming on and off for months. I can't have some random stranger touching me, even if I went into the first therapy session knowing that might be the case. The truth is, Valentine Sylver is a therapist, and there isn't anyone else I want touching me.

I don't want to work on building trust with a new person every week. I know me, and I'll never get there. Vale offered patience. She gave respect. Plus, she and I have history outside Reflexology. Not the most pleasant backstory but still a story that connects us on some visceral level that suggests I can trust her.

Still, trepidation and eagerness battle within me before my next therapy appointment.

When Vale enters the massage room, I'm already facedown, boxer-briefs on this time, and ready for her hands to be on me. The breaths I've taken intending to calm myself have wound me up instead, but I'm here and I'm prepared.

Until she touches me.

She straightens the sheet laying haphazardly over my back and settles her hands mid-spine. And my heart knocks again.

"I'm going to start the same way we did last time. This will give you a minute to warm up to me."

Thank goodness my face is in this awkward donut pillow and Vale can't see that I'm already hot for her. I haven't stopped thinking about her since the last time I was in this room. In truth, I've had plenty of time to recall a day burned into my memory. A day when I stumbled upon Vale sitting deep in the woods on the edge of the official Sterling Falls. Her legs were crisscrossed. Her eyes sprung open as I'd startled her.

What happened next surprised me as well, and in my recent recall, I realized I never touched Vale. Not properly. Not intimately. Our moment was more like an invasion than an exploration, and then I embarrassed the fuck out of myself.

When Vale's hands move in that methodic way of introduction along my spine, I'm pulled from the past and into the present moment where I mentally attempt to coach myself to relax.

Still, my mind races and the need to fill the tense silence erupts.

"How long have you worked for Reflexology?" The question sounds like I'm bored. Like the opening line to an average date, wanting all the usual information: age, education, employment, kids.

However, I'm anything but complacent. I want to know more about Vale. In twelve years, I've only had glimpses of her here and there. The grocery store where she'd offer a warm smile, and I would avoid her eyes out of embarrassment. Or a rare sighting in downtown Sterling Falls when she'd be on the opposite side of the street, talking on the phone as she walked along the sidewalk or laughing with someone beside her. Most of the time, the person next to her was her son. Then there were an even rarer occasions when I'd visit Milton Roadhouse.

Only a few seconds pass before Vale quietly replies, "We don't need to make small talk. Most people prefer *not* to talk and that's okay. Just try to relax." At the mention of relaxing, her hand moves to my lower left oblique and she begins a series of light pressure movements along my side, almost like she's prodding around the soreness.

When a zinger shoots along my side, I grunt. My body tenses and Vale stills, instantly removing her hands from me.

"You okay?" Silence fills the room like quicksand. I'm suffocating beneath the quiet tension between us, and the conflict of wanting her touch while being afraid of it. Because strange things happen when Vale Sylver has her hands on me.

My heart patters in a new rhythm, one that's chaotic but somehow lighter. My breath hitches, but it's not like I can't breathe. It's more like I'm taking the first real breath I've taken in years. And every inhale brings a soft whiff of Vale. Something sweet. Honey-like.

Next, I hear a distinct sound—the whirl of metal releasing from the lip of a container—like a jar is being opened.

"I'd like to use a special lotion on you. It's my own unique concoction. It will feel good on your skin and help keep the massage smooth. Is that okay?"

I nod, afraid to speak as she'd mentioned not talking.

Again, my auditory senses take over and the sound of flesh-on-flesh fills my ears as Vale warms up the lotion on her hands before placing her fingers on me.

Working a few minutes in silence, she concentrates on the muscles along my lower left side. I close my eyes and breathe through the process. The occasional twinge of pain. The constant conflict of Vale touching me. The slow build of arousal.

I shouldn't be getting hard. I'm not a man who likes women to be handsy with me. In fact, I'm very particular about the way I have sex, when I have sex, which has been rare in the last decade. I haven't been a monk but I'm not a guy seeking out the affection of a companion either.

Which makes my body's reaction to Vale even more befuddling.

"I started working at Reflexology about nine years ago," Vale mentions softly, almost like she doesn't want to disturb me.

However, the sound of her voice gives me something to concentrate on, distracting me from her fingers on my flesh. I want to keep her talking.

"Were you somewhere else before that?" My voice is muffled from the position of being face down and my cheeks pressed into the pillow, but Vale answers.

"This was my first job and I've been here ever since." Pride about the longevity fills her voice. "After Hudson was born, I took a year to . . . acclimate to motherhood."

I can almost hear her smile. A different type of pride fills her tone about being a mother.

My ex-wife had not been thrilled about motherhood; something that happened unexpectedly. She also hadn't been a very good mother. I fault myself in many ways. Her selfish, neglectful nature was something I saw as a reflection on me, on us and our relationship, and I hadn't recognized until it was almost too late that her behavior was simply who she was as a person.

"Anyway . . ." Vale continues working at my side, teasing out a knot I didn't even know existed. The massage is a heavy dose of pleasure and pain. Kind of like my current mental state about Vale.

"I see that Haven Exteriors has really taken off."

The comment suggests she's kept up on me. Or maybe that's just wishful thinking. Reckless hope that Vale Sylver investigated what happened to me *after* our moment in the woods. I'd certainly checked up on her.

"Yeah, Clinton and I have a good gig going."

"Until you fell off a roof." She chuckles.

I smile as well, although she can't see my expression. "Oh, I still go up on roofs."

Vale stills her fingers. The silence is almost deafening, and I wish I could see her face. I want to know what's going on in her head.

"Why would you continue to do that?" Her voice is quiet while incredulous, like she doesn't understand how I could continue the risk, when the rewards offset any potential danger.

Haven Exteriors has turned into a gold mine of success, and I'm proud of what Clint and I have built even if it is vastly different from where I thought I'd be. Not that I thought I could play professional football forever, but I still never saw, never *envisioned*, where my life would be after the pros.

"Fall down seven times. Get up eight." I've heard the philosophy several times over the course of my life.

Vale huffs. "That sounds like something Stone would say."

At the mention of her brother, tense silence fills the room again. Like something noxious and invisible has been pumped into the space. I can't breathe and I'm certain Vale is holding her breath as well. The topic of her brother is off-limits.

A painfully long minute passes before Vale settles her fingers back on my lower back and returns to working on my muscles.

So much for small talk.

The remainder of my time spirals between being over too soon and feeling like it lasted forever.

When Vale finishes, she places her hands gently on the middle of my back again.

"All right, Cort. We're finished for today."

Unfortunately, I don't feel finished with her, and I turn my head on the awkward pillow so I can see her better. She spins for the counter and types into her tablet before facing the massage table again. Reaching for the sheet over the lower half of my body, she rights the material even though I'm about to sit up. She tenderly smooths down the sheet allowing her hand to slip over my hip where I catch her pinky and ring finger before Vale can step away.

From my position, I watch as Vale glances down to where my larger fingers wrap around her two smaller ones, holding on longer than necessary. Holding on at all probably shouldn't be happening but I'm afraid to let go. Afraid of the emotions she's stirring inside me. But mostly afraid they'll disappear.

"Thank you," I whisper.

She'll never understand how monumental it's been to have her touching me. Or how stimulating in a manner more than sexual.

And by Thursday night, I find myself parked on a bar stool in Milton Roadhouse again, hoping to catch another glimpse of Vale Sylver.

9

[Vale]

When Cort asked me about my time at Reflexology, my initially snappish response was necessary. It wasn't that I didn't want to talk to him, it's just that most clients prefer the quiet and the soft hum of relaxation music piped into the room. For myself, I'd been struggling to keep my head in the process of disassociation, working my fingers along another human for purposes that are medicinal and not sexual.

Because Cort has a back that is sexy as sin. A scar near his right shoulder blade adds to the seductive edge, and my mind kept wandering, wondering what it would feel like to lay my hands on him in another manner. Spread my palms over the expanse of his back and feel his weight over my body. The thought was completely unprofessional, and one I'd never ever had before with a client.

When he asked me about myself, I'd been so lost in my head, my throat strained my answer.

A minute passed before I realized two things. Cort might have *wanted* me to talk to ease his discomfort. He also might have asked because he really wanted to know the answer. The second one seemed a bit far-fetched. Cortland has had twelve years to ask me questions and offer me some explanations.

Then again, I got the message loud and clear that day in the woods.

Unfortunately, Cort was not the answer to my prayers. He wasn't mine and never would be. It was the wake up call I'd needed to move on with my life.

Not that my life was on hold. Back then, I had one more year of school to complete my physical therapy degree and then I'd be moving on to a bigger city. Knoxville or Nashville or Atlanta. I didn't care where. The only qualification was that I be far away from Sterling Falls.

Everyone else had escaped.

Ford left to play professional baseball. Knox went into the military. Even as wrong as it sounds, Sebastian had an out by spending time in jail. Stone and Judd both had plans to leave forever but were sucked back into the vortex. Clay was the only one who never saw himself leaving.

Regardless, I had dreams outside of this mountain town.

Then I had Hudson. Stone took me in, gave me a year to spend time with my young son, *and then* I started using my degree. The furthest I'd gotten from Sterling Falls was one town over. Most days, I tell myself the distance no longer matters. My life is what it is.

However, when I find myself sitting on a bar stool in Milton Roadhouse before another book club, Kindle on the bar, and Coke in my glass, I'm struck again with how lonely my life is.

I might be surrounded by annoying brothers and a growing son and amazing new sisters-in-law-turned-friends, but I'm still missing that one component I've always wanted. *Love*. The only-for-me kind of love.

Staring down at my open e-reader, I almost curse the unrealistic romance I'm reading, realizing I've been mindlessly glaring at the digital page more than comprehending the words.

This week's Sterlets' meeting is centered around a legitimate book, and I've struggled to be swept away in it. My mind has been preoccupied instead by the reality of Cortland Haven and his body. I blame my confession to Enya for bringing him to the forefront of my brain. It's not like I've obsessed over Cort for twelve years. Eventually, I lumped him in with every other man I've sexually experienced—unable to complete the task.

Of course, I know now all the reasons why that is, and it's more about me than them.

Still, I can't help but wonder if Cort—

"Whatcha readin'?"

I glance up from my rambling thoughts to see Henry Stanton leaning casually against the bar. His elbow is perched on the counter. His hip leaning against the bar, but his gaze is outward. Despite asking me a question, his body language reads disinterested in my answer.

Inwardly, I sigh and roll my eyes, knowing he's about to *attempt* to flirt with me and I'm already exhausted by the wasted effort.

With a strained smile and a breath of annoyance, I answer him, "Smut."

Although I proudly read what some consider idyllic romance, I find the word 'smut' a bit derogatory about the genre I love, but I'm hoping shock will stun him into silence.

His head swivels in my direction and a salacious grin curls his lips. He twists his body to face the bar and settles both his forearms on the top by bending at the waist. His eyes don't leave me now, and I curse myself for having captured his attention instead of repelling it. Those same eyes blatantly scan down my seated position, lingering on my backside before flinging back up to my face.

"Interesting."

"Really? You read romance novels?" Bet Henry doesn't even read. He probably prefers pictures . . . in magazines. The thought of him pleasuring himself in such a manner makes me shiver, especially as he's standing so close to me. There are three empty stools to my right. He can take a seat anywhere else but near me.

Henry scoffs, like I've insulted his intelligence and his ability. *No romantic gestures coming from this guy.* I already know what he wants. His intention comes in every leering gaze he gives me. And it's another reason I don't like Hudson having a friendship with Atticus, which isn't fair to the kids.

The sins of the father shouldn't be held against his children. I'm all too familiar with that kind of condemnation.

With his arms still on the bar, he leans forward and back, rocking his hips in a gentle, repetitive thrusting motion. "Maybe you could read me a passage sometime."

With anyone else, the proposition might be endearing, seductive even, but not from Henry. Once again, I fight to keep a grimace off my face while a sticky, icky feeling glides down my throat. I might even throw up a little bit in my mouth at the thought of reading any such passage with this man.

"Or I could recommend the book when I'm done." *Or not.* Because I'd really prefer to have as little interaction with him as I can.

"Let me buy you a drink." He reaches for the stool to his right and tugs it closer to mine. Too close.

I scoot to the edge of my seat, frustrated that he's taken the liberty to invite himself to sit beside me, and exhausted that I must play this game with him, because small town, and my son's friend's dad, and just the bullshit of being a single woman.

Why can't I just be? Adult woman seeks love and affection; not needing a hero but wanting her equal.

Is that so hard to ask? I roll my eyes heavenward as if the goddess of love and sexual desire hears me.

"Sorry I'm late." The rugged masculine voice to my left has me turning my head so fast my neck pops. My mouth gapes, before I'm rolling my lips inward, sensing I'm caught between a rock and a hard place, and staring at the lesser of the two evils.

"Cortland." I drag out his name like I'm scolding his tardiness when we had zero plans to meet here. His name is also strangled in my throat because he looks so good. Straw cowboy hat on his head again. Silky blue shirt and dark jeans, like he *does* have plans to meet someone. Only not me.

"Weren't you sitting on the other side of the bar?" Henry asks Cort.

Was he? I hadn't noticed. I'd entered with my head down, ordered my cola from Maggie, Milton's owner, and promptly opened my Kindle as a distraction.

Cort doesn't respond to Henry but keeps his eyes on me. *He bothering you?*

I could shake my head, signaling Henry is simply an annoyance but not a threat. But then I'd be dismissing Cort and settling for Henry sidled up beside me until I can reasonably escape for book club, when I just want to sit here and sip a Coke.

Flipping a coin and happily, mentally, landing on heads, I narrow my eyes at Cort. "I've been wondering when you'd get here."

The deep layers of my statement are something I'll lose sleep over later.

"He was sitting on the other side of the bar," Henry interjects. His hand waves in my periphery toward the opposite side of the three-sided bar. His tone suggests he's offended, almost like he got here first, so Cort loses, but I'm not playing a game. At least, not with Henry.

"Hey, do you mind, I have a few things to discuss with Cort." I swivel only my upper half to address Henry. "It's about Hudson." Using my son as an excuse to soften the blow is a hopeful tactic. Like Henry will understand—parent to parent—that I need to talk privately with my kid's coach.

Henry twists his body and gives me another once over, before scrunching up his nose. He lowers his voice and leans toward me to mutter, "Don't think you can sleep your way to your son having a better position on the team."

My jaw hits the floor. I'm so taken aback; I don't respond. Like I've been slapped across the face but not associating the sting yet. I'm simply stunned.

However, Cort reacts instantly, stepping around my back and leaning in so close to Henry he presses into the bar, his back arching against the lip of the counter.

"We got a problem here?" Cort's face is close enough to Henry's that he could rub his nose against the man's. Instead, Cort has a murderous gleam in his eyes, like he wants to smash Henry's face into the countertop.

"I'm just teasing," Henry defends, holding up his arms in limp surrender.

"Did you find that funny, Vale?" Cort addresses me without taking his eyes off Henry.

I still can't talk. I'm too shocked by the venom in Cort's tone and the position he's pinned Henry in, and maybe a little turned on by this display of dominance and heroism on my behalf.

Slowly, I shake my head and swallow, wetting my mouth to form some words, but Cort continues before I can speak.

"*I* didn't find it funny," he warns. "And if I hear you say another thing like that to Vale or any other woman affiliated with the team, you and I are gonna have more than words." He doesn't bother asking Henry if he comprehends his meaning. The speck of fear in Henry's eyes confirms his understanding.

Here's the thing about men like Henry, he *thinks* he's a big fish in a small pond, when he's really a stinky, day-old fish out of water. We've got a guy who peaked in high school compared to a man who peaked . . . well . . . he's still peaking. Cort's body is as rigid as the mountain we live on and he's holding his breath like a volcano about to blow.

Henry nods once.

"Now . . . you're in my seat." Cort slowly steps backward, allowing Henry to scramble off the stool he was sitting on, which almost makes me laugh because there are still plenty of other vacant stools around me. But I'm not about to argue with Cortland.

Henry scampers off, pointing a finger gun at someone across the bar like he didn't just get chastised and chased away.

Some guys will never learn.

Settling beside me, Cort spreads his legs wide, his knee tapping against mine, while he keeps his torso facing forward, elbows on the bar. He doesn't look directly at me when he asks, "You okay?"

For some reason, his position reminds me of Henry's disinterest in what I was reading, and an edge creeps over me. Instead of gratitude, I snap. "I can handle myself."

I've been doing it for as long as I can remember.

At my outburst, Cort's head whips toward me. Those dark eyes of his narrow like he can see deep into my soul. His stare doesn't waver from my face when he says, "I know you can."

Did his voice drop an octave? Why is he looking at me like he knows a secret about me?

"But a woman like you shouldn't have to always take care of herself."

My mouth falls open. *And what kind of woman am I?* "You know you sound as sexist as Henry."

Cort shifts his seated position, setting those wide-spread legs around my stool. His knee once again touches mine. He arches one of his thick brows, eyes widening. "When we start talking about sex, it's not going to include the letters *i, s, t*." The corner of his mouth hitches. Just the slightest teasing twitch, like a blink of a smile, and then it's gone.

His expression sobers. "Seriously, though. You okay? Does that kind of bullshit happen often?"

I shrug. "Not really, but being a single mom . . ."

"You mean being beautiful."

My mouth falls open again. *What?*

"Some men think it's *their* right to say what they want to say, when and where they want to say it. I don't want you takin' that shit, Little Bee. Not on my team. Not anywhere."

I blink. Blink again. I hear what he's saying but I'm stuck on one thing.

Little Bee.

He hasn't called me that in years, and I'm caught in the crossfire between elation that he remembers the nickname he gave me and the sense he still thinks of me as that little girl. One who is defenseless and weak.

"I'm not a child," I counter, glossing over his kindness and concern.

He pins his gaze to my eyes, before his shoulders sag, like he's accepting defeat. His gaze falls like he can't fight the weight any longer. His glance slides down the slope of my nose, catching on my lips a second, before dipping to my throat.

I watch as his rolls.

There's something different in the way Cort observes me. Not lewd like Henry's disinterested review, but more like Cort is memorizing me, etching my details into a sketch book. The intensity of his eyes sends heat over my flesh while goosebumps rise.

"I remember," he says.

All the air whooshes out of me.

Not that I ever thought Cort forgot what happened between us, I just didn't think he'd ever mention it. Like it never happened if we didn't talk about it. However, my memory is a scrapbook of that moment.

His hands on me. His mouth against my throat. The rush to get somewhere I cannot get with speed. Without a strong connection. And as much as I thought I was connected to Cort in some inexplicable way, I wasn't.

It wasn't his fault. It was mine.

With his intense gaze on me, I look away from him and pick up my drink, needing a sip of something bubbly, something that will tickle my throat and reset my brain to the present situation.

Cortland Haven is sitting next to me.

"Well." I pause, setting my glass back down. "Thank you for your intervention. I appreciate you."

Cort chuffs, holding up his hand for Maggie's attention. He forms a V with his forefinger and the middle one, making a peace sign in greeting to her, but when two shot glasses full of amber liquor appear in front of us, I turn my head toward Cort again.

"Shots? Really?"

"Seems like you could use one." He taps his short glass against the lip of mine. "Take the sting out of you."

The sting? This guy has some nerve, and rising to the bait, I pick up my glass, not bothering to sniff the liquid, and down what I quickly learn is straight bourbon.

Holy F- that burns. I sputter instantly, choking on the fire trailing down my esophagus.

Thankfully, Cort doesn't laugh before tipping back his own glass and swallowing in one smooth motion.

"Thought bees liked a little smoke."

"Smoke, yes. But fire, no." I cough one more time. As an

amateur beekeeper, I know a few things about bees. Smoke is intended to calm them, not set them ablaze. And I don't need a blaze of glory in my life. Flames flicker and burn out.

"Bees prefer sweeter things." *I* want tender moments and private jokes and meaningful touches. Something long-lasting and personal. Intimate.

Cort continues to watch me before he tips his chin upward. "Like that lotion you used on me."

"My honey balm?"

"Is that what you call it?"

"I haven't come up with a better name." The combination of honey, beeswax, shea butter and grapeseed oil is the perfect texture for massages. Smooth and creamy, it works easily into someone's skin, causing my hands to glide over tight muscles and loose flesh. Not that Cort is loose anywhere.

He doesn't respond to my lack of creativity. Instead, his back stiffens and I'm about to ask if he's having back spasms, a possible side effect from the massage yesterday morning, when he slides off the stool beside me.

"Thanks for the drink," he mutters.

With long confident strides, he steps away from me, and I'm so confused, especially since he's the one who bought me the shot.

But then my eyes land on two men who have just entered Milton Roadhouse.

My brothers Clay and Knox.

Glancing toward the opposite side of the bar, I watch Cort take a seat. Possibly the one he was sitting on when Henry approached me. He gazes up at the baseball game on the big screen like it's the most fascinating game he's ever watched.

For half a second, I curse my brothers' appearance.

Then I cuss the whole lot of them for still holding a grudge.

10

[Vale]

Parents have the option of lingering during baseball practice. Rogue River isn't that far away from Sterling Falls, but also not close enough for me to run some of the errands on my list, so I sit in my SUV because of cooler temps today and wait out Hudson's practice. As much as I'd like to read the latest hot romance on my Kindle, my mind keeps drifting, along with my eyes, toward the practice field, where Cort is coaching Hudson on pitching.

Cort doesn't look over at me once.

As I've had time to reflect on his sudden appearance in the bar the other night, playing savior against Henry's rudeness, I realize Cort might have eventually been flirting with me. And I'm rusty on flirting.

My last date was almost a year ago. I can't remember when I last had sex. I don't have the energy or desire to hang out in a bar and play flirting games. Plus, there aren't that many single men in this area that I haven't already dated, or that didn't date a friend once, or marry one of them first, and there is just something about being second fiddle that strikes a chord with me.

Most days I tell myself I cannot expect there to be a man in his thirties or forties who *hasn't* experienced love with someone else first. I think I'm the anomaly.

By Wednesday, I've replayed my brief interaction with Cort last week in Milton Roadhouse over and over and concluded . . . nothing. My decision becomes clear—pretend it didn't happen. So, when Cort enters the massage room, I'm as professional and distant as I can be.

But dammit, he looks so good in faded jeans and a dark Haven Exteriors T-shirt that hugs his chest and strains over his biceps.

Why does he have to be so pretty?

"I'll give you a minute," I say, after he nods in greeting at me. Because I'm the one needing a minute for another strong pep-talk about professionalism. He's a patient. He's injured. *You will not lust after him*. And the final punctuation on the internal speech is the reminder he cannot get you off.

That should do the trick.

Only, when I re-enter the room, and see the expanse of his back, my self-talk falls to the ground like a heavy brick. His trapezius is a work of sculpted art. His rhomboid muscles are defined. His latissimus dorsi cause the perfect valley along his spine leading to his gluteus maximus. But even the technical terms are no distraction from the perfection of him and how badly I want to run my hands over his shoulders, upper back, and ass in more than a medicinal manner.

Bad, Valentine. Very, very, bad.

"How is your lower back?" I ask, reaching for my tablet to gather myself. "On a scale of one to ten, ten being unbearable."

"On a scale of one to ten, I'd say a five. The massages help but by the end of a week, the pressure is back."

I glance over at Cort and catch him watching me, his head awkwardly turned on the donut pillow.

"I'm sorry that happens to you." I clear my throat, noticing my voice is too robotic. I do feel bad for him. Back pain is no joke. "You've been approved for more visits so let's see if we can keep working out the kinks."

Cort's eyes widen, and a flash beams outward at me, like a beacon roaming over a dark sea.

Ignoring the spark, I step to his side and begin the calming work of introduction.

With my hands settled on his mid-back, I can feel his thumping heart, but he doesn't stiffen as much as he did the first time. And I have a question for him. My heart says asking Cort something personal is crossing a line; my head says it's the professional thing to do.

"Cort, may I ask you something?" The second I question him, tension occurs in his back, but I keep my hands still and my determination plows onward. "Do you have touch aversion?"

"What's 'touch aversion'?" he mutters into the pillow surrounding his face.

"It's when you don't like to be touched by anyone. Touch makes you uncomfortable. Possibly, you even have a fear of it." The thought that he's afraid of my hands wounds me and yet I know it's possible. "Technically, it's called haphephobia."

Silence follows my explanation, and I move my hands during the awkward quiet. Beneath my touch, Cort takes a deep breath. I wish I could see his face, maybe read his eyes, but I can't. With his back to me, I'd been hopeful the disconnect might make it easier for him to answer me.

A painfully long minute passes before he says, "I don't know."

While not a confession, it is an admission that touch bothers him.

"Is it me?" Because if it is, I'm willing to pass him to another therapist, like I'd mentioned during his first visit.

Cort shifts, rising up on his elbows and craning his neck to glance over his shoulder. His eyes catch on mine. "No, Vale. It isn't you." He turns his head away from me and stares at the wall in front of him. "It's me."

He offers no further explanation, and I lick my lips as he settles back into position so I can begin his massage session, concentrating on his left lat, while balancing the work on both sides.

"Did something happen?" I quietly ask, not expecting him to tell me his darkest secrets, but hoping that if he'll open up a little bit, so I'd be better equipped to help him.

As I anticipated, he doesn't answer, and I continue to work his muscles beneath the soft hum of calming music piped into the room.

"Can I ask *you* a question?" Cort finally says, breaking into my concentration on the magnificence of his back. Even that scar on his upper right shoulder blade is hot.

"Sure." I smile to myself.

"Where's Hudson's dad?"

My hands falter in the rhythmic pressure I'd been applying on his lower back.

I don't often talk about Hudson's father. Not that he was a bad man, just an absentee one. He was one more misplaced hope for love mixed with a bottle of Tanqueray and a short vacation. There's probably a love song written about such situations.

"He's not in the picture," I admit, pausing a second, deciding how much I'm willing to open myself up to Cort. "He didn't exactly want to be a dad, but then he occasionally sends Hudson stuff."

Ken never calls; he simply sends unmarked packages. He hit a few birthdays, missed the mark on a few others. I've toyed with telling him to disappear completely because the grains of sand he gives Hudson don't add up to a beach of warmth and affection. Most times, those pebbles are like that nasty pea in *The Princess and the Pea* fable. They disrupt Hudson's life, making him wonder why his dad doesn't want to come around.

Strangely, Ken also sends me gifts on Mother's Day every year.

The sad truth is that I slept with Ken in hopes to get over the heartbreak of having sex with Cort.

Ken never demanded a paternity test, he simply asked not to be written on Hudson's birth certificate. He never intended to be an involved father. *I* am Hudson's only parent. And I'm enough.

"He works on an oil rig, so he's offshore for long stretches of time, and lives in Alabama when he's on land."

At least, that was his life twelve years ago during that dang girls' trip to the Alabama shore after my friends all graduated from college and before I headed back to school for the final year of my physical therapy degree. I met a cute guy with a you-look-like-you-love-me smile, which simply meant he was open to a vacation fling, and I'd been young and foolish once again.

"Anyway, Hudson is my whole world, and I'm grateful to Stone for taking us in and giving me some time with Hudson when he was a baby."

I'd gone back to school after that reckless summer, not having known yet that I was pregnant, and had Hudson three months before my graduation.

Zero stars. Do not recommend being a new mom and finishing college at the same time.

After graduation, I took a year off from job hunting and mothered my son. Like most of my life, it took a village in the beginning and Stone has always been the president of strength.

I glance at the back of Cort's head, wondering what he thinks of me. Wondering also if he ever thinks about Stone and the friendship they once had. How they were brothers from another mother, doing everything together from birth to age twenty-two. I'd worry mentioning my brother might upset Cort, but then I recall him walking away from me the other night when Clay and Knox entered Milton Roadhouse.

Definitely does not want to discuss my brothers.

Suddenly, I feel as if I've been rambling, telling him much more than he wanted to know.

Another set of awkward minutes follow my babbling, before Cort says, "I'm glad Stone was there to look after you."

I'd scoff, but I know what he means. Stone's been watching over me like a guardian angel since I was born, and even though he flew the coop for a few years, he came home when it didn't seem like there was any other option for us. At least, not an option Stone was willing to let happen.

"Got another man in your life doing that now?"

I chuckle at the not-so-smooth transition to another topic. "Cortland Haven, are you asking if I have a boyfriend?"

He snorts, causing his shoulders to flinch. "Guess I am."

I smile but instantly chastise myself because this is not a professional conversation to have with a patient. However, the truth slips free. "I don't have a boyfriend." For some reason, my cheeks heat and my fingers stiffen against Cort's back.

Glancing at the timer on my phone, I notice our session is almost over and shift to the final stages of the massage. A calming activity where I smooth my hands over the parts I've concentrated on.

"And we're finished." I step away from the table turning for the tablet on the counter to type up my notes for today in preparation to leave the room and provide Cort privacy to dress.

But when I turn back to address him, he's pushing himself upright, twisting himself into a seated position by swinging his legs over the edge of the table while pulling the sheet over his lap. With such a quick movement, I wouldn't even guess he has a back issue.

My mouth falls open at the glorious outline of muscle on his chest and smattering of hair over his pecs before I lift the tablet like a shield before my face. *Holy hell.* "I'm just going to —" I motion toward the door with the tablet, keeping my head turned to the side despite the magnetic pull my eyes feel to inspect Cort one more time.

His fingers circle my wrist, and I lower the tablet-shield to meet coal-dark eyes, sparking here and there with a flame. My breath hitches at the warmth of his palm on my skin, and I glance down at where he's touching me.

"Does shit like what happened with Henry, happen often?"

He'd asked me a similar question the other night. He'd also told me I was beautiful, and I have not forgotten how it sounded coming out of his mouth.

I can't seem to find the words to answer him. The heat of his hand. The warmth in his eyes. The concern in his rugged voice. The combination is scrambling my thoughts.

"I'm gonna be watching out for you, too." He's referring to how my brother was there for me. How my brother has *always* taken care of me.

But I don't want his pity. His sympathy for me not having a dad, just like my son doesn't. His empathy that my brother raised me, like he helped me raise my child. The idea that I need some sort of protection.

"I don't need that," I tell him, noting the edge in my tone. "I take care of myself."

Cort stares at me long and hard, like he again knows a secret about me, or maybe he can just see into the depths of my soul. Where it says I'm a strong woman but I'm still lonely. I'm still craving something no man has ever given me.

"At the practices, and games at least, I'll have one eye on you."

I scoff. "Oh, like you've been ignoring me at said practices since seeing you at Milton's last week."

His brows hitch, eyes widening. "I'm not ignoring you, Vale. I'm keeping my distance out of respect for your brothers. There's a difference."

"Well, I don't account to my brothers." And why is he still holding my wrist? Still stroking his thumb along the sensitive flesh on the underside. Still pressing against my accelerating pulse.

"Little Bee," he whispers, soft and concerned.

"I'm not a child," I counter, sounding very much like a little girl.

"I'm well aware." With those dark eyes piercing mine, my breath hitches, and catches a second time when he slides his hand from my wrist to my palm before circling three of my fingers: pinky, ring finger, and middle one. He gives a little squeeze before he lets go, and I want to chase his touch. Like a pollinator seeks out the sweet nectar in pretty flowers.

Only, I've already been drunk on Cort, and I won't be smothered in false honey again.

Cort can never again be the buzzing awakening I experienced at ten or a blinding blip of hope I had at twenty-two.

It isn't fair to him.

And it isn't fair to me.

11

[Vale]

On Saturday, Stone takes Hudson to practice while I run errands around town. My first stop is motivational. I need coffee and something sweet, so I pop into my brother's bakery.

The Curmudgeon Bakery has black and white checkerboard tile flooring. A dark wooden bench runs the length of one wall with a scattering of tables and chairs in front of it. A display case of goodies lines the opposite wall. Near the front of the bakery is a small sitting area with café tables. The place is appropriately named for the business owned—our once surly brother—who also happened to be one of my closest friends growing up.

Trouble led Sebastian, and as I followed him wherever he went, that meant trouble found me on occasion. In my teens and the beginning of my twenties was when I was most reckless.

When I searched for love in all the wrong places, literally. I wasn't proud of what I'd done or who I'd been with, having gotten myself into a pickle a time or two with the wrong sort of character. Or rather, refusing his pickle. One time in particular was a close call, and my brother right above me in birth order played the hero. He also took the fall like a villain, serving jail time for his reaction.

For years, guilt weighed heavily on my shoulders because Sebastian was locked up while I was raising my son, living a better life than I expected. But now, Sebastian has Enya and two beautiful daughters, plus he runs a respectable business, and my pride and deep love abound for how things turned out for him.

He still has a curmudgeon look about him with the tats and dark clothing, but I know he's feeling lighter inside, and he smiles more often.

"Hey," he greets me as I near the counter where he slides a tray of brownies into the display case. "How's my favorite sister?"

"Funny, as I'm your only sister."

"And thank God for that." He looks up and winks.

I give him a sassy smirk before directing my attention to the display case. Everything looks mouth-watering today, and I take my time to glance at the variety of baby bundt cakes and brownies, plus cookies and muffins.

"What can I get you?" he asks, swiping his hands on the apron tied around his waist.

"What's new?" Still being springtime, he doesn't have a large array of seasonal berry treats or my favorite pumpkin spice anything.

"I got crack."

Certain he's joking, my head still swivels in his direction. Sebastian doesn't do drugs anymore. Further teasing me, he pulls a tray from a refrigerator. *Crack.* Graham cracker bottom with a layer of solid chocolate on top. Toffee in the middle with crumbles on top of the chocolate layer.

"I hate you," I tease. "Give me one of those." Not exactly breakfast of champions but I've got a lust for sweets today that only chocolate can fix.

After asking about the baby, Adara, and Enya, and catching him up on Hudson, I take my coffee and crack for a later snack, intending to exit the bakery, until Trinity Haven enters.

"What's up, Trin?" I ask, noting how her head is down, reading something on her phone.

She looks up at me with a weary expression before slipping her phone into her pocket. "Oh, hey, Vale. Nothing much."

I don't believe her. As Trinity and I called a truce years ago despite our brothers' situation, I take a seat on the long bench, setting my coffee on the nearest table. "Sit with me a second." She looks like she could use a friend.

Trinity simply stares at me for another second before stepping up to the counter and ordering her own morning drink and a muffin. She takes the chair opposite me and stares at the perfectly puffed-up pastry as if it offends her.

"Girl, what did that muffin do to you?" I joke.

Her blond hair shakes as she does a full body shudder before sitting upright and leaning her elbows on the tabletop. "Why are men so stupid?"

Something tells me she doesn't mean collectively. Maybe just one man.

"I hate cheaters," she adds.

I nod to agree but also find it a bit rich considering what her brother did to mine. Then again, like I said, Trinity and I have a truce.

"What'd he do now?" Eyeing her, I don't need to say his name.

Trinity swipes her hands over her face, tugging at her skin a little bit. "Nothing. Right? He's done absolutely nothing for me."

Without spelling it out, I know she's referring to her ex-husband who left our small town without a blink backward. The hardest part about their breakup was how in love they seemed. They were perfect for each other and then he just decided to leave. Or so Trinity tells us. A midlife crisis at thirty-five. He became a NASCAR driver.

"Want to talk about it?" I ask, open to listening to more details.

"Not really." She shakes her head again and stares down at her steaming cup.

Sebastian suddenly appears at the side of the table with another piece of crack goodness on a small plate. He practically drops it on the tabletop but then he slides it toward Trinity before walking away. He doesn't say a word, although minutes ago he was pleasant enough taking her order.

Trinity's eyes follow his retreat before she shakes her head one more time and turns back toward me. "Think they'll ever grow up?" She means the silent feud that is so old sometimes it's almost difficult to remember what happened. *Almost*, but not quite.

I remember. The heartbreak of my oldest brother. The loss of both his best friend and his girl. In trade he took on six siblings. It wasn't fair.

And it's a reminder why Cort and I shouldn't ever be more than we are now. Therapist and patient. Mother to a kid he coaches. Once his sessions are over and the season ends, back to our respective corners we go.

"I don't know," I admit about our siblings. They have grown in so many ways. Her brothers are just as accomplished as mine, but hers are also single later in life like most of mine have been.

"Sometimes I just want to knock all their heads together. Don't get me wrong, I know Cort was at fault, but still . . ."

This is the first time Trinity has ever spoken so directly about what happened.

Cort broke Stone's heart. He also broke mine a little bit too. While unintentionally cracking it open when I was ten, the real shattering happened later.

Cort wasn't a bad man, he just made poor decisions. Who didn't? I'd made a rash decision as well with misplaced expectations on him, so I take some responsibility for my wound. But if I was being honest, the way he'd treated me hurt. Deeply.

And the moment proved only one thing: I would never find what I was looking for through random sex.

Trinity sighs. "But sometimes, you just have to forgive and let go." She makes a heart symbol with her hands before breaking them apart and fluttering her fingers like two halves are flying away from each other. "Be free."

Somehow, I don't think we're discussing our brothers anymore, but I appreciate what she's saying. I learned to forgive long ago. Be free from my own guilt in the equation with Cort.

Letting go of him hadn't been a choice.

He'd walked away from me.

He'd also never been mine to keep.

CORT IS STILL on my brain when he shouldn't be as I stand in the beekeeping section of the Sylver Seed & Soil. Our family business started out as a dream of our mother's. She loved the outdoors. Plants and flowers. Animals, especially horses. And when the opportunity came up to buy a rundown farm and fleet business, the romantic side of our father, which I'd never ever seen, decided to purchase it for her.

Upon her death, their dream died, according to our dad.

Between his drinking, gambling, and business debts, he'd taken the start of a thriving opportunity and ran it into the ground. Clay worked his butt off for years, struggling to keep the place standing before our father died. Then the real work began. Clay turned the farm and fleet into something even greater. While farm supplies are still sold through the back of the business, the front end has turned into an empire for the outdoor enthusiast, selling garden needs and garden-themed houseware items, plus pet products. Thus, a beekeeping section.

My mind races as I stare at the two types of bee smokers on a shelf.

Forgiving Cort came with time and seeing him so often lately is triggering old feelings. The sting of his rejection. The confusion about his tears. The coldness of his second exit from my life.

While I could justify not reciprocating my crush when I was in my teens, it was harder to excuse Cort's actions as an adult.

When I was twenty-two, he'd been making bedroom eyes at me, restoring the heart emojis in mine, and that attention was enticing, refreshing, and maybe even a little vindicating. Like he really saw me. Saw what I needed.

Only everything crashed and burned as it always does when I go at sex with full speed. I'd been devastated then, but as I'm quick to react, instead of reflect, I'd been with Ken soon after Cort, and then my life flipped in other ways that made the Cort-situation almost insignificant.

But now he's back. Or at least, I'm stuck seeing him more often than I have in years.

And I'm just as befuddled.

The tender hand holds. The soft brush of his fingers on the underside of my wrist. What was he doing? Why was he doing it? And dammit, why am I stirred up by him again?

Shaking my head, I force my concentration back to the bee

smoker options, reading off once again the attributes of each one.

"Vale?"

Like I've conjured him up, the rugged, surprised voice has me turning my head, flinching a little bit in additional confusion.

"Cortland?"

The very last place I expect to see Cort is standing in the aisles of my family's business, dressed like he came here fresh from the Haven Hitters practice, complete with a backward baseball cap on his head. *Damn, he looks good.*

Taking a step closer to me, he glances at where I'd just been staring. "Smokers?"

While my insides leap at his nearness, my response is still snarky. "It's for blowing smoke up someone's ass."

Cort snorts while his gaze drops to my backside before quickly looking away. "Well, that sounds . . . hot." The corner of his mouth tips up just the slightest bit.

"Good one," I counter, turning to face him. "What are you doing here?"

Cort casually leans against the shelf. "I need to pick up a puffer." He holds one hand outward in a fist, the other a few inches away, motioning back and forth like he's pumping something up. I could make a sexual remark back at him but bite the inside of my cheek instead.

"Do you mean a powder duster?"

"Yeah, that." He snaps his fingers while the corner of his mouth curls a little higher as we stare at each other another second. "My momma needs it for her garden."

Mary Haven. "How is your momma?" I sigh sweetly, having fond memories of his mother.

"She's good." His smile falters only a little bit. Cort lost his dad to a heart attack in the time our families have been separated. Seventy-something seems too young to be a widow.

Then again, my father became a widower in his thirties.

As silence lingers, I tip my head to the side. "The puffers are in the next aisle over."

Cort exaggerates a nod but doesn't press off the shelf. Instead, he turns his attention back to the smokers.

"I've been looking at a smoker for my bees," I explain, taking the sting out of my early joke. "I'm a beekeeper." Playfully jabbing a finger in his direction, I narrow my eyes. "No little bee jokes."

Cort's mouth twitches a little higher. His arms cross and he glances back at the smokers. "A beekeeper? Really?" Disbelief doesn't fill his tone half as much as his question implies. And the curl of his mouth is still slight but teasing.

His full smile would be devastating.

When he brings his gaze back to me, a spark flickers in his eyes. "St. Valentine. Patron saint of bees."

I blink. "What?"

His face sobers a little, but that smile doesn't leave his mouth. "Don't tell me you never heard such a thing? That St. Valentine loved bees."

I have heard such a thing, but I wasn't aware *he* had.

"Where do you think Little Bee comes from?"

My mouth gapes a second before I respond. "Me being an annoying child, buzzing around you and Stone, following you everywhere." As Cort had accused me of doing on numerous occasions as a kid.

"That was never the reason I called you Little Bee."

I'm gobsmacked a moment. Had there been a deeper meaning to the nickname? There couldn't be.

He tips his head toward the smokers. "Do you even need to shop here?"

He means since I'm a partial owner of Sylver Seed & Soil, do I need to make purchases. I could have ordered something online from a beekeeping group I belong to, but I like to support our family business, even if the proceeds just get turned around as dividends paid out to me quarterly. Our brother Judd is a financial wiz and the family accountant, not to mention CFO of the Seed & Soil.

"Can't you collect compensation for years of working here?"

I chuckle. "It's been years *since* I worked here." Back in high school and during college, I spent as much time as I could helping out in some capacity or other. There was never an expectation to work at Sylver Seed & Soil just because I am a Sylver. Clay holds the honor of wanting to be here the most. Judd fell into his position because our oldest brothers worried they'd lose him otherwise, and Stone was hellbent on keeping the family together. Even Knox works here now, after his retirement from the Navy.

Thoughts of my brothers remind me why I shouldn't be so casually chatting with Cortland in our family business. Chatting in a way that's only one flimsy layer away from flirting.

Stone would be so hurt. And I couldn't be the one responsible for breaking his heart again.

"Anyway." I turn my head, aiming my focus at the bee smokers but not really seeing either of them.

Cort presses off the shelf and steps up beside me. More like just behind my left shoulder. A little closer than necessary. Close enough I get a whiff of him. Balsam fir, fresh air, and all man.

The position almost reminds me of how he stood behind me once upon a time. The things he said to me. What we did together.

Cort stretches his arm around me, brushing his inner bicep against my shoulder as he points at one of the two smokers.

"I heard this one is top of the line. Best for blowing smoke up someone's ass." He chuckles near my ear, and I close my eyes a second, breathing in the sound, sensing his heat behind me.

If anyone's blowing smoke, it's me, suddenly feeling a little overheated and a bit steamy.

He's too close. Then he moves away too soon. And I spin to face him. My heart saws against my ribs, like I've been triggered once again. Like he'll walk away with tears in his eyes and indifference in his tone.

Instead, Cort offers me a tentative smile. "See you around, Bee." He takes one step backward while still looking at me. Then another. And one more before he spins for the end of the aisle.

Then, to my surprise, he glances back one more time before rounding the shelves.

And I'm left wondering, how bad can a man really be if he's shopping for his mother? If he can tease me about bee smokers? If he can still make me weak in the knees and my heart patter and give me a final glance.

Is that enough cause to give him a second chance?

12

———

[Vale]

A week later, Hudson asks if he can go to Atticus's house for a sleepover. Personally, I'm not a fan of sleepovers unless it's family. I love my girls' nights with my three nieces—Zelle, Winnie, and June—and I look forward to the day I can have more nights with Adara and Annabelle.

As for *when* Hudson asks, it's funny how kids have this uncanny ability to ask for something in front of someone else making the situation awkward.

"Maybe Atticus could come to our house for a while?" I'd been looking forward to a quiet night at home, but the invitation will appease Hudson. Who looks at Atticus for approval.

"That's cool. My dad has a date anyway."

I'm quick to process this information which means no parent would have been present to watch the boys. Then another thought occurs.

"Did your dad have a babysitter lined up? What about Amelia?" I glance at Hudson whose cheeks turn pink. Atticus doesn't notice, because his steely eyes are narrowed toward me.

"We aren't babies, and we don't need a sitter. She'll be fine alone."

I do not like his response, nor his tone or manner of delivery, and I really don't care for this kid, but then again, his declaration sounds like something his father might have told him.

"Why doesn't Amelia come over as well?"

The girl lingers a few feet away near a friend but her attention creeps over to us before darting back to the other girl. Does she reciprocate the crush on Hudson?

Atticus looks over his shoulder and his sister meets his glance like they are having a private conversation. A twin thing. Eventually, she gives the slightest shrug but offers a soft smile. Atticus turns back toward me.

"Sure. What's for dinner?"

Demanding little shit. "Pizza."

Two hours later, Atticus isn't a fan of having to work for his pizza, as it is build-your-own style, but eventually, he gives in, and I see the child inside the tough eleven-year-old. In contrast, Amelia is sweet and gracious and had been willing to make her brother's pizza before I intervened.

"If he wants to eat, he can make his own."

"I do stuff like this at home," she informs me.

"What do you mean?" I ask as I slide the four mini-pizza pies into the oven.

"I cook for my dad and my brother."

Something tells me she cooks, not out of generosity, but because it's demanded of her. I do not like the sound of that. Not all brothers look after their sisters like mine have, but I'd assumed with the twin thing, Atticus might have a bond with his sister and respect her.

"Well, tonight you cook for you. And then the boys clean up."

"What?" Atticus grunts, horrified by the idea.

"Mom," Hudson chides like I'm embarrassing him.

But Amelia lowers her eyes and chews her lip, fighting a smile. When she finally looks up, I wink.

Us girls gotta stick together.

Throughout the night, the kids alternate between playing video games and watching a horror movie, although I don't think Amelia was thrilled by the selection.

By eight o'clock, the Stanton kids hadn't heard from their father about when he planned to pick them up or if I should bring them home.

By nine-fifteen, I am agitated by Henry's lack of response to his kids texting him.

By ten, I am pissed.

By ten-oh-eight, I make a disgruntled suggestion. "Why don't you guys spend the night here?"

Maybe this had been Henry's hope all along—date-night, kid-free evening. I'd have been all for it, if Henry had simply asked, instead of relying on, and virtually ignoring, text messages from his children.

"Dad says cool," Atticus offers within seconds of my asking.

I'm livid. How could Henry respond so quickly while he's been anywhere from radio silent to delayed reaction every other time his children have reached out to him?

Amelia glances at her brother. "But I don't have pajamas, or my book, or—" She cuts herself off when her brother narrows his eyes at her.

"You don't need Blue." His tone is quiet but condescending, like she's embarrassing him.

"Who's Blue?" Hudson asks, glancing from brother to sister.

Atticus continues to glare at his sister, who eventually, sheepishly, says, "No one."

Mother's intuition tells me Blue is someone special, or rather *something* important, and I recall sleeping with a well-loved stuffed pony as a kid. Doing so made me feel strangely close to a woman I hadn't known. My mother.

My heart softens toward the young girl, reminding myself she doesn't have a mother either and she's stuck with Henry as a father. For that matter, I muster compassion for Atticus as well.

"Let me see if I can find you something to sleep in and a book. My nieces are always leaving things here. I can put you in one of our extra bedrooms while the boys sleep in Hudson's room. It's time for bed, anyway."

With five bedrooms on the upper level, I occupy my old bedroom while Hudson has his own room. We converted one small room into a den of sorts for Hudson's gaming system slash study space, leaving other rooms as extra bedrooms.

"It's not even ten-thirty," Atticus shrieks, appalled.

"And you boys have practice tomorrow," I remind him before giving Hudson a hard mom-glare.

"Come on." Hudson turns for the staircase while Atticus looks after his friend in shock, then glances back at me, before following Hudson.

"Your mom is kind of a ballbuster," Atticus mutters as he catches up to Hudson before they reach the staircase.

"I know, but she's all right," Hudson defends.

Score for me, I guess. I doubt Atticus agrees, but I turn my attention to Amelia.

"Boys." I shake my head and Amelia rolls her eyes, on board with me.

Within minutes, I settle Amelia into the room we use for my nieces and find her a T-shirt of mine plus a too-small-for-me pair of shorts to wear. I also luck out that among the collection of books I keep on hand for my nieces, there is one Amelia wants to read. As I step toward the door, Hudson appears just outside it in the hallway.

When I give him a puzzling look, he holds up a stuffed bear. "I thought this might help Amelia."

As sheriff, Stone has a collection of Courage Bears, a bear with a sheriff star on its chest, that the department gives to kids who happen to be in the station for whatever reason.

My heart melts at the thoughtfulness of my son. "That's sweet, buddy. Want to give it to her yourself?" Even though she's already climbed into the bed, I'll wait here while he offers his gift.

"Nah." His ears turn pink reminding me how Ford's do the same thing. Thrusting the bear toward me, he says, "You can just give it to her."

I take the bear from him, smile into its soft head, and walk it over to Amelia who smiles in appreciation.

After a quick check on the boys, I remind Hudson to power off his phone and shower. I have a no-electronics-in-bed rule. Atticus groans before reluctantly turning off his.

Once I leave Hudson's room, I'm approaching mine when I hear a knocking sound. I pause a beat, thinking I've misheard the light hammering noise. When the rapping occurs again, there's no mistaking that someone is at the front door.

Certain it's Henry, I rush down the staircase ready to rip into him. *What a thoughtless father.*

Making it down the stairs in record time, I open the front door with a flourish.

"You have some— Cort?"

13

[Cort]

It's been a helluva week. On Wednesday, I missed my massage therapy session due to a roofing crisis over in Huntington. I was able to reschedule my appointment for Thursday but was assigned to someone other than Vale.

I walked out.

Thursday night, Vale was not in her typical spot at Milton Roadhouse, and within thirty minutes I'd realized I'd reached stalker level tendencies, waiting on her appearance like a Tennessee Terrors fan hoping for a glimpse of his favorite player.

However, I hadn't been able to stop thinking about the woman after our interaction at the Sylver Seed & Soil last weekend.

The way Vale was glaring at those innocent bee smokers. The way she eventually looked at me, all teasing and playful.

Her face softening at the mention of my mom who was devastated when Stone and I fell out.

At one point during our interaction, I'd lost Vale a second. Something dark and worrisome came over her face, and I couldn't for the life of me figure out what I'd said to cause the shift. Cause her sudden turning away from me, glaring back at those tin canisters like they'd offended her.

Deep down, I knew it'd been me somehow, and the anxiety was eating me up.

I wasn't a man who over-processed a look or overanalyzed a sentence, but I was second guessing everything with Vale.

Like why I felt the need to touch her in some small way after every massage. Just run my hands over her fingers or caress her skin, like some weak token of my appreciation. My gratitude for her touch. The comfort of her hands on me has been both confounding and titillating, igniting an unexplained but not unwelcome craving for more connection with her.

Earlier, I'd been at a small Italian bistro in Rogue River, seated at the bar, eating alone, when I saw Henry Stanton on a date, and it just pissed me off. Like, how is it that bastard was entertaining a woman, and I was eating alone in public, which I typically hate to do. However, I hadn't been ready to go home, alone, and face my empty house on a Friday night after this shitty week.

Afterward, I drove over to Randy's Bar, the dive located between the two towns. Making an appearance in his uniform, Stone entered, sending a signal to some of the riffraff who have been wandering into the dark place lately. Seated at another bar—alone again—Stone's entrance and exit was another gut punch on this week.

Every time I saw him was a reminder of what I'd done, what I'd lost. And it's a good reality check that I'm not worthy of Vale's attention.

Still, I relish every time Vale touches me. Every gentle placement of her hands. Every tender stroke of her fingers. Sometimes I even imagine her lingering a little longer in a spot. Like I'm not paying her to help me, but she actually wants to touch me. I'd never complain.

Thinking of her hands on me, I sit straighter on the hard wooden stool, admonishing myself for being such a damn sourpuss tonight, like a spoiled child not getting to play with his favorite new toy.

Vale isn't a plaything. She is a beautiful, considerate woman, and I'd wronged her in the past. The boundaries of therapist and patient need to be respected. Same with the off-limits lines around her as a mother to a kid I coach.

Only sitting upright, my back pinches, and I'm reminded why I need Vale in my life.

At least that's the excuse I use to stop moping and give into the pull I feel toward her. A desperate desire that started as a niggle of doubt now morphed into an anxious longing inside my chest. I need Vale's hands on me. And I want to earn the chance to touch *her* again.

So, standing on the dark porch of the Sylver family home is the last place I should be.

"I know it's late, but I need a massage." I hate how much that sounds like a proposition for more. Even hate how greedy I sound, but I can't exactly explain this newfound and unsettling, yet not wholly uncomfortable, yearning to have her touch me.

Whipping my straw cowboy hat off my head, I spin it by the brim round and round in my hands.

"Are you serious?" Vale gapes. "Now?"

She's staring at me, a queen bee preparing to sting, with one hand on her hip and the other hand holding the door like she's ready to slam it in my face.

I've been thinking a lot about what she said the other day, that I was ignoring her. The truth is, she's all I've been thinking about.

Pressing my luck, I step forward, brush past her, and enter a house I haven't set foot in for more than two decades.

Instantly, I fight the memories of trying to face my friend like a man, when I'd fucked up. When I'd been weak and betrayed him during his most vulnerable time. I've never forgiven myself. But my being here isn't about Stone. Or even me and my back. This is about Vale.

And this strange, inexplicable need to have her hands on me.

Vale steps back as I enter a living room I no longer recognize. Once dark and dingy with threadbare furniture and a slew of spent alcohol bottles, the room is now light and airy in shades of sandstone and sapphire with comfy looking chairs and an overstuffed couch centered around the fireplace. Photographs line the mantel, and the old brown brick has been whitewashed.

The soft snick of Vale closing the front door draws my attention back to her.

Coming here was a risk. A dangerous dare. But unexplainable relief also rushes through me. Or maybe that's just anxiety mingling with adrenaline, because Vale could say no, and have every right to do so.

"This is unprofessional and unethical. I don't do house calls."

While she glares at me with those cool clear eyes, I don't correct her that I'm the one calling at her home. Her eyes are the prettiest I've ever seen. To boot, her hair is pulled back in a ponytail and she's wearing a pink athletic shirt with black leggings. She takes my breath away.

"Stone could be home any minute," she adds.

"But he won't be," I counter because I saw him earlier at Randy's in his uniform.

"Where did you park?" Vale turns toward the window in the front door, noticing the absence of my truck in the space designated for several vehicles. The night is pitch black and this house is miles from town, which makes the woods nearby even darker.

"Behind the barn." I might be reckless, but I'm not an idiot. I pulled down the lane along the side of the house and parked behind the old building. *Just in case.*

"Hudson is here." She sounds like she's reading off a checklist of reasons I shouldn't be standing in this house. I have my own list, but something supersedes all my concerns.

And she's standing here, glaring at me.

"I was hoping he'd be in bed." The excuse is weak, but it's nearly ten-thirty on a Friday night.

"Mom?" Hudson calls from the upper level.

Vale steps around me like she can hide me behind her back. I'd chuckle at the scenario of her slimmer frame trying to block out my bulkier body, if I wasn't suddenly holding my breath.

"Be right up, bud," she calls out.

"Just letting you know I'm out of the shower. Atticus is going next."

My brows pinch. "You got the Stanton kid here?" *Fuck that Henry Stanton guy.* Hitting on Vale. Making snide comments. Then out on a date. Poor woman must be blind to what he's like.

"Yes," Vale whispers, turning back to face me. "And you need to go."

For a long minute, we stare at one another. Me not wanting to leave. Her . . . saying a thousand things with those eyes that I cannot read, because she's so beautiful when she looks at me, even in irritation. Plus, I don't know her well enough yet to interpret those eyes. Don't know her at all, now, as a woman, and a mother, but I want to. God help me, I want to learn more about her.

How does she kiss? Does she hiss when she's touched? Does she lose her sting when she fucks or embrace it?

I clear my throat, accepting I've gone too far. I shouldn't be here. It's late. She has kids here. Her brother hates me.

Twirling my hat in my hand one more time, I admit defeat. "I'll just—"

"Let's go to my room."

Never in my life did I think such words would cross her lips or turn me on. I shouldn't want to be turned on. I'm here for my back.

But who am I kidding?

I'm here for Vale.

14

———————

[Vale]

I cannot *believe* I am doing this. I don't even know how I'm going to get Cort up the stairs or back out of here again.

"Didn't even sneak boys into my room when I was a teenager," I mutter to myself as I tiptoe up the steps.

A soft chuckle behind me causes me to spin and place a finger over my lips to shush him. I've been walking up the stairs as quietly as I can, hoping the kids aren't in tune to the double set of footsteps climbing the treads.

Unfortunately, my bedroom is at the end of the hallway. Without direction, Cort passes me and takes the lead, moving down the hall like I'd seen him do a thousand times when we were kids. Only, back then he was headed to Stone's bedroom beside mine. Presently, he goes to the final door and lets himself into my room.

I should be cussing him out. Scolding him for appearing out of nowhere. Unannounced. Late at night.

But something inside me doused the angry fire burning in my chest while we were staring at one another downstairs. When he was spinning his hat in his hands, like a nervous twitch, and his eyes spoke a thousand words, all of which my heart wanted to interpret with more meaning than what he really desires.

A massage.

The nerve of this guy. Making a house call. To *my* home.

I don't have a massage table here and while I could use the sturdy kitchen table, I didn't want Cort exposed in a main room of the house.

Being in my bedroom isn't exactly better, though.

After I close the door, I watch as Cort takes in the soft pink walls and black and pink rug. The white comforter and the fluffy rose-colored blanket folded at the end of the bed. This room was yellow when I was a child, but the color has changed numerous times over the years, the latest being a light blush that's feminine and sweet without being childish.

"I like what you've done with the place." His mouth hooks at the corner, like he's fighting laughter.

I narrow my eyes at him. "Lie down on the bed." *Nothing* about that command sounds right.

Cort. My bedroom. My bed.

He doesn't bat an eye. He sets his hat on a chair near my dresser and sits on the edge of the bed to remove his boots.

I turn away from him, not wanting to watch him peel off his shirt, but then I catch a glimpse of him in the mirror over my dresser.

I should close my eyes, but I cannot pull them away from the sight of this man slowly unbuttoning his shirt and then shrugging it off his shoulders, exposing the wide breadth of them, and revealing his back. It's like slowly unwrapping a birthday gift and it isn't even my birthday. He tosses the shirt to the opposite side of the bed and catches me watching him through the reflection. Without a pause, he twists and lies flat on his belly, head on one of my pillows.

Everything about this scene is wrong. So wrong.

But my feet move across the rug, and I stand beside the bed. Cort is positioned lower than a massage table height and I'd ask to straddle the backs of his thighs if I didn't consider that a dangerous position. Instead, I reach for the jar of honey balm on my nightstand and lather up my hands, not bothering to ask him where it hurts.

With his head turned on the pillow, I watch his eyes close the moment I touch him. His brows pinch, signaling I've hit the mark, and I concentrate on his lower left lat. A once-a-week massage should be enough to loosen him up. He should also be doing stretches on his own to alleviate pain. However, I don't mention either method because I'm too irritated with him for barging in on my night and pissed at myself for letting him get away with it.

Fifteen minutes. Then his ass is out the door, and he owes me a huge tip for this inconvenience.

A soft knock comes to my door, and I freeze. With my hands still on Cort's back, I press down on him and crane my neck, glancing over my shoulder at the lock on the doorknob.

Dammit, I didn't lock the door.

My heart seesaws while my lungs stop working.

Please don't let Hudson come in here, I beg the Universe.

"I'll be right out, bud," I call to my son, hoping he'll respect the closed door and not barge into my room. As he's gotten older, he's become a little more reticent to walk in without an invitation and I appreciate his hesitation.

I have never *ever* experienced a situation like this one—a man in my bedroom—and I do not want this to be that first-time-for-everything moment.

"Just wanted to say goodnight."

I hang my head, thinking once again about the sweetness of my son and the kind gesture he made for Amelia.

Glancing down at Cort, I notice his eyes are open, but I'm not certain he's breathing either.

"Just give me one second, baby, and I'll come to your room." I should check on all the kids anyway and then lock my damn door.

When I pull away from Cort, he holds his position. Arms underneath my pillow. Head turned to the side. Back on display. Eyes on me.

Shaking my head, I rub my hands together, trying to blend in the honey balm on my fingers. Then, to be extra petty at his presence, I swipe my hands over Cort's denim-clad thighs, using them like a towel to remove the excess. Cort doesn't move; he doesn't even speak. With a *tsk*, I slip out my door as best I can without fully opening it and head down the hallway.

Inside Hudson's room, Atticus is fast asleep. However, Hudson is lying on his back, staring up at the ceiling.

"What's the matter, baby?" I whisper. *Please don't let him know his baseball coach is in my bedroom.* I pull up his blanket, and he tucks it beneath his arms before I smooth the covers over his chest.

"Think Amelia is okay in there?"

"I'll check on her next, buddy, but I bet she's fine. That was really sweet of you to give her the bear."

"It's not her Blue, though."

"It was still thoughtful. You're a good friend." And if he keeps up the gestures, he'll make a great boyfriend one day.

I take a seat on the edge of his bed and glance once more at Atticus in the other bed before whispering to Hudson. "Do you think there is something to worry about between Amelia and her brother and father?" I ask, prying into lives that are not my concern through an eleven-year-old.

"Like what?" Hudson counters.

I love his innocence, and shrug. "Just want to remind you that you can tell me anything. Or come to me with anything." I stroke my finger playfully down his nose and he smiles.

"Get some sleep." I lean down and press a kiss to his forehead. Before I'm fully standing, he rolls to his side, and I slip from his room, checking on Amelia as promised before returning to my uninvited guest.

Quietly entering my room, Cort remains in the same position he was in when I left. Hands beneath the pillow. Belly pressed into the cover. Back on display. Only, his eyes are closed.

"Cort," I whisper, stepping closer to the bed.

"Cort," I repeat, jabbing his tight shoulder.

"Cortland Haven," I state a little louder but not loud enough that Hudson might hear me through the wall. I smack his arm, causing him to lift his head, rub his nose against the pillow, and turn his head in the opposite direction.

He didn't open his eyes. Didn't even blink at me. And now he's settled back down, fast asleep.

"Are you kidding me?" I say in a normal tone, which still has no effect on the resting intruder. I stare down at Cort for several seconds wondering what the heck to do with him before I concede defeat and follow through on my nightly routine. With it as late as it is, I'm drained of all energy.

When I return to my room, Cort hasn't budged and as much as it's a risk to have him caught in our home, in my room, I'm also too tired to fight with him right now.

It's his funeral, I guess.

I round my double bed, of which Cort is taking up most of the space, and rest on my back at first, staring up at the ceiling much like Hudson was doing next door. Eventually, I turn on my side, face Cort, and slip my hands beneath the pillow in a loose prayer pose.

Cort's forehead is furrowed even in sleep. His nose strong.

His lips are pouty and surrounded by a trimmed layer of facial hair that's a thirsty mix of silver and ink. I slide my hands closer to him, fingertips almost touching his forearm but still respectfully distant. My thumb twitches, wanting to reach out and trace the fine lines and firm edges of his face, as if my finger is a painter's brush which can memorize this creation before me.

Instead, I hold still, watching Cort for another minute before my eyes slowly drift shut. He stirs beside me, and I sense Cort moving his arm, thinking he'll assume I'm asleep and sneak from my bedroom. Instead, his hand slides over mine, curling between my index finger and thumb so he's holding four of my fingers within his larger grasp.

We sleep like this for I don't know how long, before the heat of his hand is gone, and the warmth of a fingertip strokes over my cheek, brushing my hair around my ear.

Then, I wake to a cold, empty bed.

15

[Vale]

After my restless night, I'm sluggish despite the need to hurry. Hudson and Atticus have baseball practice, and Atticus is in a panic because he doesn't have any of his stuff. He eventually reached his father who promised to bring Atticus's equipment to the ballpark.

Henry, however, arrives late and Atticus doesn't even address his dad, other than grabbing his ball bag and cleats from his father's outstretched hand. Eventually, Henry nears where I've set up two camp chairs. One for myself and one for Amelia who is enraptured by the book she picked to read last night.

"Henry," I greet him through gritted teeth.

"Miss Sylver." He's all smiles and charm, and an I-got-laid-last-night ease.

Quickly, I stand and move in a way Henry needs to turn his

back on his child and face me, blocking her from witnessing me rip this man a new one.

"You have some nerve," I whisper, glaring at him. "If you needed a sitter for your kids, or a night off, you could have at least *asked* me." I not only feel taken advantage of, but a bit underappreciated for stepping up for *his* kids. I won't even get into the whole idea of him possibly leaving his kids alone for a night while he galivanted around.

"Well, you know how it is." He winks.

I shiver and cross my arms. "Actually, I don't know how it is." I don't have the luxury—nor desire—to dump my kid on others or let him fend for himself. Even with my brother and I living together, I don't assume Stone will care for Hudson. My son is my responsibility.

Henry's smile turns salacious, slithering up his face, and causing me to shudder. "I could help with that. Anytime. You just ask."

My mouth pops open.

"She won't be asking." The sharp, curt masculine voice behind me sends a new kind of ripple down my spine. *When did Cort come over here?* Even more befuddling is I can't decide if I'm appreciative that he's defending me or irritated he isn't letting me speak for myself. I'm not used to someone standing up for me. Not like this.

Henry glances over my shoulder but I resist turning, keeping my hard glare on his once-smug face which has turned a little sour. On the tip of his tongue is a retort. I don't have to hear it to know it will be something insinuating and insulting. However, Henry swallows whatever he intended to say.

Instead, he slips his hands into his pants' pockets—pants a little too formal for a Saturday morning baseball practice for children—and gazes toward the practice field, narrowing his eyes.

"Maybe you should get to coaching our kids," Henry mutters.

"Maybe you should be parenting your own."

Shock skitters over my skin at the strength of Cort's scolding.

Henry turns on Cort. "Don't make me report this team."

"For what?" Cort snorts, bristling behind me.

Among other things, Henry has been vocal about Kennedy Archer *as a girl* making the team.

My gaze shifts to Amelia, only a few feet away, behind her father. Certain she's no longer reading but listening to adults bicker with one another, I spin enough to share a glance with Cort and tip my head in her direction.

His eyes widen at her nearness before his nostrils flare and he walks away, the bigger man of the two.

Henry smirks. "Put him in his place." He dips his chin, pleased with himself.

He is his only fan.

"Amelia," he states sharply. "Let's go." He tilts his head toward the parking area.

"Where?" Her eyes narrow in suspicion at her father.

"Breakfast." Henry turns toward me and tweaks one brow. "I didn't get enough to eat last night."

Gross.

"I already ate at Hudson's."

Henry's weasel-eyes jolt away from me, glance at Amelia and then return to me. "At Hudson's?" The truth hits him slowly, like he hadn't known that his daughter spent the night at my house as well.

He steps closer to me. "There better not have been any shenanigans between your son and my daughter."

My mouth falls open again as I form fists at my side, wondering if I can get away with punching him in the nose like my brothers taught me as a child.

"Amelia slept in a guest room; however, I'm insulted at the insinuation. They are children and *I'm* a good parent." I jab at my chest, angered by the implication. I'd never allow something to happen to Amelia, even with my own son, at such a young age.

Suddenly, I'm vibrating. A flash of memory I do not want nor need right now whispers through my head.

"And you're implying I'm *not* a good parent?" Henry fires back.

"You know what, Daddy? I'd love a second breakfast," Amelia interjects, quickly standing and setting the book down on the chair.

I hate how she's trying to diffuse a situation between adults and a second memory crosses my mind.

Attempting to get between Sebastian and my father.

Yelling at Knox that nothing happened.

With a gut punch sensation in my belly, I glance at Amelia, full of sympathy and fear for her. She's eleven. A child. An innocent girl who missed her stuffed animal last night and slept with a bear to protect her in a strange-to-her house.

Everything in me says to intervene. To tell Amelia she doesn't need to go with him. She can stay with me, here at the park. Read her book. Ignore her dad. I did it as best I could most of my life, but the triggers have me paralyzed, and within minutes, Amelia has her father by the hand, leading him away from me. Henry isn't reciprocating her touch as much as allowing her to tug him along and I sink into the camp chair, caught in the crossfire of painful memories, shame, and confusion.

I watch Amelia leave with Henry before I glance toward the ballfield to find Cort's eyes are on me. He steps forward but I shake my head, warning him not to come near me.

If he gets too close, I'm going to shatter.

And the last thing I want is Cortland Haven seeing all my pieces.

16

———————

[Cort]

I can't believe I let that fucker Henry Stanton rile me.

And I also can't believe I slept a good portion of the night at Vale's house. It was risky, dangerous even, but I'd slept better in her bed than I'd slept in a long, long time.

The moment I saw her standoff with Henry, something inside me kicked in. *Mine.* I didn't want him near her, speaking to her, breathing the air she breathes, and I reacted. Over-reacted.

I'm well aware Vale can take care of herself. I *know* she's been doing it for a while, but I don't want Henry thinking she's available to him or propositioning her. If I thought Vale wanted Henry, I'd back off like I have for twelve fucking years, but everything in me says Vale wants nothing to do with Henry.

She wants me.

The idea is baffling and selfish, but Vale Sylver is attracted to me. I see it in the way she looks at me, a hunger in her eyes that matches the starving hollowness in my gut. Heard it in the hitch of her breath when I caressed the inside of her wrist. Witnessed her dig her teeth into her lush lower lip when I captured her fingers.

Like maybe she's as hungry for my touch as I am for hers.

If she hated me, like most of her family, she'd have declined being my therapist and kicked me to the curb last night when I stormed her house. Hell, I had one foot out the door when she invited me to her room, and that feels telling.

I just wish I fully understood what she wants.

Unfortunately, I don't even know what I want from her. Her hands on me, yes, which is confusing in and of itself. But I also want to know more about Vale. More about Hudson. The story she told me about his absentee father hasn't left my thoughts.

And all these memories are flooding back into my head.

Summer twelve years ago. Vale and the Falls. Something tempting about her despite my mental state. A momentary lapse in judgment.

I've always wondered if Vale remembers the fine details. I'm not certain she could forget. I fucking wept afterward, ashamed of myself for taking advantage of her sudden presence and willing body. Embarrassed that I wasn't in the right head space, and yet I slid into her body like it was the only place I wanted to be. I hadn't even kissed her.

Scrubbing a hand down my face, I glance over at Vale who looks like she's about to shatter. Her face is blanched. Her posture is rigid as she sits in her camp chair. She looks like she's seen a ghost, and I take a step in her direction.

With her eyes aimed toward me, she weakly holds up a hand, telling me with both those cloudy eyes and stiff limbs to keep my distance.

"Coach!" I turn in the direction of my brother, his voice questioning as he watches me.

I'm a mess today. While my body is relaxed, my mind is scattered. In general, I'm on edge more than I typically am.

"Yo," I holler back at Clint.

"Pitching practice." He tips his head toward a group of boys we've designated as pitcher potentials, among them is Hudson Sylver.

"Right." I pull my thoughts from Vale as best I can. After I corral the group toward the mound, I risk a second glance in Vale's direction, reminding us both of my promise: I'll have an eye on her.

An hour and a half later, practice ends, and Clint calls a meeting of the parents.

"This is a reminder about the Sylver Sports Camp in two weeks."

I hadn't been in favor of this decision for additional team bonding and practice time, but Clint believed the olive branch toward the new sports camp, headed by none other than Ford Sylver, former centerfielder for the Chicago Anchors, was a good move. The camp's official opening day isn't until the last weekend in May, when a grand opening celebration is scheduled. Schools break for summer around then, and the camp will be available to individuals and teams from all over the country. Clint thought it wouldn't hurt to ask Ford if he'd like a trial run with a local team, offering Haven Hitters as guinea pigs.

Small cabins. A new mess hall. A practice diamond bigger and better than this local field. The early spring temperatures make the lake on the property too cold for swimming, but in the summer, the water will provide extracurricular activities for campers.

"The weekend begins Friday night . . ." Clint continues, but I zone out on the details as my concentration falls on Vale. Her head is lowered, eyes averted from me. Is she angry that I slept at her place and slipped out of her bed in the early morning?

I'm lucky as hell Stone hadn't come home before I crept down the driveway in my truck.

"Right?" Clint claps my shoulder hard, and I turn my head in his direction. His wide eyes tell me to agree with him, so I nod, numbly.

"Okay. See you all Tuesday. Have permission forms filled out and deposits made on our website by then. And if any of you are willing to volunteer time at the camp, let us know."

To our benefit, Ford isn't charging us for more than groceries and the cleaning service needed during our short stay. If we can get a few parent-volunteers to assist, that cuts down on our costs even more. We aren't looking to be cheap, but we are on a budget, and we accept that most of our parents are as well.

Too quickly, Vale has her back to me, walking her son away from the ball field, and an unfamiliar ache settles in my chest.

How many more times will I watch her walk away before I snap?

As if Wednesday morning massage therapy sessions and weekly baseball practices weren't enough time to lay eyes on Vale, I'd returned to Milton Roadhouse on Thursday evening hoping to catch another glimpse of my new obsession. One that could hold me off from storming her house again with weak excuses like I'd done over the past weekend. When she never showed, I cursed myself for my behavior and gave in to Clint pestering me to attend a concert at a small venue in Huntington on Friday night.

I wasn't particularly a fan of country music, being more of a classic rock kind of guy, but Clint asked, and I needed to get out of my head, and away from my sudden addiction to an unobtainable single mom.

In my truck on the way to the larger city, some forty-five minutes from Rogue River, Clint and I rehash our plan for the Haven Hitters and our time at the sports' camp. To our surprise, most of the team is available to participate in the impromptu camp and four parents volunteered, among them Ronnie Archer and Vale Sylver.

When we arrive in Huntington, the city feels alive for an early spring evening. Parking is limited and we find a spot a few blocks away from the venue. Once inside the space with standing room only in front of a raised stage, we stake out a spot near a railing that divides the lower pit from a platform section. We nabbed a few beers before claiming this space. Scanning the crowd, I roam over couples on dates and groups of country music enthusiasts, bored by the scene. While glossing over people, my sight catches on a straw cowboy hat. One that looks well-loved and vaguely familiar. Could be one in a million such hats, but I know this one has a tear in the side of the brim, something I've never bothered to repair.

Because *that* is the same hat I was wearing when I crashed Vale's house a week ago and left it behind in her bedroom.

Licking my lips, a slow smile curls my mouth.

"What?" Clint knocks into my elbow with his, lifting his beer for a sip.

"What *what*?" I counter, pulling my gaze from the back of Vale's head.

"What are you smiling about?" He peers over the crowd himself. "Or better yet, who you smilin' at?"

"No one. It's nothing," I argue, but my gaze flings back toward Vale who stands sideways, talking to the woman next to her, and offering me a perfect view of her profile. A silhouette of hills and valleys. Lush breasts. Tight ass. Strong legs in a short skirt and cowboy boots. She's wearing some kind of form-fitting tank that hugs her upper body and practically matches her skin tone, making her appear almost naked.

I scrub my thumb and forefinger around my lips, and swallow back the sudden thirst I have for her.

"Is that Vale Sylver?" Clint interjects, drawing my attention to him for a second. His eyes narrow on her and the woman standing beside her. "Who is that with her?"

The woman beside Vale could be her twin. Same long blonde hair. Same height and build, and yet I could pick Vale out of a crowd. I did, actually, and I watch as the two women laugh together. Vale places her hand on her friend's shoulder. They knock plastic cups of something against each other before Vale wraps her lips over the rim of her drink.

I've never been so envious of a red Solo cup.

A warmup to the warmup band starts the show, and I stand stone-still while people sway around us. The music isn't bad, just not my scene. Clint doesn't get out much, and he wanted to see the main act. Our mother is babysitting Ruby James tonight, and she values her grammy time, which gives Clint the opportunity for an all-nighter.

When the first warmup band finishes, the crowd disburses a bit. Fans heading for the bar and the restroom in equal measure which opens the space around Vale and her friend.

"I think I'll say hello," Clint says, lasering in on where Vale stands.

A million questions run through my head. Does he typically say hello to Vale? Does he miss his old friend? Does he have a crush on her?

Before I can stop him, Clint is sliding through the crowd like he's swimming upstream.

I hold my ground, finding my feet pinned to the wood floor, and my heart as heavy as an anchor in my chest.

Within minutes, Clint reaches his destination, and Vale turns at Clint's greeting. Instantly, she looks over his shoulder toward me and I lift my beer in salute. Vale places her hand on

Clint's shoulder and leans in, pointing toward her friend, presumably introducing them.

I hate that she's touching Clint, which is absolutely ridiculous. Vale's a therapist. She touches tons of people. I just don't want her hands on my brother.

The jealous thought has me lifting my beer again and taking a hearty swig from the bottle. When I lower it, I notice Vale is no longer near my brother and her companion, and I frantically search the crowd for her.

My brother keeps his new position, like a guard stationed beside Vale's friend, before the house lights flicker and another band begins. My gaze roams the audience once more, but in the darkened room, it is difficult to distinguish anyone, even a brightly-colored straw cowboy hat on the head of a woman with sunshine hair.

With my hands on the railing, I lean forward. My shoulders are tight. Standing on this hard floor is murder on my back. Someone knocks into me, and I flinch at the contact, turning my head sharply to find clear blue eyes staring up at me.

"Looking for someone, cowboy?" Vale's voice is sweet; her drawl exaggerated.

"Not a cowboy tonight. Appears someone stole my hat." My gaze flicks up to the one on her head.

"Finder's keepers," she teases, staring up at me, placing her hand on the top of the hat.

I purse my lips, nodding once.

"I didn't picture this being your scene," she hollers over the music, taking the liberty to touch my forearm and lean closer to me. When my gaze drops to where her delicate hand wraps over my arm, Vale instantly pulls away. Like she forgot I don't like to be touched. Only, my beer sours in my belly because she's read me wrong.

I've been missing her touch, like the earth misses the sun after days of clouds.

"It's not," I holler back, leaning toward her so she can hear me. The second band is louder, more riotous than the first. Their job is to literally warm up and excite the crowd, and yet I'm feeling like an old man wishing they'd tone it down a bit so I can talk to Vale.

She nods, acknowledging my answer, before glancing into the pit in front of us. Maybe she's looking for her friend. Maybe she's enjoying the show, but all I'm aware of is her closeness. Her bare arm and shoulder occasionally brush against mine as she shifts to allow for people walking behind us. The railing prevents enthusiasts from sneaking in front of us, but they are squeezing in close at our backs.

Without thinking, I step behind Vale, slipping my arms around either side of her, placing my hands on the railing again to cage her in from the jostling crowd.

Trapped in front of me, Vale twists, almost knocking my chin with the hat. "What are you doing?"

"Protecting you."

Her mouth opens and I brace for her to tell me she can take care of herself. She's told me on more than one occasion, and I know she can handle herself. But something tells me to protect her, all the same. To take care with her.

Little Bee isn't little anymore, so that's not the reason I have this desire. The queen has risen to the top of the ranks, and my instincts tell me to keep her safe at all costs.

Thankfully, her lips clamp shut before she argues, and she turns back to the show. At one point someone bumps into me again from behind, and I press forward, brushing into Vale's back. She stiffens, and I pull away as best I can.

"Sorry," I mutter toward her ear, the brim of the hat in my way.

Vale doesn't respond, keeping her eyes forward and her hands wrapped around the railing, clutching it like she needs something to hold onto.

The band plays on, but I can't say I watch them or even register their music. My entire focus is on Vale. The hint of her honey scent, sweet and appealing, above the stench of warm bodies. The curve of her bare shoulder and the length of her arm. The curl of her hair hanging long beneath *my* cowboy hat. The swell of her ass in that short denim skirt.

At some point, my legs spread apart, and my feet are on either side of Vale's, inches away from her heels. My body is her shield when I want it to blanket her. I want to press my weight over her or feel the weight of her above me.

Taking another swig of my beer, I finish the bottle. "Want a drink," I holler over the music.

Vale glances around my arm. "I'm not sure you can make it to the bar and back before the main act."

Glancing over my shoulder, I notice the space has really filled in. The crowd is too much for me and I don't want to leave Vale, but I'm willing to get fresh beers, if she wants something.

When I peer back at her, she's watching me, checking out my profile. Our eyes lock for a second before mine dip down to her exposed throat and the peek-a-boo of her chest. The nude-color tank emphasizes the swell of her breasts.

I'm thirsty, but not for something liquid.

"Easy there, cowboy," Vale teases.

My gaze flicks back to her eyes before glancing at my hat on her head. I've never considered myself a cowboy. I'm more of a blue-collar man now, but I'll be whatever Vale wants me to be.

"You know what they say about a cowboy and his hat?" I tease.

Vale chews at the corner of her lip and I want her to dig her teeth into my flesh. "If a girl steals his hat, she goes home with him."

Would she go home with me? Can we have a repeat of what we once had? Can we do things better this round? My nostrils flare, catching another whiff of her honey-sweetness.

"However, seeing as I didn't steal it because someone left it at *my* home, I think you're safe." Vale winks.

Am I safe? I'm not so certain how much longer I can fight my attraction to this woman. Even though everything in me says stay away. Build a fortress around these newfound feelings and secure the deadbolt.

"You have nothing to fear with me." Vale watches me. Her rejection is almost as clear as her eyes.

"Why would I ever be afraid of you, Little Bee?"

Vale spins completely. Her breasts brush against my chest and I fight the groan rumbling up my throat. Crossing my arms, I attempt to calm the racing of my heart and the tingle she caused on my flesh, not to mention put some distance between us despite the cramped space.

"That." She points at my face. "Because you think I'm a child."

My gaze lowers, dripping over her body like a drizzle of honey. "I know you're not." The outside of her screams all woman, but the inside speaks it loud and clear as well. Vale *has* taken care of herself and her son. She's been a pinnacle in keeping her extended family connected. She works hard and plays soft.

When my eyes meet hers again, her chest heaves, breasts inching closer to me. My mouth waters, wanting a sip of her.

"You should probably get back to your friend," I state, giving her an out, telling her to step away from me, because my body begs for the opposite, wanting her to stay close. One of us has to make the smart decision this round.

After a beat of silence between us, I realize it won't be me, because I lean forward again, bracing my hands on the railing at her back and caging her in once more.

"If you want me to leave you alone, just tell me." Her tone turns fierce as she crosses her arms, but her body language counters the gleam in her eyes. The ones dipping down to my lips.

My mouth pops open, every warning prepared to spill forward.

She's younger than me.

She's the mother of a boy on my baseball team.

She's Stone's little sister.

And yet none of those concerns tumble out of my mouth.

My silence says everything.

I fucking want her.

I wish I could read her thoughts. Wish I knew if she wanted *me* in return.

Not the man who is older than her.

Not the coach of her kid's baseball team.

Not her brother's former best friend.

Just me, faults and all.

Abruptly, the second warmup band concludes, and Vale turns her head away from me. Like the sudden silence from the stage and uproar of the crowd reminds her where she is, who she's near, what she almost did.

"I'm going to the bathroom," she announces.

Pressing off the wood railing, I stand tall, allowing her the space to walk away. As she snakes through the crowd, I follow the weave of my hat until I can't see her anymore.

Fuck. I hang my head. She isn't going to come back. And I hate that I'm standing in a crowded room yet feel loneliness doubling down without Vale standing near me.

Scanning the pit for Clint, I send him a text when I can't find him. **Where are you?**

When he doesn't instantly answer, I tuck my phone back in my pocket and wait. But wait for what? Vale to return? My brother to magically appear? My life feels like it has been in a holding pattern for years. Like the ball has been tossed, only it's suspended in mid-air and I'm never going to catch it despite my best efforts. Then again, have I chased the ball or simply worked on blocking anyone else from catching it?

The football metaphor zaps my energy, and I reach for my phone again, willing Clint to respond to me. Time passes as slowly as sand sifting through a pin hole. I want a beer but don't dare leave my position, fearing Clint will return in my absence.

After what feels like forever, the house lights flicker once more, signaling the main act will start soon, and the crowd tightens. I'm sweaty and uncomfortable, with added irritation of bodies brushing against mine. I hate being touched on a good day. I especially hate being touched unaware, like the innocent bump of people too close together.

When someone hip-checks me, I spin toward them, ready to argue there's plenty of space not to be on top of each other, but the smaller frame is wearing a familiar hat and holding two beer bottles in one hand. She glides in front of me, wedging herself into space that could hardly fit a paperback.

Returned to her previous position, Vale faces me. Her breasts brush against me as her nearness is almost impossible to avoid. "I brought you a beer."

She holds up a bottle with the cap already removed, and she taps the long neck of hers against the length of mine before her lips pucker around the tip. As she thirstily drinks, I watch her throat roll.

Fuck.

Her eyelids flip upward, and her eyes meet mine over the base of the tipped bottle. Instantly, I imagine her in a different position. On her knees. Eyes on me. Mouth wrapped around my—

I lift my own beer bottle and take a giant gulp, needing to cool my thoughts and squelch the rise in my jeans.

Only with the first strum of a guitar, Vale spins toward the railing, setting her beer on the ledge. Her ass brushes against my thighs and I stand ramrod straight again.

A sultry song with a rapid beat starts the show and Vale lifts one arm, swaying her hips back and forth, causing that ass to paint side to side against my thighs once more.

I spread my legs to stabilize my stance and place a hand on Vale's hip, to either hold her still or keep her close, I'm not certain. What I notice instead is how the curve of her hip fits perfectly in my palm. I dip my fingers into the slant of the pocket on her skirt and dig into the soft edge of her body.

Whether I tug her back or she leans into me is undetermined, but on the next powerful swing of her hips, her ass swipes across the front of my jeans again, nearly missing where I want her, and I hiss.

Lowering my head, I aim my mouth near her ear. "Easy, Bee."

Vale doesn't respond. She lifts her arm, lowers her head, and moves her hips once more.

Right. Left. Left, left. Right.

Like a metronome counting time, only the movement is pumping up my cock. I squeeze harder on her hip and groan near the side of her neck. "Dammit, Vale."

"I love this song," she yells over the music.

My brain doesn't register the words. I can't hear any sound over the drumming of my heart.

Vale twists only her neck. Her face inches from mine. Our eyes lock again. Clear water to hard pebbles.

I lick my lips and Vale's gaze drops to them. Slowly, she lifts her eyes, climbing over my jaw and scaling my nose before landing on my eyes again.

"Vale," I whisper, not certain if it's a warning or a wish.

"You never kissed me," she shouts, pulling us both back to *that* moment.

A warm day by the Falls. I'd flipped her around, similar to

our current position, unable to look at her while still, wanting to take in every inch of her. That hunger in her eyes. A desire I don't think I've ever seen when someone was looking at me.

I'd lost my head.

Then, I was touching her, and her body was responding. Before I knew it, I was inside her, absorbing all her warmth while *my* insides were still frozen.

She's right. I didn't kiss her. Not like a man should kiss a woman. Not like a person should kiss someone he craves.

And that's exactly what this is. Vale is a craving. One I need to rid from my system.

Some might argue indulge and the craving will pass. But something tells me, another bite of her, and I'll always be insatiable.

For that reason, I fight the urge to kiss her now.

"Had other things on my mind then," I admit. The confusion of finding her in such a secluded place near the Falls. The puzzling attraction to her. The need for familiarity after so much had crumbled in my life.

Vale watches me another second, possibly misreading me again. Maybe thinking sex was all that mattered to me that day when a million other things were colliding inside me.

Number one on the list was a deep-seated desire to be close to someone again. And failing at it.

Her brows severely pinch before she abruptly turns her head back toward the stage, dropping a curtain on the show between us.

17

[Vale]

By not answering my question, Cort was fucking dodging me again. *Other things on his mind then?* He'd had sex on the brain.

And I needed to right my own head because I'm standing here practically begging this man to kiss me. And he didn't. Again.

He doesn't want me.

My irritation grows when I realize I can't find Kentucky or Clint in the pit, a sea of people that blurs for a second.

Don't you dare cry over him again, Valentine Sylver.

Logically, the prickle of tears is from frustration. Perhaps pent-up sexual tension. Definitely unrequited attraction. *Again.*

The moment was a good reminder that Cort and I should never cross a line. One recently fuzzy, but puzzling glances and playful touches do not mean he wants to fuck me.

He didn't like to be touched, and I wanted someone who could please me.

Additional warning bells dimly ring in my head, reminding me how hurt my brother would be if he learned I'd once held a flame for Cortland Haven, or had a yearning to ignite it again.

Which is all the reason I needed to get away from Cort.

"I should probably find Kentucky," I blurt as a song concludes. I really like this band and I'd been excited to have a night out with an old college friend. She's moving to Sterling Falls soon and the concert tonight was a good way to reconnect with her.

Almost as if she heard my thoughts, my phone vibrates at my hip. A crossbody strap holds a slim clear bag that meets the venue restrictions on bags, which can only fit a phone and some identification. Reaching for my phone, I notice Cort tug his out of his back pocket at the same time.

> Would it be possible for you to find a ride home?

What the fuck?

Kentucky picked me up because she was scoping out Milton County for a house. She's *my* ride.

Not to mention, women don't ditch women. Even if I'm half-happy for her—she deserves to have a little fun—the other half of me is envious that she's found some fun to be had. But another half, and I know that makes my equation dispropor-tionate, is pissed.

Pulling up her location, I notice she's still in the bar. Maybe tucked in a corner somewhere or even pressed up against an exterior wall. Still, she hasn't left me. Yet.

I should respond by telling her the truth. *No, I can't find another way home.* We're forty minutes from Sterling Falls. An Uber would be ungodly expensive if I could even get one to drive me a few towns over, not to mention that's a long stretch of highway late at night with a stranger, and I don't like the possibility.

Narrowing my eyes, I glance up at Cort, seeing his face pinched and his lips pursed, as he reads his own phone. Slowly, he lifts his gaze to me.

"Seems my brother left." He slips his phone back into his pocket. His tone is laced with disapproval. "With your friend."

Jostling my own phone toward him, I spout, "I got the message." I don't like it. Don't know what I'm going to do about it.

"I'll give you a ride," Cort offers without hesitating, but he also sounds angry.

"Not if you're angry about it," I snap. "I'll figure something out." This is not my first rodeo being out with friends who want to scamper off and get laid. Kentucky isn't a shitty friend; she really isn't. She'll come back for me. Turn tail and give up getting some when I respond back to her. Especially when this angry bear is glaring at me.

"You're right. I'm pissed. Your wing woman shouldn't have left you behind."

I stare at him, befuddled a second before realizing he isn't mad about giving me a ride. He's upset on my behalf.

"And I'm still not leaving you alone in this crowded bar." His gaze is hyper-focused on my eyes, like he's forcing them to stay linked with mine, and the intensity alone imparts his decision. He isn't leaving me behind.

"Let's just watch the rest of the show." His hand gently comes to my lower back. The motion hesitant and tender, unlike the way he was previously clutching at my hip.

He tugged me closer to him. Or maybe I just took the liberty to lean back, sizzling from his heat against me, shivering with the possibility of more with him.

I really thought he was going to kiss me for a minute there. Really wanted him to, if truth be told. But I'm not that girl anymore. The one willing to make out with just anyone or hookup with someone random.

And Cortland Haven is the last man I should take a risk on . . . again.

With a heavy sigh, I give him a final glance before lowering my head.

"I think I'd rather go home."

CORT ESCORTS me out of the venue, never removing his hand from my back, until we step outside. Like a bubble being released from a can, we both take in a breath of fresh air, until the chill hits me. I rub my hands up and down my arms when Cort drops his hand. Earlier, when we headed for Huntington, the temperature was much warmer. Now, the late-spring mountain air is giving me goosebumps and hard nipples.

As much as I'd love for Cort to wrap his arm around me to warm me up, he walks with his hands safely tucked in his pockets, keeping a good six inches between us. When we finally arrive at his truck, he opens the passenger door for me and holds out his hand to help me in. I reach for the grab handle instead and help myself.

I'm not mad at Cort. I'm disappointed in me.

Where did that reckless girl go? The one willing to make out with a guy behind a tree. The one eager to be touched and fucked by the falls. Oh, right . . . she grew up and she wants more. *Deserves* more.

When Cort enters his truck, he starts the engine and music flares to life, filling the truck with classic rock. He turns it down and hits the heat. "You cold?"

"A little," I admit, still rubbing my arms.

He reaches behind the seat, digging around before pulling forward a flannel shirt.

"I think it's clean." He brings it to his nose before holding the shirt open for me. "It will be warm at least."

He doesn't move to hand the flannel over. Instead, he leans toward me, flipping it around my shoulders and holding it, while I wrestle my arms into the longer sleeves. Once my arms are inside the warmth of the fabric, I stretch them above my head to force the loose sleeves to my wrists.

As I do this, Cort brings the two halves of the shirt together and buttons one button near my chest. Then a second button over my breasts. One more is just below them.

My chest heaves, my breath drawing deeper with each button he loops while I watch his nimble fingers dress me.

I could complain that I'm not a child and I don't need his help, but something inside me stops my protest. Something reminds me I want him to take care of me.

When I look at his face, his concentration intent, he seems to realize what he's doing and quickly withdraws his hands. Still, he remains close. His face only inches from mine. When he meets my gaze, he holds my eyes a second.

"I . . . uh . . . hope that's better."

I clench my fingers around the insides of the too-long material, making makeshift mittens. My throat is dry, just like it was earlier, when I thought he'd kiss me. When he didn't, and I stalked off to get each of us a new beer.

Now I have nothing to quench my thirst, other than the heat of his gaze and the comfort of his shirt and a swirl of emotions buzzing in my belly.

Frustration.

Confusion.

Tension.

Cort clears his throat and leans away from me. He turns down the volume on the radio and flings his arm over the seat, skillfully backing out of the parking spot, completely unaffected by his action toward me.

Meanwhile, I lift my hand covered by his flannel, close my eyes a second, and take a whiff, breathing in his scent embedded in the fabric.

Cort shifts behind the wheel. The movement pulls me from my scent-high, and I straighten in my seat.

My anxiety manifests a little voice in my head suggesting I make small talk. Fill the silence with questions about the concert or his work, but I don't have the energy. I'm still stung by disappointment.

"We should probably talk," he interjects into the low hum of classic rock playing from the radio. "About that day."

"Cortland," I exhale. "You've had the last twelve years to talk to me."

"You know why I couldn't," he says, keeping his focus forward as his hand slips down the steering wheel to clutch it at the base.

"If your reason has to do with Stone, *that* had nothing to do with me. With us."

His head swivels in my direction only momentarily before turning back to the road. "Then we should talk. About us."

I snort, dismissively. There is no us. There never can be.

"We've been quiet about it for a dozen years; we can stay silent for another twelve."

Cort is silent at first, but then, as if the stillness and quiet makes him edgy, he continues, "I wasn't myself back then. I had a lot going on."

I bite the inside of my cheek. *I* had a lot going on. My friends had graduated. I had one more year of college. I was a year out from getting away from Sterling Falls. Still, I hold back my retort.

"So, you were just using me?" I don't know why I question him. Of course he was. I was using him as well. Using him to fulfill some self-imposed ideal that he'd be the one to save me from myself. He'd be the key to turn me on.

His head whips toward me again. "Is that what you think?" He shouldn't sound so aghast. He even sounds . . . a little hurt. "Fuck, Vale. I've known you all your life. I'd never do that to you."

I don't doubt he'd intentionally hurt my feelings. What I question is everything else about that moment.

I huff. "You can't tell me you honestly remember it, right? That you enjoyed it." Like it wasn't casual and random and over within seconds.

"I fucking came like a racehorse. Of course I enjoyed it." Another glance in my direction is quick.

Then why did he fucking cry afterward? Victory tears? I doubt it. And I don't ask.

His voice softens. "You didn't like it?" He hesitates, hurt filling every word once again.

"I didn't say that." I can't say with full assurance that I did like it, though. I don't remember every detail, other than some of the finer points. Ones I considered intimate, important. His breath against my neck. His hands on my hips. The sharp rush of him entering me.

"You didn't—"

"Come like a racehorse?" I cut him off, tossing his crass comparison back at him as I roll my head in his direction.

"Well, maybe not like that, but—"

"I didn't," I respond, although I'd hoped to keep that little nugget to myself. And I quickly glance back toward the windshield.

"What?" His knuckles clutch the steering wheel so tightly I'm surprised they don't pop and crack.

Sensing him looking at me again, I stare at the windshield. "I didn't . . . then." This is the most surreal conversation, ever, and I close my eyes. Twelve years of silence and this is what we discuss? Orgasms. Who came when and how. Or not.

For the longest time after that morning in the woods, I

blamed Cort. We shouldn't have had sex. He wasn't in the right head space, like he just said. But my mind was off as well, because I'd built Cort up, made him the man of my dreams, and the reality paled in comparison, through no fault of his own. The hard truth was he didn't reciprocate my feelings. Our actions were not about emotion or connection. At least, not deeply lasting ones. Just lust and false hope and displaced trust.

Cort didn't hurt me. He hurt my feelings. Feelings *I'd* created about him. I didn't come because I can't.

Anxiously licking my lips, I decide to give him more than I probably should. "For the longest time, Cort, I had the biggest crush on you." I literally squirm on the heated leather seat with the admission. Like I'm still in my early teens and I'm revealing a secret. Holding my breath like he might return the sentiment. So juvenile. So embarrassing, because I know the truth. He doesn't.

"You what?" he whispers.

"Honestly, it felt like forever. And forever ago. But when I saw you in Milton Roadhouse that night, making eyes at me—" My flannel covered hands curl around the edge of the seat, like I need something to hold on to, something to hold me back, from pouncing like I wanted to back then.

"I knew you'd never act on anything. You'd be respectful and distant like you'd been since I was ten. But for just a blip, a hungry blink, I thought you might have noticed me. Like really saw me." My voice squeaks. "As more than Stone's forbidden sister, and more than the little kid who buzzed around the two of you."

I swallow the emotion clogging my throat and barrel on with my confession.

"And then suddenly you were there by the falls, in my sacred spot. Like what kind of weird divine intervention was that?" I chuckle bitterly. "I got wrapped up in my head, thinking the Universe sent you to me. I knew you were hurting then." His divorce. His injury. "And yet I hoped I could heal you somehow."

Like *poof!* My magical vagina would save him. One touch and I'd make him forget he ever ached over his ex-wife or lost his football career.

And one touch from him, and I'd be cured as well. I wouldn't be pent-up and repressed and fighting against what everyone told me happened naturally when a man touches you in intimate places.

"I was young." My voice falters. "Foolish." Surely, he remembers being twenty-two himself, and the stupid things he did. The mistakes he made.

But for whatever reason, I continue about me. "And I've learned that I can't get there"—I wave around my lap before quickly returning my hand to clutch the edge of the seat— "without more."

"More?" He risks a sharp glance at me. His tone is a bit firmer. Not angry. Just curious. "Like what?"

Love. Affection. Companionship. Things that can't be asked for but need to be given. Freely. Liberally. Unconditionally.

I shake my head, drained from the open confession and refusing to spell out anything deeper. "It doesn't matter."

Sneaking a peek at him, I see his jaw tick, his hand white-knuckling the steering wheel.

"I'm sorry," I whisper, although I'm not certain what I'm apologizing for. My failure during sexy times? My desire for extra from a partner? Like I'm ashamed I want more for myself. More from someone else. Suddenly, I feel sick and it's not the beers sloshing around my stomach after only having a hot pretzel at the concert.

"*I'm* fucking sorry," he blurts, glancing at me one more time before drawing his eyes back to the road. "It's bad enough that I fucking—"

Wept, I finish. My shoulders slump forward before I release the edge of the seat and slouch back, crossing my arms over my midsection, then moving my hands to the hem of my skirt, tugging at the short material that reveals too much leg while remembering more details.

Cort cried into my neck after we had sex. He apologized then, like a hundred times, but he also ran away from me without an explanation. For the tears. For the spur-of-the-moment action.

All these years, I've still wondered why we did what we did. And why he cried afterward.

My issue seems inconsequential compared to those bigger questions, but I'm talked out, wrung out, like I've confessed my soul.

For once, I'm at a loss for words and stare out the side window the remainder of our drive.

18

[Cort]

We drive in silence the remainder of the way to Sterling Falls.

Everything in me said to keep driving. Take Vale to my place in Rogue River, and get her where I failed to take her, physically.

But mentally? Emotionally? I'd been an even bigger failure. I'd had no idea how she felt about me, and I have so many questions. Forever, she'd said. Like since childhood? But obviously, it subsided, right? Her brother and I had a huge falling out, to put it mildly.

You saw me. As more than her brother's sister. As more than an annoying child.

I fucking saw her alright. I couldn't take my eyes off her in the bar the night before. Much like I can hardly take my eyes off her now.

At the massage sessions. At baseball practices. At Milton Roadhouse. I've turned into a fucking creeper.

And I've been one of too many that reinforced something Vale clearly believes is a failure *in her*. A defect that doesn't exist. She's goddamn beautiful, inside and out, and because some assholes, myself included, haven't gotten her off, is no reflection on her.

It's us. It's me. I'm the asshole here.

Why hadn't I known about the crush? Why hadn't I paid better attention to her needs?

I had all the answers. Or at least, what I thought were the answers.

The separation from Stone had me pulling blinders on to the entire Sylver family. For years, the blindness hadn't mattered because I'd moved away, but my injury returned me to the place I'd been running from and I've been back here ever since, wasting twelve years never talking to Vale, never officially apologizing, never even considering the possibility of her and me as something more.

Although I'm certain any chances between Vale and me are dead now. Crushed beneath my boots and buried in the dirt.

What a fucking tool. Vale thinks I *used* her. Selfishly, I did. But I thought—

It doesn't matter what I thought. I didn't think. I acted. Irresponsibly, immaturely, impulsively.

Too soon, I'm pulling up to the edge of Vale's driveway. It's late; the house is dark, minus a light in the front room. Stone's sheriff truck is here. If he's still awake and recognizes my vehicle, there might be hell for Vale.

And I've already put her through enough.

I place my truck in Park and pop open my door, planning to get out and circle round to Vale's side.

"Don't," she whispers, cracking open the passenger door on her own and holding up her hand.

My forehead furrows. I don't like this. Not her tone, or her refusal of me being a gentleman. I'm twelve years too late.

"Bee," I whisper. We should probably talk more, but then again, we just had half an hour to cover more details, offer explanations. The deep, dark secrets behind my actions.

And I'm still trying to process how disappointed and hurt she must have felt back then.

Spontaneous sex in the woods. Her crushing on me. Me in a bad way. Not finishing her off.

And then she's pregnant.

For the longest time, I thought Hudson might be mine. The timing worked, but Vale would have told me if he was. Despite everything between our families, if I was that boy's father, she would have told me. I believed that wholeheartedly.

But I should have asked.

I should have apologized.

I should not have let things go so long.

Because I'm learning hard truths now. Hudson's absentee father. Vale's disappointment *in me*.

At the exact time she's causing an awakening in my spirit, I've learned I crushed hers.

Vale hops out of my truck and turns back toward me. "Thanks for the ride." Her eyes are sad. The typical clear blue now foggy. Her shoulders slump forward, her body looking small in my oversized shirt.

She closes the door, and I watch her round the front corner of my truck.

Fuck it. I cut the headlights and the engine, and press open my door. Taking quick steps up the gravel drive, I catch Vale by the elbow, spinning her to face me.

"What are you—"

"I'm sorry, Vale. Sorry for everything. For taking advantage of you that day. For not satisfying you. For crying like a fucking baby afterward."

"It's—"

I press two fingers over her lips. "I'm sorry I didn't seek you out and apologize sooner, and I'm fucking sorry I never knew you had feelings for me."

I never intended to be so cruel to her.

She was my best friend's little sister. A playmate to my younger brother. And she's turned into a beautiful woman and a damn good mother.

"I'm just sorry, Vale. For all of it."

For destroying our families and breaking them apart.

Tears prickle my eyes. The sensation is something that has rarely happened in twelve years.

Dammit, what is it about this woman that makes me a mess?

"I know you are, Cort. *I know.*" She clenches her fist near her chest and stares at me in the dark night, like she really understands. Like she knows I never wanted to hurt anyone. Not Stone. Not her. Not our families.

I'd been impulsive, just like I'd been with her all those years ago, and I've paid for it ever since. Paid for that decision over and over again, but right now isn't about me, it's about the wrong I've done to her.

"Bee," I whisper, brushing a loose lock of her hair around her ear, admiring my hat on her head. It looks good on her, just like my flannel looks right, even if it is three sizes bigger than her.

I tug at the middle of my flannel shirt, pulling her closer to me.

"Vale, let me hug you." The desperation in my own voice is a whisper in the breeze. I need her closer to me. I need to feel her against me, her heart beating near mine.

I have never been a hug-it-out kind of guy. Never been someone who sought affection, especially after my ex. But right now, I *need* to hug Vale. Like bees crave pollen and lungs desire oxygen.

Vale nods, and I pull her into my chest, wrapping my arms around her neck and knocking my hat back on her head. She catches it against the back of her head, but I pull it off her, not wanting anything in the way of keeping her close.

Her body molds against mine. Her soft curves fitting against my hard planes. I breathe her in—sweet honey and mountain air—inhaling, like she's the fresh breath I've recently learned I desperately need.

Vale eventually wraps her arms around my waist, clutching the back of my tee in her fists. Her nose buries into my chest. We stand like this for a long time, sucking in deep breaths and holding on tight.

Everything in me wants to kiss her. Make it right. Make it romantic underneath the stars on this dark night.

But my chances with Vale have been checked off a list. My only hope now is understanding and forgiveness and then retreat to our corners in Milton County.

NOTHING COULD BE SO SIMPLISTIC, though. I couldn't separate myself from Vale now if I tried. She was still my massage therapist, and I was still her son's baseball coach.

On Wednesday morning, I didn't rush to undress for my appointment but sat patiently on the edge of the massage table waiting for Vale's arrival. Her son's practices and subsequent games are hardly a place to talk.

When she enters the small space, she does a double take at my seated position, dressed in jeans and a Haven Exteriors tee.

While she sets down her tablet, I reach for her hand and tug her toward me, spreading my legs so she stands between my knees.

"What are you doing?" She glances toward a corner near the ceiling.

I look up there as well then back at her. "Are there cameras up there?"

She nods and casually tries to pull her hand free from mine, but I don't let go. I spin our hands, so our palms press together and our fingers link. Her skin is so soft. Staring down at her slimmer digits slipped between my thicker ones, I lift our clasped hands and kiss her fingertips. The scent of honey tickles my nose.

"Vale, I want you to talk to me. About you and—" I point between us because something has been on my mind.

Some guys might find Vale's admission a jab at their ability, and thus a blow to their ego, an insult even. Admittedly, being selfish and unfocused, I hadn't gotten her off. But there was something in her tone the other night that suggested the issue is deeper than poor timing and a fast fuck in the woods.

She said she needed more. And I want to know what *more* means.

"Is this about the other night? What I said happened? Or rather didn't happen?"

Vale rolls her eyes and tries to pull out of my grasp again, but I hold tight. Tighter than I've ever tried to hold onto someone. Whether I openly admit it or not, Vale is important to me. *Because* she is the younger sister of my former friend, and as such, once felt like family. But also, because she's recently been patient and kind toward me. She's shown me nothing but compassion and consideration.

I don't deserve her attention or even her time. But I want it.

I want to give, not just take from her.

"Yes." I meet her eyes, steeling my gaze, so she knows I'm serious. I want to understand.

"If I have touch aversion—haphephobia—as you explained

about me, what do you have? Or don't you have? That makes . . . *it* . . . difficult?"

Another thought hits hard, that I hadn't considered before. "Did I hurt you?" My voice cracks, like I've been punched in the gut, taken unaware and can't breathe. I sit up straighter, squeezing her hand with fear that I did harm her.

"No." Her instant answer is a poor consolation. There was still something missing between us. And while I know a lot of what was lacking, I still think there is something deeper.

She's not afraid of touching someone. She's a massage therapist. But is she afraid of *being* touch?

Glancing down at where our hands are joined, and then watching her gaze upon our connected fingers, another thought strikes.

I dip my head so I can get her to look at me better. "Is this about your dad?"

Vale gasps, squeezing my hand tighter, while at the same time tugging at my fingers, like she wants me to let go. Or like she wants me to hold harder.

Either way, her head whips upright, her tone sharp. "We aren't discussing my dad."

Does she mean presently? Or does she mean ever? Or does she mean about what I know happened with him . . . and her.

"Did he hurt you?" I'm well aware of the history surrounding the Sylvers and their father. The verbal insults to the older set. The physical abuse to the younger ones. Stone wasn't half as concerned about Vale because her father basically pretended like she didn't exist.

Poor kid was treated like a ghost. But Stone made certain Vale was seen by him, as did all her brothers. As did me and my family, until I wasn't around anymore.

"No." Vale's voice is low, her gaze lowered once again, staring at our linked hands.

"Vale," I whisper.

"He never touched me." Her voice is tight. Harsh and quick and breathless. Maybe he didn't touch her. But one night, he crawled into her ten-year-old bed. Drunken fool, mistaken room. And all hell broke loose.

Maybe that was the crux. Flint Sylver ignored his only daughter. He wasn't an affectionate man. Not loving or kind. Not patient or consoling. He hurt his children on a variety of levels, and I have no doubt the abuse caused lasting implications for all of them.

Hell, I know firsthand how abusers behave and the permanent results. In my case, I repel touch. But in Vale's case . . .

"I want to understand." She's helped me in so many ways. I want to help her, if I can.

Then again, why should she trust me with more of her secrets? Why hand me her issues or her troubles? I've proven I haven't been there for her.

Twelve years of silence. She'd been willing to go a dozen more.

I'm not.

And I'll sit here for my entire session waiting for her to speak. Hell, I'll give up all my future appointments and just hold her hand until she tells me something, anything.

Eventually, her shoulders sag and her fingers loosen in my grasp. She exhales heavily. "Touch deprivation, that's what it's called. It's when someone longs for touch but gets in their head about it."

Her eyes flick up to meet mine but quickly divert staring down at my lap instead. She shrugs. "Probably stems from not being hugged enough as a child." Her voice is placating, but rough. The underlying ache is evident. The lack and absence almost suffocating.

Stone was a great big brother and an amazing mentor for his siblings, but he wasn't overly affectionate, though certainly his lack was unintentional. What twelve-year-old boy is overly hugging? Or thirteen, or eighteen, or twenty-two?

Vale's mother had been the sweet one, from what I remember of her, and Stone felt her loss greatly when she passed away, leaving six siblings below him, including a brand-new baby girl.

Valentine.

A child who never knew her mother's love or warmth or kindness.

"I just sort of get in my head," Vale whispers, head still lowered, gaze on my thighs. Her hand continues to rest in mine, I'm just not certain she even feels my fingers wrapped around hers.

"What happens in your head?" I keep my voice equally low. Patient like she'd been with me. Giving her time to warm up, to process, before she answers.

Vale closes her eyes. "There's a whole psychology behind it. Some people have high excitement. They are easily aroused."

She flicks a quick glance at me before looking away again.

"But without high intention, they can't get to the finish line. Things like 'I'm taking too long' or 'will someone hear me' or 'does he really want to do this' get in the way."

She purses her lips and twists them side to side. "It's common in couples with kids. One partner or the other worries about the kids interrupting them or walking in, and they can't keep their head in the moment."

"So in your head . . ." I wave my hand near my ear. "You start questioning everything."

When Vale doesn't answer, I add scenarios. "Like you worry that someone won't be patient for what you need? Or someone doesn't want to do what he is already doing with you?"

Vale tips up one shoulder, dismissing the situations.

Fuck, Vale, I want to scream.

She pinches her lips tight before stating, "I'm like my own cockblocker."

Then she whips her head back, eyes wide but blinking up at the overhead light. Her throat rolls, exposing a deep swallow. "And why are we even talking about this? This is your therapy session." She tips her head forward. "Your *massage* therapy session."

As I'm momentarily stuck on the roll of her throat, where I wanted to lick up the column, suck at her skin, and then lay her out on this table and show her how patient I can be with her, how very much I want to do anything she'll let me do to her, it takes me a minute to respond.

"Just to be clear, I did want you that day." Fuck, I want her now, but not like this. Not with her so raw and vulnerable. "I wanted to do what we did, and I'm sorry I didn't focus more on you." I'm sorry I didn't take more time, more care.

I was such an idiot.

Shaking my head, I glance down at how Vale's fingers fit with mine, and how our hands kind of dance together, exploring the heat of palm-to-palm contact. Lifting our fingers only to lower them back together again. I've never been a hand holder, and yet I don't want to let go of Vale.

"What happens when you're alone?"

Vale's eyes widen. "What do you mean?"

While the question might be intrusive, I power on, desperate for anything she'll give me in the way of answers. "When you are by yourself and use your toys."

"What toys?" she tilts her head.

I mirror her position. "Okay, Sterlet." *Don't play coy with me.*

"How do you know about that?" she gasps. Her brows lift. The sheen in her eyes from moments ago is gone.

"Doesn't everyone know about that?" I tease, knowing *I* hadn't until a few weeks ago.

"That's . . . personal." Her throat rolls again, and my mouth waters once more. The tension between us shifts from heavy topics and harsh realities to arousing . . . and alluring.

Because I want to be the one to help Vale explore where she can go if she only gets out of her head. I can be patient. It's been twelve years of denying any attraction I've felt toward her.

A new clock is ticking. One that is ours.

"I could help you."

"Cort." She chokes on a bitter chuckle while shaking her head.

"Look, you said you need time and patience, and I have plenty of it." Although, I'm acting impatient now. "And you've done so much for me. I want to do for you."

Vale looks at me, her eyes steady but brows pinching. "It's not just something you can give me. Like you can't hand it to me."

Instantly, I roll my lips inward, because I *can* give her orgasms with my hands, and I fight a retort until I can't hold it back anymore. "What about if I use my mouth?"

Vale's mouth pops open. Her eyes are bright a second before she narrows them. "Are you teasing me?"

"I was hoping you'd take it as flirting." I glance sheepishly at her, ducking my head while fighting a small smile.

"Cortland Haven," she scolds, tugging at her hand in my grip one more time, while attempting to step back, but I hook my feet around the back of her knees, keeping her close.

"You're helping me get over my touch aversion," I admit, clinging to her hand, proving that I might not be as averse as either of us thinks. Maybe it just took the right hands to be on me. "Let me help you never feel deprived again."

She pulls hard at our clasped hands, swatting at my shoulder with her other one. "I'm not deprived."

But isn't she? I am. I might be averse to touch, but only

because it turned hurtful and hateful. A weapon instead of Cupid's arrow of love.

With the right Valentine, everything could change.

For both of us.

19

———

[Vale]

As the conversation with Cort finally concludes, he tugs me toward him, captures the back of my head and wraps his arm around my lower back. And just holds me. Like really hugs me.

Still, I'm stiff for a second. I consider myself affectionate. I hug Hudson all the time. I'm loving toward my brothers and have offered them more hugs than they've given me. However, none of that feels like what's happening here.

The way Cort is holding me, like I'm precious, like I'm fragile. For all my insistence that I'm a strong independent woman who can take care of herself, who doesn't want to be hugged once in a while?

This is no hug, though. It's a full body experience, in which Cort's legs are still wrapped around the back of my knees, locked at his ankles. His fingers are on my nape. His palm against my lower back.

"Vale, honey." Cort pauses, still holding me. "Get out of your head."

Slowly, I release a deep breath and settle against him. Then, I let out a low exhale and fully melt. With my head on his shoulder, I hear the racing of his heart near my ear. My arms feel trapped a second, but as if sensing what I need, Cort slips the hand from my nape underneath one of my arms, allowing me to wrap around his neck. Then he returns his hand to my head and presses me tighter to his chest.

"This okay?" he whispers before tucking his face into my neck, his nose against my throat.

"Yeah." *Yeah, this is good.* My eyes fill with tears once again, and I rapidly blink at them. Feeling silly, while giddy; foolish, while light.

For a man adverse to touch, Cortland Haven knows how to hug.

However, too soon, I'm glancing back at that ceiling corner where security cameras are in place for both my safety and the safety of patients. Hesitantly, I push at Cort's shoulders, gently releasing myself from the first real hug I've had in ages.

"Your time is almost up," I whisper, hoarse and low, like I'm afraid to snap whatever is happening between us. Waiting for this weird tension to fling back at me like a rubber band and sting.

Cort simply nods, slipping his hands to my shoulders, then stroking down my arms to circle my wrists.

"We good?"

I nod without looking at him because I don't know how to respond.

Are we good? On which topic? My diagnosis? His suggestion? He wants to help me get over myself.

I'd laugh if I didn't think he was serious. I just didn't know what that could possibly look like.

Or feel like.

By the time he leaves Reflexology, I'm a mess of emotions.

Thankfully, I'm finished by noon and check out of work early. The spring afternoon is beautiful, and I need some time outdoors with my bees.

Roughly a year after Hudson's birth, a beginner's bee box arrived for me. A rare and unusual gift from Hudson's father for my first Mother's Day. At first, I was puzzled by the present. Ken never knew my nickname. It also felt ill-timed as I had a toddling son and my first job and no extra time for myself. But a year or so after the arrival of the gift, I found the box in the shed and decided to give beekeeping a try.

How cool would it be to harvest my own honey and use the surplus in homemade products?

Of course, then I had to learn how to make soaps and creams with this key ingredient. As a natural humectant, a compound that helps pull moisture to itself and retain it, honey is an ideal product for skincare. It's great for sensitive skin and perfect in massage lotions, and over the past few years, I've developed a personal line.

I don't sell it anywhere, although Clay has been pushing me to expand, offering to put my products on the shelf at Sylver Seed & Soil. I keep putting him off, telling him I'll think about it.

For now, I keep bees for me. And this gorgeous day is the perfect temperature for inspecting the hive and opening for business, as I like to call it.

The concentration I need to pull winter insulation and assess frames allows me to escape for a little while. To forget about my father, and the memories the mention of him brought forward. To not think about Cort's questions, his suggestions, or his proposition.

Let me help you never feel deprived again.

His hug certainly helped. The embrace was like none I've ever experienced before and don't expect to ever feel again.

Even hours later, though, just thinking about how Cort held me, it's like I can still feel his arms around me. His hand cupping my nape. His nose against my skin. The sensation is surreal and one I try to shake.

However, like my bees beneath smoke, lulled into calm, the feeling returns again and again. The warmth. The promise.

I'm not one to put much faith in possibilities, but there is no doubt about the strength of Cort's arms. The way he embraced me. The comfort of his body against mine. I'd like to experience it again.

Then I shake myself once more. *Nope, not going there.* Right now, it is time for me. Not my head or my heart.

Just me and my bees.

~

DESPITE MY AFTERNOON with the beehive, in less than twenty-four hours later, I'm wound up again by Hudson on the evening before his mini-sports camp.

The Haven brothers asking Ford if they could use his future camp was rather shocking, but I also hoped it was an olive branch of goodwill. Maybe fences wouldn't ever be mended between our families, but small steps had been taken to open gates of compromise.

I'd volunteered for the camp because my brother owns the place, not because I wanted to helicopter Hudson, as he has just accused me of doing.

"I'm what?" I choke, staring at my eleven-year-old which is like looking into a mirror. Thankfully, most of his features resemble mine and not his dad's.

"You're helicoptering me."

My mouth falls open as I stare at my child across the kitchen island where he sits on a stool, eating the dinner this *pilot* prepared.

"How am I helicoptering you?" I've heard the term and its reference to parents that hover over every action of their children. I know parents who behave like that, living vicariously through their child, or hyper-monitoring their kid's every decision. I am most certainly *not* that kind of parent. I'm involved, and there's a difference.

"Why do you need to go this weekend with me?"

"I'm not going *with* you, I'm going to help the team." Parent volunteers were needed to prepare meals and handle cleanup. Plus, Ford needs help with the initial setup for the boys. He's made the rooms as self-sufficient as possible, telling campers to bring their own pillows and sheets, preferably sleeping bags. The old hunting cabins on the property have been converted into bunkhouses that hold four kids per room.

Hudson snorts, lowering his head and picking at the spaghetti I made.

"Where is all this coming from, bud?"

"I'm not a baby," he snaps, and I'm taken aback. Although he's a pretty great kid, Hudson isn't perfect, and I've never boasted that I'm the ideal mother. However, we don't typically fight other than squabbles about hustling in the morning or homework at night. So, despite my shock at his tone, I tune into what he says.

"You're right. You're not a baby. You're a boy. A smart, athletic, growing boy seeking independence but still needing guidance."

Hudson huffs and that second puff of air tips me off. Atticus. That kid's attitude is rubbing off on my son, who might still be angry at me for refusing to let him go to the Stanton's house the other day after school without proof that an adult was present. When Hudson asked, I replied by inquiring if Henry was home.

"He's home," Atticus quickly told me before sliding a sly glance at my son as we stood in the school parking lot.

"Really? Let's get him on the phone." I tipped my chin at the kid, challenging him.

Challenge not accepted. He refused to call his dad, knowing he wasn't home, and I refused to let Hudson go over to their house without adult supervision at the ready to intervene should trouble arise.

Yeah, maybe I am a helicopter. I'll be fucking Stealth bomber if I need to be when it comes to Hudson.

In my anger, I didn't offer that the Stanton twins could come to our house.

"I don't need guidance," Hudson counters.

Everything in me wants to point out how he didn't make his own dinner, didn't launder the clean clothing he's wearing, or pay for the camp he's attending, but I bite my tongue.

"Well, hopefully you'll be having too much fun to bother with what I'm doing, as I'll be too busy making meals and cleaning up to be concerned with what you're doing."

Hudson looks up at me, his face befuddled, but I'm done with this discussion.

I have bigger concerns, like how I'm going to ignore his baseball coach, who gave me the hug of a lifetime, for the next few days.

20

[Vale]

When my brother was injured a year ago, his baseball career was cut short. In his late thirties, he knew his time as a professional player was coming to an end soon anyway, but no one wants to be told they can't do something they love. We all want to go out on our own terms.

To everyone's surprise, Ford gave up his home in Chicago and moved him and his girls back to Sterling Falls. It takes a village sometimes. Plus, Ford needed something to do with himself and my brothers helped build the plan Cadence, Ford's fiancée, sparked. A sports camp.

As we pull up to the old hunting camp that once housed run down mini-log cabins and an even more rundown mess hall, the difference is stunning. The smaller houses have been painted, windows replaced, and the area around them cleaned up. A new dining-slash-community building was built around what could be salvaged of the previous hall. The inside is open and airy with vaulted ceilings and a second floor where Ford has an office and a suite for special guests.

I'll have my own cabin; Ronnie Archer and her daughter have their own. Father-volunteers will be in a separate cabin, while coaches are in another one, keeping all the adults in strategic locations among the campers. Ford hired a nighttime security detail who will patrol among the cabins for extra eyes on the attendees and all our safety.

After checking in, Hudson takes his belongings to his assigned cabin while I head to mine, but within minutes Ronnie Archer is at my door.

"I *cannot* stay here," she whines with her daughter behind her looking sheepish and embarrassed by her mother's outburst.

The rooms are still rather rustic with two bunk beds and a sink in the corner. Communal bathrooms are at the opposite ends of the cabin strip. Because this simple lodging is intended for summer use, there isn't any heat. The first days of May are not cold, but the evenings can still be chilly. Bundling beneath heavy covers will be necessary.

This is a camp, not a luxury hotel, and I shrug as I roll my thermal sleeping bag over the new mattress on a lower bunk and drop my pillow.

"I'm going to speak to Cort." Spinning on heels not appropriate for the rough terrain of the outdoors, Ronnie leaves the cabin with her designer bag over her arm, Kennedy walking sullenly behind her.

Taking a seat on the mattress, I take a second look around the room, feeling like I've been transported into *The Parent Trap*. I never went to camp as a kid. Not only couldn't we afford it, but I didn't know of any in the area. My dad wouldn't have let me go anyway.

Thoughts of my father rush in, as they do on rare occasions.

All I'd ever known was a man who drank too much and swore at his children a lot. He was more physical with some of my brothers than others. Those not taking the abuse on their bodies, took it in their heads. Judd had it the worst. Ford was next in line on the rare instances he was home. He'd thrown himself into baseball, being driven and determined to get out of this town. Having given up his own dream, Stone strongly supported Ford's.

With a heavy sigh, I run my hand over the smooth exterior of the sleeping bag beneath me. Guilt riddles me at the reminder of Stone and his dreams, and the betrayal he'd feel if he knew how close I'd been with his former friend. Stone was a good boy who turned into a great man, and I don't deserve him as my brother.

With that thought, I stand and strengthen my resolve. I will keep my distance from Cortland Haven. I'm here to volunteer, to give my son an opportunity I never had. I will not helicopter him but enjoy my own slice of peace and tranquility. Although, admittedly, I wouldn't mind my *time off* being in a five-star resort instead.

Turns out Ronnie Archer isn't staying overnight at the camp but willing to drive back to her home each evening, taking Kennedy with her. She mentions it to me like it's a hardship she'll bear. She also isn't much of a cook, being grossed out by the hot dogs and hamburgers on the menu for night one. She cuts out after the meal, during clean-up duty, and disappears. Not an ideal volunteer.

Unfortunately, Kennedy misses out on the after-dinner activities as well.

During dinner, I had a sideline view of how Clint and Cort interact with the kids. It's funny how some men turn into children when surrounded by them, while others keep their distance, never forgetting they are the adult in the group. Cort falls somewhere in the middle. One minute laughing with the boys; the next pointing out how the kids need to eat the vegetables we tried to sneak into the meal.

Team building time commences after dinner, and I watch in wonder. Hudson interacts often with my brothers, especially Stone, but I still long for him to have a father of his own. Especially when I see the other two volunteers, both dads, running around the yard with the boys.

Moments like these bring back more old emotions about my own father. A man never present to play with his kids. Never encouraging their dreams or believing in their futures. Never offering a hug after a bad day or even on a good one. A man who chose to forget my birthday as it was the same day his wife died.

Tears prickle my eyes, and I fan my face wondering just what the heck brought all that on. Blinking back the water works, I look up to see Cort watching me.

"Hey, Hudson. What do you think? Should your mom be in?" Cort hollers to my son.

"Does she have to?" Hudson groans, and my heart sinks.

"Dude." Cort turns his head, interpreting the hurt.

"Your mom is awesome," one of the other boys interjects, and Hudson hangs his head in shame, being chastised by both a coach and a teammate. He kicks at the ground.

"I don't need to play." I'd planned on an early shower anyway in the private bathroom between Ford's office and the guest room in the main building.

"You're playing," Cort amends. "Everyone needs a partner, and as Coach Clint is the first to hide, I don't have one."

The group is playing Ghost in the Graveyard, a child's game where one person hides, and everyone collectively searches for him or her. Then, when the 'ghost' is found, everyone retreats to a home-base for safety. If the ghost catches you, you're the next ghost. The concept is a little disturbing when broken down, and yet, kids love it.

The idea of a partner to help you hunt the ghost is an effort for teamwork. Clint could easily pair up with one of the kids, but with Kennedy no longer present, there is an even match of participants.

I don't need to play but Cort isn't letting it go. He steps closer to me, then begins counting loudly while all the kids close their eyes a second and Clint sprints to a hiding spot.

After the count of twelve, and why twelve I don't know, Cort shouts, "Go." Kids scatter with their partners while Cort doesn't move.

"Shouldn't we be searching?" I laugh.

Cort shakes his head. "I know Clint, he'll pick some place obvious, like behind a cabin. He'll chase all the kids back to the home-base." Cort points to the flagpole just to the left of the dining hall. "And then, I'm up. We don't really want the kids hiding. They might wander too far and get lost, or we might not find them. Kids are wily like that." He wiggles his brows.

I love the thoughtfulness for the players' safety but also the spirit of the game. Cort and Clint just want the kids to have fun.

Sure enough, within minutes, two kids yell, "Ghost in the graveyard." And all the kids are running toward the flagpole with Clint chasing behind them, arms wide and bent, like he's a great big scary ghost, when he looks more like a leprechaun.

He over-exaggerates that he didn't catch anyone and he's out of breath, bending at the waist, inhaling heavily before standing and pointing at his brother.

"I nominate Coach Cort next." Clint motions like he's setting an arrow in a bow and aims it at his brother.

Suddenly, Cort grips my hand. "I'm taking a prisoner." He starts jogging and I have no choice but to keep up despite my feet initially tangling.

"Cort." I laugh. "What are you doing?"

He doesn't answer me, only starts running faster as his brother loudly counts from one to twelve.

Although the coaches previously told the boys the woods are off limits minus the trees between the dining hall and lake, Cort leads us just beyond the edge of the boundary, tugging me behind a tree and then positioning himself in front of me, like he's shielding me from sight.

With my back to the rough tree trunk, I giggle, all breathy and giddy thanks to the rush.

"Shh," Cort whispers, covering my mouth with his hand while his other arm is braced over the top of my head. He peeks around the tree before looking back at me.

"Hi," he whispers, his eyes dancing in the dimming daylight.

"Hi," I chuckle with my hands behind me, fingers picking at the tree bark.

"Thanks for your help tonight. With dinner. It was delicious."

I smile extra wide. "It was hot dogs."

"I had five of them."

I glance down at his belly, where his abs are tight. "You did not."

He shushes me again, slipping his hand back over my mouth and peering around the tree once more. But when he looks back at me, his smile is wide. His teeth dig into his lower lip, and he slips his hand around to the side of my neck. With his backward baseball cap and the lean happening, he's yummy to look at.

"I don't recall ghosts taking prisoners in this game," I whisper, while my chest heaves from rushing to keep up with Cort's longer legs. My heart continues to hammer.

"New rule," he teases. His eyes dancing once more before

he focuses on my mouth. "But the truth is, I just wanted to be close to you. Wanted a moment alone with you."

"Oh." I swallow thickly but can't stop my smile. One that expresses how tickled I am.

"Yeah. Oh." Cort glances around the tree quick but then returns his attention to me. "I'm having trouble staying away."

The admission is surprising. I've struggled with my own pull toward him, feeling guilty despite the number of the pep talks I've given myself to keep my distance. But with his body merely inches from mine, it's impossible to remember why I should be staying away from him.

The ease of his lean. The brightness of his smile. The hint of exertion.

Cort is in his element as a coach and mentor. It's a version of him that I hadn't known before now, because people change. They evolve. They move on.

Staring up at his face, with my head tipped back against the tree, I take in this older, more mature man in front of me. A sexy version with gray in his beard and heat in his eyes as he looks at me. He's still the Cort I remember and yet totally different from the boy I once crushed on. Even different still from the younger man I willingly gave my body to once upon a time.

This Cort is charming and sweet. And I admit, he's got the whole DILF thing happening because nothing turns me on more than to watch him interact with my son. The positive influence he has. The protection of me around Hudson.

"You didn't have to say anything to Hudson when he didn't want me to play." I sound like an ousted child, like when all my brothers played a game with their friends, and their friends didn't want *a girl* to play as well. The only girl in the family.

Cort scans my face a second. "I remember being eleven or twelve or thirteen. No one wants to be seen as a momma's boy, even if he is a momma's boy. But I didn't like his tone. You're an awesome mom. You're here, supporting him, volunteering for his team. You're the only mom here."

I dip my head. "Ronnie was here."

"And she had to be because of Kennedy. Plus, she left." Cort tips up my chin using the side of his hand. "He's lucky to have you."

"I'm lucky to have him," I whisper, caught between the sudden frog in my throat and the intensity of Cort's gaze. The pride in them. The acknowledgement. I'm not always certain I'm doing it right, but I'm trying. God knows I'm trying, and it's nice that someone other than family sees it.

"Thank you," I mouth, afraid I'll break whatever we have going on here, because Cort is still holding up my chin and his focus is on my lips. He leans forward just the slightest bit, causing his breath to tickle my mouth.

My heart speeds up again, like we're running once more toward the edge of these woods. Toward the edge of something. And I want to stay here in this hidden spot and explore all the possibilities with Cort.

"Ghost in the graveyard!"

Cort springs back from me and I collapse forward, as if his presence had been holding me upright. I also need a minute to catch my breath because whomever just found us, scared the bejesus out of me. Cort might need to climb this tree to pull me back to earth.

"Holy—" I gasp while Cort gives me a final glance before yelling past the trees, "Run!" Then he's off and I'm quick to follow, chasing after boys scattering here and there, hollering that Coach Cort cheated.

We were outside the boundaries but only by a tree or three.

Still, Cort makes a growling noise and runs behind the boys, following them as they race willy-nilly back to the flagpole.

As for me, I'm laughing like a fiend, running behind the lot of them as most are out-sprinting me. Once they've all collected around the flagpole, touching it as best they can, or one another in some special rule considering themselves safe, Cort and I accept defeat.

I bend at the waist, similar to how Clint did previously, only I'm not exaggerating. I have an ache in my side from running and I need a second to catch my breath between the fright of being found . . . and the near kiss with Cort.

By nine-thirty, the lights are out in the cabins. The boys have been warned that tomorrow holds a full schedule of calisthenics and drills. I finally take a shower in Ford's suite and return to my cabin. The security guard's flashlight sweeps a beam across my window. The quiet of the night suggests the camp is secure and calm.

However, I'm wound up. The exhilaration of playing a child's game. The thrill of Cort pressing me up against that tree. The near kiss and miss . . . again. And I know the perfect way to relax. To release this buzzing inside me. Reaching into my bag, I pull out my *special* travel wand.

A fantasy already plays out in my head. Cort and I against that tree. His hand travels down my chest and squeezes my breast before lowering to—

A sharp rap on my cabin door causes me to squeak. With my imagination running wild, I feel caught, exposed even, especially as I'm clutching my magic wand while standing in the middle of the room.

It's after ten and all the campers should be in bed, still I worry Hudson snuck out of his cabin to see me. In a rush, I shove the wand beneath my pillow, giggle from the tension humming around me, and step toward the door, sweeping it open to find my visitor is a little too large to be my son.

"Cortland?"

Quickly, he bypasses the two steps in front of my cabin and presses his hand against my belly, gently forcing me backward. He shuts the door behind him then exhales once his back hits the wood. His head tips back a second while I stare at him.

"What the heck are you—"

Suddenly, Cort is cupping my face and kissing me into stunned silence. His mouth doesn't hesitate. This is no ordinary first kiss. This is captivity. I'm his willing prisoner again, and I don't want to be released. His torture is the hunger of his mouth. The deep suction on my lips. The sweep of his tongue.

Then, he presses his forehead gently against mine. "I had to kiss you good night."

That's ... sweet.

"Are you also here for a little turn down service and to tuck me in?" I tease, reminding him this isn't a hotel.

Cort pulls back, keeping his hands on my jaw. "Maybe." Then he's kissing me again, slipping his hand around the back of my neck while the other slides down my arm until our hands are clasped together. Lifting our collective fingers, he tucks them against his chest while continuing to spell out his desire.

Cort and I are clearly attracted to each other. An unexplained magnetism that I should resist, but with the way he's kissing me I can't think straight.

Before I know it, Cort is walking us the short distance to the edge of the bunk bed and tucking me beneath the upper berth.

I giggle as I take a seat. "Why do I feel like I'm breaking rules at summer camp? Like I have a boy in my cabin after lights out."

"You have a man in your cabin," Cort snorts, staring down at me. "And is that my shirt?"

He's caught me. After showering, I tugged on a pair of black leggings and his flannel shirt from last weekend, minus a bra.

"Maybe," I tease, chewing my lower lip.

"Looks good on you."

I wait for him to say it would look better on the floor, but he doesn't speak. Instead, he lowers to climb onto the single bed, forcing me to lay back. Partially covering me, he wedges his leg between both of mine.

"You're so beautiful, Vale." He brushes back my hair and kisses me despite my face heating at the compliment.

When he bends his knee, he forces my legs to spread wider and I curl one of my legs over his thigh. Cupping his face, I run my fingertips over the bristly scruff on his jaw.

Cort hums. "I like having your hands on me."

I like having my hands on him, too. Pulling my head back so I can see him better, I stare into his deep eyes.

The room is dark other than a light on the nightstand replicating a camp lamp. I'd previously dimmed the switch, preparing for my personal relief moment. Now, I have this man winding me up even tighter and spitting out compliments.

He swipes through my hair again, glancing at my hair line a second. His voice is low when he speaks. "Maybe I was never afraid of touch. Just hadn't experienced it with the right person." His dark gaze falls to my eyes.

My heart skips a beat. *Am I the right person?* I want to be.

Brushing my hand along his jaw, I pinch his chin and bring his mouth back to mine.

While we kiss, I'm sensitive to his thigh pressed against my center and my breasts crushed beneath his chest. The partial weight of him is soothing, calming even, despite the racing behind my ribs and the beat between my legs. If I'm not careful, I'm going to end up humping his thigh.

Deciding we need a small break, I pull back, catching Cort's eyes. I've been kissed speechless. This moment has been knock-your-cabin-socks-off and kick-off-the-baseball-cleats delicious and I'd be happy just to continue to stare into this man's eyes for eternity.

Until Cort stretches his arm underneath the pillow beneath my head and suddenly goes rigid over me. His gaze falls to the pillow, where he slowly withdraws his hand, holding—

"Oh, shit," I whisper.

Between his hasty entrance and the dizzying kisses, I forgot all about what I stashed and where.

Cort perches up on his elbow, examining the small, purple wand. Not my finest toy but one that gets the job done.

"Cort, I . . ." I actually don't know what to say or how to defend myself.

"Did you just use this or where you about to use it?" His voice is raspy and rough, urgent even, licking up my spine and leaving a path of goosebumps in their wake.

When the vibrator turns on, I flinch a little, releasing a nervous giggle.

"Answer me." The strain in Cort's command suggests he's suddenly holding on by a thin thread. A thread only as thick as the clothing separating me from that vibrator.

Swallowing down my nerves, I'm uncertain which answer will sound better, but decide to go with the *cleaner* of the two options. And the truth. "I was about to use it."

With Cort holding the vibrating wand, I clench my legs around his. Like Pavlov's dog, my body knows what the sound means and what that toy will do for me. I'm practically salivating for him to touch me with it.

Cort brings the tip to the side of my neck, slowly dragging it around the column of my throat and notching it in the space between my collarbones.

My breath comes heavy and quick as I tip back my head, fighting against the tickling vibration. Even slower than before, he glides the tip down my chest. Wearing his shirt, I've buttoned the same three buttons he did when he first put this shirt on me. Thus, he easily slides to the top of my breasts.

Then, removing the device from my chest, he leans forward and presses a kiss to the spot he tickled.

The vibration is suddenly against my belly, moving south, until my leg is forced off his, spreading my thighs wide. Cort drags the humming toy down my lower abdomen and slips it between my legs.

"Cort," I whimper, as he presses the vibration against my legging-covered core, thrumming against my clit.

"Were you going to think of me while you used this?" His voice is thick, choked and strained, as he glances down at what he's holding between my thighs.

"A girl never shares her secrets," I tease, closing my eyes as he nudges harder, intensifying the pleasure.

Another minute passes with the hum buzzing in the room, drowning out the hammering in my chest, and the whimpers in my throat.

"Vale." Cort hisses, leaning forward and running his nose along my throat. At my ear, he quietly asks, "May I be so bold as to ask you to show me how you use this thing? Show me how your body responds to it?" He sounds almost as desperate as I feel. On the verge of unraveling, but not yet.

I need the magic closer to me. Hooking my thumbs in the waistband of my leggings, I tug them down revealing black boy-cut panties. I pull a panel of his flannel shirt over my belly, but Cort uses the wand to push aside the material, giving him a clearer view of my spread legs and dark underwear. And the vibrator he holds against me.

He nudges my inner thigh, so I bend my knee and rest my leg against his. I shift my other leg closer to the wall. The space is tight, intimate even, like we're in a cocoon.

A sports camp cocoon.

"Out of your head," Cort warns after watching my face a second. I lick my lips and close my eyes, nodding once.

With only the thin material between my skin and the vibration, I'm still turned to full watts. My clit hums and when Cort does a little twist with the thumping tip, I cry out and turn my head away from him. He latches onto the side of my exposed throat, sucking my flesh while teasing covered bits.

When he pulls back, his voice is rough once more while he appraises me. "Look at you." He hums. "Little Bee and her stinger."

I roll my eyes. This isn't a time for jokes, but before I can scold him, he slips the toy to the side, nudges the inner thigh of my boy-shorts over, and the musky aroma of my arousal slowly wafts upward. He taps my clit, and I whimper once more.

Cort hums again. "My sweet bee. Dripping. Desperate. Taking this wand like a queen." Awe fills his voice. Then he slips it lower, inward and teasing, and my back bows off the bed.

Rolling my head to look at him, I find his gaze pinned between my thighs, concentrating on where he's teasing me. His fingers don't meet my skin, but he might as well be touching me. What he sees. How I smell. How I'm reacting.

"I've never used a toy with someone else," I blurt, wanting him to know this moment is special to me. Important even. I'm in a vulnerable state. A position I never thought I'd be in with anyone, let alone Cortland Haven.

Cort swivels his head, his coal-dark eyes meet mine. "I've never touched someone like this either."

I want to believe him. Want to think this moment is significant for him as well. The thought throws me off course again.

Cort's gaze returns to my center. "I'm not leaving this room until you're satisfied, Queenie."

I laugh, sharp and quick. "Oh, have I earned a new nickname?"

Cort only chuffs, his concentration back between my thighs. "Take this wand, sweetness. Show me how you use it. Show me how it makes you wet and wild." His voice thickens, the command more demanding. A certain level of yearning rings from him and my attention returns to what he's doing to me. How he's moving the tip against my clit before slipping inside me, filling but not full enough. That sensation is reserved for a partner, one I haven't had in too long to count.

Eventually, Cort tugs his flannel up my belly, exposing more of my lower half. He leans forward and kisses my lower abs while he holds the wand against my clit. His slow kisses become more frantic. Open mouthed and scraping teeth right over the soft material. He shifts, moving his body down the length of mine, and my head takes over in the best way.

I imagine Cort dipping his head between my thighs. His mouth working me in the same way he's sucking at my belly. The lap of his tongue against sensitive folds. The pressure of his lips against—

"Cort," I cry out as my body contracts and then relief washes through me. Like the first harvest of honey, sticky and sweet and mouthwatering. My legs fall to the side as I ride out the pleasure, clutching the sleeping bag beneath me. I long to touch Cort but don't want to startle him.

He holds the wand steady, letting it do the sexy work, never wavering from watching me. When I'm wrung out, he only gives me a moment reprieve, before he slips the wand lower, forcing it deep inside me and I cry out again, covering my mouth with the back of my hand.

I blink up at the bunkbed above me. Doubleheaders are hard to win, but a few weeks ago, while fantasizing about Cort after book club, it happened.

The reality of him pleasuring me with this thing is so much better than the fantasy.

Cort keeps his eyes on my lower body, watching as he dips the wand in and out of me. My legs tremble. My fingers fisting the sleeping bag once more.

"You don't have to—"

"You're gonna come again," he demands, grit and grizzle to his voice. Sheer determination to make it happen a second time.

"If I touched you, would you sting or melt like honey?" he asks, moving the vibrator faster. "Would you want me to fuck your pussy or make love to you?"

"Oh Jesus," I mutter, a spiral building inside me again. Bees in a frenzy to be set free to explore the world.

"Makes no difference to me, just let me be your plaything, Vale. Use me for your needs."

The thought alone brings me up short, and I fling over the edge once again. My legs straighten. My head turns. I grip the edge of his shirt, the one *he's* wearing, holding on as sweet release drips from me. Not as powerful as the first but a cleansing drizzle of relief, nonetheless.

Spent, my body sags, legs wide, while my hand lets go of Cort's shirt.

He pulls the wand from my body and shuts it off, tossing it toward the end of the bed for now. Then he climbs back over me, balancing on all fours above me.

"I mean it, Bee. Use me for good."

I could argue that he doesn't like to be touched and my desire to be caressed are at odds, but I chew my lower lip instead.

"Like I said, maybe it was never the right hands on me." He seeks my hand and lifts it, pressing a kiss to the tips of my fingers. "Maybe we could help each other."

My heart soars, and I shouldn't like the feeling. Shouldn't allow the hitch in my breath. Shouldn't even consider the possibility of something more with Cort.

But right now, I'm honey-drunk, on a self-imposed Cortland-high and wiped out from a double orgasm. A fantasy come to life.

"I'd like that."

21

[Cort]

On the second night of camp, I find my way to Vale's cabin despite how tired I am. Our team's enthusiasm has run me ragged but as I near the small lodge with Vale inside, my energy revives.

After a soft knock, Vale answers the door. "Lost, coach?" she teases.

She has no idea how lost I've been.

I don't answer, other than skipping up the two steps and gently forcing her back into the room. Once the door is closed and locked, my hands are in her hair and my mouth against her lips, desperate like the starving man I've become. When I called Vale a craving, one I was certain wouldn't be satiated after one taste, I wasn't wrong. I have a sweet tooth for her.

For the longest time, I refused to kiss women. The intimacy was too much. No lips. No excessive handsy foreplay. Flip her over and do my thing. Easier to compartmentalize then. The defense mechanism was a way to keep my ex out of my mind.

But this is Vale. My sweet honeybee. A fucking queen. And I have ideas on how to give her pleasure. I want to please her.

Guiding her backward, I press her to sit on the lower bunk. Not exactly the most romantic location, but something about the rustic space renews my spirit. Like I'm a kid again, while not truly being a child.

"Still stealing my clothing, I see," I tease about her wearing my flannel shirt again. She still has my straw cowboy hat. If I'm not careful this little thief might make off with a few other items belonging to me. For now, I'm here to steal from her. Her kisses. Her breath. Her orgasms.

Vale chuckles while tugging the shirt forward. Whether she planned to give me a peek of her breasts or not, a hint is there. No bra again tonight. She isn't wearing pants right now either.

When I kneel in front of her on the hardwood floor, I rub my hands up her outer thighs, skimming all the way to her hips to discover no underwear.

"Expecting me?" I arch a brow.

Vale shrugs, lowering her gaze. "Hoping."

Damn. I do not miss the extra blip in my heart rate. I also don't want to disappoint her. From what she's told me, I already have, along with every other guy she's ever been with. I'm determined to be the exception.

"Came to play again," I admit, running my finger down the side of her neck, tracing over her collarbone, like I did last night with her magic wand. I dip my finger down her chest and hook it into the opening of my shirt on her, only three buttons looped again tonight, revealing a hint of her cleavage once more.

"Want to steal more bases?" Her voice is quiet, low and sultry.

"Looking for another doubleheader." I hum, watching my

fingertip glide over her flesh. I'm aware that my breathing is exaggerated. My voice commanding when I add, "Spread your legs for me, Vale."

Instantly, she complies, spreading her knees wide. I reach for her backside, dragging her to the edge of the bed.

"Good girl," I whisper.

Vale's breath hitches.

"You got a praise kink, Bee?" I reach for the looped buttons on the flannel covering her, needing to unbutton them and see more of her luscious body.

Vale shrugs. "Who doesn't want to be told once in while they're doing well?"

It strikes me that as much as Vale proclaims she can take care of herself, she might not be complimented for the jobs she does. Mother. Sister. Friend. Worker.

"You're doing more than well." I chuff, peeling apart the two sides of my flannel shirt and revealing the beauty of Valentine Sylver. The swell of her breasts. The valley of her belly. The curve of her hips.

Vale is already a work of art, yet I want to sculpt her body with my hands. My fingers shake as I place them on her belly which she sucks inward. Faint lines stretch across her skin. Hudson's doing. It's beautiful.

Softly, she giggles. "Sorry."

"Ticklish?"

She shakes her head and chews her lower lip. With both of us watching my hands, I climb up her body, cupping the weight of each breast in my palms before fully squeezing one, lifting it and lowering my head to take a sip. Sucking the swell, I eventually nip at the sharp peak, then move to the other breast and repeat.

Pulling back, I glance up to meet Vale's eyes. "Sensitive?"

"A little," she lies, as her breathing grows heavier, and her answer is raspy.

I want to touch Vale in other ways, but tonight, I also want to play again. I'm in no rush to prove what my hands can do, or my mouth, or my dick. I want every second to be about her.

"You have another magic wand, or should I use the same one?"

Vale nods toward her pillow where she stashed her vibrator last night.

Reaching beneath the fluffed item, I find what I want plus a small tube of lube. Vale didn't need it last night. Pushing her knees wider apart, I stare at her pretty pink center, already milky and wet, but if she wants something extra, I have an idea.

I lift the fake cock for her lips. "Open."

With strained willpower, I watch as Vale follows my command and wraps her lips around the silicone dildo. Her eyes are on me as she rolls her tongue around the tip before pulling it into the warmth of her mouth.

Fucking hell. I'm hard as a rock, like I was last night, and I'll be taking care of that later with images of this moment in my head.

"Little tease should be your nickname."

Vale chuckles as I pull the toy away from her mouth and settle it against her. With a flick of a switch, it comes to life and Vale flinches. A soft gasp escapes her lips as she watches where I'm touching her with her toy.

"You like that, sweetness?" I ask, speaking to her center.

Vale hums and I look up as her lids drowsily close. Her hands have been gripping the edge of the bed, but she slides them backward, tipping her body.

"Just want you to relax, Vale. Let me do the lifting." Her gaze falls to my face for a second but when I move the wand to her clit, her lids close again. I want her eyes on me, but she mentioned how commands can shut her down and I want Vale worked up. I want her so wound that she only thinks about me and the pleasure I'm pulling from her.

A queen giving herself to her subject.

Vale's toes are pointed on the floor and one of her knees begins to bounce. Mentally, I catalogue all her tells. A soft purr. A sharp gasp. How her legs eventually stiffen, and she digs her hands into the sleeping bag beneath her.

"Fuck." Vale hisses, coming fast and furious. Her essence coats the tip of this wand.

My mouth waters, thirsty to lap her up, but this isn't about me. Not yet.

Capturing her ankle, I bring it up to my shoulder, thus causing Vale to fall back. She chuckles once before my mouth kisses the knob of her ankle. She's open in a new way in this position, and as my mouth trails over her calf, I shift the wand to enter her, craving that doubleheader I told her I sought.

"Cort," she whimpers.

"Take your time, Bee. I have all night." I don't really, but I'm not leaving this room until she's satisfied a second time. Moving from her calf to the underside of her leg, I nip her skin.

"That feels good," she admits breathlessly.

"A little pain with the pleasure? My bee likes the sting."

"Just a little." She bites her lower lip, and I tally another item on my mental list.

Working the wand in and out of her, I move closer and closer to her center with my mouth, inhaling the tangy musk scent combined with her honey essence. Wanting a taste but resisting.

Vale reaches above her head, gripping the opposite edge of the slim camp bed and grinding on the wand inside her.

"Look at you," I encourage as her hips slowly roll. "You like this, honeybee?" Her body says she does.

"Gonna let my dick be here instead one day?" I ask, hoping, praying, teasing her as I drive the vibrator faster.

"Cort," she groans.

"Vale," I counter, my thumb wanting to play with that pretty nub, the trigger to tip her over the edge. Instead, I pull the wand from her body, swipe her clit, and then slip inside her again, watching as Vale detonates. She goes off like fireworks against a dark sky. So bright, so beautiful, like nothing I've ever seen before.

I sink my teeth into her inner thigh, letting her ride out the celebration within.

I'm so hard, I can't resist, gripping myself over my athletic pants, running the heel of my hand down my rock-solid length.

Eventually, Vale whispers, "Enough."

Withdrawing the toy, I power it off and drop it to the bed. Then I reach for her waist and tug her upright, needing to taste her mouth again.

Vale kisses like she's putting all of her into it. Her arms wrap around my neck, and I don't pull back, don't even flinch. We kiss for long, languid seconds before Vale leans away and settles her forehead against mine.

"Let me play with you." Her tone is desperate, hungry and begging as she clutches my T-shirt.

"You don't need to do that," I assure her, despite how primed my body is.

"I want to," she hums, risking a kiss to the corner of my mouth. Then another to my cheek and one to my chin. "I need to taste you."

Shocking me, she licks up my lips.

I want this. I fucking want this so badly, but my head instantly gets in the way. Ghosts creeping in about being in such a vulnerable position.

Get over yourself, Cort. Slowly, I rise, my knees popping as I do. I grip the base of the upper bunk for leverage and stand to my full height, gazing down at Vale. Sweet Vale. All innocent and untouched in her own way.

When she reaches for my waistband, though, I flinch. Unwarranted. Unknowingly.

Shit.

Vale holds her hands outward, like she's frozen in freeze-tag, the game we played earlier tonight.

"I'm sorry." Her apology is hesitant, while concerned eyes glance up at me towering over her. Like she doesn't know what she's done wrong when it's not about her at all.

"*I'm* sorry," I mutter, knowing it must be confusing. Last night, I was all in, not thinking about anything but pleasing Vale. Tonight, I want the same thing. She looks hungry to take me, and I fucking want to be taken. But I have rules.

Swallowing hard, I lick my lips. "Could . . . could I ask you to . . . sit on your hands?"

Vale is quiet a second before stating, "You don't want me to touch you."

As far as I've come, I'm still a mess. All of this is new to me. Her kindness. Her tenderness. Her understanding, and I hate asking her for this concession. I don't want to fuck this up.

"Just tonight. Keep your hands to yourself." I try to soften the blow with a tease in my tone.

Vale doesn't hesitate, slipping her hands beneath her thighs, and I release a breath I didn't know I was holding.

Quickly, I shove down my track pants and boxer-briefs. My dick springs free like it's been contained too long. Hard and hot and pointing at Vale like a neon sign reading: desperate and horny.

Don't hurt me, Vale. My heart rumbles so loud I swear she can hear it.

"Step closer to me." The command in her sultry voice has my cock twitching, and I cup the base, rocking my hips forward.

"Feed me," she whispers.

FUCK!

This good girl has a naughty streak I did not see coming, but like the queen she is, I obey her demands, guiding my tip to the seam of her lips, where her tongue sneaks outward and she licks around the crown.

I hiss at the contact.

"Want me to stop?" Vale whispers, her breath a soft breeze over my dick. Her gaze dropped to the appendage that's long and stiff, and weeping for her attention.

I can't speak, don't know any words. Instead, I shake my head.

Vale kisses the tip again, and I jolt forward, the magnetic pull almost overpowering.

"Sorry," I mutter. "Sorry, sorry, sorry." I grip the base of my cock tighter, attempting to hold myself steady. My other arm braces on the frame of the upper bunk and I press my forehead against my bent arm, watching Vale hunger for me.

She rubs her nose along my length. "Don't apologize. You're doing so good."

I snort at the reverse praise, recognizing that *I* appreciate the encouragement as well. I want to be good for her.

When her mouth opens and she glides down my length, my eyes instantly close, the sensation too great. Her warmth. Her strength. Her comfort. It's too much, yet I don't want to miss a second of this experience. Forcing my eyes open, I stare down at Vale, catching her watching my face. Releasing my base, I comb my fingers through her hair, fist it at her nape, and watch her glide up and down my length, coating it in heat, giving me all her strength, caring for me in this moment.

My ass clenches, taking great effort not to thrust forward to the back of her throat.

"Gonna be embarrassingly fast," I warn, already feeling the tightening of my balls and a pull in my lower back. I grip the edge of the upper bunk with my hand and lean back, rocking my hips forward only two times before I'm holding Vale's head and jetting off down her throat.

"Fuck," I cry out, too loud, too overwhelmed.

Vale swallows hard, drinking me in, before eventually pulling back, letting her tongue lap along my length before popping off the head.

"Sweetness." I choke, bending and ducking my head beneath the bunk to take her mouth with mine. I don't know that I've ever kissed a woman after what Vale just did, but I want to taste myself on her lips, want to savor the sensation of her mouth. The gift of it.

Eventually, I grab a tissue from a box on the small nightstand between the bunks and clean up, then pull my pants back into place.

Last night, I didn't spend the night and tonight I can't either, but I need a minute to come down from this high Vale has me on.

I climb onto the slim mattress, Vale giggling as we attempt to fit both of us on a twin-sized bed again. My feet dangle off the edge near the bottom and Vale presses her back against the wall, while we stare at one another for a long minute. Her clear eyes are refreshing and bright.

"I want to see you again," I blurt. Two nights isn't enough.

Instantly, Vale's brows pinch, worry dances over her forehead. "How would that happen?"

"I don't know," I whisper, sorrow clogging my throat. I don't want to stop whatever is happening between us, but I understand Vale's concerns without her even expressing them. Her brother is top of the list.

Vale continues to stare at me, no answers herself.

"Can you hand me that pen on the stand?" She nods toward the low nightstand that holds the tissue box and the miniature camp lamp. A Sharpie pen and a notebook are also on the stand.

Puzzled, I awkwardly stretch for the marker, nearly falling off the narrow bed. Vale laughs, clutching my forearm like that could prevent me from slipping off this slim mattress. The sudden burst of joyful noise dissolves some of my worrisome thoughts and I hand her the marker.

Braced on my elbows, I watch as she pulls the cap from the permanent pen and flips my arm so my inner forearm is upward.

Vale draws on my skin, and I flinch.

"Ticklish?" She returns my tease from earlier.

I simply smile. There are so many ways to touch someone, but I never considered drawing on a person. Never thought how sensual it would feel.

Her artwork is quick and when she pulls back, she blows on the small design.

"A bee?" I softly chuff about the cartoon-looking insect with flowery wings, stripes over its back and a little stinger for a nose.

"So you won't forget me again."

My gaze leaps to her face, catching on her eyes looking back at me. "I've never forgotten you, Vale."

Not how she was as a young woman. Not how we came together by the falls. Not how she's been the first to bring me out of a hard shell, making me want to be soft.

For her.

When I sneak out of Vale's cabin, I have no idea what time it is other than the camp is quiet, and the hour must be late.

And I'm startled by the sudden appearance of the overnight security guard just off the corner of Vale's cabin.

"Cort?" He shines his flashlight directly in my eyes, blinding me a second before I recognize his voice.

Andy Whitehall is a deputy for Sheriff Stone Sylver. Rumor has it he'd been on probation for a while but has been reinstated on the force. Apparently, he moonlighted as a security guard while on that probation period and continues to offer the service. Ford hired him for our weekend here.

"Andy," I counter, holding up a hand to shield the light he continues to shine in my direction.

"Deputy Sheriff Whitehall," he corrects, like I'm disrespecting the man who is younger than me. He's nearly Vale's age, which is something I've been forgetting.

Vale is twelve years younger than I am. The age gap hardly seems to be an issue until you consider she's the *younger* sister of my former best friend. Guilt smacks into me, despite the relaxation of my body.

"Whatcha doin' out here?" Andy asks.

"Just needed some air."

Andy probably sees right through my lie. It's late. Very late. But he doesn't need to know the air I needed was Vale.

"Well, I better get some rest. It's been a long day." I sound too chipper and completely unlike myself.

Good head can do that to a man. So can a woman like Vale.

"Thanks for your service," I add, stepping closer to Andy and offering him my hand.

He glances down at it, hesitating a second before clasping mine in a firm grip, and shaking once. "Any time."

On that note, I pass him, slipping my hands into my pockets and holding my breath as I slowly eek open the door to my cabin.

Last night, Clint questioned where I'd been, and I'd told him I went for a walk. He'd be shocked to learn where my steps took me.

Hell, I'm still a little stunned myself, but there is no turning back.

Glancing down at the outline on my inner arm, I smile to myself.

There must be a way to see Vale again.

22

[Vale]

When Wednesday rolls around, I'm nervous. I haven't seen or heard from Cort since the weekend. A weekend that was both an eye-opener and sexy as hell. But I don't know where that leaves us, other than as therapist and patient again.

Most of the time Cort and I were in private, he didn't seem to mind my touching him. He even appeared to welcome it, until it came to the more intimate moment of me undressing him and taking him in my mouth. I have no doubt he enjoyed himself immensely, but the fact he had me sit on my hands was worrisome.

Having touch aversion is typically a symptom of some past trauma and I shudder to think that Cort has been hurt in some deep, dark, disturbing way that's caused him to be afraid of physical contact. I doubt it was his parents. Mary and Franklin

Haven were good people, kind people, and very loving toward their children. The mystery lays elsewhere.

And these thoughts rumble through my head while Cort lies face down on my massage table. His beautiful shoulders on display. His triceps tight while his arms are at his sides. The curve of his backside beneath the sheet. The suggestion of what's on the front of him vivid in my memory.

My mouth waters when I consider what we did. What I said to him.

Feed me. I've never been so bold. So direct. Demanding from him what I *wanted* him to do.

The memory sends a shiver licking up my spine. An empowering shiver. One that has me smiling while I pull down the sheet covering him mid-back and lower, including his arms.

Instantly, I notice a bandage on Cort's arm.

"What happened?" I ask. The wrap isn't something small. It's wide and thick and circling around his lower left arm.

"Just a little scrape on the job," he mutters, his face buried in the circular pillow as I start our warmup routine.

"You need to be more careful," I scold, frowning although he can't see me.

He's in this position in the first place because he fell off a roof. He needs to take better care of himself.

The thought brings me up short, because I want to take care of him. I want to wipe away whatever fears still linger about being touched. I want to erase the pain and give him pleasure. I want him to learn that hands are for love, not harm.

Massaging methodically along his side, I'm lost in this thought when Cort turns his head on the pillow.

"I can almost hear you thinking, Bee."

I softly chuckle. "Just wish you wouldn't take risks with yourself." Maybe just take a risk on me.

"I'll pay better attention," he says, his eyes open, peering at me as best he can in his current position. Somehow the words feel telling, like he means something deeper. Like he'll note details better with me.

I don't want to act like this weekend didn't mean everything to me, but I also don't want to come across like I want more. I'll take whatever Cort offers. I'm just happy we're still talking. He didn't walk away from me this time. He didn't disappear.

He was all sweet smiles and tender kisses, giving me one last, lingering one before slipping from the cabin late at night, leaving me to slumber in a sleeping bag surrounded by his scent.

Like a love-sick teen, I slept in his flannel again.

"Your hands feel so good, Vale," he murmurs, sounding drowsy from my work. I'm so pleased he appreciates the massage, and he's content with my touch.

Then I circle back to his hesitation when it came to placing my hands on him when we were more intimate. I wish he'd open up with me. Tell me what happened to him. Asking deep questions feels like crossing a line, though. One that moves us from just having fun to something more serious.

I'm so lost in my head, time passes quickly and before I know it, his session is over.

Stepping back to type up my report on this session, Cort shifts, rolling before swinging his legs over the side of the table and sitting upright, dragging the sheet over his lap.

"Look at you," I tease. "Almost ready to hop off that table without a hint of back trouble."

For some reason, I think about us crammed on that narrow twin bunk. I hope he didn't hurt himself then. Or when we were running around the yard at camp, playing childhood games. Or—

I stop my thoughts and catch Cort watching me.

"Anyway, no more falling off roofs." My gaze drops to the bandage on his arm. Roofing is clearly dangerous work.

"Yes, Queenie," he teases, fisting the sheet over his thighs, while his legs swing back and forth once. His voice is light. His smile sweet and slow.

"You only have a few remaining sessions," I remind him. His insurance only covered so many. "How are you doing with the exercises at home?"

As a physical therapist as well, I've assigned Cort movements to help stretch his back and keep his muscles loose.

"I don't know. I might need another home visit to check on my progress."

I chuckle at his playful tone. But he probably shouldn't pop over to my house again anytime soon, and I'm instantly saddened by the thought.

I can't date Cort. We can't be seen in public and there isn't anywhere to meet in private.

Cort reaches for my hand, and I easily give it to him. He tugs me closer. "You feel so far away."

"Guess I'm just in my head a little bit today."

Cort dips his head to look at me, the corner of his mouth curling upward. "You know I want to help you get out of your head."

Which is exactly what he did this weekend, giving me orgasms like I've never had before. His physical fingers never left the edge of that magic travel wand. Still, it was all Cort.

High intention. Total focus. All patience. Some hidden skills for a man who claims he's never used toys on companions before.

"Vale," Cort squeezes my hand. "I want to take you on a proper date." He purses his lips and twists them a second before adding, "Even knowing the risks. I haven't been able to stop thinking about what we did this weekend."

"Me either," I whisper, lowering my gaze to where he holds my hand, linking our fingers together.

I'm reminded how his touch started small. A brush of our pinkies. A finger hooked around two of mine. Then three. Then my hand cupped in his. And then our fingers entwined together.

We've come so far, and I don't want it to end. "I just don't see how we can do something public. Dinner. A movie." Because of my brother. Keeping my gaze lowered, I dig my teeth into my lip. "We probably shouldn't be seen together outside of you coaching my son." Public baseball games for children.

"Then maybe we could do something more private," Cort suggests. "Come to my house, Vale. Let me make you dinner."

My head pops up. The suggestion is so much sweeter than taking me to a restaurant. The date would be personal, intimate, private.

A secret.

23

———

[Vale]

That night, I tell my brother I have a date on Saturday, sticking as close to the truth as I can.

"It's new, and I'm not certain it will go anywhere, but I've agreed to go on this one date." My tone suggests it's a hardship while my insides are a riot of excitement.

I have a date with Cortland Haven.

"Anyone I know?" Stone arches a brow like Cort does.

I shake my head. "I'm not ready to share yet."

For all Stone's questioning of me when I was younger, he trusts me now, which builds another layer of guilt on the already existing pile.

However, Stone and I also respect each other's privacy. He doesn't share with me what the hell is going on between him and Emerson Milton, the town's mayor. He also knows I don't have much of a dating life. This is my first one in forever.

By Saturday night, I'm a bundle of nerves.

My brother Knox has a stepdaughter named Violet. The irony of her name being our mother's name did not escape anyone in the family. She's a pretty redhead who looks just like her mom did as a teen. She's also a junior in high school and can drive, so I ask her to watch Hudson for the few hours before Stone will be home. While Hudson isn't too thrilled to spend time with a *babysitter*, I try to rationalize that she's his cousin, making her family. He doesn't fall for it. When her younger brother Tim agrees to come over as well, turning the night into a pizza-slash-video game competition for the older 'cousins', Hudson changes his tune. He hero-worships the four-teen-year-old boy who loves soccer as much as Hudson loves baseball.

"Bless you," I say to Violet when they arrive, and I can finally slip out the door.

"You look . . ." My niece wiggles her brows then taps the tip of her tongue with her forefinger making a sizzling sound. "Hot."

I laugh, needing the chuckle to settle my nerves. "Do you think I look all right?" I might be a tad overdressed in a slinky black number that is more appropriate for a wedding than a stay-at-home meal. Not to mention, I'm asking the opinion of a sixteen-year-old.

"Honestly, Vale, you look beautiful." Her reassuring smile sends me on my way.

Cort lives in an A-frame house tucked in the hills around Rogue River. When I park in his driveway, the soft echo of the river comes from somewhere behind his home.

He steps out onto his porch before I've even exited my car, and I inhale. He looks amazing in a dark, silky shirt and black jeans, and he smiles sheepishly when he sees me. I no longer worry about being overdressed. He looks as anxious as I feel.

On the drive over, I've given myself a pep talk. How I shouldn't be nervous. This man has seen intimate parts of me but there are deeper layers we don't know anymore. Years of absence from each other's lives.

What if he doesn't like me? Quickly, I shake off the negative thoughts, smooth my hand over my belly, and cross the walk to his porch.

"Vale," he whispers like his tongue is too thick. His eyes roam up and down my body, and he holds out a hand as soon as I step onto the porch. Right there, he twirls me around so he can see me from all angles.

"Fuck. You're so beautiful, Bee." He cups my cheek and kisses me sweetly. Not like his typical hunger but more like he wants to savor the moment.

A mental image of this Cort is certainly going into the scrapbook of my heart.

After leading me inside, I get a quick tour of the house. The living room opens to a large kitchen that curves right and faces an open concept sitting area. Through the sliding glass doors, a view of the river down below is visible. A loft is above us with the same view.

Cort points out that one end of the house has two bedrooms. The primary bedroom is in the opposite direction. Brushing over that information, he offers me a glass of wine. "I have white or red or rosé."

His voice trembles a little, and I round the small kitchen island and slip my arms around his waist.

"Hi." I focus on his eyes. His shoulders relax and his arms wrap around me as well.

"Hi." He chuckles softly, blowing out a breath. "I don't want to fuck this up."

"You won't." I smile to reassure him. I'm here. He's here, and we're alone.

Pressing a kiss to the top of my head, he pulls away. "Hope you like steak."

"I love a good hunk of meat." I wink and Cort laughs,

bursting the initial bubble of nerves surrounding us.

As Cort prepares the steak and pulls pre-cut vegetables out of his fridge, we chat about his family, a safer topic than mine.

"Tate is still a punk ass while Clint is . . . well . . . Clint. A good guy at heart, trying to raise his daughter on his own."

Ruby James is five years old and in kindergarten with my niece June. The two girls are becoming fast friends, and their connection might be a rebuilding bridge between the families.

"Trinity is still a spitfire." Cort shakes his head.

I'm well aware of what he means. After her divorce, she really went through a glow up and opened up herself. She's very *vocal* at our Sterlet meetings about how a woman can meet her own needs. Often spoken like a woman truly scorned.

"I see your mom sometimes, at the grocery store." I smile as I twirl my glass of wine in my hand, watching the liquid gently swirl from side to side. "She has always been nice to me."

When my mother died, her friends tried to rally around our family. Seven kids ranging from twelve to newborn was a lot to tackle. My dad decided not to handle it; instead, sinking himself into bottle after bottle. From what I've been told, my mother's friends stepped up and tried to step in, but Dad shut that down over and over again.

Mary Haven was particularly close to our mother, especially as several Sylvers line up in age to the Haven kids. Stone and Cort. Judd and Tate, who never got along. Sebastian and Clint. Trinity is between Knox and Ford.

"Your mother taught Sebastian and I how to bake," I remind him, still smiling down at my glass of wine with fond memories of standing in the Haven kitchen mixing up ingredients and rolling balls of dough for holiday cookies.

"When I was little, I wanted to be adopted by your family." I shrug and lift my glass, hoping to disguise the emotion in my voice. The memory has come out of nowhere, but it's an honest recollection. Before I crushed on Cort, before everything fell apart, I wanted to be a Haven.

Their home was warm and bright, and full of laughter and love, not harsh words, physical repercussions, and dirt.

"You know my dad wasn't much of a loving man," I continue, lowering my glass to the counter.

Cort stands on the other side of the island, his arms spread wide, and hands braced on the top. He's stopped moving and given me his full attention.

"I remember," he whispers. He'd been a witness many times to the way my father spoke to Stone, but Stone, and Cort for that matter, were gone when the true wrath of our father was unleashed. When insults turned to injury. He cut Judd the most with his words, skipping to Ford next. His physical abuse went to the scrappier set of Knox and Sebastian. Somehow, Clay knew how to deal with our dad, but he'd left the house as well.

Cort keeps his gaze on me. He's already admitted he remembers what happened between my father and me. Ten years old, and my father was drunk. Crawled into my bed, his breath hot at my ear. I'd been frozen in place, uncertain how to react, my throat clogged with fear.

Sebastian's voice is what I heard first, yelling *you sonofabitch*.

Knox was next.

I'd closed my eyes, squeezing them shut, knowing they were about to fight again. My dad and Knox went at it constantly the year before he left for the Navy.

That night was the catalyst for our father's death.

He took his own life.

I lick my lips. "Probably why I was such a wild child in my late teens and twenties," I weakly attempt to joke, referring back to my dad not being a loving man. "Chasing love in all the wrong places," I add, huffing and dismissively waving my hand. "I think there's a song about that."

Cort tilts his head, sympathy in his eyes. "Little Bee."

"Anyway." I bitterly chuckle, picking up my wine but pausing before taking another drink, "That got heavy fast."

Phew, I don't know where any of that came from, and I feel itchy and exposed, like I've revealed too much about myself.

Cort doesn't take his eyes off me, watching me in that way he does, like he can see inside me. However, I don't want him to see all the broken pieces.

Slipping from the stool, I round the counter. "Put me to work." It's the best way to take my mind off the memories and bring me back to this moment, where I'm safe, standing in Cortland Haven's kitchen.

"Tonight"—Cort watches me—"I take care of you."

I chuff, prepared to tell him I take care of myself. On the tip of my tongue is a secondary retort: *I don't know what that would feel like.* I have no idea what it means to have someone take care of me.

Cort certainly took care *with* me last weekend, but I mean on a deeper level. Someone looking out for just me. My needs. My wants. My dreams.

As if knowing I'm about to argue, Cort keeps his steely eyes on me and unbuttons the cuffs of his shirt. He methodically rolls up the right side and then the left.

My gaze instantly drops to his forearm. "Oh, you got your bandage off. Let me see." Without thinking, I reach for Cort's arm.

He pulls back and I'm reminded that touching him comes with caution. No sudden movements. *Noted.* While I'm curious why that is, I don't ask because I've already dampened the evening by bringing up my dad.

In an attempt to brush off the twinge of hurt at his retraction, I weakly smile and glance up at his face. "Well, I'm glad you're better." That was some bandage he had on his arm before.

Slowly, Cort lowers his shoulders and stretches his left arm toward me. He closes his eyes a second and flips his arm so I can see the inner part of his forearm.

Prepared for a deep cut or a nasty burn, I gasp when I see what's really present. Swallowing thickly, I say, "That permanent marker should have washed off." Because a week out from drawing that silly bee on his inner arm, there shouldn't be any trace of the mark. What I see isn't anything made with a marker, though, but definitely permanent ink.

"Cort," I whisper, looking up at him again.

"Told you I'd never forget."

My gaze falls once more to the tattoo etched into his skin in a perfect replica of what I drew.

A buzzing bee.

That's forever, my head registers but my heart warns, *don't you dare hope*.

With his arm steady, I point at the permanent artwork with a shaky finger, before pressing my forefinger to his warm skin and skimming over the bee and the little trail of dots behind it.

I want to throw myself at this man. Wrap my body around him, tackle him to the floor, and beg him to take me.

Thankfully, he's saved by the beep of the timer on the microwave.

"Grill should be ready." He clears his throat, and I wonder if he'd been thinking the same thing I had.

I want him to mark me, in a way that's better than the first time. I want to have a permanent reminder of him as well.

WHEN WE EAT at the kitchen island, Cort sits sideways, having pulled my stool close to his, and spreading his knees to bracket me in on my stool. His left foot is casually on the low rung of my stool while his right knee is pressed against mine, keeping us connected somehow while we eat.

The steak is great, grilled veggies amazing, and the company exceptional. The date is the best I can ever remember having. With history between us, both good and bad, we easily recall shared moments as kids or similar experiences from having grown up in a small town. An ease exists that's always been there and the magnetic pull between us becomes a strong force.

When we finish the meal, Cort and I linger, finishing off the bottle of wine and laughing about stupid pranks and former dates on my side. He admits he hasn't dated much in the past.

"Bailey sort of took the wind out of my sail." It's the first time Cort's mentioned his ex, and as much as I want to learn all about him and what happened, I'm not ready to discuss *her*.

"Anyway," Cort sighs, reaching out and tucking my hair behind my ear. "Tonight is about you."

From the wine to the meal and even the conversation, I certainly feel like the center of his attention.

"Let me take care of the dishes," I say, slipping from my seat and breaking our knee-to-knee connection, before Cort catches my wrist.

"Vale." Our eyes lock. "Leave 'em."

"We don't have to."

But Cort is already shaking his head. Just a slight left-right. "Bee, who takes care of you?"

"I do," I tease flippantly, but something dark in Cort's eyes chops up my laughter.

"No, who really takes care of you?"

"Cort." I blink, pulling my eyes from his, and tugging at my arm. We don't need to get heavy again. It's been a great night.

Slowly, Cort stands and removes the stool between us. He steps up to me, cups the side of my neck and leans down to kiss me. Just once, soft and sweet, like when I first arrived.

I want him to ravish me instead.

And I think that's where we're headed when Cort leads me

to his bedroom. Only once there, I'm met with a collection of candles on the bedside stand along with a jar of *my* honey cream.

"Did you steal that from me?" We don't sell my stuff at Reflexology, so the only place he could have gotten a jar of my homemade balm is by taking it from the massage room. Or my bedroom.

"I wouldn't say stealing," he teases.

"Oh, are you gonna give it back?" I joke.

"In some way, yes." Cort nods toward the bed. "I want you to lay down, head on the pillow."

"Cortland," I groan.

With his hands on my shoulders, he presses me to sit on the edge of his large bed covered with a dark-colored comforter.

"Tonight, it's your turn for a massage."

From my seated position, I stare up at him, thinking he must be kidding. Then I glance at the candles and the cream and accept that he's not.

"Do you even know how to give a massage?" I counter, wanting to sound playful but my throat is thick again.

"You can teach me." He nods toward the bed. "Lie down."

My dress isn't exactly massage friendly, but I do as Cort asks, swiping my hair to one side as I place my cheek on his pillow. Instantly, I'm surrounded by his scent. Balsam fir and a twinge of asphalt. I want to press my nose further into the fragrance but resist.

"May I?" His fingers touch the zipper pull, mid-back, on my dress.

I nod and blow out a deep breath. He's taking this rather seriously, so I try to relax. Unfortunately, the slow unzipping of my dress is like butterfly kisses against my skin, triggering flutters in my lower belly.

Cort spreads the two sides of my dress apart and unclasps my strapless bra with a quick snap. With my back fully exposed, and my head on the pillow, I hear Cort open the jar of honey balm. He rubs his hands together and then places them on my back the way I initially touch him.

"This is kind of an odd angle."

"Sit on my legs." The invitation comes out sultry and rich, and the second he straddles my thighs, I'm in trouble. The river outside his window doesn't compare to the wetness that pools at my center.

Cort does as I suggest but doesn't put his full weight on me somehow. Then he rubs his hands up and down my spine, digging his thumbs into my upper back and stroking up my neck.

Damn, that feels good.

He continues kneading his thumbs into my muscles, working one side to the other along my upper back before moving downward, along my spine, and eventually digging into my lower back. My dress only spreads so far near my backside, above my hips, so Cort slips his hands beneath the material, squeezing at my lower lats.

I flinch and giggle.

He stills. "Ticklish?"

"Maybe." As I told him once, a girl can't give away all her secrets.

Cort softens his touch but still works on muscles I didn't know were aching. I stand on my feet most of the day but wear comfortable, supportive shoes for the task. Still, my body isn't as young as it used to be, though I work at keeping it strong.

Eventually, Cort removes his hands from the inside of my dress, and I think the massage is complete but then his palms settle on my ass. He squeezes over the silky material of my dress, and I tense my legs.

"No-go zone," he questions, instantly lifting his hands.

"I'm good." I'm more than good. I'm melting into this bed.

Cort massages the globes of my ass but then shifts his body

lower, cupping underneath the swells and moving on to my thighs. Starting at the back of my knees, he shimmies my dress upward to where the curve of my backside meets my legs and wedges himself between my spread legs. He digs in once again, kneading the back of my thighs, working down to my calves and stroking over my bare feet.

With my eyes closed, Cort's scent on his pillow filling my nose, and his hands laid gently on me, I could fall asleep, if I wasn't also turned on.

"Feel good, Vale?"

I purr in response.

Cort slowly slides his hands up my legs, humming to himself as he strokes featherlight over my flesh.

"I've got another way to make you feel good, sweetness, but there's no pressure."

I'm in a vulnerable position here. Belly down on his bed. Legs spread around his knees. Hands beneath his pillow.

"I didn't bring a toy," I admit, recalling he never actually touched me the other night and there's nothing I want more.

I blow out a breath, trying to settle my apprehension.

Cort climbs over me, presses a kiss to my exposed shoulder, and whispers at my ear. "Let me touch you." He kisses my shoulder blade next. "We'll go at your pace. I just want to make you feel good. Take care of you."

He means right now. Tonight. And tears prickle my eyes, but I nod, giving him permission to play.

Sliding his hands over my hips, he hooks his finger into my panties and drags them down my legs. He rubs his hands back up my calves and thighs and then dips between them.

In this position, I feel both exposed but exhilarated. And when Cort swipes up my seam, I bend my knees a little bit, chasing his finger.

"It's been so long," I mutter, revealing more about myself.

"Same," Cort whispers as he continues to explore. He pops

up on his knees and leans over me, balancing on one arm while his other hand traces lazily up and around sensitive parts, driving me nearly mad, before settling right where I need him.

I whimper in relief and arch my back, pressing against his fingers, hoping to stay out of my head.

As if Cort senses my hesitation, he leans closer to my ear. "You're so beautiful, Vale. Sweet and soaked. I can't wait to taste you one day."

I could beg him to taste me now, but I'm too turned on by his words, by his touch. By the possibility of another date with him.

"One day . . . you gonna let me put my dick in you, Bee? Gonna let me savor that sweet honey dripping over me, coating me, marking me again?"

"Oh God," I groan, lifting my backside higher, wanting him to go deeper. Cort slides a finger inside me but quickly pulls out and returns to the sensitive bundle of nerves where I need him.

I'm wound tight again before he drops two fingers inside me.

"Jesus, Vale. The way I know we'll fit."

I grind back against his hand before he withdraws his fingers once more and meets my clit, rubbing in sharp, short circles that cause me to cry out within seconds. I bury my face into his pillow and scream as an orgasm like no other rips through me.

"Oh my God." I turn my head, not even certain what's happening to me, feeling wetness spread, as I continue to ride out the two fingers Cort slipped back inside me.

Eventually, I collapse back to the mattress, a sprawled-out mess. "Did I . . . did you make me . . ." I can hardly ask. I think I *squirted*.

Cort leans forward and kisses my shoulder, his lips lingering a moment. "Can't say that's ever happened before." He smiles against my skin, and I picture a smug, proud look on his face.

"I'm so embarrassed," I admit, but everything about that orgasm was better than anything I've ever experienced.

Cort slips to my side and our eyes meet. "I never want you to be embarrassed with me. I enjoyed that." His fingers tickle up my back. "Why don't you close your eyes a second, while I clean up?"

I nod because I honestly don't think I can move. The back rub. The new-to-me release. I'm weightless and spent, and within seconds, I'm dozing off.

24

[Cort]

Vale didn't spend the night, and while I understand all the reasons why she can't, it still felt wrong that she eventually snuck out of my place. After cleaning her up, I'd left her lying on my bed and went through the house to lock up. When I came back to my room, I curled up beside Vale, held her wrist, and stared at her for the longest time, wondering how we got here.

Her and me. My former best friend's younger sister. Her needing touch, me repelling it, until recently. There is so much I should explain, so much I should ask; instead, I just relish the beautiful woman in my bed, having gotten her off so extremely and from my hand.

A few days later, a text arrives from an unrecognizable number, but I quickly identify the caller.

> You don't happen to know where my panties
> are, do you?

I chuckle knowing exactly where they are.

> Seems only fair to keep them as you stole my
> hat and a shirt.

Although, there is something about knowing Vale has kept them both.

> Plus, you stole from my bed.

While we didn't discuss Vale spending the night, knowing all the reasons she couldn't, I still want to make it clear I didn't like her absence. Which is ironic considering I don't cuddle or spend nights with women.

> You were sleeping.

I could tell her I was dreaming about her, but I keep things light instead.

> Just concerned about you sneaking off so late.

Somehow that sounds even heavier.

> You worried about me, Coach?

> Yeah, you need a better nickname than that.
> Makes me feel like a creepy old man, and I'm
> already older than you.

> Could call you beekeeper. <wink emoji>

> You're the beekeeper, not me.

You're beekeeping age. An attractive man in his forties. Like a DILF. A beekeeper. <insert crying laughter emoji> <insert a bee emoji>

I stare down at my phone, shaking my head, feeling like this conversation is proof that I'm older than her. Maybe too old. I have no idea what she's talking about.

Gotta take care of my bee.

I hit send before I realize I've called her mine.

Always available to be tended to.

Not only is she flirty, she's fun, and turning me the fuck on when I have work to do.

Beehave. <insert wink face emoji>

Good one.

Then moments later.

I've got to buzz off. Next client is here.

I snort, shake my head once more, ignoring the pang of concern that Vale might be attracted to another client of hers. Another man who's of beekeeping age. Or maybe someone more her age without so much baggage.

"What're you smiling about?" Clint's voice startles me, and I stand from my desk in our shared office, tucking my phone into my back pocket.

"Nothing. Mind your own business," I snap.

His expression is instantly stricken before he slowly smiles.

"You gotta girl, big brother?" His lips roll into a huge grin, knowing I haven't been with another woman in any serious manner since my divorce twelve years ago.

"Like I said, mind your own business."

"Geez. Who put a bee in your bonnet?" Clint counters referring to my unnecessary irritation.

He sounds like a geezer with such an old-fashioned saying, and yet I don't want him to have any idea that there *is* a bee buzzing around my head. A beautiful queen filling my thoughts with hope. "Okay, *grandpa*. Get to work."

"Yes sir," Clint salutes me and stands as well to go our separate ways for the day.

I set Vale's number in my phone under Bonnet, hoping to keep her a secret for a while longer.

DURING THE WEEK, we have a Haven Hitters game. Our pitchers are on a rotation, because their young arms can only handle so many pitches per game. Hudson Sylver is in the middle of our mix.

The pressure to perform well at such a young age comes from multiple places, including the drive within a kid and pressure from a parent. In the case of Atticus Stanton, his ambition is derived from his father.

Typically, I tune out the cheers or jeers from parents on the sideline. I'm here for the boys, like my father was once there for me. Like I hadn't been enough for my own son. But Henry Stanton takes pressure to a whole other level.

"Come on, ump. That was clearly a strike," Henry hollers at the man behind home plate, making calls against Hudson's pitching.

Which clearly was a strike.

"Maybe you need your bifocals checked," Henry continues taunting the official.

"Jesus," Clint mutters under his breath while shaking his head as the opposing team hits a single.

"Henry," I snap, turning toward the stands and leveling him with a shut-the-fuck-up glare. He's one more shout from being kicked out of this game and I'd love nothing more. Mr. Stanton clearly needs a reminder of our zero tolerance for negative taunts. Banning him from our sidelines would give me great pleasure.

Instead, my focus returns to Hudson.

When he walks a kid after four thrown balls and then hits a kid in the ankle on an attempted curveball, also walking him, the bases are loaded. The next hit is a grand slam, and our opponent scores four runs. Sensing Hudson's discouragement, Clint approaches the mound, giving him a pep talk and the option to sit out. But somehow Clint always finds the right words to keep a kid in the game and Hudson buckles down. When he eventually gets us out of the inning, his shoulders slump and his head is lowered as he nears the dugout.

"I suck," he mutters, entering the fenced in area and tossing his mitt at the cage around the dugout before throwing himself onto the end of the bench.

"Hey," I counter, hoping to catch Hudson's attention. I don't like to see any kid down on himself. Typically, Clint is good cop to my bad cop, so to speak. He's comfort and encouragement while I'm more about instruction and discipline. With a quick glance toward the stands, I see Vale staring at the back of Hudson's head, concern etched between her brows.

Sometimes we let the kids stew; other times we intervene. It isn't unheard of for a parent to step forward and speak to their child. In this case, I feel the need to say something positive, and I take a step toward Hudson inside the dugout just as I see Stone round the short set of bleachers. This is a public field, and most parents bring their own chairs or blankets to sit along the edge of the baselines and watch their kids, but a wooden set of three risers sits behind the first baseline. I hadn't noticed Stone standing next to it.

Our eyes catch a second before he quickly looks away, glancing down at his sulking nephew, and I'm caught in this weird quandary. Do I step forward? Do I step back? Stone freezes in position as well, before glancing up and giving me a short, sharp nod. If anyone respects the dynamics of coach and player, it's Stone. He doesn't step back but he also doesn't move forward. Instead, I move.

"Hey," I mutter again quietly, crouching in front of Hudson, attempting to draw his gaze away from his lap where he's aggressively twiddling his thumbs.

I'm not one to coddle kids. Baseball is a game. The object is to hit a ball and outrun your opponent. My competitive spirit enjoys the thrill. But I also remember the pressure I'd put on myself when I was young. The way I saw every bad situation as a personal failure. A missed hit when I played baseball as a kid. A missed catch or tackle when I played professional football.

"We're still in our early games," I remind him. "We're all a little rusty." Despite skills practice and team scrimmages for weeks, we still haven't figured out who fits best where and that's the challenge of our level. This is a time for kids to explore different field positions and their feelings about the game. Our hope is these kids love baseball enough to continue to play in high school and pursue the sport in college.

As the recipient of a football scholarship, I appreciate the benefits of being a student athlete. My parents were grateful as well.

"Dust off the rust. Steel underneath." I tap the side of my fist on his knee, reminding him of our team's motto. A metaphor for scraping off the bad stuff and finding strength within yourself. I'd like to take credit for the slogan but it's all Clint.

Hudson weakly nods, signaling he hears me, even if he's still struggling.

"I see you applying what we taught you about the four-seam fast ball. You had some good throws."

"My curveball stunk."

"So, we work on that in practice."

Hudson purses his lips tight and moves them side to side before slowly nodding. He's a good kid, great team player, and a natural leader. He'll get where he needs to be, both physically in the game, and mentally.

"One minute," I state, standing to give him time to regroup on his own. The initiative is something Clint wanted to instill for mental health reasons, asking kids to count down from sixty to settle their emotions. We had an incident two years ago with a kid who angered easily, throwing tantrums, and baseball bats, and having crying fits with every failure. Clint feared for the kid's mental stability in competitive sports and read up on ways high schools and colleges were practicing mental health checks among athletes.

I hiss as I stand, feeling a familiar ache in my knee as it cracks. Immediately, I notice Stone has stepped back to his spot near the bleachers. The ache in my knee is a reminder of all I had, and all he gave up. The thought has my gaze seeking Vale, who is still watching Hudson. With a tip of my chin, I convey that Hudson will be okay. He's strong, like his mom, and he'll build the armor he needs to handle sports at this level.

Returning to my position beside Clint, he mutters, without looking in my direction. "He okay?"

"He will be."

Clint nods once, squinting in the direction of Kennedy Archer up at bat. The girl has a nice swing. Too bad she can't stay in our league after she turns twelve, although we've recently learned a Women's Baseball League is opening and the hope for a professional league will open avenues for younger girls.

"What'd you say to him?" A hint of fear laces Clint's question, like he's worried I'd tell the kid to buck up or something. Soothing egos or skinned knees is not my forte.

"Pulled a Clint." I chuckle, slapping my brother one time hard on his shoulder blade in an effort to brush off my own concerns for the kid.

Clint turns his head at the comment, watching me. "Huh."

"Huh?" That's all he's got to say? But I don't miss Clint's glance over my shoulder before the corner of his mouth ticks upward, fighting a smile that suggests he's onto me, when there's nothing to be *onto*.

Hudson Sylver is a kid on our team. I'm concerned for him like any other player. And it has nothing to do with his hot-as-sin mother who makes me want things I shouldn't want. Like to take care of her *and* her son.

"Stone's here," Clint adds, as if I hadn't already seen him.

"Yep."

The discussion of reconciliation has been an on-again off-again topic for decades. As we've all aged and matured, Clint and Trinity both think I should try to speak to Stone. Maybe explain how I was young and foolish and made a grave mistake.

But that ship has sailed.

Stone and I won't ever be friends again, although I've greatly missed his friendship, especially in the early years when I was drafted and married with a newborn baby. However, those three things in combination are also a reminder of all Stone lost; all the things I'd stolen from him. Of the three, the only one I regret is my marriage.

I can never ask Stone to forgive me for stealing his girl.

I can never forgive myself either.

25

———————

[Vale]

From our first official date, two weeks pass before Cort and I can coordinate schedules and meet at his house again.

I'm barely inside his front door before he has it closed and pins me against it. Cort's lips cover mine in an eager greeting and I melt into a gooey sensation I've missed since the last time we kissed.

I like kissing Cortland Haven.

In the two weeks since our first date, we've shared both flirty texts and filthy phone calls, one in which I brought myself to completion while Cort spoke the dirtiest things, and I used one of my toys to get off. The man has a mouth, and I love it. His words in my ears. His lips against mine. I'd love to explore the possibility of that mouth in other places on me.

Too soon, Cort is pulling back and glancing down the length of my body, taking in my vibrant sundress, cowboy boots and his straw cowboy hat which has been knocked back on my head.

"You look pretty." While being called beautiful is always nice, there is something about the word pretty that makes me blush. As a flirty word, it makes me feel all bubbly inside, especially when accompanied by the hunger in Cort's eyes.

I tug the sides of the skirt outward and gaze down at myself. "Told Stone I was going dancing." I tap my right foot side to side to emphasize my boots.

When I glance back up at Cort, his brows are pinched. "I don't like that you had to lie."

I'd told Stone I was giving my first date a second chance, but I still wasn't ready to share more about my mystery man. Stone gave me a questioning look, making me feel like a teenager under pressure to offer more information to a concerned father. Sensing I owed him some explanation, I told him I was going dancing at the country bar in Rogue River. Shenanigans hosts theme nights, which include line dancing on occasion, and it wouldn't be an uncommon place for a second date.

I don't like the worry lines near Cort's eyes, and I press my thumb to the corners, loving how he doesn't flinch from unexpected caresses from me.

"Well, I *am* in Rogue River, and I *could* dance." I hitch a brow teasing him with the possibility. I'm not opposed to a lap dance or any other dance that involves us rhythmically moving together. However, I press pause on my libido when Cort chuckles.

The rumbly sound causes me to smile. "You have a nice laugh."

The compliment leads to me being pressed up against the front door again. His hands on my jaw. His mouth on my lips. The gooey sensation of kissing him starts to simmer again as I clutch at his snazzy shirt. Cort dressed up for me again in a short-sleeved, denim shirt with pearl snaps. We look like we might go out dancing but going out isn't a possibility.

And there's nowhere else I'd rather be than tucked into his arms inside his home.

Eventually, Cort pulls back again. "Let me feed you." There is nothing sensual in his offer and yet I'm hungry for him as well.

He catches my hand in his and walks backward toward his kitchen. "I cheated tonight. Picked up Italian."

Rogue River has an amazing Italian bistro-style restaurant and my mouth instantly waters.

"Chicken parmesan?" I question when Cort pulls the prepared meal in a tin pan from his fridge. Nonna's freshly packs ready-to-bake meals to be heated at home. "My favorite."

Cort smiles, pleased with his selection. Setting the meal in the oven to heat, he then pours me a glass of wine and opens a beer for himself.

"Want to sit on the deck a while?" He tilts his head toward the long deck that runs the length of the back of the house.

"Sure." Cort and I each take a seat in Adirondack chairs, where the river softly rolls between the gap in the hills below the deck.

"I want to thank you again for being so patient with Hudson." In the past two weeks, I've seen Cort during his therapy sessions and Hudson's baseball games, but we've kept our distance, especially at those public events. I might catch him looking at me or offer him a soft smile, but then I second guess myself, worried someone else might notice the private exchange between us.

Regarding Hudson, Cort seems to be taking an extra interest in coaching him on how to be a better pitcher. Hudson can't stop talking about Cort. How great he is as a coach. How *nice* he is. If my son catches the soft grunts or questionable quietness of his uncle whenever he raves about Cort, Hudson hasn't mentioned it to me.

"However, I don't want you to do him any favors," I remind him, worrying he's giving special treatment to Hudson because of me.

"I'm not." Cort looks directly at me over his shoulder. "He's a great kid with a lot of potential."

I smile and nod, agreeing about my son.

"Was Josh good at sports?" Cort's son was already a teen when I had Hudson, and as our paths didn't cross then, I don't know much about his boy.

He stares toward the river again, the sky turning darker with the dimming evening light. "In a small community, it isn't unlikely that kids play all the traditional, seasonal sports. Football in the fall. Basketball in winter. Baseball in spring. And Josh did all three. I'd hoped he'd go to college on a scholarship for something, but he opted out of playing at the collegiate level. He played intramural sports, though. Less pressure. More time to study." Cort snorts and turns his head toward me. "I think he meant more time to party."

He smiles softly thinking of his son who is on the verge of graduating college with a master's degree. "He had a rough go of things when he was young. I wasn't around as much as I should have been. His mother was home too much with him."

Cort doesn't speak about Bailey, ever, and that's fine by me. I am not a fan of her because of her history with my brother. Which is a major reason Stone would never forgive me for being with Cort.

"I'm so proud of him, but don't take any credit for who he is." Cort turns his attention back toward the river.

"You have to take some credit," I tease, not liking his self-deprecating comment and hoping he'll open up more about why he came back to the area, as a single father, Josh in tow. "You're one side of parenting him. Bailey being the other." I cringe at giving her praise for anything, but I don't want to dismiss that she is Josh's mother.

Cort's head quickly whips in my direction. "Bailey didn't do anything for Josh, other than fuck him up." The strength in his statement speaks volumes. I'm intrigued and curious by the sharpness of his tone and the dark look in his eyes, but I don't pry. I don't want to hurt Cort by dragging up his murky past, but I hope one day he'll talk to me.

He looks back at the river and lifts his beer, taking a deep swallow before setting the bottle back on the wide armrest.

"Was it difficult to give up football?" I ask next, still tiptoeing around another difficult topic. "I remember it being hard for Ford when he had to give up baseball."

My brother had a career-ending shoulder injury.

Cort squints into the darkening sky and softly says, "Yeah." He pauses before adding, "My body has taken a beating over the years. As a tight end, you either tackle or be tackled. And as much as my hamstrings and ankles took the brunt, it was my knee that eventually gave out." He absentmindedly squeezes his right kneecap.

"I'm sorry you got hurt." Recalling once again how my brother Ford handled his injury, which wasn't well. I can only imagine how Cort felt both physically and mentally. The pain in his body; the loss of a game he loved. Cort had been recently injured and released from his team right before our interlude *that* summer. His mind must have been a mess.

"It happens." He doesn't sound bitter as much as melancholy over the loss.

We both remain quiet a second, letting the peacefulness of hushed evening sounds flow around us. The gentle roll of the river below. The soft call of night creatures coming to life. Unexpectedly, a string of fairy lights flickers on along the underside of the railing around Cort's deck. The ambiance is lovely.

Glancing over at Cort after the sudden illumination, I catch him looking at me.

He stands and holds out his hand. "Want to dance with me?" He smiles softly. "I don't want to make you a liar."

I set my hand in his but pause a second, glancing down at his leg. "What about your knee?"

"I think I can handle a dance with my girl." With a sharp tug, he pulls me upward, and I collide with his firm chest.

"Your girl, huh?" I tease, stroking my hands up his shirt and over his shoulders.

"Want me to call you my Little Bee, instead?"

My gaze leaps to his eyes, seeing he's teasing me with the childish name. "Want me to call you my beekeeper?" I snark back, arching a brow. "Although I do call you that. In my phone." Keeping Cort my secret, I have him listed in my favorites as The Beekeeper.

"Because I'm a hot man over forty?" He chuckles, under-appreciating how very handsome he is.

"The hottest." I wink.

He laughs even harder, and I'd wager his cheeks are heating with the compliment.

With his hands on my hips and mine on his shoulders, I state, "There's no music out here."

"Yes there is. Just listen." Tugging me closer to him, he slips his hand behind my back and takes my other hand in his, pulling our joined hands upward. Then he moves us side-to-side to the melody of the evening around us. A soft breeze, chirping crickets, and the river. Only this isn't some high school dance movement. Cort sweeps us across his deck, taking slow, measured steps before larger, dramatic ones. We spin and he twirls me away from him and pulls me back. He knows how to lead a girl, and quickly, I'm lost to the magic around us and his eyes on mine, drinking me in.

Eventually, he dips me, and I tip my head back until Cort

brushes his nose along the column of my neck. As he pulls me upright, his lips skim my jaw until we face one another. We stop dancing, but other movements take over.

Our hearts beating. Our lips savoring. And I'm in real danger of falling in love.

Cort is no longer the fantasy in my head but a real man. One who rebounded after his injury. Raised a child as a single father. Built a business and gives back to his community.

He's a man who sweeps me off my feet and kisses me like I'm the air he needs to breathe. As our kissing heats, Cort uses his firm hands on my sides to tug me closer to him, holding me against him. I wrap my arms around his neck, breathing him in with every twirl of our tongues.

Beep-beep-beep.

The sudden sound has us breaking apart and glancing toward his kitchen. Cort left the sliding glass door open, and the noise alerts us that the chicken dinner is ready.

Taking my hand again, Cort leads me into his house, and we settle in for another meal together. We sit at his island counter, him seated sideways with his legs spread, locking me in with his knees.

"Why are you sitting like that?" I ask, thinking it must be uncomfortable.

"I want to look at you while I eat." He winks, like I'm in on some secret, and then he digs into his chicken parmesan.

Once we finish eating and clean up, Cort suggests we sit on his couch. He turns the television on, flipping to a Tennessee Terrors baseball game. He sets the volume low before he reaches for my ankle and tugs off one of my boots.

I gasp, then giggle. "What are you doing?"

He reaches for my other boot and removes it as well, then lifts my legs so they drape over his lap. I shift so I'm seated sideways beside him. He tugs off the low-cut socks I wear and presses his knuckles into the arch of one foot.

"Ew. My feet are all sweaty and probably stink."

"*Ew*?" Cort laughs, wrinkling his nose as he mimics me. "You sound like you're twelve." He continues to press the hard edge of his fingers into the soft curve of my foot and my leg jolts.

Damn that feels good.

"Well, I am younger than you, old man."

"Do *not* remind me," he chuffs, concentrating on how he uses his knuckles against my foot.

I hope he isn't thinking what I'm suddenly thinking. This man changed my diapers.

Resting my head on the back cushion, I ask, "Does it bother you? The age thing? Because I feel one hundred some days."

Cort's head whips in my direction, never missing a beat as he cups my foot and squeezes, digging his fingertips into the top of my foot. "You're stunning."

I give him a pointed look, like I don't fully believe the compliment.

"Look, I get it that some women worry about aging. Hell, men worry about it, too."

I snort, taking in the contrasting color combination of hairs on his jaw and the strong length of his nose. His lush lips and dark eyes. *Cort* is stunning.

"But our bodies are our story. Every freckle and line, every mole and scar." His brows pinch at the mention and I think back to the stitched line near his shoulder blade. "And without them, we aren't who we are."

Cort pauses while plucking at each of my toes, tugging them one at a time.

"I think true beauty lies within and radiates outward."

I smile softly at the concept.

"And *you* are fucking sunshine."

Tilting my head to the side, I reach for the side of his neck and stroke my finger along it. "That's sweet."

With his lids lowered, staring at my foot in his hand, he swipes his other hand up my calf.

"*You*'re sweet," he mutters, watching as he cups the back of my knee.

He moves to my other leg and repeats the massage. Knuckling my arch. Squeezing my foot. Tugging my toes. And then stroking up my leg.

Only he doesn't stop at the back of my knee. With my knees bent, my dress falls to my lap, exposing more of my legs. When Cort glides up my inner thigh, my dress rides higher.

"And I'd like to see how sweet you are, honeybee." With that, his eyes leap up to mine, watching me as his fingers tickle the inside of my leg. Willingly, I spread my thighs, and my dress collects in my lap.

"Lay back," he softly commands, and I sweep my hair up the back of my head and lie down, resting the back of my neck on the armrest. I lift my hands above my head and hang onto the armrest behind me, stretching out my body.

"Fucking perfection, Bee." He hisses, gazing up my body, like he's watching a river weave through the hills. He slips his hands to my hips and drags my underwear off me in a torturous tease, taking his time to remove them before pushing my dress up to my belly so he can see me.

Cort shifts, spreading my legs wider and positioning himself between them. Staring down at where I'm wet and waiting for him, he licks his lips. "Gonna devour that honey-covered cunt."

I gasp at the word, then lose my breath as his mouth meets my center and he swipes up my seam. I buck upward, chasing his tongue. Cort does not disappoint, quickly bringing his mouth against me and swirling his tongue around my clit.

"Oh God," I cry out, unable to remember the last time someone did this to me. Not often. Not any time in the last few years. The sensation of his thick tongue parting folds and sweeping over sensitive skin is like no other.

My knees fall farther apart as Cort holds one thigh steady, keeping me spread wide for him. His tongue paints broad strokes over my most tender parts. His fingers join the mix, dipping into the wetness, spreading it around me, and slipping into me.

"Cort," I call out, holding onto the armrest above my head, afraid to let go. Afraid to touch him for fear he'll stop touching me.

"Pure honey gold," he mutters, peppering me with soft pecks before diving in again with that tongue, taking his time to lick and suck and tease me.

"Dripping all over me," he hums, pressing his fingers deep while continuing to devour me like he's ravenous. "Sticky sweet."

He laps up my seam again, catching on that triggering nub, focusing on where I need him most.

"Oh Cort. Right there. Don't stop." I whisper, afraid he will. Afraid I'll lose the bliss he's building, winding me up like a tight string, ready to unravel at any moment.

"Not gonna stop until you soak my face, honeybee. Until you're dripping on my tongue and clenching on my fingers." He slips two up my channel and presses on a spot no one has ever discovered.

"So close," I whimper.

"Gonna get there." It's not a question but a fact. He's not giving up until I'm finished. Until I'm wrung out.

Soon enough, I break. My legs clamp around his head and my back arches off the couch. I cry out as an orgasm like no other rips through me. My lower belly is a swarm, buzzing and fluttering, and zipping through me like nothing I've ever experienced. The rush continues, dipping and diving, like I'm riding the wind, until finally I settle, lowering my hips and releasing my knees from around his head.

With his fingers still inside me, softly stroking in and out, he presses his lips to my inner thigh before pulling his fingers free.

"Honey gold, like I thought." His beard is damp. His eyes gleaming. He's so damn proud of himself.

"It's never been like that," I admit, as he already knows I've struggled to find relief with a partner.

"I know, sweetness." He kisses the top of my knee, keeping his eyes on me. "I know."

26

[Cort]

I know.

Because I've never felt anything like this either. This yearning to please her. This desire to take care of her. And it's not just the sexual side of things, because I like feeding her and massaging her and dancing on the deck beneath the stars with her.

She's flirty and funny and makes me feel so damn light-hearted. I hadn't realized how heavy my heart was in my chest until Vale re-entered my life.

"Let me touch you," she whispers, reminding us both of my apprehension. In the times we've been together, it's been more me exploring Vale than the other way around. Even back at Ford's camp, where Vale took me in her mouth, I didn't allow her to touch me with her hands.

She sits upright, holding my eyes with hers. "Please." Her

plea asks for more. She wants me to trust her. Trust she isn't going to turn on me, isn't going to hurt me.

Slowly, I nod, falling back on the couch.

Vale scrambles off the cushions and stands in front of me. She wedges herself between my legs and folds down to her knees. With her eyes still on mine, she lifts her hands for the snaps on my shirt. I dressed up for her. If we can't go out, I want to look nice while we stay in.

With the pop of the first snap, I flinch. The sound is almost too loud despite the low volume on the television and the hammering of my heart.

Vale drops her gaze and we both watch her fingers unsnap the next closure on my shirt. Down she goes, working her way through the snaps until the two sides of my shirt fall apart.

She places her hands on my lower abs, holding them still like she did when I first started massage therapy. She's letting me get familiar with her touch. With her hands on me.

I suck in my abs and Vale's gaze flicks up to my face. With hesitant hands, she brushes aside my shirt, exposing more of my belly and chest.

She hisses, the sound more a sizzle of appreciation. "You are magnificent."

Dammit, she's always complimenting me, making my face heat and my heart saw faster.

Cautiously, she runs her hands up my midsection. Over my abs, beneath my ribs, across my chest. With her eyes still on mine, she lowers her head and presses a soft kiss to my sternum.

My breath hitches.

Vale pulls up, checking on me once more, her eyes speaking volumes while neither of us utters a sound. I'm afraid I don't have words; she looks afraid she'll break me.

And God, I want her to shatter me. I want her to tear apart

the pieces and put me back together. Make me feel again. Make me whole.

Reaching up for her face, I swipe my thumb over her cheek, then tuck her hair behind her ear. She's so good for me. Too good to me.

"Bee," I whisper, my throat rough.

Sweetly smiling, she leans forward again and peppers my chest with soft, deliberate kisses, taking her time to cover every inch. Her tongues swirls around my nipples. Her fingers comb through the dusting of hair between my pecs. Eventually, she reaches up for my shoulders and presses at my shirt, forcing me to sit forward and allow the material to fall off my arms. I shrug out of it and lean back again, waiting for this queen on her knees. However, I'm at her service. I'll let her do anything to me.

When her palms skim back down my chest, reversing the pattern she originally pressed, until reaching the waistband of my jeans, she pauses.

"May I?"

I nod, watching her take further control by unbuckling my belt and popping the button on my pants. In short time, Vale has the sides lowered and me kicking out of the denim. In only my boxer briefs, I boldly sit on my couch, Vale between my knees, her hands on my thighs, staring at where I'm long and hard, thick and bulging behind thin cotton.

"Let me touch you," she whispers again, addressing my dick with hunger in her eyes.

I tip up her chin with the side of my hand. "My eyes are up here."

Vale lets out a sweet, light laugh. "But you're so pretty down there." With a steady finger, she strokes the length of my dick, over my boxer briefs, and I close my eyes, tipping back my head.

"Cortland." Her voice trembles, as if her desire is strangling her.

I lower my underwear, revealing myself to her. Hard and proud, my dick stands at attention, ready to do whatever bidding this woman wants from me.

Please don't hurt me. I swallow thickly, fighting back fears I don't need to have with Vale.

Wrapping her hand around my heavy cock, she squeezes, and I'm lost. Closing my eyes once more, I give in to the sensation. The sweet tug. The slight pump. The light tickle of her tongue on my tip.

My eyes fling open, and I stare down at Vale, who is watching me. Eyes up. Mouth open. I don't think I've ever wanted anything more than for her to take me.

Not disappointing me, she lowers and draws me into the heat of her mouth, sucking, swirling her tongue, licking up my length.

"Oh Jesus," I groan. My eyes falling closed once more before I force them open, not wanting to miss a minute of this woman —*my girl*—worshipping me.

"Sweetness," I grunt, stroking over her hair, petting her head while my other hand fists at my side. Enjoying every lap, every deep suck, and yet struggling not to lose myself, buck my hips, and go wild within Vale's mouth. That fucking mouth.

Thankfully, I last a little longer than I did a few weeks ago when Vale had her lips wrapped around me the first time. She sucked the life out of me in under thirty seconds then. However, I don't hold out much longer, and within a few short minutes, I'm warning her.

"Vale. You're so good, honeybee. I can't hold on." I didn't want to hold out. I wanted to fucking come down her throat.

"That's it, sweetness," I encourage, wrapping some of her hair around my hand and holding it at the back of her head. Whether to keep me steady or keep her on me, I'm not certain.

I'm lost to the sensation of Vale. Her care. Her patience. Her fucking tongue.

"Vale," I groan, choking on her name as my lower back tightens and my balls pull up, and then I'm jetting off, jolting against her tongue.

Vale swallows and gags a bit, and I feel every fucking movement.

"Baby," I moan, as my head tips back, and my dick pulses again before Vale slowly pulls up the length and pops off the tip.

I lift my head to look at her. She swipes the back of her wrist over her mouth before a smug smile graces her lips.

"You little vixen," I tease.

"Thought I was a little bee?"

I pull up my boxer briefs and then scoop her up, tossing us down to the couch to face each other on our sides. Brushing back her hair, I watch my fingers trace her face. "How much longer do you have?"

It's not like Vale has a curfew, but she does have Hudson, and Stone is watching him for her.

"A little longer," she says with a sigh. If I didn't know better, she sounds as disappointed as I feel. I don't want her to leave.

"Let me get something to clean you up." With a swift kiss to her lips, I hop over her and return with a warm cloth then hand her underwear to her.

"I'll be right back." I scoop up my clothes and head into my room, changing into something more comfortable. Joggers and a Haven Exteriors tee.

Once back on the couch, I tuck behind Vale, keeping us both on our sides and wrap my arms around her. With my lips on the back of her head, I stare at the television, not really watching the silent game.

Time passes too quickly until Vale has to leave and I'm walking her to my front door. I hate this part.

"I don't like you traveling alone in the dark this late at night." I don't want her to leave and yet I can't ask her to stay.

Giving me an understanding smile, she tips up on her toes and kisses me. Long and sweet, showing me she doesn't want to go either, but she must.

"Call me," I say when I pull back and rest my forehead against hers.

"As soon as I get home," she states for confirmation, softly smiling at my concern.

"No. When you get in your car. Keep the phone on while you drive home."

"Cort." she giggles. "That's silly. It's late."

"We don't have to talk. I just want to know you're safe. Play the radio and keep me on speaker."

Vale smiles wider and tips up once more, wrapping her arms around my neck like she doesn't want to let go. We kiss again, seeking extra seconds with ever suck of our lips and clash of our tongues, until finally Vale whispers, "I have to go."

I know. I know she does, but I hate separating from her. I hate being her secret.

Yet I have no one to blame but myself.

27

———

[Vale]

Attending book club has been a bit rare for me as the Haven Hitters' season seems to take up most of my evenings and weekends. Thankfully, I finally have a Thursday night free.

I'm running late and miss the weekly pre-game established at Milton Roadhouse, but as soon as I enter Meredith Mulligan's second floor, a wine glass is in my hand, and a strange sense of calm I hadn't known I needed settles over me.

Not that the room is calm. The collection of select women from Milton County is like standing in the middle of a gaggle of geese. Chatter and squeaks, excitement and gasps. These are my girls.

As the only sister in a family of brothers, I appreciate these times with women and I've missed being somewhere that doesn't involve baseball, laundry, and rushed dinners.

"Hey, lady." Enya smiles softly. "Welcome back."

"I could say the same to you." Enya has struggled just as much as me to consistently make it to our 'book club' with the new baby, although Sebastian practically pushes her out the door, claiming he wants alone time with his girls. The younger set at least. He's turned into a huge cinnamon roll for his babies.

With a hand on my forearm, Enya leads me to a couch Meredith pushes up against a wall to provide more space in her apartment. We collapse in giggles as the couch is a bit lower than either of us anticipated.

"So . . ." Enya takes a sip of the wine in her hand. "How are things?" She gives me a pointed look, like she knows I have a secret. When she knows a few of them already.

"I don't know what you're talking about," I tease, bringing my own glass to my lips to disguise a smile.

"Vale," she admonishes.

"Enya," I tease before looking over at her. Her eyes search my face, seeing signs I'm certain are confusing. But I can't help my smile, brought about by thoughts of Cort which constantly creep into my head.

"Who is he?" she asks, no preamble. The family knows I went on a date a few weeks back, and a second one more recently. My brothers are a nosy bunch and gossip worse than women sometimes, so it doesn't matter who told whom what. They all know one date turned into two, plus I'm constantly getting busted glancing at my phone.

"I'm not ready to tell." The moment I lie, my insides rumble, because I'm desperate to talk about *who he is*. I want to tell everyone how happy I am and how I'm finally getting good orgasms from something other than my own hands. But I can't. Not because that's an overshare but because of *who he is*.

No one in my family is going to understand.

"We're just having fun." Not a total lie the second time, but it's more than just fun. More than fucking around fun. Cort listens to me, and he talks to me. We laugh. He makes me smile, like the goofy grin I can't seem to fight right now. He makes me feel sexy, but more so, he makes me feel appreciated and special.

Enya continues to watch me, looking for signs of who he is, but instead only seeing evidence of what he does for me. "You look happy."

"I am." The first full whisper of truth coming from my lips. I really am happy. Maybe I'm still in the this-is-new phase but I'm not rushing for it to be more. New . . . is nice and I'm content to linger in this feeling for a while longer, however much longer we can keep up the secret.

Suddenly, a blonde storm flings herself onto the couch beside me, wedging herself into the barely-there space between me and the corner.

"I'm getting the Cliterature Stick tonight," Trinity announces, like she isn't interrupting anything. Spinning her head in my direction, she adds, "It actually comes with a book." She giggles, suggesting she's already had a few glasses of wine tonight. "I need a new book boyfriend."

Enya laughs and I smile at the curvy girl beside me who has an infectious spirit about her. Her ex-husband is an idiot for letting this bubble of energy go.

She goes on to describe some book I might need to check out as well, especially if it comes with a built-in sidekick, AKA, the Cliterature Stick.

"It's all clit stick instead of chic lit," Trinity guffaws at her own joke. "Oh," she suddenly shifts, sitting up straighter. "And get this. I think my brother Cort is dating someone."

My breath hitches before I catch it and hold. I can't breathe. Since the Trinity-Vale truce, we don't typically discuss our brothers and their lives. At least not something personal like this.

Enya stiffens on my other side. "Really? Who?"

"I don't know yet. He's being his typical mysterious self, but over the weekend, he was at my mom's for dinner, and he was constantly on his phone. Typing messages and then smiling to himself." Trinity makes a face like she's horrified by the thought. "I mean . . . oh my God, my older brother is dating again, and I'm here purchasing another personal pleasure plaything."

The double whammy in Trinity's confession hits hard. Her brother is dating someone and the upsetting part to Trin is that he has *a person* in his life. She's fine being an individualist, like I've been for years, but we both know, having a man handle our intimate parts adds something extra to sexual endeavors.

Someone who reads our body and knows the nuances is a game changer.

And I can only hope I'm the someone Cort is dating because we haven't discussed exclusivity. Not that I think he has time for anyone else, we just haven't confirmed anything.

Should we confirm our status? What exactly are we? Secret lovers? Friends with benefits?

"Sending text messages, huh?" Enya says to Trinity, but the heat of her gaze is on the side of my face. "Think it's something new?

"It must be new. Like in the last few weeks because two months ago he was still his grumpy old self."

Cort isn't grumpy, just quiet, reserved even. He has an air of *don't mess with me* because he's been messed with in the past. Also, in a small community, our hearts forgive but our minds never forget. Despite the time that has passed since the fallout between Stone and Cort, people still bring it up on occasion.

"Interesting," Enya purrs beside me, lifting her glass for another sip of wine. Her gaze isn't leaving the side of my head, though, so I don't dare look at her.

"Remember when we were kids, and I wanted us to be

sisters?" Trinity continues, the ramble of this conversation diffi-cult to follow.

"Um, actually, I don't recall that," I admit, having never known she thought such a thing. Trinity is older than me. Somewhere in between Knox and Ford area.

"Of course, I wanted a sister," she says a little louder. "Brothers are the worst."

She knows I don't *really* agree with that sentiment.

"And I always thought one of us would marry into the other's family and then we'd be linked together forever." Trinity lifts her wineglass, like she's toasting the room.

What would she think of that scenario now? If it were to happen? The thought is a gut punch to my belly because it could never happen. Never be a possibility. While Cort and I might be intersecting, our paths will eventually diverge again. They must.

Because my oldest brother isn't the worst. He's the best. And he'd never forgive me for my recent behavior.

"Whoa, girl. How much wine have you had tonight?" Enya teases our friend.

Trinity lowers the glass and stares absentmindedly into it. "Not enough." Her voice softens and I think back to weeks ago when she was staring at her phone, a scowl on her face, thinking about her ex.

"What'd he do now?" I lower my voice as well, gently nudging her arm with my elbow.

"Nothing." She sighs. "And isn't that the point." Lifting her glass, she finishes the rest of her wine in one swallow and stands. Or attempts to, using the couch armrest and my thigh to force herself upward before taking a staggering step forward, then righting herself, and heading to the help-yourself-bar in Meredith's kitchen.

"Oh my," I whisper, watching Trinity stumble away.

"Valentine Sylver." Enya hisses beside me.

"What?" I turn toward my sister-in-law, hoping for an innocent expression, but certain guilt is written in every line on my face.

"What are you doing?" she whispers, knowing without asking.

"I don't know," I admit with a heavy exhale.

Playing with fire feels too crass of a comeback. I'm not a twenty-something girl anymore. I'm not looking to tempt fate or be reckless or push boundaries. This is more than sneaking off behind a tree and making out with a cute boy for an hour.

Hearts are on the line. Mine. Cort's. And Stone's.

"I really don't know."

28

———————

[Vale]

Cort's final massage therapy session is upon us. He had to reschedule his typical Wednesday morning one for a Friday. His health insurance has only approved so many visits, and he'll be on his own to exercise and stretch to strengthen his back and keep his muscles loose.

While he sits on my massage table for the final time, I stand between his spread legs. "You should do yoga."

He laughs. "You aren't serious."

"I'm totally serious. Many athletes do yoga to strengthen their flexibility and settle their minds." I tap my temple.

Between work and raising my son, plus Hudson's intensive baseball season, I still find time to sneak in a yoga class at the local studio near Reflexology.

"I'm going to miss my Wednesdays," Cort softly says, holding my hand and linking our fingers together, staring at them joined as one, like he's still surprised how well we fit. Still surprised at how comforting touch can be.

"I'm going to miss them, too." These rare moments of privacy beat staring at him across a crowded baseball diamond full of kids and their parents.

With a too-quick, parting kiss, Cort exits Reflexology.

But to my complete surprise, I find him standing next to the front desk around noon.

"Cortland?" I glance at Derrek, who is seated at the desk, and glances suspiciously between me and Cort. "Did you forget something?"

"I wanted to leave you a tip. I forgot to earlier."

"A *tip*?" Derrek drawls, turning his attention from Cort to me, and drawing out the word like he's stretching a string.

I scowl at Derrek.

"Wanted to thank you for all your hard work," Cort adds, keeping his sights on me.

My cheeks flame as Derrek parrots Cort one more time.

"Hard work." His perfectly sculpted eyebrows lift. "Did you hear that, Vale? You worked him *hard*." Our desk clerk exhales the word like he's blowing his breath on a window.

Glaring at him again, I defend, "That's not what he—"

Cort clears his throat. "I thought maybe I could take you to lunch."

My attention swings back toward him. To ask me out in front of a co-worker is bold. Plus, we'd be seen in public, even if this is Rogue River. Most of my friends and all of my family are the next town over, but you never know who you'll run into midday on a Wednesday.

"A little afternoon delight?" Derrek questions me. "Everyone deserves a noon-time meal." He glances back at Cort. "Vale's a carnivore. She likes meat."

Did he just gnash his teeth?

Chewing at my lower lip, I shake my head. "Ignore him. I do."

"Seriously, though," Derrek interjects. "Go. Get laid."

"Der-*reek*!"

"I mean, get a latte." He waves, dismissing all his innuendos, then flicks his hand like he's shooing me out the door. "And lunch. No need to rush. Your one o'clock canceled."

Derrek winks at Cort, like the two of them share a secret.

Before I know it, Cort is leading me outside and insists I ride with him. "I promise where we are going, no one will see us."

On the one hand, I'm relieved and appreciate his understanding about my apprehension. It's not like I *want* to keep Cort a secret. It feels so unfair that we have to hide what we are doing. Then again, I'm not exactly certain what is going on between us. It's clear we have a physical connection. We're *exploring* with one another, but are we more than friends with benefits? I can hardly be a booty call. I have Hudson to consider.

While I try not to define us, and simply revel in the fun, I'm confused sometimes by the things Cort says or the way he looks at me. Like he really wants me. Wants more from me. Then, I worry I'm projecting onto him, because I've never felt what I feel when I'm with him. How he makes me laugh. How hot he can be with simple words. How sweet he is in person.

Like making me stay on the phone when I drove home the other night.

Or sending a small bouquet of flowers to my work one morning.

Or a lunch delivery another day, from Nonna's, after I told him how much I love their antipasto salad.

When we pull into Cort's driveway, I laugh. "You really took Derrek's suggestion for afternoon delight to heart."

"As much as I'd like to give the guy props for some solid

sexual innuendos, this lunch comes with no expectations." With his hand dangling over his steering wheel, he smiles at me. "It's a beautiful day and I thought we could eat on my deck."

Cort reaches for a white paper bag between us that I'd noticed but hadn't commented on. Picking up the bag, he pops open his door, and I hop out of his truck as well.

Once inside his house, Cort sets the bag on the island countertop and spins toward me.

"Hi," he says, cupping my face and leaning in for a more proper greeting.

My belly buzzes and I smile against his lips. "Hi," I mutter amidst the kiss.

Cort smiles as well. "Lunch?"

"What are you making me?" I tease, glancing over at the paper bag.

"Just give me a minute to put the ingredients together." Cort pulls what looks like a homemade loaf of bread from the bag. Next, he spins toward a cabinet, retrieving a plastic container of peanut butter and a jar of honey. The glass container with a clasped lid is common enough. Your average kitchen storage jar. But the ribbon around the lip gives it away as something special. Something made with love.

"That's my honey," I whisper, staring at the pink and black ribbon I personally tied around the top of the jar.

"I know," Cort says, his voice low as he pops the lid.

"But how do you have it?" I make jars of honey each year in the fall and distribute them as gratitude for any nicety that's offered throughout the year. The homegrown honey mainly goes to my family and some book club members, but a few jars get delivered to—

"Did you steal that jar from your mother?" Every year I remember Mary Haven as well for past kindness.

Cort smiles, unscrewing the lid to the peanut butter container. "She willingly gives me a jar."

I don't know whether to be flattered she shared or hurt that she's regifting my honey.

"She knows it's my favorite." He winks.

What?

"And . . ." He pauses to grab a bread knife from the knife holder on his counter. "She knows I love it best on her home-made wheat bread with peanut butter."

A memory hits me so hard I almost fall over. Mary Haven in her kitchen making sandwiches like she was working an assembly line, going through an entire loaf of her homemade bread, slapping together two pieces for each kid. One side peanut butter; one side honey. I'd never tasted anything so good before or since.

Cort pauses his moments, watching me. "I know it seems like a kid's meal, but I still love honey on whole wheat."

And he's making one of his favorite meals to share with me. He's making me lunch and he's using my honey, his mother's bread and—

I glance back at the white bakery-style bread bag. "Did your mom make this bread for you?"

"Picked it up this morning. It was still warm in the bag." He smiles like a kid who's stolen a cookie before dinner, or bread before it has cooled. The childlike grin along with a giddy gleam in his eyes has me rounding the island and wrapping my arms around his midsection.

Cort stills at the suddenness, before slowly wrapping his arms around me, tugging me tighter to his chest. Silly tears sting my eyes at the memory of his mom and the sweetness of this moment.

He presses a kiss to the top of my head before I pull back and stare up at him.

"Don't look at me like that." His voice tight.

"And how am I looking at you?" I bat my eyes.

"Like you want that afternoon delight after all. With me."

He isn't wrong. I desperately want to have sex with Cort. But I also want this PB and H on Mary Haven's homemade whole wheat.

"Feed me first?" I tease, pulling free of his arms. "I need energy for stamina."

Cort chuckles. "Well, as I've already proven I can't last more than a few minutes with you, I think it's safe to say, it'd be over quickly."

"And I think practice makes perfection." The challenge flag is tossed and Cort stares back at me, gripping the edge of the island countertop and glancing at me over his shoulder.

"Vale," he warns.

"I'm just saying . . ."

"Stop talking."

As we're about to share a kid-like meal, and memories of being a child are fresh in my head, I say something equally childish. "Make me."

Before I can blink, Cort sweeps the lunch ingredients aside and hoists me onto the countertop by my waist. His hips wedge between my knees and I spread my legs to accommodate him while his hands delve into my hair and tug me to him, kissing me like I'm the first course to our simple meal.

Within minutes, my shirt is removed, and my pants slipped off. Cort presses me back to the countertop and strips me of my underwear. I cry out at the cold surface, but the warmth of his hands has me quiet again. Then he swipes a finger up my seam, parting me and slipping in.

"Cort," I groan.

"What was it you explained to me." He pauses, tipping two fingers into the nearby honey jar. "High excitement but you need high intention."

Removing his finger from me and then bringing those two

fingers coated in honey between my legs instead, Cort contin-ues. "My intention . . . is to make you my new favorite meal." He swipes the sticky sap over my hot center and dives in, licking at the mess he's making, creating more of one, and my arousal mixes with my homemade brand.

"Holy shit," I cry out at the hunger of Cort's lips, the eager-ness of his tongue. For all my talk of needing time, I'm on the edge within seconds and crying out his name within minutes.

My orgasm slams into me so hard, the intensity causes me to choke on air, trying to catch my breath. Cort's name on my lips is a stuttering mangle of syllables.

With a final lap between my legs, which involves a generous swipe up and around to lick me clean, Cort pulls back. His beard is coated with a combination of me and sticky residue.

He *looks* like a child, who has eaten a messy meal.

"Dammit, Cort." I chuckle before draping my arm over my eyes, still trying to catch my breath after such a rush. My feet dangle off his counter, tingling asleep.

Cort grips my hand and pulls my arm free from my face, then gently tugs me upright.

"Now, why don't you head to my bathroom, and I'll clean up, then make us an actual lunch." He kisses me quick with his messy lips before swiping at his mouth and sucking the tip of his finger. "Never a fan of leftovers, but this isn't bad."

He winks and helps me down from the counter. Then he slaps my ass, and I yelp as I gather my clothes and head to his bathroom.

When I return to the kitchen, the distinct scent of bleach and a spray bottle of kitchen cleaner near the sink tells me Cort sanitized the countertop before getting to his original plan of making sandwiches. With plates in hand, he nods toward his fridge. "Want to grab the iced tea and follow me?"

He has no idea I'd follow him anywhere he wants to lead me.

29

[Cort]

Eating lunch with Vale, or eating Vale for lunch, becomes my new obsession. With her working in Rogue River, I meet her as often as I can on her lunch break. Thankfully, I'm not on top of roofs as much as I used to be, but in more of a supervisory position for our jobsites and can slip home at my leisure.

I've even given Vale a key, so she doesn't have to wait for me, if I'm running late.

In many ways, I'm happy Vale and I take things slow in a sense. These past few weeks, I've felt like a teenager again, getting away with sneaking around and meeting up with my girl. We make out a lot and get off by hand jobs and oral play, but I'm eager to put my dirty talk to further practice, as Vale said, and have sex with her.

Only one afternoon reminds me why that shouldn't happen.

"Stone isn't able to watch Hudson for me after all. I can't get away on Friday or Saturday," she mentions after we've had lunch one day.

Vale and I haven't had a more formal date at my house in weeks. One where we aren't on the clock, and I can take more time with her.

The reminder of Stone is a damper on my desire.

"And Sundays are always out because of Sylver Sunday."

"Sylver what?" I chuckle without humor, instantly sour that I'll be missing out on another date, spending another weekend without her.

"Every Sunday. Stone set the tradition back when he took over the family." Vale isn't looking at me as she straightens her Reflexology polo over her black leggings.

She doesn't need to clarify for me what *took over the family* means. At twenty-two, my best friend was about to graduate from college. He had a deal signed with a professional football team out west and was on his way to success. More money than his family had ever seen running their small-town, family-owned seed and soil business, which his brother Clay was frantically trying to keep afloat despite their dad having gambling debts and bar tabs all over the county.

Stone planned to take care of his siblings, financially, from a distance.

But when old man Sylver killed himself, Stone didn't feel like he had any other choice but to return home and become guardian to his younger siblings, especially Knox, Ford, Sebastian, and Vale who were all under eighteen at the time.

"Sylver Sunday," Vale continues. "Enya started calling it that when she started coming around. Every Sunday, Stone insisted on a family meal. Like a weekly check-in. It was a time for him to write up the family schedule on a calendar and get a read on where everyone was at. Homework. School functions. Basic needs." Vale fluffs up her long locks and then swipes them back, collecting them in one hand and using a hairband from her opposite wrist to secure her hair in a ponytail.

The hair style makes her look young and reminds me how much younger she is than me.

Twelve years.

At twelve years old, Stone became guardian of Vale in a different way. Violet Sylver died giving birth to Vale, and Stone felt responsible to care for his only sister because his father was failing at parenthood.

I tried to help as best I could. He was my best friend. His mother had been a good friend to my mom. Our families were meshed in so many ways.

I often brought Stone home with me. I brought the Sylvers meals. My mom taught Stone how to change diapers, wash a baby, and feed her with a bottle. Instead of abandoning my friend who had taken on this incredible responsibility, I learned along with him.

He had been a good kid who turned into a great man.

And I'd shit all over that friendship in a moment of weakness.

"Anyway," Vale continues, swiping a finger underneath her eyes, seeking stray mascara while I simply stare at her.

We've moved many of our make out sessions and lunch time shenanigans to my bedroom, preserving the kitchen for actual meals. But on occasion, we've christened other locations in my house. On the living room floor. On an island stool. On the deck.

"Stone kept up the tradition even as we aged. Even as people moved out. Of course, for the longest time, it was just him and Clay, plus me and Hudson."

My mouth opens to ask about Judd, their brother who lined up in age with Tate but never became friends with him. Judd works for Sylver Seed & Soil, alongside Clay who still oversees the family business. He turned their simple farm supply store into a small empire, not only selling farm necessities but also fashionable garden gifts and housewares along with pet products. While I've only been in the place a handful of times, having felt guilty for even crossing their property, I was so fucking proud of the family for breaking through barriers and rising up from the ashes of the loss of their parents.

One from a medical condition. The other from mental illness.

"Judd hadn't attended until recently," she clarifies, as if reading my thoughts.

While I've been quietly watching her pull herself back together, she's filled the silence. "But as each brother started dating and falling in love"—she rolls her eyes— "the family gathering has grown enough we needed to add a second picnic table out back."

The reminder of an original picnic table fills my head. The one where Stone and I often sat, me trying to sympathize with the shit life kept throwing at him. The loss of his mom. The care of his sister. The slow trickle of abuse from his dad.

In college, Stone worried things had gone from bad to worse, but he didn't know what he could do about it. He needed to pass classes and graduate. He was driven and his vision was to cross the goal line, collect a large check, and help them all.

With me as his best friend at his side, and a girl he loved in his corner, I had no doubt Stone would achieve all he dreamed of accomplishing.

I wasn't jealous. I was right beside him, only I was fucking every girl who came my way, while reaching for my own golden ticket to a professional football future.

Then everything went to hell.

"So Sundays, I'm home. Making side dishes and covering cleanup while drinking as much wine as I can swallow." Vale smiles like Sunday is the best day of the week despite all the hustling, and suddenly, I *am* envious of the Sylvers. Of family time gathering their favorite people. Of *them* spending time with Vale. Even spending time with Hudson, who I've grown closer to through coaching, but wish I could know even better.

The truth is that I can never be part of their world.

"Stone's a good man," I blurt, releasing twenty-plus years of my opinion. "A better man than me."

Vale straightens and stares at me. Her hair now in place. Her makeup no longer smudged. Her clothes righted.

"Why would you say that?"

"Because I fucking slept with Bailey." It's the same confession I shouted at my best friend in his front yard, needing his forgiveness when I didn't have a right to ask for it. His world was literally crumbling around him, and I piled another heap of debris on the rubbish of his life.

Vale stares at me, knowing my hard truth. My shameful and inexcusable decision to sleep with my best friend's girl. Bailey and I were both grieving. We were losing Stone to something neither of us could comprehend. Taking on the responsibility of six younger siblings when we were hardly out of childhood ourselves. He was so much more mature than me. More responsible. More level-headed. A better person, like I said.

"It happened. You both made a choice. Good or bad. Right or wrong," Vale says, as if it's that simple. "Sometimes we act irrationally through our grief."

She speaks like she understands. Like she's not here to judge me even if she isn't happy with my indiscretion. Grief makes strange bedfellows.

Like Bailey Cummins coming to my room, both of us devastated and leaning on each other, which led to us to being naked in my bed.

And then to add broken bricks to the already crumbled building, she was pregnant.

One time. They teach you that shit in sex education as a

kid. I had not believed it. Condoms. The pill. No way through that kind of protection.

But Bailey had been sick the week before we were together and taking prescription antibiotics. She claimed her and Stone hadn't had sex in a month. She was lonely and sad and none of it was an excuse for what we did, where we ended up or what the future flipped on us.

"I married her," I remind Vale. "She's the mother of *my* kid."

Josh. The reason I wouldn't ever change any of it. Despite my deep remorse over imploding a life-long friendship, severing family ties, and marrying Bailey, I could never ever regret my son. *Never.*

Josh was an entirely different kind of mess I couldn't tackle with Vale right now. Not while we were discussing the destruction with Stone.

"And you divorced her because something was never right between the two of you." Vale glares at me, strong in her conviction, although we've never discussed the reason behind my failed marriage. "And you brought Josh here. To Rogue River. To home and family." Vale points at the floor, like coming back here was some kind of atonement for what I'd done, and not me tucking my tail and hanging my head for the wrong I'd done.

Sterling Falls had been our initial destination, but I couldn't live in the same town as Stone, as the Sylver family, so I selected the next one over and raised my son here.

"You came back for—" She falters and clamps her mouth shut.

As much as I want to know what else she thinks I came back for, I'm equally afraid of some misplaced misconception she might have about me. I'm not a worthy person.

A crush, she'd admitted the night of the concert. *She* has blinders on, not seeing me for the villain I am in her family's history.

"I don't think we should keep doing this." I stand taller, shocking myself as well as Vale with the sudden decision, even as my stomach pitches and my chest squeezes.

"Don't say that." She steps toward me, but I step back, needing to keep some distance before I do something stupid, like pull her to me and beg her to never leave me. Beg for forgiveness I shouldn't ask from her. Put her in a position where she feels she must choose me or them, and it will never be me. She should *never* pick me.

"I have to go," I lie, glancing at the clock on my stove, like I have some pending appointment when I simply need to get out of my house, away from all the memories that cover every corner here. Away from her.

Vale has been like a new roof over an old worn one, once neglected, weathered and battered. She was shelter and protection and a revival I hadn't known I'd longed for.

But now, I need to move on. For *her* own good.

30

—————

[Vale]

He was lying. He was also scared.

But I was pissed.

After another blissed-out lunch break, Cort pushed me away, and at first, I couldn't leave him behind fast enough.

But by the time I'd returned to work, I'd had time to reflect on what he'd said. The emotion and anguish in his tone. The pain of what he'd done *twenty-plus* years ago and the unforgiving nature of its aftereffects.

Cort's sudden absence was like a vacancy in my heart. He hadn't reached out to me after making his bold declaration and I didn't want to appear like a heartbroken woman, desperately clinging to a fling. However, Cort never felt like something flimsy and fleeting. Maybe he wasn't forever, but we were more than sex. We had history, and we were maximizing the present.

On Monday, I called in sick. Something I rarely ever do and

then played hooky from life. It had been too long since I'd gone on a hike in the area surrounding Sterling Falls, the namesake of our town, and I longed to be outdoors. I could have been mothering my bees, but I'd spent time checking on the hive over the weekend, and being home wasn't an option if I wanted to skip out on life for a little while.

Once I reached the forest park, I quickly found the trailhead leading to the falls. A variety of routes existed to reach the glistening destination. An easy walk around the water. A steep climb up the nearby boulders. Or a moderate hike through the trees and along the river's edge a few feet above the shallow canyon. On one side of the lower river was a notch of space that wasn't particularly deep but rather tall. A foot path proved that others had frequented the trail to the natural grotto.

I was hopeful that on a Monday morning the space would be vacant, and I could just sit and meditate, and attempt to regroup. Far too much time has passed since I'd done something like this to center myself. Thinking about Cort was not an option. I didn't want to focus on how angry I was, feeling tossed aside once again by him. I didn't want to lean into this negative energy swirling in my gut and clawing my heart.

With each step I took, I tried to separate myself from my thoughts, giving my concentration to the sound of falling water and the soft rush over large river rocks. Embracing the whisper of the trees and the speckled sunlight filtering through the canopy over my head. Up the narrow incline, that barely allowed for the width of one person, I hiked among the mystique of nature, anxious for the magical destination. With each placement of my feet, I felt lighter.

Until I round the large rock formation and stumble upon a familiar-looking man.

He'd been standing just inside the open space, his hand widespread and bracing him against a boulder. His head is lowered as if he is praying. I make a quick note of where he stands, as if I am looking from the outside into my past. At the spot where he pressed me face-first toward those boulders and entered me from behind, shielding my body from the possibility of a rogue hiker seeing us, filling me with his lust and momentary desire.

"Cortland?"

At the surprised call of his name, Cort drops his hand and spins to face me. My first inclination is to smile. To express relief in seeing him. To question the strange destiny of stumbling upon him in the place we shared history together.

But the stricken look in his eyes and hard clench of his jaw reminds me that he'd told me he was done.

"Cortland." I cross my arms, displeasure in my tone; like he should have known *I'd* be here, and he shouldn't be.

Cort rubs his thumb and forefinger across his eyes and pinches the bridge of his nose for a second before sharply lifting his head and staring back at me.

"Vale." He steps toward me, and I'd take a step back, but I don't have anywhere to go. The wrong footing and I'll be sliding down the embankment into the shallow waters below.

Instead, I hold my ground.

"What are you doing here?" he asks.

I could ask the same of him, but I don't. Even way back when, I'd been open to forgiveness. I'd been willing to make amends. Back then, I'd asked Cort how he was, knowing about his recent injury, hearing about his impending divorce. He'd been hurting, and he hadn't even had to tell me. I felt it in the way he spoke. Seductive and sad. Maybe even shock and spite. If he taunted me, I'd turn tail and run away.

Only, I've never been afraid of Cortland Haven.

And now, I don't answer him.

Instead, I turn my back and stare out at the water falling from a higher elevation. Mystery surrounds this place. Rumors as well. Some say you can see the face of a maiden in the water.

Others mention a couple hidden behind the falls. Destined lovers, unnecessarily killed by a perceived enemy; each other's family. Very *Romeo and Juliet*.

Knox once told me if you drink the water from the Falls, your true love will be revealed. He'd also told me how he had sex on the higher ground near the river's edge and almost gotten eaten alive by bugs. The story was probably supposed to be a precautionary tale. It failed. I'd had sex here once. With the man behind me.

His presence is suddenly closer to me. His breath against the side of my throat. I close my eyes.

"Vale," he whispers.

The last time we were here, he cried in the space between my neck and shoulder. He was so broken, and all I wanted to do was fix him. Hold him together. Promise him things would get better.

Instead, he walked away and never looked back. And I hate how I've come to realize I might have always been waiting for him to return. To me. To us.

Shaking my head, I straighten my shoulders and force my eyes to stay aimed at the water rushing over the rocky edge above and plummeting to the shallower river below. If ever there was a metaphor for love—

"I didn't want to marry her," he begins behind me, as if picking up where he left off last week. "I didn't love her, but it felt like the right thing to do after so many wrongs."

I close my eyes to the devastation. Stone's girlfriend and his best friend cheated on Stone with each other.

A man who was prepared to propose to his girl.

A man who desperately needed his friend. His brother from another.

Yet, the three of them were irreparably torn apart through a poor decision and reckless hearts.

They fucked up—Bailey and Cort—and in their wake was

my twenty-two-year-old brother, saddled with six younger siblings when he needed them most.

"The marriage was shit from the start," Cort continues.

I never liked Bailey, but my brother loved her and later admitted he never could have asked her to join him on the path he took. Guardian to siblings. Giving up a career. Changing the course of his life.

"Things were . . . volatile between us. Hostile." His voice trembles, anxious and hesitant, while I'm suddenly holding my breath as if sensing the worst is still to come. Wanting him to continue but also wanting him to stop.

My eyes stay pinned to the opposite side of the river.

Cort exhales behind me. "You mentioned touch aversion." He pauses a beat. "Bailey is the reason."

I feel the hard pinch of my brows. The confusion at his admission.

"She wasn't loving or nurturing. No compassion. No comfort. She preferred . . . submission. Abuse, actually."

I spin to face him. My mouth falling open with a thousand questions, and yet, none tumble off my tongue

"She'd scream and yell. Insult." He closes his eyes a brief second. "Throw punches."

"What?" Fists form at my sides, while my mind races in circles.

"Bailey *hit* me."

At first, I can't see it. Cort is bigger than her. He's stronger. Surely, he would have held her off. Or fought back. But Cort doesn't strike me as the kind of man to harm a woman. The anguish in his eyes confirms it. The confusion. The frustration. The struggle he must have felt between keeping her at bay and hurting her.

Men can be victims of domestic violence, and I know this. I'm a little ashamed of myself that I hadn't thought of it. Most people believe a big, burly man couldn't possibly be abused by his smaller wife. A sense of implausible, when it's very possible. It's a reason there is a stigma and shame attached to such behavior.

My heart breaks for Cort in an entirely new way.

"When I didn't do what she wanted, didn't say what she needed—" Cort flinches like he can feel the effects of her hand on his face. "God, I felt so weak at times." He hangs his head, again the conflict weighing on him.

"She drank. A lot." He lifts his head again but stares over my shoulder. "And I'd made too many excuses for her, enabling her. I let it go on for too long."

He eventually looks back at me. "How could I teach my son to be a fighter, to know his worth, when I didn't know how to respond to his mother's behavior? While he witnessed her act in such a degrading manner? How do I teach him to respect women, while equally teaching him to stand up for himself? But don't fight back. Don't touch her."

I don't have an answer for him.

Cort shakes his head. "Bailey and I fought constantly. Sometimes, she'd even toss Stone in the mix. Tell me how he was a better man. How she lost him because of me. She even blamed Josh."

Cort snorts, incredulous, as if an innocent baby was ever to blame for adult decisions. His gaze latches on my face, imploring me to understand.

"So, you left her because of what she did to you?" I confirm quietly. Of course he did. Whatever strength he needed to finally walk away, he found.

"I left her because of what she did to Josh."

"No!" I gasp, while shaky fingers cover my mouth. No, *no, no, no*. Not his son.

Cort gazes over my shoulder again. His eyes distant and glassy, and full of regret. "I never had a clue how rough he had it. I mean, I knew she said things, and I didn't like them, and we'd fight about her words toward him as well, but I never *really* knew the truth until he had a bruise on his arm."

"Oh my God, Cort." I step forward, reaching for him, but then halt, retracting my hand and forming fists at my side again to prevent me from touching him.

"He was only eleven," he chokes on a strangled sob.

The same age as Hudson. The same age as his entire twelve and under baseball team.

Cort crosses his left arm over his chest and taps at his right shoulder. "She stabbed me when I told her we were leaving."

"Cort, that's just . . ." What word describes it best? Awful isn't strong enough. Deranged doesn't cover it.

"The season had just finished. I was on the IL without a decision on whether I'd play again or not. I'd been sticking things out for Josh, thinking I was providing a good life for him, doing the right thing for him. I didn't want to separate a mother and her child."

He exhales, the sound raspy and rough. "Then I'd learned she'd been smacking him around for years, and he never told me. He was fucking afraid of her. My boy scared of his mother, and he never mentioned it to me."

A heavy sob leaves his throat, but he quickly coughs to clear it.

"I've been so selfish." His head lowers for a second, shaking it side to side before whipping it upright, gathering inner strength, forcing his voice to steel. "And I tarnish everything I touch."

His friendship with Stone. His marriage. His poor son.

"I won't do that to you, Vale. I can't."

Unable to stop myself, I reach for his left arm, the one I drew on, and now bears a permanent mark. With my thumb, I swipe lightly over the bee.

"You did what you thought was best for Josh, both at first and then later on." It's all we can do as parents. The best we know how in the moment, until we learn more, or better, or accept what's best for our child.

"She'd already done so much damage." Cort's voice cracks.

Bailey probably had. Recalling where I was at twelve, even at ten, so much irreparable harm had happened and the trauma was buried deep within me, yet I've carried on. Persevered. And from what Cort has told me about Josh, he's moved on as well. Perhaps never forgetting, but making peace with his past, focusing on his future.

"Where is Bailey now?"

Cort glances over my shoulder again. "After the divorce, she had no legal claim to Josh, handing over full custody when he was still young. She had a restraining order placed on her. She wouldn't come anywhere near Josh or myself ever again. The last place she'd visit is Sterling Falls. I don't have any idea where she is now."

After a heavy sigh, Cort glances back at me. His face wiped of all emotion other than weariness and drain.

"I'm sorry I never told you. It's embarrassing." He hitches one shoulder. "I should have told you all this the first time we met here. But I wasn't in a good place. And I never should have taken advantage of you."

"Is that what you think happened? That you took advantage of me?" I'm taken aback by the thought.

"Didn't I?" His eyes peer at mine, full of contrition and fear. Apology and regret.

"I didn't stop you. I didn't even complain," I remind him. I could tell him I liked it, and I did on some level, but I've already admitted to him that it wasn't an equal experience. Honestly, afterward, I was too confused to give the moment deep thought, other than accept disappointment and chastise myself for putting false hope on Cort and failing at orgasms again.

"I forgive you, Cort. I forgive us." For what happened twelve years ago in this very spot. For being impulsive and reckless, and making a decision. Right or wrong. Good or bad. We need to live with the consequences. *Live* being the key word. Something tells me Cortland Haven hasn't been living. He's been existing.

He's had decades of regret and remorse, isolated and lacking in love. The suffering comes from never forgiving himself or moving on from the pain of the past. Never accepting he made a huge mistake. Or rather, accepting it and living his life anchored by it.

Cort lowers his head again, slowly nodding while watching my thumb stroke over the bee inked on his arm. The memory of me. The reminder of us. In a different time, at a different place, making a different decision.

"Everyone deserves a second chance, Cort." At the very core of me, I believe that. "We all falter and fail and then we dust ourselves off and start over."

Dust off the rust. That's the Haven Hitters motto. Look beneath the tarnish for strength. *Find steel underneath.*

"You know, every spring, I awaken my bees. Re-assemble their hive. The first year or two, I was afraid of them." I'd been scared to death I'd get stung. "But bees remind me it's okay to be a little bit scared. Of change. Of new beginnings."

That a little sting isn't going to set me back. Big pain shouldn't either. Hearts heal. I believe that as well, but only if we move forward.

"Sometimes you need to step out of your comfort zone and into something new to really live."

Not that Cort is comfortable with his past. His mistakes are strangling him, holding him in a chokehold. He needs to let what's behind him go and forgive himself. For Stone. For Bailey. For Josh.

"You did what you could," I remind him. "For Josh."

One of the most important things we can do as parents is

admit our failures and then move on, righting wrongs the only way we know how, until the next time we falter.

"But did I?" He stares at me, his eyes glistening.

"You loved him, more than anything. And that's the greatest thing we can do for our children." He left an abusive marriage to save his child. "You gave him a place to start over. A *second* chance. Perhaps it's time you give yourself that chance as well."

"I just don't know, Vale." His eyes are cloudy as he stares at me.

"I know," I whisper. As a survivor of an abusive father, without protection from my mother through no fault of her own, *I know* that what Cort did was in the best interest of his child.

My knowing can cover the both of us.

With that, I step forward, tugging Cort to me and wrapping my arms around him. At first, he doesn't respond, just lowers his head to my shoulder and presses his weight against me. But eventually, his arms loop around me and he tugs me tighter and tighter, until I almost can't breathe.

I inhale, catching my breath on the sharp scent of balsam fir and man coming off him.

Perhaps this round, *my* hug is the one he hadn't known he needed.

31

[Vale]

On Friday night, Stone is gone for the weekend. A rare escape with Emerson Milton although he refuses to talk about her or what's going on between them. In another rare incident, I've allowed Hudson to spend the night at Atticus Stanton's after speaking with Henry, who assured me he'd be home all evening.

I'm giving myself a night off.

Despite our tight embrace earlier in the week, Cort and I went our separate ways. An alarm on his phone went off and he told me he had to get to a job site. As for me, I'd needed a few minutes to process what I'd learned.

I sat in nature while my mind raced. Like the bees I tend, my head buzzed here, there, and everywhere.

Five days after his explanation, my brain is still swirling.

Other than a quick text from Cort, thanking me for listening to him, it's been radio silence. I'd like to call bullshit on us being done with one another, but I don't have the band-width to argue with the man.

Instead, I'm baking a cake.

While Sebastian is the true baker in our family, my skill isn't too bad either. After having peanut butter and honey on whole wheat on more than one occasion lately, I've decided to bake a honey lemon cake, which reminds me of Cort's mother.

Mary Haven is the closest example I have of what a mother should be like, other than living my own experience. As a child, her love and affection toward her children was something I'd longingly stare at, puzzled by it, envious of it.

While mixing all the ingredients for my cake, including three heaping tablespoons of honey, I receive a text.

> I want to be stung.

A bee emoji follows the statement, along with a heart. I could interpret that request a million ways, and probably none of them would be correct.

I tap my phone with my knuckle because my hands are messy and stare down at the message.

A week ago, he tells me he's done.

Days later, he nearly cries.

Men?!

I wash my hands, giving him a second to stew over my initial lack of response.

> Is this a booty call?

On another occasion, the response might be flirtatious, even fun, but I'm just not in the mood.

> I can't. I'm baking a cake.

The excuse is almost as weak as washing my hair in order avoid a date with someone or claiming to be in the shower and unable to take a phone call, but the cake is a legitimate reason not to chase Cort and with the irritated energy suddenly buzzing around me I just don't have patience for him right now.

I've given him compassion. I've expressed my concern. I've forgiven him for past transgressions.

Three little bubbles pop up and then disappear. Three more appear and then vanish.

"Guess that's that."

Even if I had been tempted to run to Cort's house, I promised myself I would never pursue a man, and this baking cake is my sign to stay put.

Stirring up the ingredients again, I pour equal amounts into three separate round tins. I'm making a three-layer cake with raspberry preserves and butter cream frosting in the middle. The secret ingredient is a homemade lemon-honey glaze that soaks into the layers. Fresh raspberries would be a better garnish, but store-bought ones will do as well. The final result will be a naked cake. No frosting on the sides but heaps of it in between the layers.

The timer on the oven goes off thirty-five minutes later and I pull the three tins from the oven, setting them on wire racks. While they cool, I begin the honey glaze which involves heating honey, freshly squeezed lemon juice, and lemon zest. As I pour the concoction into a pot, a knock comes to the front door.

As I'm alone, miles from town, and it's getting late, I'm not expecting anyone, and there isn't really a reason for someone to stop by without a specific purpose. So, I hesitate, sneaking a glance through a small gap in the living room curtain before approaching the front door.

With a flourish, I open the door and stare at the man on my front porch.

"Another house call? Need a massage?"

Cort gives me a sheepish smile, twirling a baseball cap in his hand. "I deserve that."

He's taken a risk to come to the house again. Hudson could be here. Stone too. Tilting my head to the side, I state, "This is dangerous."

His dark eyes meet mine through the screen door barrier between us. "You told me to be a little bit scared."

I can't fight the smile curling my lips as I open the exterior door. He should be *real* scared to openly stand on the front porch of the house I share with Stone.

"How do you know if I'm alone?" I ask as he crosses into the living room.

"Heard a rumor Stone was out of town with Emerson. Saw Hudson in Rogue River earlier with the Stanton's getting pizzas. Took my chances there was no one else." He pauses in the living room and faces me. "Despite that lame cake excuse."

"There's no one else, Cort," I confirm quietly, lowering my gaze. He's the only one I want. "And the cake wasn't an excuse. I'm really baking one."

He inhales and turns his head in the direction of the kitchen. "Smells delicious and like something is burning."

"Shit." I race to the kitchen, finding my honey glaze boiling when it should be simmering. "Crap." I quickly turn off the burner and whisk the ingredients, hoping I haven't overdone it but the browned edges in the pot say I have.

"I'll need to start over," I mutter to myself, taking the pot from the stove and setting it on a hot pad near the sink.

Cort stands on the opposite side of our kitchen island while I work, mixing up fresh ingredients before pulling out a clean pot.

"The house looks nice."

I glance up to see him looking around the kitchen. Long gone are the dingy, dark cabinets and scuffed countertops.

"Thanks. Years ago, Stone gutted this place, and I designed the renovation." We went with open concept as best we could, maximizing the space to include the island but still allowing for a kitchen table. A formal dining room exists off to the left, although we hardly use the space other than for buffets to accommodate Sunday meals in the cooler months or the holidays.

After mentioning Stone, I hesitate. I've had time to process that my long explanation about Sylver Sundays was the tipping point with Cort. However, if I can't even mention my brother, Cort and I aren't ever going to have something deeper. We will only be surface level, like on countertops and king-sized beds, and again, I'm just not in the mood.

"What are you doing here?" I ask, flicking my gaze toward him before just as quickly looking away.

"I wanted to see you, Vale."

"Get a good look last night?" I comment, turning toward the stovetop and pouring the honey glaze into the fresh pot. When Hudson had another baseball game yesterday, Cort saw me, and I'd missed another book club.

Suddenly, I feel Cort behind me. "Not enough of one."

I close my eyes, caught between his words sounding like a pickup line and a seductive plea.

"Cort," I sigh, twirling a wooden spoon around the glaze. "What do you want?"

"I want to be a little scared. With you."

At his reference to my first beekeeping years, my head pulls up so fast, I knock the spoon against the pot, startling both of us. Turning back to the glaze, I give it another stir, staring into the gooey mixture that suddenly matches the consistency of my insides.

Cort's hand hesitantly comes to my lower back as he steps even closer to me.

"I don't know how this will work, Vale. Hiding out in my

house makes it seem a bit sordid, but then again, our business isn't other people's business. However, I'd like to be more open about us. I want to tell my mom and Clint. Hell, even Tate and Trinity."

The reference to his sister adds to my guilt. I pretended I didn't know Cort was dating anyone.

I tip my head, glancing at him over my shoulder. "You know what this might mean for me, though, right?"

"You're going to catch hell from Stone." Anguish fills his eyes a second. He doesn't want me to hurt my brother any more than I want to hurt him.

"I'm not worried about my brother." Maybe I could reasonably talk to Stone. Maybe he'd understand that we don't choose who we love, we just love. And I want to love Cort. I've *been* loving him my entire life, faults and all.

"Okay, I'm a little bit worried about him," I admit.

"I could talk to him." There are several reasons why Cort should talk to my brother, but I'm flattered that he's willing to go to bat for me. For us. "I don't want this to be difficult for you."

"The difficult part has been you shutting down on me for a week." I speak before I can hold the words back and turn to tend the heating honey glaze.

"I'm sorry I hurt you again," Cort whispers behind me.

I nod once, accepting the apology but still stung by his rejection. I don't need a marriage proposal, but I'm also not looking for a rollercoaster ride with this man.

Cort swipes his hand up my back and squeezes at the nape of my neck. He clears his throat. "Can I help somehow?"

"I've got it. This just needs to cool a bit, the cakes as well, and then I can apply the glaze and frost them." I turn off the stove and step over to the island with the hot pot.

Cort follows me and reaches for the open bottle of wine on the counter to refill my glass.

"Want a beer?"

"I'd love one." His sly smile lights up his face. Like I'm offering him something more than a beverage. I'm giving him time.

After getting him a beer, I set the glaze in a glass jar to cool and clean up the mess I've already made. Cort helps himself to a dish towel hanging off a hook and dries all the bowls and utensils. We work mostly in silence, just taking up space with one another, which is different, of course, from sharing a kitchen with my brother. This sensation is foreign but nice.

"Think your brother will tell you that you can't see me?" Cort eventually asks, his tone heavy.

"Think I still don't listen to my big brother all the time," I sass like the teenager I once was, frustrated when Stone tried to tell me what to do. "I respect my brother, but I don't kowtow to him."

Cort roughly chuckles. "I bet you've been a real pain in the ass over the years."

I snort. "Bees sting, Cortland."

"The queen especially." He winks.

I laugh as I scrub down the sink and turn off the faucet. "Want to watch a movie?" Next on my night alone list was watching a rom-com.

Cake. Wine. And mindless romance. A perfect combination.

Cort shrugs, picks up both his beer and my wine glass and follows me into the living room. Within minutes, I queue up a movie and we watch the hero fumble around his attraction to the heroine. The acting is weak and when the sex scene begins, I pause the film.

"Why do men think they can say such a thing?"

"What thing?"

Cort and I are sitting next to each other, but we feel miles apart. I'm curled over the armrest with my knees bent and feet against his thigh. His hand holds my ankle, but we still feel disconnected.

Pulling up a deep masculine voice, I mock, "I'm so hard for you."

Cort sputters. "What?"

"You never hear or read a woman say, *I'm so wet for you*." I use a false soprano to mimic my own kind.

Cort's been holding his beer bottle on his upper thigh, and he lifts the glass to his mouth, muttering, "Jesus," before he takes a sip.

I lift the remote, aiming it toward the screen, when Cort cuffs my wrist. "What else?"

"What else what?"

"What are other things men get away with saying but women don't?"

I shift on the couch, dipping my toes beneath his thigh, taking a second to think of a few other statements fictional men make.

"*I can't wait to fill you up*," I mock in a rugged voice then drop to my own. "Never hear a woman say aloud *I can't wait to be filled by you*."

Cort shifts slightly, draping his arm over the back of the couch as his upper body faces mine. "And why is that?"

"I don't know," I nearly shriek. "Like women should get to be just as vocal. Turning all those phrases around."

"Agreed." Cort nods, his eyes gleaming, humoring me, before setting his beer bottle on the floor and covering my ankle again. "What else?" His voice drops lower as he tugs my foot into his lap and knuckles the arch of it.

"Guys are always like, *I can't wait to see her lips wrapped around my cock*." My masculine impression isn't wavering. "How about a woman says, I can't wait to see your head between my thighs?"

Cort arches a brow at me.

"It's not an invitation. I'm just saying—"

"Why isn't it an invitation?" Cort questions, looking up at me at the same time he adds pressure against the bottom of my foot. My leg jerks, kicking at him.

"So, this is a booty call?"

When Cort doesn't immediately answer, I throw my legs off the couch and rise. "I need more wine. And it's time to glaze the cake."

What is wrong with me? I'm not trying to pick a fight with him. I'm also not trying to seduce him. I just don't understand what he's doing here. And I don't know why I'm tossing out sexual comments, when my brain keeps saying don't go there.

Once back in the kitchen, I reach for the bottle of wine, but Cort is right behind me, and he covers my hand.

"Vale," he whispers near my ear. "I'm here because I've missed you." Sincerity fills his voice, and I turn to face him. He's so close. Too close. Close enough I get a strong whiff of his now-familiar scent. Balsam fir and a hint of asphalt. Beer and mint on his breath. I close my eyes fighting the pull to him.

"I need to glaze the cake." My comment rumbles in my throat, choking down the admission of how much I've missed him.

"Bee." He cups the side of my neck with one hand, and I glance up at him. His mouth is inches from mine, holding still, waiting for my permission. And I gently push against his chest.

"Cake," I whisper. The weight of his absence still weighs heavily on me. I need more time to pull myself together and tap down my conflicting desires.

I want him. I want him not. I just want him to want me.

Cort steps back, giving me the space I need to brush the honey glaze on the top of each layer, allowing the sticky sweetness to drip into the spongy cake. He has refilled my wine glass and leans against the counter while I work, diligently watching me stroke the pastry brush back and forth over each layer.

"Ready for round two of the movie?" I ask after cleaning up by sealing the glaze in a jar and lightly placing plastic wrap over each cake layer.

When Cort doesn't answer, I glance at him, feet apart from me between the kitchen island and the sink counter.

"I want a second chance," he states, holding his gaze on me. "With you."

No words have ever surprised me more, and I don't know who moves first, but suddenly our mouths clash. We are a frenzy of lips and tongues, roaming hands and the removal of his short-sleeved shirt. Ideally, he'd pick me up and pin me to the wall, but with his bum knee and bad back, I have another idea.

"Let's go to my room."

32

[Cort]

Never had an invitation been so sweet, nor had I expected to hear it a second time.

Following Vale to her bedroom the first time I made a house call was like an out-of-body experience. I'd walked the halls of this house thousands of times but always stopped at one particular bedroom door. My best friend's.

Just like the last time, I breeze past that doorway, and head to the final room.

On that other night, Vale was mumbling under her breath about never sneaking boys into her room before, and as much as I wanted to remind her then that I am a man, Vale is well aware of that point by now.

When she walked through the house, locking doors and turning off lights before climbing the stairs tonight, I had a strange sense of doing this every night with her. Maybe not in this house, but mine.

Once we reach her bedroom, Vale remains silent. The space is tight. Her double bed takes up most of the room along with a slim dresser and a wicker chair in the corner.

"Having second thoughts?" I ask as she stands near the foot of her bed, still not speaking.

"Just seems so strange, right? You in my room. After all this time."

The corner of my lip curls upward. "You getting' shy on me now?"

I've seen every inch of this woman in some manner or other. I've sucked her breasts and fingered her sweet center. I've tasted her and swallowed her moans, but we have yet to cross a certain line and I'm happy to keep both feet planted on one side of it if it means I can keep touching her in other ways. Keep holding her close.

Last week, I told Vale I didn't think we should continue seeing one another. But a week without her has been torture. And I've thought a lot about what she said. How I did the best I could, after making one of the worst decisions of my life. I couldn't ask Stone to forgive me, but I needed to forgive myself. I needed to finally face the future more than focus on the past. And while I've been coasting these last twelve years, I'd like to really swim. Move forward. Move on.

And I want to do that with Vale.

Like I told her, I don't know what that will look like. *How* to make us work. But there's nothing I want more than to try. I could speak to Stone, like I offered. Or she can talk to him first, giving him fair warning. I'd been impulsive once before around a Sylver, but I'm not going to be reckless again with one.

I'm not giving up on Vale and me. Not without a valiant fight.

In answer to my question about her shyness, Vale tugs off the sweatshirt she wears, revealing a light pink bra. She shoves down her leggings, exposing a matching set of panties. I'd ask if she wore the set for me, but she didn't know I'd be here tonight. I didn't know I'd be here either until I couldn't take one more lonely night without her.

"Does it make you feel sexy to wear such pretty things?" I tip my chin, acknowledging her silky attire.

With a gleam in her eyes, she says, "I want you to make me feel sexy."

Fuck yes. Recalling her words earlier—her *reverse* of words—I say, "Can't say I've ever had a woman tell me so boldly what she wants. It's hot, Bee. Very hot."

She already pushed my shirt off downstairs, so I step out of my jeans, leaving on my boxer briefs. We remain feet apart, staring at one another, taking each other in, and I inhale the first real breath I've taken in a week.

God, I've fucking missed her.

I'm also a little bit scared. Frightened for Vale. Afraid for me. I've never felt this way before. This desperate pull to look at her. This constant desire to touch her. And I don't see a way of giving her up.

Our future might be uncertain, but I want a future with no one else but her.

She's stolen my heart; we can continue to share stolen moments as well.

I step toward her while she steps toward me and our mouths meet again. The kiss is hungry. Open lips and seeking tongues. I cup the side of her neck and her hands land on my shoulder blades, pressing me closer to her.

Vale backs toward her bed and then breaks the kiss, scooting up on the mattress and climbing back on the bed. I follow after her; a worker bee chasing his queen, eager for her attention. Vale falls back against her pillows, and I reach between her legs, pushing aside the thin scrap of fabric over her center.

"Can't decide between stripping you bare or leaving all this on? You're so beautiful either way."

There's something equally sexy about hidden parts as there is about revealing ones. The swell of her breasts just above the cups of this rosy silk. The tease of her sex soaking the thin strip at the apex of her legs.

As my fingers enter her, Vale tips back her head, her lids fluttering shut a second.

"Talk dirty to me again, Bee," I tease, struggling with all I want to say to her and hearing all she said earlier to me. "Tell me how you feel. What you want."

Her eyes ping open.

"It feels so good when you touch me. Like no one ever has," she admits.

"And no one else ever will." I can't fight the declaration. I want to be the only one to ever touch her like this, ever please her.

Vale cups the back of my head as her breath hitches. Her hips rock, responding to my touch, my fingers deep inside her. Pressing my thumb to her clit, I watch as her eyes glaze over and her mouth falls open.

"I've missed you, too," she finally admits. She doesn't mean only sexually. Over the past months, all the texts and phone calls, the open conversations and unspoken ones, have brought us closer together. Closer than I've ever been with anyone.

With every catch of her breath, I feel Vale drawing near the brink.

"Take your dick out. Let me see you touch yourself." The bold command has me choking a second. We've done this before. Performed for one another, watched each other, but something about tonight feels different.

"Let me see you." Her gaze holds mine as I push down my boxer briefs with one hand and grip my hard shaft. Vale tilts her head, watching me stroke myself while I finger her.

"Cort." She's so close and I can't wait to feel her come in my hand. "Fuck me," she whispers.

I stare down at her, pliant and pleased, melting beneath me and squeezing at my fingers inside her. With her pretty eyes staring up at me, she adds, "I mean it, Cort. I want to ride your cock, slick it with my—"

I cover her mouth with mine, swallowing down her dirty commands, living out the fantasy in my head. Her sweet pussy wrapped around me. Her legs hitched over my back.

Vale pulls back. "Now, Cort. *Please*. I want to come around you."

"Fucking dream," I mutter, as my thumb moves faster, and my fingers deeper, while I'm tugging at myself.

Vale reaches for my wrist, on the arm holding myself. Then she's shoving at my forearm of the hand between her thighs. With her legs spread wide, slick and dripping from her center, she begs me again.

"Please, Cort. Inside me."

Vale and I have already discussed our sexual history. How long it's been for each of us. How safe we've always been as well. I know she's on the pill for her periods. She knows I had a vasectomy in my mid-thirties.

"Are you sure?" I question one more time because there will be no turning back. Once I go bare inside her, I'll never want anything else. I'm already certain of how this will feel, how this will change everything.

Vale already has her hands on my hips, guiding me to lower between her thighs, and I grip myself once more to line up with her. She's so wet, I easily slip forward, gliding into her depths until we're as close as we can be.

"Sweetness," I choke out, desperate to move, to unleash what's been held at bay for too long, but also holding still, needing a second to catch my breath.

"Move," she softly commands.

Rocking her hips, Vale unleashes on the first stroke of my cock. Pulling back and thrusting in again, she comes around me in a sudden burst. Her fingertips dig into my ass and her mouth hangs open, moaning my name as I surge inside her. Back and forth I go, coating myself like she asked, feeling her clench around me.

Too fast. We're moving too fast, and it's been too long, and within seconds, I'm on my knees, pulling her lower half up my thighs and hammering into her, going off like a dormant volcano as I bury myself to the hilt.

Vale chuckles beneath me while we're still connected, and I fall forward, catching myself on my extended arms. While most men wouldn't appreciate such a reaction from the women they just had sex with, I embrace the crack in the tension.

"We're quite a pair," Vale teases.

"High excitement," I remind her, how we've been riding the accelerator for a while now.

"High intention," she adds. We'd been focused only on each other, only on what we were doing, and how it felt.

"My intention . . ." I tease, lowering to kiss her nose. "Is to do that again, in about a half hour." I'm going to need some time to recover.

Only as I remain inside Vale, she clinches, and I find I'm still hard.

"Vale," I whisper, surprised myself.

Hastily, I pull out of her and reach for her nightstand. "Where are they, Vale?"

"Where are what?" she asks confused.

"Your toys."

After a hesitant look, Vale points toward the second drawer of the stand. Buried beneath notebooks and a soft set of lingerie, I find what I'm looking for.

With her still on her back, I climb over her again and set the tip of a clit vibrator against her.

"It's new," she chokes as the vibration hits her just right. She stutters in ecstasy as she explains, "It's called a Cliterature Stick."

I don't care what it's called as long as it gets her off. Adding tease to torture, I set my dick at her entrance, holding steady as I regroup, and Vale grows wild and hungry again.

"Got another one for me." It isn't a question. Vale's been giving me doubleheaders for weeks, and now that I've had a sense of what she feels like wrapped around me, I want to feel it again and again.

Hard once more, I glide into her, where she clenches around me while the vibration continues to tickle that sensitive nub on her.

"Oh God." Vale's eyes roll back, and she whimpers at the sensation. Inside and out, she's a bundle of nerves.

"Pure honey gold," I hiss, slipping through her folds and pulsing beneath the squeeze of her heat. The vibrator brushes against me as well, adding a strange new kind of stimulation. But my focus is all on Vale. How she clenches around me. How she's slick from this additional touch.

We take a little longer this round while still racing the clock. Vale eventually screams my name, squeezing her thighs around mine, and dragging me over the edge with her.

"Holy shit," I holler, surprised myself, but loving it. Loving every minute of her wrapped around me, holding me inside her, soaking my cock.

Loving her.

I collapse on top of her a second, before rolling us both to the side, keeping us attached.

"I could sleep for a week like this." While my heart is racing, I'm spent. My arm lies loosely over Vale's waist, but she nestles closer to my chest and purrs.

"I like the sound of that."

33

―――――

[Vale]

We'd fallen asleep exactly as he suggested, his softening shaft eventually slipping out of me. We were a mess and yet I didn't care.

Until my phone suddenly rings. A lamp is still on in my room. Cort is still wrapped around me. Fumbling for my phone on the stand, I quickly read the time and the caller ID.

"Hudson?" I shift, pressing up on my elbow, while Cort tightens his arm around my waist.

"Miss Sylver." The quiet female voice has me even more alarmed.

"Amelia? Honey, what's wrong?"

With a heavy sob, the girl tries to speak. "Hudson told me to call you."

"Are you okay? Is he?" I sit upright, as Cort's arm loosens around my waist but doesn't release me. The tension in his forearm suggests he's awake as well and listening.

"Mom." Hudson's voice is both relief and fear. "Can you come get me?"

"Of course." I'm already pushing at Cort's arm and rushing off the bed, trying to juggle the slim phone between my ear and shoulder as I reach for my clothes. The phone slips free.

"Shit." I reach for it and press the speaker button. "You're still at the Stanton's, right?" My fear is the kids have snuck out of the house, like something I might have done when I was a tad older than their present age and have gotten in over their heads somewhere.

I have a no-questions-asked policy with Hudson, reminding him often that he simply needs to call me for help. I'll ask questions later. I've never had to indulge that promise until now, and it takes everything in me to not bombard him with an inquisition.

"We're here. But hurry, okay?"

"Okay. I'm getting dressed." I should ask where Henry is? What were they doing? Why was it Amelia who called first? But I keep my composure, hastily dressing. Cort has sat up as well and slowly slips off the side of my bed, stepping into his pants without underwear and tugging on his shirt.

"I can keep you on the phone," I tell Hudson, worried that he's hurt, as he's clearly afraid of something.

"I'm okay. Just come and get me."

"I'm on my way." I click off the phone with trembling fingers.

Cort covers my hand in the firm grip of his own. "Stanton's, right?"

"I've got to go," I say, looking at him.

"I'm going with you."

"No." I can't handle explaining what he's doing with me or why at this late hour.

"Not arguing with you, Vale. I'm not letting you go to that prick's house alone. I'll drive."

I do nothing but nod. No-questions-asked. I'll explain myself to Hudson later.

WHEN WE PULL up in front of the Stanton's house, all three kids are outside, huddled together. Hudson has his arm around Atticus who leans forward with his head on his knees. Amelia sits close beside Hudson on his other side.

Cort and I hop out of his truck at the same time, and I race up the sidewalk, instantly cupping Hudson's face to inspect him.

"I'm fine, Mom." He exhales heavily. "It's Atticus."

Reaching for the child, I lift his head and discover a large welt beneath his eye. "What happened?"

Atticus doesn't speak but Amelia whispers in a quivering voice. "Daddy."

Cort is up the porch stairs in one giant step.

"Cort," I cry out as he thunders across the wooden planks and opens the screen door with so much force, it hits the exterior of the house. He helps himself to enter and I glance back at all three kids.

"Stay right here. Hudson, call 9-1-1 if you hear anything."

"Mom," he gasps.

I step around him and rush up the porch steps myself. I don't want to imagine what might happen, but Cort has entered the Stanton home, Henry unaware, and as Henry is clearly unhinged, I can't risk Cort surprising him.

"Cort," I quietly call out, searching the lower-level rooms before he thunders back down the staircase, meeting me at the bottom.

"Fucking bastard. He's out cold." He breaths heavily.

"You hit him?" I shriek.

"Passed out drunk," Cort clarifies with a shake of his head. He glances toward the front porch. "Let's get them out of here."

As we step toward the front door, I suggest, "We should call Stone."

Cort simply shakes his head. "You need a sheriff report now." Which reminds me Stone is out of town. "I'm a mandated reporter, Vale."

As a coach, he's obligated to report abuse to the authorities.

As Cort approaches Atticus, he crouches in front of him. "Hey, buddy. Want to tell me what happened?"

Atticus rolls his head side to side. "Can we just get out of here?" He shivers in his thin shirt and pajama pants, minus shoes. Hudson still has his arm around his friend while only slightly better dressed in pajamas plus his gym shoes. His back-pack is on the step behind him. Amelia clutches a blue bear to her chest and is dressed like she's headed to a sporting event. Leggings, gym shoes and a large, zippered sweatshirt.

"Let's go," I whisper, reaching down for Cort's shoulder in his hunched position in front of Atticus. "We can talk later."

Hudson and I share a glance, and he nods once, then stands and guides Atticus to follow his lead. As Atticus steps toward Cort, Hudson takes Amelia's hand, and I wrap my arm around her as we guide all three kids to Cortland's truck.

Once in the backseat, Atticus closes his eyes and tips his head against the window. Hudson stares out the opposite window while Amelia sits between them.

I have so much I want to ask but bite my tongue other than to whisper to Cort, "Thank you."

He reaches for my hand across the center console and gives my fingers a squeeze, then holds on. I risk another glance at the kids in the back seat but don't pull free from Cort's hand, needing his touch to ground me.

When we got back to the house, Cort follows us inside, and I don't argue with him. I retrieve a bag of peas and hand it to

Cort for Atticus's cheek, then I take Amelia to the guest room she was previously in. Cort leads Atticus and Hudson to my son's room.

"Okay, sweetheart. Did he hurt you?" I ask, running my hand over Amelia's head while inspecting her face.

She shakes her head and her lips quiver again. "He's never done that before. He yells a lot and makes threats, but he's never hit us." She swallows around a sob. "I don't even know what happened. I just heard him yelling and then Atticus screamed. Dad slammed his bedroom door, and I waited a few minutes before I snuck into my brother's room."

She leans forward, covering her face while she cries, and I tug her to me, wrapping my arms around her thin frame.

I'll kill Henry Stanton for frightening his daughter and hurting his son. There will be no mercy for him.

Finally, drying Amelia's face and offering her the same clothes she wore weeks ago to sleep in, I tuck her into bed. She still hiccups, but exhaustion eventually settles over her while she clutches her blue bear.

Stepping into the hallway, I pause when I see Cort standing outside Hudson's door.

"How is Atticus?"

"Shaken and scared. Pissed, too." Cort bitterly chuffs, leaning against the wall. "Kid's got a mouth, and I know where he gets it." He lowers his gaze and purses his lips. "I've got to call the sheriff."

"I know."

Cort nods and steps toward the staircase.

"I just need a minute," I state, pointing toward Hudson's room.

"Of course." Cort descends the stairs while I open Hudson's door.

Once inside his bedroom, I approach Hudson's twin bed. He's rolled toward the wall, and I don't want to disturb him. I just need to see him, check on him. When I swipe my hand over his hair, he rolls to face me.

"Hey, bud. How are you doin'?"

I lower to the edge of his bed as he sits upright and flings his arms around me. "I didn't know what to do."

"It's okay, buddy." I hold him tightly. "You did the right thing by calling me."

"His dad just came out of nowhere, screaming at us to turn down the video game. It wasn't even that loud. Atticus told him to go to bed, and his dad picked up a baseball and flung it at his head. It happened so fast."

Hudson holds onto me harder.

"It's okay now, baby." I stroke the back of his head. "You're home now, okay? Coach is going to call the sheriff, and I'll talk to Uncle Stone."

Hudson pulls back. "Will their dad go to jail?"

Sadly, I don't think so. There probably won't be any repercussion other than a harsh warning and a strong suggestion to seek counseling. For now, Atticus and Amelia are safe. Only for tonight.

"No, bud." At least, not yet.

Hudson nods and folds down to his pillow.

"Try to get some rest." I run my hand along his face and cup his cheeks. "I love you. You did the right thing tonight by calling me. I'm always here for you, Hudson. Always."

He shouldn't need the reminder, but I tell him anyway. I'll never be like the Henrys of the world. Or the Baileys. I'll never be like my father either.

After pressing a kiss to his forehead, I stand and step over to the other bed. Glancing down at Atticus, my original dislike of the kid is now peppered with guilt. He's who he is *because* of his father. Lying there, he looks so innocent, and I reach down and brush back his hair as well, hoping I won't disturb him while praying for protection over him and his sister. Their road is not going to be easy.

Exiting Hudson's room, I silently close the door and head down the stairs. Cort sits at the kitchen island, holding his phone. Coffee brews in the machine.

I'm wired while exhausted, and the last thing I need is a cup of coffee. I'm already jittery.

"What did the sheriff's department say?"

"They'll investigate. Send a mediator to interview the kids. Send someone to talk to Henry. I told Andy the kids are here."

I nod. Andy Whitehall works with Stone, but I'm not a fan of him. He can hold a grudge, and he's done so against Sebastian and his past, even though everyone else in the community forgives Sebastian for his transgressions.

Cort shifts on the island stool and holds out his arm. I step into his embrace, wedging between his legs while wrapping my arms around his neck.

"How are you doing?"

I blow out a deep breath. "Tired." I chuckle sorrowfully before pulling back from his much-needed hug. "And kind of feeling like our night was ruined." Only an hour or so ago, Cort was in my bed.

"There's going to be questions about why I was with you."

I nod slowly. "I think I'll cross that bridge when I get to it." I pause a second. "But I'm grateful you were here."

While I could have handled this situation on my own, I'm relieved I didn't have to.

"I hate to leave you to the firing squad in the morning, but I've got Josh's graduation later today."

I press back while holding onto Cort's shoulders. "Oh my gosh." Glancing at Cort's phone, the time reads two a.m. West Virginia University is three hours away. "You need some sleep."

Cort meets my concerned eyes. "I don't want to leave you

alone with them yet. I'd already planned that if I leave by five, I'll make it to Morgantown by eight. The graduation is at nine."

"Cort, I'm so sorry I forgot." Weeks ago, he mentioned this achievement for his son. The Haven Hitters don't have practice this weekend because of Cort's commitment.

"Why don't you head to bed? I'm gonna hang on your couch for a while, then I'll head out."

Everything in me wants to invite Cort back upstairs and return us to our previous position, him wrapped around me, but too much has happened in such a short period.

"You don't have to stay," I whisper, contradicting all I want.

"I'm not leaving, Vale." He swipes his finger down my nose. "Go to bed, sweetness."

Cupping his bristly jaw in my hand, I lean forward and kiss him, slow and deliberate, hoping to convey how grateful I am that he was with me tonight. That he came to me, despite the risks, and we shared ourselves with one another in a new way.

Pulling back, there's no doubt about what Cort would hear if he could read my mind.

I love you.

34

———

[Vale]

The following morning, Cort was gone and as much as I tried to remain hopeful, making pancakes and bacon and plastering on false positivity, the inevitable happened.

A mediator came to talk with the kids and then Deputy Sheriff Andy Whitehall took Atticus and Amelia back to their home despite my offer to let them stay with me a while longer.

"Got no immediate reason to keep them with you." Andy leveled me with a hard glare, upset that I removed the kids from their house without their father's permission—according to Henry—despite the shiner on Atticus's cheek.

Henry claimed the boys were horsing around and Hudson threw a baseball at Atticus. Atticus missed the catch.

There was no way my boy lied.

"Waste of money being on that expensive travel team if they

can't even teach boys how to toss a ball or catch one." Andy repeated Henry's accusation.

I couldn't believe Henry had done such a thing: dismissing his own crime and blaming it on my son. Even with each of the kids telling their truth and my statement about their obvious fear, Andy didn't listen.

"You had no right removing those kids from their father." He spoke with a patronizing tone, like I was some busybody meddling in family affairs. He said I was fortunate Henry wasn't pressing charges against me.

"On what grounds?" I'd demanded, glaring at Andy like he'd lost his mind.

He shrugged. "Kidnapping."

"What the hell, Andy?"

"Deputy Sheriff Whitehall, Valentine," he corrected me.

"Where's Stone?" Even though I knew the answer and I didn't really want to bother my brother with this situation—he'd learn about it soon enough—but I did not appreciate how Andy was handling things.

"Don't you worry. The sheriff will hear all about this." Andy spoke as if that sheriff wasn't my oldest brother, and I didn't know his position in the law. *And* implying my son had done something wrong, as well as I had.

Insufferable ass.

When Stone did get home, late Sunday morning, we hosted our weekly family gathering and didn't have time to speak about the incident until later that evening.

Entering his office on the first floor of our home, I feel like the angsty teen I once was, needing to ask my older brother for some necessity, or money, or help. In this case, I don't need his help as much as his compassion.

Atticus and Amelia Stanton need help.

Of course, in my explanation about Hudson calling me, I can't leave out Cort's presence. I don't want to tell Stone about Cort and me like this, but I can't avoid Cort's involvement.

"I called Cort," I lie, bold-faced and straight to the face of my hero, because whether Cort was in the house or not isn't the issue right now. Henry is.

If Stone questions why I didn't call any of my brothers instead, he doesn't ask.

Instead, he sits back in his swiveling chair and stares at me from across his desk, listening while I explain how Cort drove to the Stanton home, what we saw, what Cort saw of Henry's condition, and then how I brought the kids back to the house, glossing over how Cort stayed here.

As Cort made the call to the sheriff's department there was no way to skip over his involvement, plus considering his position as a coach, Cort was obligated to report what he'd seen.

Eventually, Stone leans forward, locking his eyes with mine. Ones that mirror our momma's, or so I'm told. All of us Sylvers have blue eyes in some shade or other, and it's been repeatedly mentioned how they were one of her best features. Kind and sweet, loving and honest.

Stone's eyes are a combination of those characteristics mingled with other traits, original to him. No-nonsense. Steadfast. Protective.

If he has further questions about Cort's involvement, he doesn't ask. He simply states, "I'll have to corroborate Cort's story with yours."

"Of course," I swallow hard, knowing I've put all of us in a difficult position. Cort and me. Me and Stone. Stone and Cort.

This isn't going to end well for anyone, but the people I'm most concerned about are the Stanton kids.

"What will happen to Atticus and Amelia?" I stare at my brother, certain he reads the fear in my eyes. "They can't stay with Henry."

Stone sighs. "They can, unfortunately. And they will, for

now. But we're keeping an eye on the situation." Stone leans forward. "*I'm* keeping an eye on things."

His words bring me little comfort. The current situation is the voice of three children against an adult, and the adult won this round. I don't want Atticus and Amelia to eventually be the losers, though.

When I was a kid, any adult I turned to for help was eventually chased off our property by our drunk father. I don't want that kind of lifestyle for the Stanton children. Or any child.

But as Stone continues to stare at me, leaning forward with his hands clasped on his desk, I sense he's trying to impart some deeper meaning to his words.

Like he isn't only keeping an eye on the Stanton kids, but me as well.

35

———————

[Cort]

Henry Stanton was a motherfucking motherfucker, and I couldn't believe Andy Whitehall bought that shit about boys being boys, and Hudson tossing a ball at Atticus, that Atticus caught with his cheek.

Unfortunately, Henry withdrew Atticus from Haven Hitters, and I had to remind Hudson that he did nothing wrong.

"Not one thing, bud," I tell him when I pull him aside during our first practice after the weekend. Hudson is standing, but I kneel on one knee so I'm closer to his eye level.

"We know the truth." I point at my head and then my chest. "And you did not lie."

I doubt the boys were horsing around that late at night. Sneaking in late night video games? Having the volume too loud? Yelling into headsets forgetting others can hear you? Absolutely guilty. Maybe. But I don't believe Hudson threw a ball at his friend, that pegged him in the face because Atticus was a lousy catcher.

Fucking Henry.

"Other kids are talking," Hudson reminds me of the chatter among the parents and the kids before practice began.

I nod once, glancing down at the ground to collect my thoughts before looking at him again. "Hudson, I get that you're walking a fine line. You should always tell the truth, but sometimes that truth does not belong to others. It's no one's business what you witnessed, except for your mom, and me, because I was there. And the people who can make it better for Atticus and Amelia, like your uncle." I leave off Andy because he's another motherfucking motherfucker who is clearly on some power trip with some backward-ass sympathy for Henry.

"But will they get help?" Hudson asks, with concern written all over his young face.

"I hope so, bud." I really do, but I also don't have much hope unless divine intervention strikes Henry, or a miracle occurs before something more severe happens to the Stanton kids.

"Now, you ready to pitch some awesome pitches?" I ask, hoping to distract him from deeper worries and get him back to being a kid for at least the next two hours.

"Yeah." His enthusiasm isn't there yet, but it will be. Kids are resilient like that.

I hold out a fist and Hudson bumps his knuckles to mine before I stand, grunting as I lift myself upward because of my knee.

"You okay there, old man?" Hudson teases.

"Hey." I jokingly point at him. "Easy kid."

Hudson finally smiles. The first one he's had since arriving at the ballpark. He turns and takes a few steps away from me, before turning back around.

"And, Coach." Hudson adjusts his ball cap on his head.

"Thanks for being there. For Atticus and Amelia. With my mom."

I try to steady my expression. Hold back my surprise, wondering what Vale said about me being present. We haven't had a chance to really talk other than quick check-ins with one another.

"Of course. I'm always here for you, Hudson." Always have been.

As Hudson turns back around, I watch him walk back to the practice field and then glance over his head where a man dressed in a brown uniform catches my eyes.

I've been waiting for this moment, caught between dread and apprehension, neither emotion particularly good.

With a deep inhale, I make my way across the field, telling myself I just need to get this over with. This is community business. I'm a mandated reporter, as I'd told Vale. I *must* report my suspicions or findings to the proper authorities. Stone isn't Vale's older brother in this case. He isn't even Hudson's uncle. He's the local sheriff.

I stop several feet from him, fighting the urge to look away from him, knowing I need to look him in the eyes.

"Sheriff," I address him formally.

"Cortland." His responding tone is just as tight.

When he doesn't say more, I speak. "Need more information about the Stantons?"

"Nope. Andy got your statement." Stone stares at me, with eyes unlike his sister's. I've seen varying shades on Vale from clear to cloudy, foggy with lust and filled with laughter, and none of those colors match this hard, cold glare.

For half a second, I expect him to shout that he knows what I'm doing with his sister. Instead, he keeps a steely gaze on me, weighty and watching, assessing. Like he *does* know the truth and he's waiting on me to explain myself. But I'm not making a move without Vale's permission. Without her knowing what I'd say and when.

I continue to hold my ground a second, thinking he'll ask for more clarification or an additional detail about the case. After what feels like an eternity, when he doesn't say anything else, I rub my hands together and break. "Okay then. Let me know if you need my help in any way."

While I know a lot about the abuse the Sylvers suffered at the hands and foul mouth of their father, I'm doubtful Stone has any hint to the abuse I suffered from Bailey and what ultimately led me to leave her. *I* understand what the Stanton kids are going through, and the last thing I want is two helpless children living with their worthless drunk dad. But this isn't my jurisdiction to moderate or meddle in.

Without salutation, I turn on my heels and stalk away from Stone, feeling the heat of his glare burning into my back, right along that old stab wound from my ex-wife, possibly adding his own indentation to match her mark.

Stone has no idea how lucky he is he didn't end up with Bailey. There's no forgiveness for what we did to Stone, but he'd escaped a level of hell by losing her. One he should be grateful for. Not grateful to me, just gratitude in general. Stone Sylver has suffered enough in his lifetime.

Stepping onto the ball field, I shake off Stone's cold glare and get back to business as best I can.

Coaching kids on how to be team players and strong individuals, like Hudson Sylver.

36

[Vale]

While Hudson had seen the Stanton twins in school, he was suddenly on the outs with Atticus, who kept his distance. The separation hurt Hudson and confused him. As much as I'd wished for the friendship to end, it broke my heart that by trying to help his friend, Hudson lost him.

Fortunately, when our family eventually learned all that happened between Hudson and the other kids, Knox invited Hudson to come over to his place to hang with Tim, his four-teen-year-old bonus son, on Friday night. Thanks to a case of hero worship for the older boy, Hudson was thrilled to spend time with his newer cousin. The distraction would do him good.

The time also offered me the freedom to sneak to Cort's house.

Even though I have a key, I hadn't planned on using it. I intended to knock. But Cort was already walking out his front door when I arrived as if he'd been anticipating me, as if he'd been as eager to see me as I was to see him.

I fight the urge to run up his front walk and throw myself at him, like a giddy teen. His bad back and injured knee are a reminder that catching me wouldn't be a good idea for him. Still, as I step up his stoop, he reaches for me and pulls me toward him by my hip, cups the side of neck and welcomes me back to his home with a searing kiss.

"Hi," I eventually say, pulling away to break the temptation to wrap my legs around him and dry hump him on his front porch.

"Hi." He swipes back my hair, holding it at the base of my neck. After pressing a kiss to my forehead, he releases me and sweeps his arm toward the open front door. "Come on in."

Once inside, I kick off my shoes, making myself comfortable like I have on so many of our lunch dates.

"It's such a beautiful night and I have a hankering for burgers. Is that alright with you?"

"As long as you're cooking, I'll eat whatever you make." I make meal decisions most days, then prep them and clean up afterward. It's nice not to have to decide what's for dinner once in a while.

A wine bottle already sits out on the countertop and Cort points toward it. "I can pour you a glass, but I was also thinking a margarita might go better with a burger."

"Cortland Haven, are you trying to make me love you?" I laugh until I see Cort's brows pinch. Licking my lips, I immediately backpedal. "I mean, you know, in the you-make-a-mean-margarita kind of love."

Cort arches one brow and leans against the kitchen island. "I didn't know there was such a way to love someone."

"Oh, yeah," I dismissively wave a hand, as my cheeks grow warmer and warmer.

Cort only shakes his head and offers me a lopsided smile, humoring my ridiculousness.

"A margarita it is then." He turns toward the opposite counter and begins making the drink from scratch. None of that pre-mixed combination I buy because I don't need an entire bottle of tequila in my house. He even salts the rim, and adds lots of ice, and I'm grateful I don't have to drive home tonight.

At least, I hope I'm not going home.

Turning back toward me, Cort hands me the margarita in a tall glass and taps his against mine before we each take a sip.

"Dang, that's good," I hum in appreciation.

However, Cort's attention is on my wrist. "What's that?"

I glance down at the bracelet I'm wearing. A silver band with a bee charm dangling from it.

"Oh, this?" I brush off the gift. "Every year, Ken sends me a gift for Mother's Day."

Cort's arms are spread, bracing him on the island opposite me, and he arches a brow at the explanation. He remembers who Ken is and his absence.

"The first anniversary, if you will, of my being a mom, I got a beehive starter kit from him." I'm reminded once again how I'd thought it was such a strange gift for a busy new mom.

"Most years the gifts are impersonal but always themed around bees." A beeswax candle making kit. A journal with a bee on it.

Cort lowers his head, the corner of his mouth ticking upward. I can't decide if mentioning Ken's thoughtfulness lands like a brick between us, or if Cort is pleased by the kindness.

I jangle my wrist. "Then, last year this gift arrived. Must have marked the end of an era. Ten years as a mother. Ken didn't send something this year."

Mother's Day passed a while back.

"Just this final gift. An Alex & Ani bracelet with a little bee—"

Glancing back at the charm dangling from the thin silver bangle, I finger the delicate insect. *All bee-themed items.* Little Bee. When Ken didn't know the nickname. Didn't know a thing about Cort and the tag he'd given me.

Snapping my head upright, I stare at Cort standing on the other side of the island, head bowed.

"Cortland," I whisper, my throat suddenly thick. "It was never Ken, was it?"

It never made sense. Why would a man who didn't want to be a father acknowledge Mother's Day for me. For that fact, why would he bother sending gifts on his son's birthday when he didn't want to know his child. Yet, I'd never given it a second thought. In my refusal to believe Ken was a bad man, I'd given him too much credit as a good one.

Continuing to stare at Cort, he finally lifts his head. His eyes are a storm of emotion. Struggling with the whirlwind spiraling inside myself, I can't read his expression. Out of all the questions I have, I settle on one.

"Why?" My voice remains quiet but filled with confusion.

Cort shifts his eyes away from mine. "For a while, I thought Hudson might be mine."

"What?" I whisper again.

"When I finally got my head out of my ass, and learned you had a child, I did the math. The timing felt about right. A March baby, counting backward, landed roughly in June. It made sense, but I also believed you'd tell me if Hudson was mine." Cort levels me with a serious stare. "Even though I'd fucked up, made an ass of myself by the Falls and all, you'd have told me."

I nod, assuring him I'd never have kept a secret like this

from him. Even with fear of Stone's disappointment, I would have never kept Hudson from Cort, if I believed in my soul, he was Cort's child.

A piece of honesty falls out of my mouth before I can stop myself. "I wanted him to be your son."

At first, I'd hoped Hudson did belong to Cort, giving me a permanent reminder of him.

"But he isn't." I'd been a little hussy that summer and *I'd* done the math. Conception was closer to the fling with Ken than the morning with Cort.

Cort nods to accept the hard truth and another thought hits me.

"March?" I continue watching Cort. "How did you even know his birthday was at the end of March?"

"Trinity." Cort's sister works in the NICU at the local hospital, but before moving into the specialized department, she worked the regular maternity ward, where I had Hudson. She hadn't been my nurse, but there was no doubt she would have known of his birth.

"So, if Ken never sent Mother's Day presents. He also never sent Hudson . . ." *birthday ones either.*

Cort is already shaking his head, lowering his gaze once more. And I don't know whether to laugh or cry. *I'm so stupid.*

Instead, I stand from my stool and round the island, extending my hand toward Cort. He twists, leaning his hip against the counter, and stares down at my offered hand a second, before glancing at me. He doesn't take my hand but instead continues to watch me.

"Aren't you mad?"

"Mad? No, anger is not the emotion I feel." Am I upset that he's been keeping *this* secret all these years? Was I a little stung that the gifts hadn't come from Ken? The answer to both was overruled by the immediate understanding that Cort had been trying to atone for what he considered a shameful moment by celebrating both Hudson and me. My son's birth and the honor of being his mother.

I wasn't mad. I was overwhelmed by emotion for this man. Ten years. Eleven, if I included Hudson's recent birthday. Mentally, I flip back through the gifts in my head. A Tennessee Terrors little slugger baseball onesie. Cort's favorite team. A tee-ball mitt. A pair of baseball cleats. And this year's gift, a pair of tickets to a Terrors versus Anchors game.

"Take my hand, Cort," I instruct, my voice quiet, knowing the only way I can show this man my gratitude and appreciation. My forgiveness for something he doesn't need to be forgiven for.

Cort still doesn't reach for me. Instead, he stands upright.

"Hold that thought." He holds up a finger to emphasize his point before he disappears down the hallway and then comes back with a small square box tied with a ribbon in his hand.

"What's this?"

"Year eleven," he whispers, staring down at the box he presents to me.

Hesitantly, I take the gift, pull the ribbon, and slip the lid from the top. Inside is something labeled a bee revival kit along with a bee ID tag.

"It holds bee food syrup for tired bees."

I flip the item, but my eyes don't register the instructions. It's like I've forgotten how to read, and I glance back at Cort who gives a soft shrug before slipping his hands in his jeans' pockets.

"It reminded me of you. Your sweetness has revived me and brought me back to life."

My eyes instantly water.

"I should have given it to you a while back, I just didn't know how—"

"It's so precious, Cort." The small vial is rose gold and

dangles from a keychain. "Thank you." I hold out my hand again. "Maybe in the future, you can give me these gifts in person."

This time, Cort slips his hand in mine. "There are lots of things I want to give you, Vale. All of them in person."

37

[Cort]

After giving her this most recent gift, Vale leads me to my bedroom. Tugging me behind her, I take in some of her best features. Her bare feet, so comfortable in my house. Her ass, in a skirt that unfairly hugs her. Her hair hanging to the middle of her back. And her hand holding mine.

When we reach my room, Vale spins to face me and tugs up the hem of my shirt which is easily pressed up and over my head. Standing bare-chested in front of her, she takes the liberty to run her hands from my abs up my middle and around my pecs, combing her fingers through the short hairs tickling up my sternum.

I suck in a sharp breath. Not because I'm afraid of Vale's touch, but because I appreciate it so much. I trust her with everything in me.

I rub my hands up her arms and tug at the straps of her

tank top, pulling them off each of her shoulders before lowering my mouth to her neck, dragging my bristly jaw from the side of her throat up over her jaw. She shivers, signaling how much she enjoys it.

Vale Sylver likes my touch as well.

We continue to express our appreciation for each other by taking our time to undress one another before folding down to the bed, where our hands don't stop their lazy exploration.

Her breasts in my palms. My balls in hers.

My fingers circling her sacred places. Hers wrapping around mine.

The buildup is slow, but our hearts are racing. Even though I've already touched Vale in a thousand different ways. Kissed her in all the places. Fingered her. Tasted her. Every touch is a new experience. Every time added to the catalogue in my heart where I'd written every detail about her.

Her lush mouth. Her firm breasts. Her honeyed heat.

"Vale," I whisper near her ear as my fingers slip inside her, finding her slick and ready, but still wanting to drag this moment out. Because I know what this moment is going to mean.

Vale doesn't just love me in a you-make-a-mean-margarita way. I don't love her like that either.

I want to love Vale with my entire being, faults and all, because Vale accepts me as I am. I've made mistakes. Huge ones. And she'd forgiven every one of them. She means more to me than anyone, except Josh, ever has.

Even Stone, who I will no longer let be a barrier to keeping Vale in my life.

But for now, my intention is to worship Vale.

My *high* intention is to marry her one day.

With focus on the present, I dip deeper into her, knowing what she likes. "A little sting for my bee."

She hums.

"Need a taste of that honey, sweetness."

Vale purrs again, her body telling me how relaxed she is while winding up. Kissing my way down her middle, I stop to suck her breasts and teasingly bite each of her nipples. Down her center I continue until I reach where she's hot and ready for me to devour her. With a lash of my tongue, then a tickle to her clit, Vale bucks against my mouth. It isn't a jolt so much as her chasing me. Wanting me.

"Only me, Bee," I tell her, the meaning even deeper than this moment. It's been me all along looking out for her and her son, celebrating them both. Wishing I could be part of their world while knowing all the reasons I needed to keep my distance.

But no more. I want to be the only one to experience her cries and wishes. Meet her needs and desires. I want to be present for Vale. Be her future.

With that thought, I dig in, making a feast of her until her thighs are slick and my face is coated in her sweet essence. And she cries out my name in the sweetest voice I've ever heard.

Then I delve into round two, making my fingers her pleasure. Vale knows I like to bring her to a doubleheader, as we've come to call it. However, . . .

"Today, we're going for a grand slam," I tell her after she's wrung out by what only my hand can do for her.

Vale chuckles. "No pun intended."

As I skim my hands over her hips and climb back up her body, I cage her in a second and explain. "I don't plan to slam anything today, Vale."

I'm going to fucking make love to her.

Sliding my hands up each of her arms, I let my dick fall between her thighs, the tip bobbing at her entrance a minute while I kiss Vale until I'm a stirred-up mess.

Reaching between us to angle myself better, I swipe the tip

of my dick through her slick folds, teasing us both with where I intend to go.

"Cortland," she whimpers, wrapping one leg around my hip.

"Soon, baby," I warn, squeezing the base of my shaft to hold myself back, counting from sixty backward to keep myself from coming too soon. "I want you to go off on the tip."

"You know I'm not like that," she groans. She can't come on demand. But she will.

"Want to feel you dripping on my cock. Giving me all that sweetness. Teasing me with your sweet sting."

I kiss along her neck. "You're gonna squeeze me so hard." I moan as well, fighting the building sensation, the anticipation of having her wrapped around me again. "Your sweet little cunt is so ready for my dick."

The words spur Vale on. She likes it a little dirty, and I twirl the tip of my cock against her clit, holding back until we're both ready to break.

Thankfully, Vale tips over the edge again and the second she lets loose, I slam into her, though that hadn't been my intention. I just want to feel her going off around me, igniting that spark that radiates my world, and adds an additional thump to my heart.

Because that's what Vale does to me. She's sunlight and new life and the buzzing in my chest.

"Yes, Vale," I groan, sliding my hands back up her arms, lifting them both above her head where we clasp hands. Fingers mingled with fingers, gripping each other hard, holding on like we'll never let go.

I don't intend to. Never again will something come between us. Not me, not her, not outside forces.

"Bee." My back seizes and my balls tighten, and I go off inside her with a sharp cry that makes no sense.

I might have cried once before, into her shoulder, out of

shame and frustration and disappointment in myself, but today, the clouds in my eyes are this overwhelming emotion of faith and trust and love for her.

Vale gives me my moment, releasing inside her, filling her up with all this pent-up emotion and sensual sensation, and then she's cupping my face, and we're kissing like we didn't just expel every ounce of energy between us.

Until the kisses turn soft, and our bodies are a replete tangle of legs and arms wrapped around one another.

A private hive between a queen and her humble worker, who plans to serve her all the days of his life.

Vale and I linger in bed another few moments before I suggest a shower. Our margaritas are probably melted, and our burgers await us. I need food energy for all the ways I plan to continue worshipping this woman tonight.

Our shower is playful, but perfunctory, and Vale eventually exits wearing only a towel around her midsection.

"I'm going to get my bee revival kit. Later, you can fuck me while I wear only it."

"Jesus," I hiss, swiping a hand down my face, as I step out of the shower as well, already growing hard and hungry for her again. She's got a dirty little mouth that I love and I'm planning to tell her exactly how I feel later.

When she's wearing only that keychain tied to a ribbon and riding over me.

As Vale pads down the hallway, still wearing only a towel, I wrap one around my waist.

Maybe the burgers can wait. We have all night to eat a meal.

Then I hear Vale scream, and I rush to the middle of my house, finding a very startled Vale and an even more surprised son.

"Josh?"

38

[Cort]

I step toward my twenty-three-year-old son after taking another minute to process he's standing in the house where Vale and I both wear only towels. Extending my arm, while still clutching the material about my waist, I bring him in for a bear hug.

Just as it's been hard for me over the years to be physical with women, it took some time for Josh to accept affection from me. We'd always had a good relationship although I wasn't an overly affectionate father. However, eventually, I became more generous with hugs, wanting Josh to know I was here for him whenever he needed me.

And standing in my kitchen, late on a Friday, it is clear my boy needs me.

But Vale . . . I release Josh and step back, turning toward Vale who still has a ghostly look on her face and clutches at the towel around her breasts.

"Um, Josh, this is Vale. Vale Sylver." This is not how I expected to introduce Vale to my child. But it's also time to start letting people into our circle. Letting people know how we feel about one another. How we are together.

"Hi." She steps forward, hesitating as she holds out a hand to shake his. "I'm a hugger. But . . . um . . ." She glances down at her attire. "Yeah." A nervous giggle escapes her.

"Vale Sylver? As in Sheriff Sylver?" Josh's head turns toward me, eyes questioning. Over the years, he's learned what happened between me and my best friend. He's also been told he's neither a cause nor effect of that fallout but a reward.

"Younger sister," Vale announces pointing at her chest which splotches pink.

"Ah." Josh nods, raising his brows and giving me a weary smile.

"I think I'm just going to . . ." Vale points over her shoulder toward my bedroom. "I should probably go."

Fuck. No. I didn't want Vale to leave. Nights with her are rare. As much as I cherish our afternoons together, I want to hold her overnight in my bed.

I glance at Josh.

"Maybe I should come back."

Fuck. I don't want that either. He's driven three hours to get home.

"Just—" I give Vale a pleading look before glancing back at Josh, holding up my hand. "Just stay here. Let me get dressed."

I spin toward Vale, setting my hand on her lower back, nudging her toward my bedroom.

"It was nice to meet you," she calls out over my shoulder to Josh.

Once we're in my room, I close the door and Vale falls flat on the bed, staring up at the ceiling. She lets out another anxious laugh before covering her face with both her hands. Then she jackknifes upward and stands. "I'll just leave."

Stepping into her space, I cup her shoulders. "*Please*. Stay. Just give me some time to talk to him. I'm just as surprised as you are to see him here."

Vale glances down at her towel before looking at my bare chest. "Well, maybe *we're* a little more surprised than he is." She offers me a shaky smile. "This is so embarrassing."

"But it's also perfect, because I want to tell him about us." I want him to see how happy I am with Vale. How she makes me a better person. I'm also hoping it will show him by example that life moves on. Love exists.

"I know it's a lot to ask, but can you stay? Please." I'm thinking I'm going to need her close after I talk with my son.

Vale examines my face, her eyes as weary as Josh's for a minute. Then she cups my jaw, and I lean into her touch. "Okay, honey. I'll stay."

I kiss the inside of her hand before leaning in for her mouth, kissing her with gratitude and relief. Pulling back, I tip my forehead to hers.

"And would it be too much to ask that you put on that Tennessee Terrors jersey and nothing else?"

"What about the bee revival kit?" She's left it out in the kitchen a second time.

"Later." I wink. I want her in my fan jersey and nothing else.

Vale narrows her eyes. "Now, you're really pushing it." Her follow-up grin is pure sunshine.

Yeah, I plan on pushing it again, once I know what my son needs.

I quickly dress in fresh joggers and a white T-shirt and head out to the kitchen where Josh is sitting on a stool, drinking a beer.

"What's going on?" I ask, while helping myself to a beer.

"Why's there got to be anything going on? I just thought I'd come home to surprise you."

"And I am surprised." I tease, tapping my beer bottle against his and lifting it for a sip. "I'm also grateful. But it's late, kid. What's really on your mind?"

His surprise is amazing because my time at his graduation last weekend was too short. He plans to remain in Morgantown before heading to Memphis in August for his first real job, where he'll be even farther away from me.

"I didn't take you for having sleepovers." He nods toward the hallway leading to my bedroom.

I could argue that I don't. Or defend that Vale isn't just a one-and-done. Taking in a deep breath, I exhale and announce, "Vale is my girlfriend."

Josh's brows lift again. "Since when?"

"Since . . . April." Because from the moment Vale and I started this thing, there was no one else. And while I get that the younger generation wants relationship statuses to be a formal asking, Vale is mine and I'm hers.

"You haven't mentioned her," Josh reminds me.

"It's . . . complicated." I sigh, leaning against the island counter on my forearms and cupping my beer bottle in my hands.

"I imagine it is." Josh chuckles, like he's put two and two together with the Sylver last name.

"As much as I'd love to talk about it, let's get down to the real issue. You. Here. Talk to me, Josh."

I'm thrilled that he's home, but showing up like this still isn't like my son.

With a heavy sigh, he lowers his gaze to the beer bottle in front of him and stares at the rim a second.

"I got someone pregnant."

Holy shit. That is not what I expected him to say at all.

"I didn't know *you* had a girlfriend," I reply first, feeling as stunned as he might have felt finding Vale here.

Josh has always been a bit tight-lipped about any women in

his life, and I don't push, because, well, we're men, and we aren't always the best at talking about our feelings. But I've tried to remind him often he can come to me with anything ... although this surpasses *anything*.

"I don't. We're more like friends with benefits and—" Josh cups his forehead, shaking his head against his palm. "I'd like to say I don't know how this happened, because I mean, I know how it happened, but I mean, just what the fuck, Dad?"

"Sounds like that's what happened." I chuckle softly before taking another sip of my beer.

"Now isn't time for jokes," Josh adds, with no spite in his voice.

"You're right." I pause a beat. "Do you love her?"

Josh shrugs but then shakes his head. "We're friends. She's fun, but I just graduated, and I'm starting my first real job in August. She's got plans to move to Alabama." Josh exhales. "It's her body, her rights. I don't want her to give up her life or feel trapped by a kid."

Fear fills Josh's eyes as he looks at me, knowing that's how his mother felt. That's what she said to *him*.

"But I also ... I don't know ... Is it wrong if *I* want the baby? I want my son." He swallows thickly. "Or daughter."

Tears fill my son's eyes. He's so young, and looking at him, I'm reminded of myself at that age. This is everything I didn't want to happen to him. He has his future ahead of him, but perhaps his future includes a child. Now.

"Do you think you want to ask her to have the baby, and then you keep him or her?" *Holy shit*. A baby boy or girl. I'd be a— I can't even think the word. I'm too young.

Josh sighs heavily again. "Fuck, I don't know, but I think I'd like the option." He glances up at me, confusion cluttering eyes that match the color of mine.

"How will that work?" His new job. Him in Memphis.

"I don't know." His breath is heavy. "How did you make it work?"

I stare at Josh, knowing I didn't make it work. I married Bailey because I thought I should, and she saw my future in professional football. If she hadn't wanted Josh from the start, I never had a clue until after he was born. Until her life changed significantly while mine hardly did, other than a seven day work week, with either practice or games, including travel and media runs. She'd been alone, a lot.

Reaching forward, I cover Josh's hand. "I'm here for you, for whatever you decide to do." I swallow thickly before adding my advice. "I don't recommend marriage without love, Josh."

He stares back at me, knowing all the reasons why it's a bad idea.

"If you can be amicable with one another and want to co-parent, I'll help any way I can. And if you decide to stand by her while she has the baby, and then raise your child on your own, you will never be alone, Josh. You got me? We'll figure it out. Together."

I don't want him or his partner to have regrets. But I also want Josh to know he has my support.

He nods once before pinching at his eyes and stroking down his nose then glancing up at me. "I didn't know who else to talk to."

"That's why I'm here." I round the island and hold out my arms again, while he shifts on the stool. Tucking my grown boy into my chest, I lower my head to his and hold onto him, wishing I could turn back time in so many ways. Erase every misstep. But I can't. And the one thing I'd never trade is him. I can only support him now and in his future.

I press a kiss to the top of his head. "I love you, bud."

"I know, Dad. I love you, too." He pulls out of my embrace and reaches for his beer again. Tipping the bottle toward my bedroom, he says, "I guess I'll let you get back to . . . you know."

"Easy there, buddy." I point at him, teasingly.

"Wow, Dad. A girlfriend? I never thought I'd see the day."

I chuff but can't help the smile curling my lips.

"Love looks good on you." He smiles as well.

I could argue that I'm not in love, but the truth is written all over my face.

When I climb on top of my bed, Vale is tucked under my covers, the hint of my jersey on her arms above the blankets. I wrap myself around her.

"Everything okay?" she asks, sleepily.

"I—" I swallow thickly, scared out of my mind for Josh. "I'm going to be a grandpa." I can hardly say the word.

Vale spins in my arms. The soft glow of the lamp on the nightstand gives a halo effect around her blond hair.

"What?"

I quickly relay what Josh told me.

"Oh, sweetie. This could be a great thing," she eventually says.

And it could be. *It will be.* Josh will not be alone in whatever decision he makes.

Vale sits up a little bit, pressing her back into the pillows and tugs my head to her chest, stroking her fingers over my hair. "And here my biggest concern was what you would tell Josh about me?"

I chuckle bitterly, because my son does have bigger issues. "I told him the truth. You're my girlfriend."

Vale stops stroking and cups my face, so I tilt my head and look at her. "Really?"

"Yes, really," I quip before softening the words with a smile. "And one day, I want everyone to know."

Not that we need to broadcast the news and announce it on social media, but I don't want to always sneak off to my home for time with her or worry that someone will pop up and catch us. I want to hold her hand and not be concerned about who sees it happen. I don't care about their opinions, other than one man, and only because of how he'll react toward Vale.

"I don't want us to be a secret, Vale."

"I don't either," she admits.

And it's time to stand up for ourselves.

For our love.

39

[Vale]

That night, Cort has his way with me in his Tennessee Terrors jersey, despite the seriousness of Josh's sudden appearance.

In the morning, he makes all three of us pancakes before I go home.

The secrecy of our relationship is coming to an end, and the revelation is a tad bittersweet. Our time alone has been something special, something just for me. But I also don't want to hoard Cort. I don't want to hide our relationship.

Deciding the women in my life should be the first to know, I call an emergency meeting of the *Sylver* Sterlets.

Enya and Cadence. Halle and Mavis. And our newest addition, Genie Webster, Judd's sudden fiancée, whom we met only six weeks ago.

While Stone should be the first person I tell, I value these women for their advice on the best way to explain to my brother I've done the forbidden.

I fell in love with Cortland Haven.

Picking Milton Roadhouse as our emergency meeting place, Genie, Enya and Cadence all arrive together. I've ordered pitchers of margaritas and water in a margarita glass for Cadence.

"Is this meeting about what I think it's about?" Genie asks, taking a seat at the table I picked near a wall. The wavy hair of her chocolate and vanilla bob gives her a jovial glow. My brother calls her Firefly.

"What do you know?" Enya asks, sitting beside me but turning toward Genie. With surprise on her face, she glances between another future sister-in-law and me.

"Who knows what about who?" Cadence counters, after taking the chair across from her sister, and glancing between all of us. Ford's very pregnant fiancée is practically glowing as well. Pregnancy agrees with her and soon Ford will be a father of four.

"I love good gossip," the superstar teases, sarcasm in her tone, while she rolls her eyes.

"Vale *is* gossip," Genie adds, playfully wiggling her brows.

"*Vale* has some explaining to do," Enya adds, keeping her eyes on me, sensing the pressure inside me. The need to talk. The reason for this meeting.

"Can I just add, I love our new name? Sylver Sterlets." Cadence wiggles jazz hands toward all of us. "We need a uniform. And a team motto."

I groan, but the smile on my face eases the tension of what I have to say.

"We need to make a special date. Just for us," Genie adds. She loves calendars.

"I think . . ." Enya places her hand on my forearm. "We should let Vale talk."

When Halle and Mavis arrive, I'm an open well, pouring out all that's happened minus a few private details. The basics are covered. My long-standing crush. My recent transgression.

"I love him," I finish, sounding like a love-sick girl, begging for their understanding.

"God, it's so fun to watch you Sylvers fall," Cadence teases, a gleam in her eye at the latest of us to be in love.

"Yeah, well, I'm worried about Stone," I admit.

A heavy haze covers the table, the truth weaving between all of us. I'm going to hurt my brother.

"I think you just need to talk to him," Enya says after a few quiet seconds. She has a special place in her heart for my brother. A bond formed when Enya had trouble shortly after she met Sebastian.

"Keeping secrets is never a good idea," Mavis adds, another sister-in-law with a soft spot for Stone. Her secrets once almost got her killed, so she knows how important honesty is.

"The truth *might* hurt, but love heals all wounds, right?" Halle offers, her encouragement full of sympathy as her own love story is full of compassion.

"Stone only wants the best for each of his siblings." Enya keeps her eyes on me. "That means he wants them to be happy. And it sounds like Cort makes you happy."

"He does," I interject, glancing down at the silver bracelet with a little bee charm dangling from my wrist. Fingering the delicate jewelry, I smile to myself.

However, happiness has levels, and passion for my job doesn't compare to passion for his former best friend.

"Stone values honesty above all else," Enya adds.

The statement is a reminder of Cort's past with Stone. He came to Stone after everything that happened and admitted his fault. It destroyed their friendship.

And if anyone has lied recently, it's been me.

"You just need to tell him the truth," Genie reiterates. "Lies never lead anywhere good."

Says the girl who faked an engagement with Judd, only to learn they actually were in love with one another.

"I'm not saying it will be easy," Enya tries to sooth. "Just tell him what you told us. How happy Cort makes you."

"And now is your opportunity." Mavis nods and I look up to see my brother in his sheriff's uniform entering the Roadhouse.

"He's probably on a dinner break." I hesitate. "I should wait until we are somewhere private." Then again, in a public place, Stone is less likely to make a scene. Not that he is a scene-making kind of guy, but you never know about those silent types.

"No time like the present," Cadence encourages.

"You got this." Halle reaches across the table and gives my arm a reassuring squeeze.

"I got this," I state, slowly rising and taking a final gulp of my margarita.

This is Stone. My oldest brother. A man who has loved me unconditionally from infancy to ornery teen to single mother-hood. He's been by my side literally every day of my life. He wasn't my father; he's been so much more, and that's why this situation felt so much worse.

But I also believe what every important woman in my life has told me. My brother only wants the best for each of us. He wants us happy and whole, loved, and I am all those things . . . with Cort. And honesty is the best way through this situation.

"Hey, big brother," I tease, slipping into a chair across from Stone. He took a seat at a high-top table closer to the bar and he holds a menu like he hasn't eaten at Milton Roadhouse enough times to have memorized their offerings.

"Hey." He gives me a slow, kind smile. One that feels reserved just for family.

"I was wondering if I could—"

"Hey there. I didn't know we'd have company." Andy White-hall sneaks up behind me and rounds the table, pulling out a stool next to my brother who shifts to accommodate Andy's position.

Shit.

"You joinin' us for dinner?" Andy adds, offering a smile that makes my blood boil. After how he botched up the Stanton situation and believed Henry over Hudson, I don't want to even look at him.

"I was just looking to speak to Stone a second, but it can—"

"Are you kidding me?" Andy mutters, glaring over my shoulder. His harsh undertone forces me ramrod straight.

Then I get a sense of what Andy is looking at, or rather *who*, as he takes a seat behind me. The tables are tight in this section, and I heard a chair scrape against the wooden floor behind me but hadn't given it a thought. When I catch a whiff of balsam fir, man, and asphalt, I know exactly who is seated at my back.

With Josh witnessing us straight out of the shower, we realized it was only a matter of time before rumors would start. We could hardly keep our eyes off one another during Haven Hitters' practices or games. Keeping our hands to ourselves has been torture.

When I'd told Cort I was going to come clean to the females in the family, he'd asked if I needed moral support. I hadn't known how badly I might need him at my back until this moment.

"We can do this another time." Because now might not be the ideal time to speak. With Andy present, and Cort behind me. Plus, this *is* a public place, and I should have this discussion privately with my big brother.

Stone immediately stands despite what I'd said. "I'm going to wash my hands."

This leaves me awkwardly seated at the table with Andy,

knowing I shouldn't leave until Stone returns, but desperately wanting to slink away.

"My, my, my, isn't this complicated," Andy smirks, glancing over my head at Cort behind me. Then he leans forward, lowering his head and his voice. "Because sister here has a secret."

Andy's like a villain in a B movie, with poor acting skills and exaggerated motions. When he licks his top teeth, I want to punch him like my brothers have taught me.

But I'm also curious what Andy *thinks* he knows, and I hold still a moment, knowing a man on a power trip, like him, is all too eager to share.

"I know all about you and the late night visits during your son's sport camp."

Initially, I have no idea what Andy means. Seconds later, I recall that Andy was the night patrol during the Haven Hitters weekend on Ford's property. And of course, I remember what I did with Cort.

Which means—

"Since you're spreading your legs for just anyone, maybe you could spread them for me."

I gag. And everything happens lightning fast.

A stool falls over. The table jostles. And I'm catching Cort's arm as he leans over the table, reaching for Andy.

Fumbling off my stool, I stand while still clutching Cort's forearm.

"You fucking watch your mouth," Cort snarls, pointing at Andy. His finger nearly underneath the deputy's chin, like Cort intends to throat punch him.

"He isn't worth it," I whimper, still trying to process that Andy might have seen Cort and I together. He was watching us.

I'm going to be sick.

Cort and I have discussed Andy's incompetence and grudge against Sebastian. We've also talked about how he mishandled the Stanton case. But this infraction is on an entirely different level of disturbing.

"Is there a problem here?" Stone is suddenly standing near the opposite side of the table. His gaze falls to where my hand grips Cort's arm.

As Cort stands to his full height, he nudges me behind him, and I keep my hand on his arm, sliding it up to the crook of his elbow. The last thing I want is a physical altercation between my boyfriend and the sheriff.

"Maybe Andy would like to share the problem." Cort sneers in Andy's direction. The edge in his voice as sharp as a knife. "Want to repeat that disrespectful, vulgar shit you just said to Stone's sister?"

"It's Deputy Sheriff Whitehall." Andy stands, ignoring all the rest of what Cort said, and runs his hands along his belt, before settling it on the gun holstered at his hip.

With a gasp, I glance at Stone. *How does someone like Andy work with my brother?*

However, Stone hasn't taken his eyes off Cort. The two of them are locked in some battle of wills, or worse, a conversation of truths.

Eventually, Cort tips up his chin.

"Alright," he mutters, slipping out from underneath my touch without a glance in my direction. As he spins and disappears behind me, I stare at Stone a second before glancing at Cort's retreating back.

Swallowing hard, I make the only decision I can.

I follow Cort.

40

─────────

[Cort]

"Hey." The call follows me as I slam open the door to Milton Roadhouse and step out into the early evening sunlight. I round the corner onto Corner Street and head for the lot behind the building where I parked my truck.

"Hey. I'm talking to you," Vale calls out again.

As much as I love her, I'm not in the headspace to be with her right now.

"And you shouldn't be," I snap as I spin to face her, witnessing the instant hurt in her eyes. Those beautiful clear eyes that smile up at me when I'm over her. That stare at me across my kitchen island. That laugh with me seated on my couch.

Dammit.

"Vale, I just can't—" Cause issues between her and her brother. Love her. Lose her.

"What?" she quips. "Be with me?" Vale crosses her arms. "I call bullshit. And if you walk away from me again, Cortland Haven, then I'm just going to have to—"

"What?" I taunt, goading her. Will she close the door and toss back my key? Will she walk away from me? Will she stop loving me?

I feel sick at all the possibilities.

"Dammit, Cort," she whispers. "Fight for me, not against me."

Once again, I'm disappointing her. I hear it in her tone. This isn't some failed orgasm during a quick fuck. This is heartbreak. I'm letting her down and I know it.

It's just that the way Stone looked at me. The hurt in his eyes. The *knowing* in them.

I hang my head a second but pop it back upright at the crunch of gravel under firm boots. Glancing up, I catch a glimpse of Stone, feet behind his sister, glaring at me like he did inside Milton's.

Are you fucking kidding me?

You piece of shit.

You were my best friend.

I'm at an all-time low here, man, and you just buried me.

The words echo through my head as if they happened yesterday, not twenty-three years ago. And I'd taken all of them to heart. I held them in my chest, knowing he was right. I'd done him a huge wrong.

Dressed in his uniform, Stone looks more imposing than I know he is. Or at least, the man he once was. He'd always been large, solid even. He was a damn good football player with a bright future ahead of him. But his heart is soft, and he didn't have a choice, or so he'd said. He couldn't leave his siblings behind without their father, even if the man had been a piece of shit. Stone felt he'd already walked away once by going to college.

"I'm trying to let bygones be bygones here, Cortland." Stone crosses his arms then unfolds them again. "But my sister? Really? Why Vale?"

Vale spins at the harsh tone of her brother. A voice I'm certain he reserves for sheriff duty.

"Why *not* me?" Vale counters, narrowing her eyes at her sibling, letting her hands fist at her side as she faces off with her older, *bigger* brother.

Not taking my eyes off Stone, I answer, knowing exactly what he means. "You're too good for me."

Vale swings her head back toward me, her voice lowering when she says, "Don't say that."

Then she glances back at her brother. "You knew, didn't you?"

"Think I don't know what happens in this area?" Stone stares at Vale. "With my sister?" His jaw is tight. He isn't exerting his authority like Andy, where power has been misplaced. Stone looks angry. And hurt.

"Why didn't you say something?" Vale's voice drops again, hesitant and puzzled.

I almost hear Stone's rebuke before he speaks it. "Why didn't *you*?"

Why hasn't Vale told him the truth?

There wasn't a plan for Vale and me to keep a secret. There wasn't even a plan for Vale and me, period. But it happened. And I could say for right or wrong, for good or bad, it happened. But Vale is right for me. She's good for me. I'm not accepting an end. Not like this.

Stepping closer to Vale, I set my hand on her lower back. A sign of possession but also a sign of my protection. I don't intend to hurt her. Not like I hurt him. Even back then, it wasn't intentional. It was being young and stupid, making regrettable mistakes with heavy consequences.

I've paid enough.

"I never thought you'd lie to me," Stone lowers his tone, addressing Vale. A fatherly edge laces the words. Disappointment as well.

"I—" Vale chokes, blinking at him before looking at me and then back at her brother.

She might not have told the whole truth, but omission is still considered a lie as well.

"I'm sorry," Vale hangs her head, and I slide my hand up her back, squeezing her nape. "I should have told you sooner."

Not ask for his permission. Just been honest with him.

Stone doesn't ask how long this has been going on. I'm thinking he doesn't care. Something is happening here between his sister and me, and that's all that matters.

"I was . . . scared." She glances up at me once more before looking back at Stone. "I didn't want to hurt you."

"Vale." Stone's rough voice softens while his bushy brows rise, surprised by her admission.

"You've done so much for me." Her voice thickens and she clears her throat. "*Everything* for me," she admits, giving him the credit he's due. "And I love you, Stone. I *appreciate* all you've done, and everything I know you'll ever do for Hudson."

Licking her lips, she glances at me over her shoulder before looking at her brother. "But if you truly love me, and want me to be happy, like you always say you do, then you'll accept this. Accept that I love Cort."

My breath hitches and I glance at Vale, who twists to look up at me.

"Because I love you, Cort." Her eyes are full of hope and desire and a speck of fear.

Fear that I won't reciprocate the feeling, but I never want her to doubt me. I never want to disappoint her again. Any hesitation I ever felt was never about her.

"I love you, too, Bee."

Vale flings her arms around me, and I accept the embrace, wrapping my arms around her as well.

Still, I risk a glance at Stone, beseeching him to understand. I don't need his blessing, but I want grace for Vale.

Stone only stares back at me, his expression one I can't read as we are no longer brothers from another. Two decades of harm and silence separate us now. So, I don't linger on Stone's face. I tuck my nose into Vale's neck, inhaling her honey scent and holding her tighter against me.

This amazing, confident, strong woman has chosen me. She loves me as I am, and I want to love her in return with all I have.

When I hear the crunch of gravel beneath retreating feet, I don't glance up. I close my eyes and hug Vale as close as I can get her to me.

With happiness wrapped in my arms, I don't ever plan to let her go.

WITH OUR RELATIONSHIP out in the open, I don't waste any time doing something I feel is only right. I'm not looking to rub Vale and me in Stone's face, but there is someone even more important than all of us to speak with.

With a few hours before Haven Hitters' practice, Vale is home early today, so I climb the stairs to the Sylver family home in broad daylight.

My chest holds a weight on it, but it isn't heavy like that time more than two decades ago when I was here. Standing in the yard, confessing one of my greatest sins to the young, newly appointed owner of this property.

Nope. Today I'm here with a rumble of nerves in my gut for a different reason. After a short, sharp rap on the front door, I step back, rubbing my hands along the sides of my jeans.

When Stone opens the door, he narrows his eyes at me. "What do you want?"

Not the greeting I expected, though certainly one I should anticipate receiving every time I step on this porch. But I'm not here to profess to *him* all the promises I plan to make Vale.

"I'm here to see Vale." I'm not asking his permission. While I'd like his blessing, that might take time, if I ever earn it. However, Stone isn't Vale's father or keeper. She is her own headstrong person who can make decisions for herself.

There is someone else I'd like to get approval from.

Within seconds, Vale is behind Stone. Her smile is sweet and hopeful, because she knows this is important to me. Hudson is right beside her.

"Hey, Coach," Hudson addresses me before glancing up at his uncle who has hardly moved. His broad hand still holds the edge of the front door like he intends to slam it in my face any second now.

"Hey, pal." As I don't want to do this through a screen door, or even with Stone standing like a centurion in front of Hudson, I ask, "Can you step out here for a second?"

Vale tugs at Hudson's shoulders to get a better look at his face and smiles, before tipping her chin toward me. Hudson gives one more glance to Stone before stepping past him and onto the covered porch.

"Want to take a seat?" I point toward a swing at the end of the porch.

"Am I in trouble?" His eyes never leave my face after he takes a seat, and I lower to one knee in front of him.

"No, Hudson. You aren't in trouble." I chuckle lightly, glancing over my shoulder to where Vale has stepped outside as well. Stone stands behind her.

With my arm perched on my thigh, I turn back to Hudson. "I'm here to see your mom, but I have something to ask you first. Hudson . . . " I swallow thickly and lick my lips. "I'd like permission to date your mom."

"What the—" Stone mutters somewhere behind me.

Vale giggles.

"Your mom and I are old friends, and we've become friends again. More than friends. And I'd like to take her on a proper date. Dinner. A movie maybe. Or dancing." I glance over my shoulder at Vale and wink.

Looking back at Hudson, I add, "But I want your blessing first."

Hudson peers over my shoulder at his mom. "This is going to be weird, isn't it?"

"It doesn't have to be," I state, drawing his attention back to me. "We don't need to be telling our truths to the whole town." Like I told him about the situation with Atticus. "But I don't want to be sneaking around behind your back. I like your mom, a lot." I love her, as Vale and I have admitted to one another, but baby steps are needed with Hudson.

Vale steps closer to us, setting her hand on my shoulder, while I continue kneeling.

"Are you gonna marry her?" Hudson asks, looking from his mother to me again.

I glance up at Vale. "I don't think we're there . . . yet." I wink again, expressing my hope with a flutter of my eyelid.

Behind me, the screen door opens and closes with a slap against the door jamb. I ignore the sound as the hammering in my heart supersedes everything else.

"So, what do you say, bud? Can I take your mom out? Maybe the three of us can even do something together sometime."

"Like what?" he instantly asks with the typical attention span of a kid.

I chuckle and glance back at Vale before pressing up from the wooden porch floor, using the swing to lift myself.

"I don't know. Maybe a Terrors game? Or bowling?" I remember all the things I did with Josh at this age. I should have done more. Should have paid better attention to the details because the time went too fast.

But I'm focused now.

On my girl. On her son. On our future.

"Sounds good," Hudson says before looking at his mom. "Can I go text Amelia now?"

"You got it." She holds out her arms and Hudson stands, stepping in for a quick hug from her. "Thank you, Hudson." She presses a kiss to the top of his head.

I hold out my fist and he bumps his knuckles against mine before crossing the porch for the screen door.

Vale and I both watch him enter the house.

"Well, that went better than I expected," she says, reaching for my hand and taking a seat on the swing. I follow her down to the cushioned seat and rest my arm along the back of it.

The swing is a replica of the one that once hung here and eventually fell from the ceiling. With a press of my heel on the floor, I rock us gently back and forth.

Can't say I ever imagined myself sitting here again. Never imagined it like this with Vale at my side. But I also can't say I've ever been happier.

"I love you, sweetness," I turn my head to find Vale watching me.

"Damn right you do," she teases before leaning toward me for a quick kiss.

Too quick. But as much as I feel like celebrating, and tackling Vale back on this swing, getting her naked out here, it probably isn't in our best interest with her son and her brother inside the house.

"I love you, too," Vale says back, smiling at me like it's her favorite thing to say.

It's become my favorite thing to hear.

"So, Amelia, huh?" I glance toward the screen door again.

"Yep. Although her daddy isn't allowing her to speak to Hudson, they talk through texts almost every day." Vale air quotes. "*They're text-dating.*"

"What the hell is that?" I ask, glancing back at my beautiful woman.

Vale giggles and shakes her head. "I don't even know. Kids these days." She laughs harder. "Sneaking around and dating behind backs."

"Valentine." I narrow my eyes without any heat. "We're gonna be open about this relationship."

"But not too open," She smiles, dropping her gaze to my shirt and smoothing my collar.

I catch her meaning and lean over to kiss her again.

"It's going to be the right mix of public dates and private time."

Because this feels right. Love is good. For the first time, everything perfectly happens.

EPILOGUE

[Vale]

With our relationship in the open, I didn't think I could be happier. It was the little things, like *not* having to keep my distance during a Haven Hitters baseball game. Or *not* being able to approach him at Milton Roadhouse.

Cort was even more affectionate in public than I'd anticipated, always holding my hand when we walked anywhere or putting his arm around my shoulder, keeping me close.

He even braved joining me for coffee at Curmudgeon Bakery one morning, where Sebastian narrowed his eyes at Cort with a strong warning. "I know people."

He isn't lying. He served time in jail and I'm certain he has questionable connections, but the threat isn't warranted. Cort took the warning with grace, placing his hand on my lower back before sliding it up my spine in that way that always makes me tingle, before cupping the back of my neck.

"If I hurt her, I'll be the first to ask you for someone's number." Cort kissed my temple right in front of my brother, whose eyebrows I didn't think could rise any higher on his head.

Ford and Cadence were too hectic with their three little ones and a baby on the way to give Cort and I much thought. Although Ford knows about the split between Stone and Cort as well as the rest of the family, he wasn't as fazed by a union between Cort and me.

Knox and Halle joined Cort and me along with Hudson and Tim for a hike one day. As reunited lovers, they are big on second chances and graciously offered silent support of whatever makes us happy.

Cort makes me deliriously happy. I'm pretty certain I do the same for him.

Judd was the surprising one. He gave an open invitation for Cort and I, along with Hudson and Josh, to come to his place and enjoy the lake behind his house.

And Clay, as both the easygoing one and the closest to Stone, had simple words of advice: "He'll come around."

I wanted to believe that was true. That, eventually, Stone would accept Cort wasn't the same Cort of his youth and their friendship. He'd had his own demons to conquer during their split making him the strong, reflective man he is today.

As for me, the relief at my brothers' casual acceptance and the bliss I feel being with Cort is like honey-lemon glaze on a honey cake.

Sweet and satisfying.

ALTHOUGH THE HAVEN Hitters will have a Fourth of July tournament, the actual holiday is a break for the team, but not from baseball.

A new tradition has developed for us Sylvers. After the parade in town, which honors both Stone and Knox for their service as the Sheriff and a local fire fighter, the family meets back at the house for what's become a rather competitive baseball game.

The teams were once random because of our second generation being so young but as a few of them have aged up, the family teams have reshuffled.

We've added more players recently, like Mavis and Dutton, and Genie. But Judd also had a request to include Trudy Wallace and her grandson, Simon. Trudy admitted she'd be more of a fan than a participant as she's roughly the age our mother would have been. The two women were best friends when our mom was alive. Trudy's an icon in our community for raising many of her nieces and nephews as well as a handful of foster kids.

Because of these additions, I've decided to make a few invites of my own to our annual game. Might as well make it a party because this year we plan to host fireworks on our property, being that Knox is well trained in fire safety. Stone's going to look the other way on whether it's truly legal to have our own celebratory display.

I'm nervous as I've only mentioned the additional invites to a few of my family members. Not that the art of surprise will win over Stone, but I figure he won't make a scene in front of the entire Sylver clan.

Or Mary Haven, Trinity, and Clint, with his daughter, Ruby James.

As Ford's daughter June and Ruby James are pals, I figured there is no harm in them being included.

And it's been too long since Mary Haven has come around.

During one of our first public dates, where Cort took me dancing at Shenanigans in Rogue River, he told me he'd mentioned to his mother that I was his girlfriend. *Cort's girl-*

friend. We're in no rush for other labels, even though he hinted to Hudson that one day we might marry.

I'll be saying yes faster than a cat leaps off a hot tin roof.

The family slowly makes their way toward the former penned-in area, once used for horses we didn't have when I was a kid, but now an official baseball diamond thanks to Ford's vision and my brothers' determination to bring one more family member back to the fold.

Anxiously, I await my extra guests.

When Cort arrives, he approaches me, cupping the side of my neck and giving me a kiss that lets everyone know we are together.

When he releases me, my face is heated, and I don't dare risk a glance at Stone. Hudson, however, has seen Cort give me more chaste kisses around his practices and ball games, and he's come to simply roll his eyes at the public display of affection.

Cort glances over my head and nods once. "Stone." He doesn't take his hand off my shoulder blade, but turns toward his mother, who is already approaching my oldest brother.

"Stone Sylver, it's been too long." Mary Haven steps right up to my brother and opens her arms, like she's welcoming home a long-lost son. There's no doubt that Stone has seen Mary over the years but I'm not certain if they've ever spoken about what happened.

"Thank you so much for having us," Mary says, still holding onto my brother's shoulders, keeping his attention on her a second before he glances over at me.

"Of course," he says rather tightly, knowing that I might have, *maybe*, included Mary Haven in this invitation to smooth rough water.

Stone eventually greets Trinity, along with Clint and Ruby James, who quickly runs off to find June.

"Now, where is Trudy?" Mary questions. "I heard she and I are team moms. One for each team."

Stone smiles softly at the mention of Trudy.

Cort chuckles. "We're a little old for team-moms."

"Says the man hiding behind his," Stone mutters.

I'm certain everyone near enough to hear holds their breath before Stone swipes a hand down his face like he didn't mean to say the words aloud.

"Don't be a dickhead, dickhead," Cort says, without a hint of malice in his tone and surprising everyone. He said it like one of my brothers might say to another in jest.

Or like old friends might say to one another as a joke.

"I'm not a dickhead, dickhead," Stone says, his expression serious for only half a second before the sliver of a smile cracks his mouth.

"Okay now," Mary interjects, swinging her head from one grown man to the other. "That's enough talk about dickheads."

"Mom," Trinity scowls while laughing.

"I brought my famous lemonade with me." Mary winks at Stone. "One for the kiddos and one for adults who aren't dickheads."

Hudson used to be a swear-word sheriff, charging by the word, and thank goodness he isn't close enough for this interchange or he'd be making bank.

"I call Mary," Stone hollers, breaking a little bit of the tension while spinning to face the rest of our family, who have been standing around in various positions near the newish baseball field watching this slightly awkward arrival. Stone slips his arm around Mary and leads her toward everyone else.

"Mom for the win," Cort scoffs, shaking his head. "But now she's the enemy." Because Stone isn't going to pick Cort to be on his team, and their old competitive streak is about to kick into high gear.

As self-appointed team captains, Stone and Clay each head up the two halves of our family, keeping the teams as equitable as they can. It's exactly how they raised us, because the bottom line is I was raised by my brothers, mainly the two at the top.

As Cort and I approach the field, another car pulls into the drive that's already overflowing with vehicles. Once the car is parked, the back passenger door flies open and out rushes Simon, a dark-haired boy who hero-worships Judd. With a mitt and ball already in hand, he runs from the car but quickly does a turnabout when Trudy steps out of the vehicle, admonishing him for his manners.

"I'm not raising no Tasmanian devil here," she comments on the whirlwind of excitement the kid displays before he swings back to close the car door, then spins again for the homemade field.

Trudy circles the vehicle and takes one look at me under the arm of Cort.

"Well, as I live and breathe," she mutters, her eyes wide as she approaches us, offering us a collective hug. Pulling back, the dark-skinned woman cups my cheek while keeping her other hand on Cort's shoulder.

"Your momma would be so proud."

The comment brings instant tears to my eyes. My looks have been compared to my mother. Sometimes, my temperament is even compared to hers, but this moment means the most to me. Because I know Trudy means my mother would be happy to see me happy.

Cort tugs me tighter to his side and kisses the top of my head while I fist his Terrors jersey in my hand.

"Thank you, Trudy. It's so nice to have you here today." It's going to be a great day.

Behind her, another car door shuts, and Trudy releases Cort and I, stepping aside to wave an arm toward a stunning, deeply-tan-colored woman with wildly curly hair piled on top of her head. She's a cross between glamourous, with large sunglasses on, and artsy, wearing bib overalls with a tank top underneath.

She pulls the dark shades from her face revealing smokey gray eyes.

"Vale, I don't know if you remember my niece, Tallulah."

"Of course, although it's been a while." I step forward to offer her a welcoming hug. She's slim and taller than me and smells amazing. I also know she's around Judd's age.

Releasing her, I hear the crunch of gravel behind me and turn to see Stone standing on the edge of the drive, roughly a foot to the side of Cort.

For a half a second, my breath hitches because the two men I love most in this world are so close to one another.

But Stone looks like he's seen a ghost, and his eyes don't leave Tallulah. His slightly summer-tanned cheeks are almost as white as the beard on his jaw.

"Stone?" I question at the same time Tallulah gasps.

I glance between her and my brother then back at our new arrival.

Stone finally finds his feet and steps forward. "Um. Hey. Welcome to my home." He extends a hand toward our guest, who stares down at it a moment before hesitantly slipping her hand into his.

They don't shake as much as hold still, clasping hands a little longer than might be socially acceptable.

"Hey. The name is Taxi."

Trudy scoffs. "Tallulah Alexander," she chides.

Only Taxi doesn't break eye contact with Stone. "Nice to meet you."

Stone blinks, like he's taken aback. "Yeah. Nice to meet you."

Trudy chuckles. "You two have met, you just don't remember." Trudy waves a hand. "She was the one always running around the yard, trying to take her clothes off as a child."

"Aunt Trudy," Taxi shrieks, embarrassed, while still holding Stone's hand.

As if realizing they are still clasped together, she tugs her arm free.

"Think I'd remember if I saw you naked," Stone states, quietly chuckling afterward.

"Yeah," Taxi says, slipping her sunglasses back on her face and glancing around Stone. "Heard there's a baseball game. Are we going to play ball or what?" Impatience is clear in her tone, but she remains stone-still, slipping her hands into her overalls.

My brother's gaze follows the motion before he says, "Oh, we're going to play alright."

I sputter a cough and glance over at Cort, arching my brow. *What the hell is happening here?*

Cort simply smiles, like he's read the room, or rather the driveway, and he's picked up on something no one else is privy to about his former best friend. A story just waiting to be told.

As Stone steps aside, he waves out his arm, inviting Taxi to step forward. When she does, holding her head high, hands still in her pockets, Stone follows a little too closely behind her.

"Oh, boy." Trudy chuckles, suggesting she's picked up on the weird vibe between those two as well. She follows her niece and my brother while I step over to Cort, wrapping my arms around his middle.

"What do you think that was all about?"

"I can't say for certain, but I'm going to guess your brother was just thunderstruck."

Stone? Thunderstruck? Not my unflappable brother whose personality perfectly fits his namesake. He epitomizes calm and control. Even with Cort and I being in love, he's still rather standfast, even if he's not fully onboard yet.

And I'd love to see a woman who rocks his world.

My glance leaps to Taxi taking steps toward Clay's team, while Stone watches like he's just lost an all-star player.

"You two playing or what?" Sebastian calls out, pulling my attention away from observing our eldest sibling.

"Put me in, Coach," I call out as Cort, and I start walking toward the field with his arm draped over my shoulders.

Cort chuckles. "Somehow you've made that sound real dirty, Bee."

"We can round our own bases later," I tease him, poking at his hard abs.

"I like the sound of that, sweetness." He leans down, pressing another kiss to the top of my head as we step closer to my family.

And I smile because all my favorite people in the world are in one place, and I don't think I've ever been so happy.

Thank you for taking the time to read *Sterling Touch*.

Please consider writing a review on major sales channels where ebooks and paperbacks are sold and discussed.

If you'd like a little bit more of Vale and Cort,
read their proposal scene HERE.

Sterling Touch BONUS

Up next in Sterling Falls . . . the oldest brother finally gets his happily-ever-after in *Sterling Stone*.

MORE BY L.B. DUNBAR

Sterling Falls

Seven small-town siblings muddle their way through love over 40.

Sterling Heat

Sterling Brick

Sterling Streak

Sterling Clay

Sterling Fight

Sterling Touch

Sterling Stone

Chicago Anchors

When your eyes are on the silver fox coach more than the ball.

Elevator Pitch

Catch the Kiss

Parentmoon

When the mother of the groom goes head-to-head with the single father of the bride.

<u>Holiday Hotties (Christmas novellas)</u>
Holiday novellas certain to heat the season.
Scrooge-ish
Naughty-ish
Grouch-ish

<u>Road Trips & Romance</u>
Three sisters. Three destinations. All second chances at love over 40.
Hauling Ashe
Merging Wright
Rhode Trip

<u>Lakeside Cottage</u>
Four friends. Four summers. Shenanigans and love happen at the lake.
Living at 40
Loving at 40
Learning at 40
Letting Go at 40

<u>The Silver Foxes of Blue Ridge</u>
Small mountain town, silver fox brothers seeking love over 40.
Silver Brewer
Silver Player
Silver Mayor
Silver Biker

<u>Sexy Silver Foxes</u>
When sexy silver foxes meet the feisty vixens of their dreams.
After Care
Midlife Crisis
Restored Dreams
Second Chance

Wine&Dine

Collision novellas
A spin-off from *After Care* – the younger set/rock stars
Collide
Caught

The Sex Education of M.E.
The original sexy silver fox.
When a widowed professor decides she'd like to date again,
and a local fireman volunteers to give her lessons.

The Heart Collection
Small town, big hearts - stories of family and love.
Speak from the Heart
Read with your Heart
Look with your Heart
Fight from the Heart
View with your Heart

A Heart Collection Spin-off
The Heart Remembers

BOOKS IN OTHER AUTHOR WORLDS

Smartypants Romance (an imprint of Penny Reid)
Tales of the Winters sisters set in Green Valley.
Love in Due Time
Love in Deed
Love in a Pickle

The World of True North (an imprint of Sarina Bowen)
Welcome to Vermont! And the Busy Bean Café.
Cowboy

Studfinder

THE EARLY YEARS

<u>Legendary Rock Stars Series</u>
A classic tale with a modern twist of rockstar romance and
suspense.

<u>Paradise Stories</u>
MMA romance. Two brothers. One fight.

<u>The Island Duet</u>
Intrigue and suspense. The island knows what you've done.

<u>Modern Descendants – writing as elda lore</u>
Magical realism. Modern myths of Greek gods.

ABOUT THE AUTHOR

www.lbdunbar.com

L.B. Dunbar loves sexy silver foxes, second chances, and small towns. If you enjoy older characters in your romance reads, including a hero with a little silver in his scruff and a heroine rediscovering her worth, then welcome to romance for those over 40. L.B. Dunbar's signature works include women and men in their prime taking another turn at love and happily ever after. She's a *USA TODAY* Bestseller as well as #1 Bestseller on Amazon in Later in Life Romance with her Sterling Falls, Lakeside Cottage, and Road Trips & Romance series. L.B. lives in Chicago with her own sexy silver fox.

To get all the scoop about the self-proclaimed queen of silver fox romance, join her on Facebook at Loving L.B. (Dunbar) or receive her monthly newsletter, Love Notes.

+ + +

CONNECT WITH L.B. DUNBAR